To P[...]
W[...]
[...]rem Hm.
Happy reading

The Blue Bay

Café

Ann E Brockbank

Ann E Brockbank

Front cover 'View From The Blue Bay Café'

by © R W Floyd, from an original oil painting

ISBN-10:1511879564
ISBN-13: 9781511879569

:

For Peter

Forever in my heart

Also by Ann E Brockbank

Mr de Sousa's Legacy

Ann E Brockbank

ACKNOWLEDGMENTS

I couldn't have written this book without the help and support of some very special people. To my beloved partner Rob, your love and encouragement has kept me writing and your beautiful paintings add a special quality to my books. Thanks to Roger, for your time and expertise. Your sensitive editorial suggestions are always wise, and your honesty and encouragement have improved the book enormously. To my good friend Wendy, for always being the first person willing to read my work. Your astute advice is always helpful and appreciated. Enormous thanks to Cathy and Karen for giving their time to help to make a silk-purse out of my prose. You have all helped me launch this book with confidence.

Thanks to the staff at Poldhu Café and at Kynance Cove Café, for letting me hog your beachside tables for hours and for sustaining me with frothy coffee. To Liz, Kim & Lizzy, who helped and encouraged me with their expertise and advice whilst writing this second book.

A big thank you to all the wonderful new friends and readers I have made since writing my first novel, Mr de Sousa's Legacy. Your enthusiasm, kind words and support inspired me to keep writing.

Finally to my darling late husband Peter, your spirit is woven into the pages of this book; my life will be forever blessed for the love you gave me. You have not gone, just out of sight and always in my heart.

As always the most nerve-wracking part of writing a book is letting it go out into the world, so I'd like to thank every single reader who has spent their hard-earned money on this book. Without each of you, I'd be a very miserable writer without an audience. I am honoured that you have selected my story to read.

Ann E Brockbank

Prologue

Andover Country House Hotel,
Andover Hampshire
Friday March 24th 1995

Trembling with rage, Jasmine ran the length of the car park, kicking back gravel in her wake. In her haste she stumbled, losing one of her shoes. Swiftly dipping to retrieve it, she snatched it from where it lay and hopped in an ungainly fashion towards her car. She glanced angrily towards the hotel as she fumbled for her car keys, then wrenched open the door of her brand new Mercedes. Once inside, she barely noticed the heady smell of new leather as she flung the crumpled registration documents onto the passenger seat. The luxurious softness of the cream leather interior could not dispel the fury building within her as she yanked the rear view mirror towards her and quickly checked her appearance. Her perfect features harboured small high, angry red spots at her cheeks, and her lips betrayed the smudge of the rough kiss she'd so vehemently resisted a few moments before. Furiously wiping the back of her hand across her mouth, she was incensed at the way he had treated her. She would not allow him to spoil her special weekend. She tossed her blonde hair proudly. Tomorrow, everyone would know of her. Her face would grace the covers of all the glossy magazines. Her image would be projected into the homes of millions of TV viewers. Because tomorrow, she would be revealed as the new 'face' of Lemmel, London, as they launched their new fragrance 'Infinity'. She congratulated herself, as this was no mean feat for a girl from a small

Cornish town at the edge of England.

She slammed her hands furiously on the leather steering-wheel. This beautiful car was her reward; she had earned it, as part of her amazing contract with Lemmel. Today should have been the start of her celebrations, but he had ruined it, cheapened the whole occasion. She was so fractious she could hardly think straight. He had lured her to this place, on the pretence of a pre-launch meeting, only to humiliate her. She held her hand to her décolletage. She could still feel the rawness from where he had pushed the Mercedes registration documents down the front of her cleavage. She shuddered with indignation; he had made her feel like some sort of whore, accepting favours. "I will not be treated like this," she yelled defiantly. "I owe him nothing, absolutely nothing." She seethed inwardly. He may have threatened to ruin her career, but she would fight him all the way!

Twilight was falling as she checked her watch. It was four p.m.; she was going to be really late now. She groaned, as great spots of fat raindrops began to pelt her windscreen. It was going to be a long wet drive down to Cornwall tonight. She quickly reapplied her lipstick, adjusted her skirt, and took a deep breath. Turning the ignition, she revved the engine, selected a CD on the stereo and turned up the volume. Jasmine Quintana never saw the hay roll which had worked loose from the tractor, leaving a long black ribbon of plastic fluttering from the tractor forks. Nor was she alerted by the farmer's frantic shouts, as he chased the hay roll down the steep wet field behind the hotel car park. There was nothing anyone could do, destiny would prevail. The hay roll struck the wall at the bottom of the field with an almighty thud, bounced majestically into the air and landed with a sickening thump on top of the silver Mercedes SLK.

The distraught farmer, along with a smattering of hotel guests, watched in hushed numbed silence, as the fire brigade cut Jasmine from the wreckage of her car. No one noticed the vehicle, which surreptitiously inched its way out of the hotel car park, the driver casually averting his eyes from the carnage.

1

Cornwall

Faye Larson failed to see the tree root; consequently, her quiet amble along the cliff path high above the peaceful village of Zennor on the Penwith peninsular suddenly took a turn for the worse. Unable to stop herself, she realised she was falling, and falling hard, executing a spectacular face-first dive into a clump of yellow gorse. The impact on her bare knees was painfully jarring and she knew there would be blood. Taking a moment to catch her breath, she quickly glanced about, hoping that no one had witnessed her humiliation; the path was thankfully deserted. Pulling her hands from the gorse, she sat back to inspect her grazed knees. Not since she was a little girl had she bore the scars normally associated with playtime. Carefully picking the grit from the bleeding wounds, a man's voice from behind startled her.

"May I be of any assistance?" He crouched down to her eye level.

Flustered slightly, Faye smiled, shook her head and began to scramble to her feet. Her head swam dizzily, and quite unintentionally, she grabbed her Good Samaritan by the arm to steady herself.

Closing a protective arm about her shoulder, he said gently, "Please, come and sit down for a moment. I have a studio nearby; we could clean the wound there." He gestured towards a thicket of ferns, but Faye could see no visible building.

Recovering her composure, she declined his offer. "Honestly, I'm fine; my car is in the village just over the hill. I'd like to get back there, if that's okay? Thank you for your help though." She smiled warmly into his kind eyes, and began to limp painfully away.

Seeing her struggle, but not wanting to be a nuisance, he caught her up. "I'm walking back that way, please take my arm and let me help you. I'm heading home anyway for lunch and it seems ludicrous for me to follow without helping you."

Faye smiled thankfully, knowing full well the walk would be a struggle unaided. She cheerfully accepted his arm and they walked back to the car in relative silence. Dutifully delivered safely to her car, he said, "Are you sure I can't do anything else to help? My cottage is just there." He pointed towards a pretty, stone built cottage, which was smothered liberally in Virginia creeper.

For the first time Faye really took the time to look at the man who'd helped her. He was handsome, in a rugged sort of way. His hair was a mass of unruly dark curls which were peppered with signs of grey. This gave him a wild, outdoor-all-weathers look. And his eyes, she noted, were blue and seemed to glisten cheekily as he smiled. She declined his thoughtful offer with a shake of the head. "Thank you, I'm fine now, you've been so very kind."

"I'll say goodbye then," he said, bowing his head slightly. He held out his hand to her. "Nathaniel Prior at your service. Have a safe journey home."

"Oh," she said in recognition of his name. "Thank you again Mr Prior," she called after him.

*

The noise of heavy machinery craning a yacht into the Helford River brought Faye back into the present. The memory of that day two years ago, when she had fallen in Zennor, had been prompted by reading The West Briton's obituary about Elizabeth Trent-Prior, the sculptor and wife of the artist Nathaniel Prior. Nathaniel had been so kind to her, but with the pain brought on by the fall, she had been slow to recognise him that day, and was sorry now that she hadn't been more responsive towards him.

As she finished the article, a weight of great sorrow lay

13

heavily on her. How sad that such a lovely man should lose his wife, and so young as well. The obituary said that she was forty-five, and from her memory of Nathaniel, he didn't look much older. Yes, his hair was greying slightly, but his face had been void of lines and his clear blue-grey eyes had sparkled with vitality. She almost felt as though she knew him personally and felt his grief keenly. In the interim years since she had encountered him, Faye had attended one of his exhibitions, and as a budding artist herself, was much taken with his style of work. He was a photorealist figurative artist first and foremost, but he also painted landscapes and seascapes with equal passion. Faye loved them all, but her favourite was a seascape called: 'View from Blue Bay Café'. She was astonished when she realised he had created this particular painting, because for many years she had carried a photo of it in her purse, not knowing the artist. She'd found the photo in between the pages of an art book about Elizabeth Trent. The dedication inside the book was to Philip Morton, which proved it had belonged to her father, who had died when she was four years old. She'd found it by chance, in a box of books in the attic. It seemed to be the only memento of her father's existence. For some reason her mother had thrown everything else of his away, as though he had never existed. She had questioned her mother on several occasions, about what he did for a living, how he'd died and where he was buried. But all she ever gleaned from her was that he was a photographer, he had died in a car crash and was cremated. There was no headstone anywhere to even visit. In the end Faye gave up her quest for information, and surmised that they must have had a very unhappy marriage for her to be so resolute about him.

Thinking of the photo she remembered that she had picked up Nathaniel's business card from the desk at the gallery where he had exhibited. She probably still had it somewhere she thought, rummaging through her bag, though goodness knows why she kept it, she would never be able to afford to buy any of his work, not on her wages anyway. She flicked the card between her fingers and read the address of his studio. She would send a card of condolence, it was the least she could do.

She quickly read through the other obituaries, not for any morbid reason, but for the short accurate account of the lives of interesting people. She enjoyed reading about them, the structure of their lives, their achievements and condensed biographies.

Faye removed her coat and placed it on the ground beside her. It was unusually warm for March, but the shade of the chestnut tree on Gweek Green kept her cool. She continued to flick through the paper, to read the local news which had a full centre page spread of the previous week's storm. The gales and high seas had caused havoc here in Cornwall, causing substantial damage to many of the boats and yachts already moored down on the Helford. Now, the sky was pale blue and cloudless, daffodils were raising their battered heads to feel the warmth of the sun, and the Gweek boatyard bustled with anxious yacht owners watching their beloved vessels being craned into the water in readiness for the sailing season.

Faye sat quietly against the gnarled roots of the great tree, and began to studiously observe a rather nice looking gentleman on the quay. Linking the yacht to the owner, she drew the assumption that this must be the enigmatic Liam Knight.

For a moment Liam turned his attention from the crane which was lifting his forty foot Moody yacht 'Ina' into the channel, and appeared to look directly at her. Faye took a sharp intake of breath, but Liam's gaze was suddenly averted as the yacht touched down in the water.

She lowered her head shyly and glanced at him from under her lashes, pushing a wisp of hair away from her face. Her study of Liam determined that he was approximately six foot two, and possibly in his mid thirties, though his boyish looks questioned her supposition. His hair, which was dark and tousled, framed a fine bone structure, and the short stubble beard emphasised his tanned good looks. His attire was casual, but notably expensive, dressed in a royal blue Musto shirt, white trousers and deck shoes; all in all, he was quite the most handsome man Faye had ever seen.

As a yacht broker in the Gweek Quay boatyard, Faye had spoken to Liam many times on the telephone over the winter. Building up a friendly repartee with him, she often wondered about the face behind the voice. Her eyes twinkled; she was not disappointed.

With Liam now aboard his yacht and out of sight, Faye unscrewed her flask, poured a cup of coffee and returned to her newspaper. Local girl Jasmine Quintana's beautiful face, adorned the front page, under the heading:

'Local woman, Jasmine Quintana, dies tragically in a freak accident, just days before launching her glittering career as the 'face' of Lemmel, London.

The story went on to reveal the whole horrible scenario of the poor girl's demise, and Faye's heart went out to her distraught parents, pictured pale and thin-lipped with grief. The article preceded the inquest report and Faye read on:

The parents of a beautiful, healthy young woman, on the brink of a lucrative cosmetic contract with Lemmel, London, paid a heartfelt tribute to their daughter.

On Friday March 24th 1995 Jasmine Quintana (19) died when a round hay bale escaped from the tractor transporting the load. The bale rolled down the hill opposite the Andover Country House Hotel in Hampshire and struck her stationary car, which was parked in their car park.

Holding hands with her husband David, at the family home in Carbis Bay near St Ives, Cornwall, Sarah Quintana said: "Jasmine was a truly beautiful and wonderful model daughter; she was always kind and blessed with the sweetest nature. She worked hard, and the contract with Lemmel, would have been 'just rewards' for her fantastic work ethic, as she worked her way up to the top of her modelling career. We have no idea why she was in the Andover Country House Hotel car park at the time. She was on the brink of a huge advertising campaign as the 'Face of Infinity' which was to be launched internationally on March 25th. She had just taken delivery of a new Mercedes as part of her contract and was looking forward to driving down to see us. We had spoken to her earlier that day by phone, where she confirmed she would be at our family home in Carbis Bay at 8.00 p.m. for a special family party. We were absolutely shocked to the core when we heard of the accident, and we cannot understand why she had checked into the hotel that evening. It's an absolute mystery.

A spokesman for the Andover Country House Hotel confirmed that the penthouse suite had been booked in the name of Jasmine Quintana, though there was some confusion at reception when Miss Quintana arrived. However, a hotel source, who would like to remain anonymous, suggested that Miss Quintana joined a gentleman at the bar and then a few minutes later, heated words were exchanged. The gentleman appeared to push some papers towards Miss Quintana, which she grabbed from him just before she stormed off. The gentleman bent down to retrieve a book Miss Quintana had dropped during her departure, but instead of following her, he finished his drink. The next thing we knew was that there had been a terrible accident in the car park. When we all returned to the bar area, the gentleman had gone and the key to the penthouse suite was still on the bar.

The article continued:

Woman on the brink of a glittering career.

Jasmine had been a model with the Sirocco model agency in London since she was sixteen, when she was spotted by a scout working for Lemmel, looking for a 'fresh face' to front their new high profile advertising campaign. This was her big break with huge financial rewards. The campaign had taken her to Bali and Thailand in January to shoot photographs, which would have had blanket coverage in all the giant glossy magazines. She had also shot a TV commercial, which was to have been aired on the 25th March. As a mark of respect, the campaign was immediately pulled on word of her death.

A spokesman for Lemmel said: 'We are deeply shocked at this appalling accident, which took the life of such a beautiful and gentle young woman.' The spokesman for Sirocco Model Agency could shed no light on why she was at the hotel that evening. 'Jasmine had been looking forward to the family party and had been in high spirits when she left the London office at lunch time. She was thrilled at the prospect of picking up the car of her dreams from the Mercedes Garage in Reading.' She added, 'Our thoughts and love go out to her family. Jasmine was a wonderful young woman on the brink of a glittering career'.

An initial post-mortem found she had sustained catastrophic crushing injuries, including a broken spine and shattered pelvis. These injuries were consistent with the impact on the car by large round hay bail found at the site of the accident.

At the inquest into her death last week the coroner recorded a verdict of accidental death following multiple injuries after being crushed by the hay bale.

With an uncanny sensation that she was being watched, Faye's eyes lifted from the newspaper to meet those of Liam Knight. He smiled warmly and moved towards her.

"Forgive the intrusion. You're obviously on your lunch break. It's just that I noticed you watching me earlier, while I was having my yacht craned in." He gestured towards the Moody, now moored alongside the quay. Faye coloured slightly, and observing her uneasiness, he said, "Forgive me, I must have been mistaken." He began to move away, and then hesitated. "It's just…" He laughed softly. "I just thought you must know me, you know, by the way you were watching. So I thought I had better come over to say hello." He raised his hand apologetically. "Never mind." He laughed again. "Just ignore me and I'll go away." This time he turned to leave.

"No," Faye said urgently, folding the newspaper and placing it by her side. "Please don't go. You're right, I admit it." She smiled shyly. "I was watching you." Easing herself up from where she sat, she held out her hand in welcome. "I do actually know who you are!" She blushed again, this time more profusely.

Liam raised his eyebrows in interest. "I'm intrigued," he said, his eyes devouring Faye as though she was the most exquisite creature he had ever seen. He'd watched her from the quay for quite a while before he approached her, trying to make out her features, for she looked - he searched for the word - ethereal, yes, that was it, ethereal, and on closer inspection he found that she was the most perfect specimen of a woman he had ever come across. He reached out to shake her hand. "Enchanted," he said, gazing at her long auburn hair which seemed to glow like sunshine as it framed her beautiful face. Her creamy pale skin held a hint of blush at her cheeks, and her soft dark lashes lowered slightly in coyness to shield her emerald eyes from the intensity of his gaze.

His was not an unusual reaction for Faye to witness - she had attracted a great deal of male attention since she had turned fifteen and most of it was quite unwelcome. The innate sexuality which went with her delicate beauty seemed to give most men carte blanche to behave improperly towards her, which in turn, made her wary of men. She knew some women would revel in the attention, but she found it quite unnerving.

Aware that he was staring at her, he quickly held out his

hand to shake hers. "I'm Liam Knight, but then you seem to know that fact."

Faye smiled and shook his hand, which was firm and warm. "I'm Faye Larson, from the boatyard."

"Faye? Goodness, isn't it funny, you can never guess what a person looks like by their voice!"

"True." She smiled wryly. "You're nothing like how I imagined."

"Am I not? Why, what did you imagine?"

Faye smiled inwardly, remembering her good friend Pippa's comical description of Liam. 'Oh you won't like him one little bit,' she'd said, every time Faye swooned as she took a call from Liam. 'He has short fat bow legs, a beer belly and a comb over.'

"What are you smiling about?" Liam asked searchingly.

"Nothing," Faye said dismissively. "But I'm very pleased to meet you at last."

"Likewise, I hope we meet again very soon." He searched in his pocket for his wallet and produced a business card. "Call me and we'll meet up for a drink."

She took the card and read the bold lettering - Mr Liam Knight Advertising executive, Lemmel, London.

She raised her eyebrows and looked directly at him. "Lemmel, how strange is that? I was just reading about that poor girl who was crushed by the hay bale last week. You know the one who was to be the new face of Lemmel? I suppose you knew her quite well?"

Liam cleared his throat and shook his head. "No, I didn't really know of her to tell you the truth. Terrible business though. Anyway, call me, on that number, if you fancy a drink or something one evening." He winked in a self assured way.

Faye watched him walk away, glanced at the card and tucked it into her handbag. The call would never happen; she was much too reticent to be so forward.

*

The boatyard and chandlery was a hive of activity that

afternoon. Last minute preparations were being made to the various vessels which now sat alongside the quay, in readiness for their voyage down the river. Frantic yacht owners rushed in and out of the chandlery, purchasing everything from ropes, lines and marine paints, to safety equipment, deck hardware, fenders and engine spares.

At four-thirty p.m. Joe breezed into the office. "My God what a day, I'm glad that is over. Anyone fancy a Pizza at Poldhu tonight?"

"We're in, aren't we Faye?" Pippa said brightly.

Faye leaned back from her desk and stretched her arms in the air. "Sounds good to me, how are we getting there?"

"My van, I got the short straw this week." Joe grinned.

Faye loved the social life attached to the boatyard, everyone was so friendly. There was a regular quiz every other Thursday at the Black Swan, Pizza night on Friday at Poldhu café and folk music down at the Cadgwith Arms on Tuesday, where she, Joe and Sid played and sang together, collectively known as 'Three Fold'. Life was never dull. On her days off she would take her sketchbook and paints out onto the cliffs and if Pippa had the same day off they would be down on Poldhu beach attempting to surf - 'attempting' being the operative word. No matter how many times she tried, Faye could not stand on the board, whereas Pippa, who had lived in Cornwall all her life, was a true water baby.

*

The Black Swan at Gweek was as deserted as a greenhouse in a heat-wave when Liam Knight walked through the door at seven p.m. He settled himself on a bar stool and ordered a gin and tonic, helping himself to a handful of peanuts from the dish on the bar. Every time the door opened, he turned, ever hopeful that Faye would walk in. Presently, he said to the landlord, "It's quiet in here tonight!"

He checked his watch and nodded. "It'll get busy later when the boatyard lot come back from having their supper at Poldhu."

"I see." He sighed gloomily.

"Are you on holiday then?" the landlord enquired.

"No," Liam answered nonchalantly.

He waited for a moment, then realising conversation with Liam was not forthcoming, the landlord smiled and moved to the other end of the bar.

At ten p.m., Joe's bright green VW camper van drove noisily into the boatyard and seven people spilled out of the side door laughing.

The tide had risen and dark murky water, illuminated by the almost full moon, lapped lazily against the hull of Liam's yacht. He stood motionless on the deck and watched as the group exchanged hugs. The two women parted company, shouting their goodbyes to each other. Liam watched with interest as the streetlamp illuminated the long flowing hair of the remaining woman. She casually linked arms with one of the men, and they chatted and laughed gently and intimately with each other as they crossed the bridge and disappeared from sight.

2

Zennor, April 3rd 1995

Nathaniel Prior screwed his eyes tight shut, his stomach churned and his mouth was dry and sour with the terror of his never-ending nightmare. How he would get through this coming day he had no idea. This was the day he would bury the love of his life.

Calm, I must stay calm. He willed his trembling body to be still. He began to take deep breaths, in through the nose, out through the mouth, slowly he relaxed and peace ensued momentarily. As he lay in quiet desolation upon the bed, unease prevailed, and unable to keep the horrors of that night at bay, his mind, once again began to replay the whole scenario.

It had been exactly one week since that terrible night, and the memory of it tortured his sleep and his waking hours. That long dreadful night had been filled with terror for both him and his darling wife Elizabeth. The hours had been punctuated with sudden desperate episodes of breathlessness as she gulped air from her oxygen mask. He knew in his heart that that had been the beginning of the end.

A storm raged all night and he slept fitfully, only to be woken by the sudden grasp of Elizabeth's hand on his wrist as she gasped for breath. Anxiously she watched as he rushed to her side of the bed. Swiftly the oxygen bottle was changed and the syringe drive was pressed and a shot of morphine was administered into her stomach.

"Oh Nathan, is this it?" she said, a small tear trickling down her cheek. She closed her eyes and waited for the pain and panic to ease.

"It's all right my darling, I'm here," Nathan whispered as he sat on the bed, tenderly stroking her emaciated hand. His sadness deepened as his fingers unconsciously played with the gold wedding band which moved freely along the length of her thin finger.

The rain lashed against the windows and great gusts of wind shook the window fastenings. He looked around the bedroom they had shared for twenty-five blissful years. It was cosy and cluttered with an array of soft silk cushions and a lifetime of framed memories. His eyes rested on the marble sculpture of a woman and child crafted by Elizabeth's own loving hands. But the constant exposure to the marble dust had undoubtedly caused the problem in her lungs. He shook his head. How could something so beautiful, be responsible for all this suffering? He felt the emotion rise from the pit of his stomach, as he fought back the tears which welled in his eyes. He must be strong for Elizabeth. He must match her bravery and help her through today, otherwise he would cry, and that, he feared, would be the ruin of them all.

When the end came, it had been swift and unbearable. Wrapping his loving arms around her, he whispered words of love into her ear, nuzzling into her soft neck, praying to God not to take her. When inevitably the last desperate breaths came, he whispered softly, "Don't leave me Elizabeth. Please don't leave me." Then silence ensued, and the world suddenly became very still, broken eventually by a long drawn out howl. Nathan closed his eyes and clamped his hands to his ears, willing the noise to stop, and then he realised the strange keening sound was from his own throat as grief engulfed him.

As Elizabeth passed from this life to the next, their twenty year old son Greg had sat in stunned silence at his mother's feet. His head held low, as tears fell onto the quilted eiderdown he'd watched his mother make when he was just a small boy at her apron strings. Elizabeth had battled with lung cancer for the last two years, but on that day, she had finally lost the war just before dawn. The cold grey morning laid bare the stark reminder of the loss and hopelessness Nathan felt within him. She had gone, and he could stay indoors no longer and took himself off to stand alone on the cliff edge in his shirt sleeves. His feelings, like the weather, were raw and volatile. The storm still raged without losing any of its ferocity from the previous night. Sheets of driving rain pushed in from the ocean, driven by the strong south-westerly wind, inflicting havoc on many a spring garden in the tiny village of Zennor. The gales had ripped the Tinners Arms public house sign from its fastenings and it now hung precariously by one chain, smacking intermittently against the granite walls of the *hostelry, much to the irritation of landlord Duggie Martin, who was trying to sleep inside.*

In the distance the bell from the church rang out to those of the faith. Nathan laughed scornfully. Faith! He had no faith in a God who could take someone as wonderful as Elizabeth from the loving arms of her family. What sort of God could do that and let the evil element of this world live?

In the bay, tiny fishing boats yanked furiously at their moorings as the tide, high and angry, whipped at the shingle beach. He ran his hands through his wet hair in desperate frustration.

"Elizabeth," he roared her name in anguish, but the wind caught his words and they skittered across the valley to be lost along with Elizabeth for infinity.

Greg had found him and tenderly placed his hand on Nathan's shoulder. Nathan turned to meet his only son; his wet pale-faced misery mirrored his own. How young he looked, almost like a child and as diffident. Over Greg's shoulder, Nathan could see the black hearse waiting outside the gate of Gwithian Cottage.

"They have come to take Mum away," Greg said tearfully.

*

Nathan wiped a tear away from his tired eyes. The previous week's incessant rain, which had poured from leaden skies and pounded with such ferocity against the windows of the cottage, had now been replaced by warm sunshine. Despite the sun streaming through the bedroom window, Gwithian Cottage felt cold and eerily silent. Gone was the constant hiss of oxygen and gone was the rasping cough that had plagued Elizabeth for so many months.

Nathan sat in his best suit on the crumpled bed and surveyed the cosy cluttered room. As always a vase of flowers adorned the dressing table, today they were the remains of long stemmed red roses and white gypsophila, elegant and beautiful, but hot house forced and void of any scent. Never again would Elizabeth breeze into the house with her arms full of wild flowers and happily arrange them in each and every room, Nathan thought wistfully.

*

Elizabeth Trent-Prior's funeral was well attended; a great many of their friends had come to pay their last respects. Elizabeth's father, himself a widower for a great many years, had driven down from his home in Scotland to watch his beloved daughter make her last journey. His grief, like Nathan's, was deep and all consuming.

Elizabeth was well liked among the small community of Zennor, and much admired for her work as a sculptor and artist throughout the art world.

Nathan requested donations to a cancer charity instead of flowers, but the mourners sent both. Elizabeth was beautiful and flowers were indeed a necessary tribute to adorn her on her last journey.

Within the ancient walls of the church of St Senara's in Zennor, Greg cried softly for his mother. A river of helpless tears flowed down his cheeks throughout the moving ceremony, none more so then when Nathan read the Eulogy. Nathan had spent night after night pouring his heart out into the words he wrote, and as he stood in the pulpit, his hands trembled as he began to speak:

"I am now among the thousands of people who have lost a loved one to the ravages of cancer. I walked hand in hand with my Elizabeth in life and then to the far end of death with her. And there I had to leave her and walk the lonely road home by myself. Thankfully I have the love of family and friends and I thank them for being there to help me through this painful journey.

Elizabeth struggled so hard to stay with me; she never lost her fighting spirit. I look back and see through the mist that shrouds my world, and realise that Elizabeth gave me a very special gift; she gave me many years of profound and enduring love and I will treasure the memory of her forever.

During the last two years that she endured this terrible disease, we had the special opportunity of living our lives to the full and showing our love to each other in very special ways.

We must all succumb to death someday, as death is a certainty, and you cannot fear a certainty, and watching someone you love die, makes us lose the fear of going through the dying process ourselves

Losing my darling girl and the intense and painful emotions which followed, coupled with the helplessness I feel will last forever, I am now left to dig down deep within myself to find the spiritual strength that will help me to go on living a productive life without her. Maybe one day we will learn not to dwell on our loss, but to give thanks for the time we were given to share our life with such a special person. One day I hope we will truly look back and only see the good things in our lives spent together, and then I'll know we have recovered from our loss. But until then, and I know I speak for myself, my son and Elizabeth's father, our hearts will bleed.

Elizabeth endured her fate with courage and fortitude and never lost her wonderful sense of humour, even at the very end of her life."

He paused and looked down at the lily clad coffin.

"Goodbye my darling girl, until we meet again, another time, another place."

As he stepped down from the pulpit, Nathan observed his handsome son, his mop of dark glossy curls, worn long, but pulled back and tied with a band. Greg's face emulated Nathan's feelings, but now tears failed to fall so freely from his own eyes - he felt dazed and confused, life had become surreal. He could not comprehend his wife's death. It was not possible that she had left him, it was too much to contemplate that she had gone forever. As he neared the church door, his eyes fell upon his good friends the Quintanas, themselves deep in their own grief at losing their beautiful daughter Jasmine. They embraced with a shared loss so deep it was unfathomable. When Sarah

Quintana had rung the previous week to tell Nathan of Jasmine's tragic accident, and knowing how close to death Elizabeth was, they had agreed between themselves to keep the dreadful news from her, in case it accelerated her own death.

In the bright Cornish sunshine, Greg and Nathan held each other as they stepped out of the church gates and made their way to the plot of land where her headstone would stand. A wake was laid on in the Tinners Arms, which all the mourners would attend before Nathan, Greg and Elizabeth's father accompanied the coffin to Truro for a private cremation. As they led the procession of mourners across the road, Nathan noted that every house in the village had closed their curtains in respect.

Nathan took a deep breath before he entered the hostelry. "Be strong," Nathan could hear Elizabeth's voice in his head. "Be strong and brave my beautiful boys."

3
Gweek

April was one of the busiest months at the boatyard. Yacht owners were fussing about, putting the finishing touches to their vessels in readiness for the sailing season. The office diary was full of yachts waiting to be craned in. Sid, the crane driver, barely had time to snatch a cup of tea and sandwich before the next anxious client appeared ready to watch their beloved vessels being transported from hard standing to water. The chandlery was a constant hive of activity, selling and re-merchandising stock, cutting lengths of rope and chain, phones ringing constantly, and frayed tempers to deal with. When lunchtime arrived, Faye invariably escaped to sit at the river bank whenever the weather permitted.

Settling down against her favourite tree, the sun was warm and the sound of water rushing from under the bridge to meet the oncoming tide was punctuated with the sound of children playing at the waters edge. Two swans glided majestically up the river, bowing their long willowing necks deep into the water to feed. Suddenly the children's shrill laughter slowed the creatures to a halt, and then with a flap of wings, they took themselves off towards the peace and solitude of the island in the middle of the river.

After a cold lunch of humus, bread and olives, Faye reflected on her weekend. Life was good down in Cornwall, the beach at Poldhu was only five miles away and she and Pippa had spent most of the weekend there swimming and drinking coffee. Closing her eyes she let the sun warm her face. How wonderful spring was in this beautiful part of the world.

She'd been twenty-one when she'd arrived in Cornwall, just over four years ago. She had left her parents' home in

Burndale, North Yorkshire on a whim. The artist in her felt drawn to Cornwall, though she did have a connection with the county, having been born here - though her family had moved away when she was very young. Though her family never returned to holiday, Faye felt it was her spiritual home. So, much to her step-father's disapproval, she left her safe job as a bank cashier, packed her bags and set off for a better life.

Cornwall was her home now. Not once in the four years she'd been down here, had she wanted to return to Yorkshire.

Faye had always yearned to live by the water, so the move from a quiet little Yorkshire village, some ninety miles from any coastline you could call decent, to the majestic splendour of the beautiful Cornish coast, was her 'dream-come-true'.

After several part-time jobs working in beach cafés and pubs, Faye had finally settled happily into a full-time job in the Chandlery at Gweek Quay Boatyard. She rented a small but adequate house on Post Office Row in Gweek, which had become her sanctuary. A place of her own where she could relax and enjoy the freedom of life without the restrictions that came about when one still shared a home with a domineering step-father. As she watched the comings and goings in the boatyard she smiled inwardly. This was not what she had envisaged doing, but she had settled into it quickly and thoroughly enjoyed the people she worked with. Faye's dream was to be an artist, though her parents had done their best to suppress her talent, telling her that she needed a proper job. In truth, she wanted to own her own beachside café, with space to hang and sell her own artwork. But for now she was content. Gweek was a wonderful place to live, and she had time to paint and enjoy life with her work colleague and very good friend Pippa.

Pippa was a blonde bubbly petite twenty-three year old, with a wicked sense of humour, a good-natured personality and a permanent smile. She was the second child of Edwin and Carole Ferris-Norton, who ran the local veterinary practice, which had been in their family for the last two generations. Though her brother Charles had entered into the family business, Pippa had forged a different career for herself. She loved boats, and being a yacht broker at Gweek Quay was all she ever wanted to do. Faye had taken to her instantly, forging a friendship that she believed would last a lifetime.

The boatyard was managed by Owen Barnes and his wife Gloria who worked as yard manager and cafeteria manageress respectively.

Owen was forty-nine years old. He was not a tall man, but stocky with a thick neck, kind eyes and an abundance of thick dark body hair, that was evident from the tufts which grew upwards from his stiff white collar. Every morning he would breeze into the office and greet the girls with a cheery, "Good morning my lovelies."

Gloria was equally lovely and mothered the girls to death, supplying them with ample amounts of cake to have with their afternoon coffee. "You two are as thin as sticks," she would say, thumping her fists into her own ample hips.

Faye checked the time, drained the last of her coffee which had gone cold, screwed the cup back onto the flask and stored it in her bag. She stood up and stretched the stiffness from her long legs, yawned lazily, picked up her lunch box, then made her way back to work.

*

Faye had been back in the office about half an hour, so too had Amos Peel.

Amos was a loner, a tall scruffy twenty five-year-old, who emitted a strong unpleasant odour of oil and unwashed skin. He lived alone in the boatyard, aboard the houseboat he was born on, the rest of his family having moved out long ago on the receipt of a family legacy. To Faye's frustration Amos spent a great deal of time in the

Chandlery part of the office, mostly wasting time, but today he was being particularly irritating. After Faye had spent most of the morning neatly re-stocking the shelves, Amos, as usual, was engaged in his annoying habit of moving things from one shelf to another whilst he was browsing. Suddenly there was a loud crash. Faye shook her head and glanced at Pippa.

Putting down her pen, Pippa asked wearily, "Are you at a loose end Amos by any chance?"

Amos moved to the counter. "Yeah," he answered scratching his lank hair. He looked intently at Faye, but she did not look up.

"What about your boat Amos? Isn't there anything you can do on her?" Pippa suggested.

Amos snorted loudly as though he was about to spit out the contents of his throat. Neither girl could hide their repulsion. It was a disgustingly annoying habit that Amos had, which turned their stomachs whenever he did it.

"Do you have to do that Amos?" Pippa asked.

"Do what?"

"That disgusting noise you are always making."

Amos shrugged his shoulders.

Pippa shook her head. "Oh never mind. Can't you go and work on your boat or something?"

"No, the boat is finished." He rested his elbows on the counter and continued to gaze at Faye. After a few moments he said, "Hey, Faye?"

"Mmm?" Faye answered patiently, not looking up from her work.

Amos willed her to look up at him, but she carried on working. Faye was without doubt the most beautiful woman he had ever seen and over the last few months his adoration for her had become almost an obsession. Amos chewed his bottom lip then spoke her name again.

"Yes Amos?" she answered despairingly.

"I was just thinking. Now I've finished the repairs to my boat 'Odessa', she's ready to sail again," he declared proudly.

"That's nice," Faye answered absentmindedly.

Amos drew a deep breath then asked brightly, "Would you like to come for a sail on her? I could have her craned into the water if you said yes."

Pippa shot Faye an amused glance.

Faye looked up from her work and smiled kindly at him. "No thank you Amos. Don't do that for me. I'm not a very good sailor, but thank you for asking me."

Pippa sniggered and Amos shot her a cold look. He cleared his throat and said, "Oh don't worry Faye, I'll make sure it's a calm day. You'll be absolutely fine, I promise."

Unable to contain her amusement, Pippa shot Faye a large toothy grin.

Faye glanced at Pippa from the corner of her eye, and with great effort to hide the irritation in her voice she politely said, "Thanks Amos, but no thanks."

Reluctant to accept her refusal, Amos stood silently at the counter for a moment, his mind working overtime. Determined not to give up, he said, "What about a drink then, or dinner? Come over to our house, I'll get Mum to cook some Ostrich, you'll like that, it's posh."

Pippa grimaced. "Ostrich! Who the hell eats Ostrich?"

"Lots of people eat it!" he declared. "My Dad breeds them and keeps them at the far end of Post Office Lane! Haven't you seen them?"

"Nope, can't say I have. How long have they been there?"

"About two months. Bloody funny looking things they are too. They have gigantic feet and beady eyes. My Dad says that everyone will be eating them soon."

"Ugh, what do they taste of?" Pippa asked. "Oh don't tell me, I bet it tastes of ….Chicken!" The two girls said the last word in unison and grinned at each other.

Amos sighed heavily. "So, what do you say, eh Faye, an Ostrich dinner and a nice glass of Blue Nun."

Unable to contain it any longer, Pippa burst out laughing.

Faye bit her lip and said as politely as she could, "No thank you Amos. Now I'm really sorry, but I'm terribly busy. I'd really appreciate it if you could let me get on with my work."

Amos smiled thinly but made no attempt to move. Eventually the pungent smell that was wafting from Amos's direction became too much to bear and Faye could take no more. She sighed heavily and pushed her chair violently from her desk.

"Fancy a cuppa Pippa?" she said, scurrying off to the back room to make some tea.

The back room was an untidy array of odd chairs and obsolete display stands. There were boat magazines and dirty rags strewn across the floor, as were coils of used rope and half eaten food which had been tipped from the upturned waste bin to be used as a makeshift seat. Faye shook her head; it hadn't been three hours since she'd cleaned this place. She glanced at the washing up bowl full of dirty cups, and blew out an exasperated sigh, rolled her sleeves up and ran the water from the boiler until it came warm. Oh the joys of sharing an office with a crowd of marine mechanics and boat builders, she thought wistfully. Just as she filled the kettle she heard the telephone ring.

A moment later Pippa hit the mute button. "Faye," she shouted in a sing-song voice, "It's for you."

"Who is it?" Faye enquired, trying not to inhale as she squeezed past Amos who had followed her to the back room.

"It's Liam Knight." She grinned broadly. "He wants to talk to *you*." Pippa raised her eyebrows and passed the phone over.

Faye's heart skipped a beat. It had been three days since she'd met him on the river bank and he had never actually left her thoughts since then. She took the telephone from Pippa and felt the blush rise from her neck and colour her cheeks.

"Hello," she said softly, trying to ignore Pippa, who had seated herself at the end of Faye's desk and was gesticulating wildly at her. "I'm sorry Mr Knight, could you just hold for a moment," she said, covering the mouthpiece with her hand. "What do you want?" she mouthed to Pippa.

"Do you know you've gone bright red?" Pippa grinned.

Faye's blush deepened. "Stop it, you're making it worse." She quickly fanned her face with her hand then returned to her call. "Hello Mr Knight, I'm so sorry about that."

"No worries, but please Faye, stop this Mr Knight business, call me Liam, okay," he said brightly.

"Okay, thank you," she answered softly.

"So, how are you on this bright sunny day?"

She smiled at his cheeriness. "I'm fine thank you," she answered politely, pulling her blouse open at the neck to release some of the heat from her blushing body. "And you?"

"Splendid thank you. So, why didn't you call me then?" He kept his voice light, but in truth, it had puzzled him that she hadn't rung. Normally when he gave out his business card to a woman, and she saw what he did for a living, they practically threw themselves at him. He couldn't remember ever having to follow up one of his invitations before.

Unsure of what to say, Faye fell silent.

"Faye, are you still there?"

Nervously she cleared her throat. "Yes, I'm here."

"Did you misplace the card I gave you?"

"No." She thought of all the times she had looked at the card and placed it back in her bag.

"So, why didn't you call me then?" he teased.

She grimaced. "I don't know," she said, trying to calm her pounding heart.

"I see." He laughed, and then choosing his words carefully said, "Well, I'll ask you again, would you like to meet me for a drink?"

She bit down on her lip then forced herself to say, "Yes. Thank you, I'd like that very much."

Liam sighed with relief. "Well, thank goodness for that, I thought you didn't like me."

Feeling more relaxed now, Faye laughed lightly. "No, believe me, it was a nice surprise to meet you the other day, especially after Pippa told me you had short fat bow legs, a beer belly and a comb over," she joked, glancing at Pippa, whose face was aghast.

"She did, did she," he answered humourlessly. "So, when is your next day off?"

"I'm off tomorrow."

"Good. Maybe we could have a lunchtime drink on my yacht then?"

Faye laughed nervously. "Yes, maybe."

He was struggling now to hide his irritation. What the hell was wrong with this woman? "Well, I'll let you decide," he answered evenly. "I shall wait in anticipation. You know where I'll be, I'll be there from 1 p.m."

"Okay, thank you. Goodbye Liam." She put the receiver down, leaned back in her chair and fanned the heat from her face.

"Ha ha, do I detect a little love interest here?" Pippa enquired mischievously.

Faye put her finger to her lips and smiled sweetly. But the gesture hadn't gone unnoticed.

Amos closed his eyes and leant heavily against the wall of the back room. As he'd listened to her telephone conversation, each soft word and tinkle of laughter Faye gave broke his heart into a million pieces. Unable to stand it any longer, he emerged crestfallen into the office, cast a mournful look in Faye's direction and stormed out, almost colliding with Owen Barnes at the doorway.

"Oh hello, what's up with him? He looks like he's lost a

pound and found a shilling," Owen asked.

"He wants to take Faye out for a drink, but she has other plans."

Faye's eyes widened with embarrassment.

"Ah, they're queuing up are they? Well, that's what you get for being so beautiful my lovely." Owen winked at Faye.

A moment later he left the office and Faye threw a Yachting Weekly magazine at Pippa. "Can I have no secrets?"

"Nope." Pippa said, perching herself on Faye's desk again. "So, tell me more about this short fat balding man you've taken a shine too," she asked with a twinkle in her eye. "Was it his bow legs or his comb over which took your fancy?"

4

Lifting her eyes to the ceiling, Faye carefully administered cooling eye drops into each of her dry and scratchy eyes. She blinked furiously and shuddered. She loathed having to do anything to her eyes, but needs must today. She had experienced a shockingly sleepless night. For all her yawning and rubbing of tired eyes, sleep had evaded her for most of the night.

It was the thought of meeting Liam, she knew that. She was wary of men, and questioned herself relentlessly about whether to meet him or not. After all, she hardly knew the man. For all her beauty, Faye had been very shy and cautious when it came to dating. She had only once before been on a proper date with someone and that had been when she was seventeen. The boy in question seemed really keen and to be truthful Faye had enjoyed the attention from him. She hadn't planned for anything other than a romantic date, but a little too much to drink resulted in a rather unpleasant experience for both of them. It seems he too was inexperienced, and with his pride hurt he had turned on her in a most vicious way. She still shuddered to this day at his harsh words. 'You whore, you pushed me into that before I was ready…and on the first date,' he'd spat the words venomously at her. She remembered with fear, his face white with anger, as he snatched his clothes into a bundle and stormed away, leaving her laying on her coat in the grounds of a deserted park, reeling in sick emotion.

Funnily enough she had been quite relaxed and chilled at the close of the previous evening. She had enjoyed a rather superb baked lasagne, Pippa's 'signature dish', and the girls had consumed copious glasses of red wine, the latter taking its toll on her aching head this morning. It's true to say that Pippa had probably been more excited about her date with Liam than she was, and couldn't understand Faye's reservations.

Settling down to eat in Pippa's cosy kitchen, Pippa dished up a portion of lasagne. "He's rich you know! Life could change for you tomorrow," she enthused with much aplomb.

Faye narrowed her eyes. "I'm not interested in rich, you know I'm not," she said, adding a generous amount of salad to her plate.

Pippa raised her eyebrows. "Be that as it may, but he could certainly give a girl a good time," she said, waving the spatula in the air.

Faye sighed heavily. "No doubt," she said crisply.

"I don't know what your problem is," Pippa said, slapping her playfully on the shoulder before sitting down to eat. "He's rich and gorgeous, what more could you want? You'll have to go a long way to find someone else as dishy."

"I know, I know. I hear you."

A mouthful of lasagne rendered Pippa silent for a moment, but the furious waving of her fork in the air preceded another reason why she should go. "Oh come on, I know you like him, I can see your face light up every time his name is mentioned."

Faye smiled and lowered her eyes. "It's true. I do like him, it's just....."

"It's just what, for goodness sake?" Pippa said, almost spilling the contents of her glass of wine.

"I don't know, I'm just being silly, I know."

"Yes you bloody well are! Well dear girl, it's either him or Amos, the choice is yours."

"Oh well if you put it like that, it's a no brainer. It'll just have to be Amos. Where else will I find anyone with such animal magnetism?" She grinned.

Pippa sputtered gleefully. "Where else would you find anyone with such animal smells more like?" Faye screwed up her nose at the very thought of him. "Well, I'm telling you now lady, if you're not down on that riverbank in the morning, there had better be a bloody good excuse."

*

After selecting one of the first outfits she had pulled out of the wardrobe, she dressed quickly as it was almost one p.m. She couldn't help it, but part of her hoped he wouldn't be there. She took one last look in the mirror, picked up her handbag, gave the house a quick once over to check all was tidy and opened the back door. Momentarily stunned at the unbelievable image before her, she stopped dead in her tracks, let out a piercing scream, and tried in vain to shut the door on the encroaching creature. Suddenly the door was wrenched from her hands and the kitchen was full of a five foot ostrich, feathers flying, wings flaying, as it ran about knocking everything onto the floor as it went. Faye screamed hysterically as the bird zigzagged slowly towards her, its small black beady eyes latched onto its target. Suddenly it came at her and she grabbed for the pan trivet, the only available thing to hand to defend herself.

"Oh no," she screeched. "Get away. Oh God, someone help, please someone help!" she wailed. The bird pushed a leg out towards her and she fell to the ground knocking her head on the cooker. Cornered now, she made several attempts to get up and run away, but she was repeatedly pecked on the head and kicked in the chest by its enormous prehistoric feet. Curling up into a tight ball, she heard Joe her neighbour, at the door threshold.

"What the f......" Faye heard Joe shout, and then heard the thuds as he began to beat the bird with her umbrella to drive it back out of the kitchen. Almost at the back door, it turned again, rushed past Joe and burst through into Faye's lounge. Not daring to move at first, she flinched when Joe grabbed her by the arm to pull her out of the kitchen. "Come on love, you need to get out of here," she heard him say, as he dragged her to the safety of the communal back garden, quickly pulling the back door shut behind them. They could hear the destruction the bird was causing inside, and then suddenly she heard her front window smash and all fell quiet.

Dazed and stunned at what had just happened, Faye lay groaning on the back lawn as several of her neighbours milled around fussing and making her comfortable. She hugged her arms around her sore ribs, moaning with every breath. Losing all track of time, she was barely aware of the ambulance men, and the journey to The Royal Cornwall Hospital at Treliske.

She'd been lucky, she was told by the police, who interviewed her in casualty. Although she had sustained multiple cuts, bruises, concussion and a cracked rib, an attack from an ostrich often proved fatal. As for her assailant, she was told it had slit its own throat with a shard of glass when it smashed through the window. Amos's father, who the bird belonged to, had been arrested and cautioned for allowing the dangerous creature to escape from his ostrich farm.

*

Liam had his yacht 'Ina' moored alongside the quay, and by the time his watch said one-thirty p.m. his mood had turned sour. Not used to being stood up, his anger festered like an open wound. Disliking the idea that she would do it again, he was torn on how to proceed with her. She was something special, he knew that. In his line of work a woman of this calibre was not to be passed over under any circumstances. He settled down to seethe into his gin and tonic.

After reading the newspaper, he drained his glass and glanced again at his watch. He wondered where on earth she could be, and why she hadn't shown up. He would have thought a drinks date on a yacht had to be a hundred times more appealing than spending her time with that provincial lot she hung around with all the time! There was just no accounting for taste he thought, as he gave an exaggerated sigh. Banging his glass down on the table, he climbed out onto the deck and squinted into the bright sunlight.

There was some sort of commotion going on in the centre of the village, several people were milling about, but being indifferent to the goings on of these people, who were so insignificant to him in the grand scheme of things, he chose to ignore the gathering crowd. He turned and slammed the hatch shut, climbed out onto the quay and looked down the river. Just another couple of days and the tide would be high enough to sail away down the Helford, where he could enjoy the splendid isolation he craved away from everyone. He threw his overnight bag into the boot of his Range Rover and pulled out of the boatyard at top speed, leaving a cloud of dust in his wake. As he approached the bridge, an ambulance came swiftly down the hill with blue lights flashing and siren blaring. He quickly pulled onto the verge and gave a short derisive snort. 'Someone must have died of boredom in the village' he thought to himself.

*

"She was attacked by a what?" Pippa screeched, when Joe rang her from the hospital.

"No kidding Pippa, it was an ostrich. The bloody thing was enormous. It's completely wrecked her house!"

"Oh my God! Is she all right?" she said, reaching up to clasp her hand to her throat.

"Battered and bruised. She's just having some x-rays, but they are keeping her in overnight for observation. Will you let Owen know where I am? Tell him, I'm sorry I missed high tide, he'll understand, I'm sure."

"I'm sure he will," she said pouting, remembering the rather colourful language Owen had used when he couldn't locate Joe half an hour ago. "Send her my love. Tell her I'll come and see her tonight." She put the phone down just as Amos walked into the office. She raised her eyebrows at him knowingly.

"What?" he said in bemusement.

"One of your bloody ostriches has attacked Faye and nearly bloody killed her," she said tapping her foot in annoyance.

His face paled significantly. "They're not my ostriches," he said shaking his head. "Tell her they are not mine."

*

Armed with grapes, magazines and sandwiches, Pippa sat at Faye's bedside and studiously surveyed the battered face of her friend. She had several cuts and bruises to her face and one of her eyes was blackened and closed. "Blimey Faye, you look like you've done ten rounds with Muhammad Ali!"

Faye lifted her head so she could see out of her good eye. "I might have faired better in a boxing ring."

"What the hell happened then?"

"I just opened the door and whoosh. It was in the kitchen before I even registered what it was! I didn't stand a chance; it just set its beady eyes on me and kept battering me with its enormous feet. If it hadn't been for Joe coming to my rescue, I don't know what would have happened. He was amazing, but I swear I'll have nightmares for years about it. Ouch," she said holding her hand to her ribs. She had never felt pain like it. Every sharp intake of breath or slight movement sent a searing pain through her chest.

Pippa held her hands to her face. "Oh you poor thing. If it wasn't so horrific, it would be funny though, wouldn't it?"

"Well it's not funny. It could have killed me you know!" she said, catching her breath again as a pain jabbed at her ribcage. "It wasn't like Rod Hull's emu attacking Michael Parkinson you know. It was really frightening, all those bloody feathers beating down on me." She looked up at Pippa who was trying to stifle a laugh.

Pippa held her hands in the air and said, "Sorry, sorry, I know it's not funny. But I'm going to frame your sick note when you send it into work; it's got to go down as the best excuse for a sickie ever. "

"Oh go away you horrible woman," she moaned.

"So, you didn't make it to lunch with the delectable Mr Knight then?"

"Nope. Goodness knows what he must think, and I'm in no fit state to see him at the moment. I must look an absolute fright."

"Rubbish, you look beautiful even with a black eye, and you know it," she winked. "Will they let you home tomorrow then?"

She nodded. "Joe will pick me up after high tide. I hope he didn't get into trouble today. To tell you the truth, I'm not looking forward to going home. God knows what sort of mess I'll find when I get there. Joe said the bird absolutely destroyed the house."

"Well don't worry about anything, we'll all help you sort it out, but for now come over to mine, you know where the key is!"

Faye smiled gratefully.

*

When Pippa opened up the office the next morning, she made straight for the telephone. She sat down and drummed the desk with her fingers for a moment. Should she, or shouldn't she? She'd pondered all night as to whether to intervene in Faye's love life. Suddenly she was decided. Why not? What harm could it do? Somebody had to get these two love birds together she thought, as she pulled the contact number book from the drawer. Tracing her finger down the list she dialled Liam's number.

Liam was still in bed nursing a monumental hangover when his cell phone rang. After several attempts to locate the phone with his eyes shut, he managed to hit the talk button. "What?" he grunted.

Pippa pursed her lips at his tone. "Mr Knight?"

"Yes, what do you want?"

"It's Pippa from the boatyard," she said cautiously.

"Oh yes," he said sarcastically, not in the mood to speak to anyone connected with the boatyard.

"Sorry, am I disturbing you?" she said trying to keep the sarcasm out of her own voice.

He sighed heavily. "No, what do you want?"

Pippa swallowed hard. "I just thought I would phone you in case you were wondering why Faye didn't turn up yesterday for a lunchtime drink."

"Lunchtime drink?" he answered nonchalantly.

Pippa was puzzled now. "Err, yes, Faye was under the impression you invited her for a drink at lunchtime!"

He gave a short derisory snort. "It was hardly a lunch date," he answered flippantly. "Anyway, in answer to your question, no, I wasn't wondering, because I wasn't there, I was called away on important business," he lied.

Pippa was losing patience with him now. "Oh that's okay then, she must have been mistaken. Faye doesn't like to be rude, and she didn't want to have upset you," she said coolly.

"Never gave it a thought." He gave an exaggerated yawn.

Pippa bristled indignantly. "Oh well, I was just phoning to say she should be out of hospital later today."

He sat up in bed with a start. "Hospital?"

Pippa clenched her teeth and said, "Yes, she had an accident yesterday, that's why she couldn't meet you for the lunch date…. that never was," she added unable to stop herself.

"What sort of accident?"

Pippa detected the alarm in his voice and proceeded to tell him what had happened.

"Damn it," he said under his breath. "Is she disfigured, are there injuries to her face?" This could ruin all his plans.

"Yes, but nothing that won't mend," Pippa answered suspiciously.

"What time is she coming home? Does she need picking up?"

Pippa frowned when she heard the panic in his voice. "No. Joe is picking her up."

"Who's Joe?" he asked bluntly.

"Joe is her friend." Pippa quipped. "Anyway, I'll have to go. Goodbye Mr Knight. Sorry to have disturbed you. I just thought I'd let you know." Pippa put the phone down on him before he could answer. Something deep inside her caused her great concern for her friend, and she wished with all her heart that she hadn't made the phone call.

5
Zennor

In his eerily quiet bedroom, and only three days after burying his beloved Elizabeth, Nathan once again donned his black suit to attend yet another funeral.

It was all too awful to comprehend, that today his beautiful goddaughter Jasmine Quintana would too be buried.

"You look terribly pale Dad. The Quintanas won't expect us to go you know if you're not feeling up to it," Greg had pointed out over breakfast.

"Your Mother would though," he'd answered quietly.

Adjusting his black tie at the mirror, he closed his eyes momentarily. Tired and weary he wondered if he would ever sleep peacefully again. The bed was so cold and empty without the warmth of the woman who had spent twenty-five years by his side.

Greg knocked softly on the bedroom door. "Are you ready?"

He turned to Greg and nodded sadly.

As they sat amongst the grief stricken congregation, the beautiful white coffin, draped in a carpet of flowers, was carried in and placed at the altar. The perfume from the lilies was overpowering and everyone shook their head in disbelief at the loss. How could someone so young and beautiful be dead? As the service commenced, Nathan barely took in the words being spoken by the vicar. Lost in his own cavernous grief, his mind drifted back to the very moment Jasmine had entered the world. It had been a sunny Thursday morning. Sarah and David had spent the night at Gwithian Cottage after enjoying a small but intimate dinner party - probably the last one they would have before Sarah gave birth. A short walk to the sea had preceded a visit to the post office for the morning papers. The three of them had waited outside chatting in the sunshine while Sarah bought the papers. Suddenly Tom the postmaster ran into the street ashen faced. He stood open-mouth with his hands clamped against his balding head.

"What is it? What's happened?" Nathan asked.

"She's asking for someone to take her knickers off," he said breathlessly.

"What?" They all exchanged puzzled glances and Nathan ran indoors, swiftly followed by the others.

Sarah was lying by the bread counter crying, "Help me get them off." She pulled frantically at her undergarments. "The baby's coming."

David immediately ran and knelt down, pulling his jacket off and propping her head up. Elizabeth ran with the postmaster to the back room to phone an ambulance, leaving Nathan at the business end with the task of removing the undergarments of the woman he had only ever kissed on the cheek in friendship. With a quick pull, the garment was removed, only to be confronted with the blonde haired crown of a baby's head making its swift entry into the world. Not knowing what else to do, he took on his old rugby stance and cupped two hands as Sarah cried out in pain. Nathan emitted an equally loud wail as baby Jasmine shot out into the world, slipped through his hands and landed in a sack of potatoes by the till. The image had amused him for the past eighteen years, and they had all had some mileage out of the story. While Nathan swiftly covered Sarah's modesty with a copy of the West Briton, Tom the postmaster, now recovered from the shock, picked up the baby from the potato sack, weighed it on the post office scales and pronounced, "Seven pounds four ounces, that will be seventy-six pence to send her anywhere in the country."

Suddenly Nathan laughed out loud, rousing himself from his reverie.

Greg jumped as if electrified at his father's outburst of laughter. They both looked up at the congregation only to be confronted by a sea of astonished faces.

Realising his faux pas, his hands shot to his mouth as he mumbled, "Oh my goodness, I'm so sorry. I'm so very, very, sorry." He looked up towards Sarah and David Quintana and shook his head. "I'm so sorry", he mouthed pleadingly. He quickly stood and stumbled out of the pew and made haste towards the church door. Once outside he rushed towards the gate, fell to his knees and covered his face in shame.

A moment later Greg knelt at his side, circling his arm about his father's shoulders. "Dad, what the hell was that all about?"

"Oh my God Greg, go back inside. Tell them I'm so sorry," he said breathlessly. His face buckled. "I was just remembering......" He choked on his words. ".....something.... a better time than this, I err, oh God, what a terrible thing to do at a funeral."

Pulling him to his feet, Greg pleaded with him, "Come on Dad. Let's go home. I knew we shouldn't have come. We'll explain later, I'm sure they'll understand."

Once back at Gwithian Cottage, Nathan refused Greg's offer of making them both a strong cup of tea, and set off towards the sea, wanting only to be on his own for a while. For a good hour, he sat on a patch of grassy earth, his eyebrows set low upon his eyes as if intently observing the deep crevices of his mind. Initially, tears of humiliation had streamed down his face, his body shuddering occasionally as though to rid himself of horrible thoughts. What on earth the Quintanas must think of him he did not know. He had known them for years, but even the familiarity of the close friendship they shared would be severely tested by his outburst. He hoped with all his heart that they would understand when he explained, and perhaps in a few weeks this awful feeling would wear away and the humiliation would diminish in time.

So deep in his reverie, he barely noticed when Greg appeared by this side. A hot cup of strong tea was offered and Nathan took it gratefully, warming his hands on the cup. With cloud and sun alternating, the two men sat in silence for a long time. Nathan in his unfathomable grief and Greg lost in his own deep thoughts, which was only partly to do with the loss of his mother. He was desperate to speak to his father on a pressing issue, but now was not the right time.

6

The journey from the hospital back to Gweek had been uncomfortably unpleasant. Each corner Joe took and every bump in the road was felt keenly in Faye's ribs, therefore all conversation between them had been punctuated with gasps and moans of agony.

It was with great relief to both parties that Joe pulled up outside Post Office Row. He ran to the passenger's side and helped Faye as she gingerly climbed out of the car. Once he had her upright they embraced gently. "Come on sweetheart, let's get you indoors. I do wish you would let me take you straight round to Pippa's though. You'll be shocked when you see yours."

"Honestly Joe, I'm fine, I need to pick some things up. I'll have to see the place for myself sometime; it might as well be now. Thank you for getting me home though." She kissed him on the cheek. "You had better get back to work, I'll see you later."

He gave a comforting squeeze of her hand. "Okay, if you're sure. I'll be back later to help you clear up. *Don't* do anything until I get back. " And then he set off towards the boatyard.

"I won't," she said, feeling a twinge of pain in her ribs. "I can't," she added sotto voce.

Her foot slipped on the slimy floor as she entered the kitchen, triggering another searing pain from her rib. Hardly daring to breathe, she cradled her arms to her chest to give some protection. Her bleached white kitchen table was upended, and one of her chairs now sported only three legs. Not a single cup or kitchen utensil had escaped the onslaught of the mad bird, and everything lay strewn and broken in the ostrich faeces which covered the floor. Beyond the kitchen, her lounge was equally devastated. A large gaping hole where her window had been was now covered in a large hardboard sheet, and the shredded curtains lay limp on her tattered sofa. Her eyes swept over the clothes which were strewn across her carpet. The clothes horse, which had been airing her fresh laundry, was now devoid of any of the garments she had placed on it. All the artwork on her walls now hung at drunken angles and the canvas she had been working on for the last month now lay in the grimy mess of her carpet. She rubbed her forehead in despair. "What a mess," she murmured. She glanced at the clock on the mantelpiece as it chimed four-thirty; it appeared to be the only thing that had avoided the destruction. As she reached down to retrieve what remained of her best white jeans, a sharp knock on the door startled her.

"Hello, can I come in?" called the unexpected visitor as he stood in the doorway.

Conscious of her battered face, she reluctantly beckoned Liam into her house.

"Good God Faye." He moved towards her. She flinched thinking he was going to hug her, knowing her ribs would protest keenly. But he cupped his hand to her shoulders. "You poor thing, look at the state of you."

She looked up into his handsome face and his gentle words brought tears bubbling to her eyes. "I take it you'll forgive me for missing our lunch date yesterday?" she said softly.

He nodded gently and looked around the room. "This is dreadful. You can't possibly stay here!" It was an order rather than an observation.

Faye smiled thinly. "It's okay I'm going to sleep on Pippa's bedroom floor, just until I can get things sorted."

"The devil you are. I have a house at Mawnan Smith; you'll stay there tonight until we can get this fixed up."

"Oh!" She laughed in surprise. Her mind went quickly over this; the statement had taken her completely by surprise. "Thank you so much for the offer, but I'll be fine at Pippa's. Anyway, she's expecting me."

He shook his head. "You don't have to worry about that. I've sorted everything out with her."

Faye opened her mouth to protest, but closed it again as three people appeared behind them dressed in white overalls.

"Oh good, you're all here. I want this ship-shape by the morning, you hear me?" he barked the order at them.

Faye looked nonplussed, as he pulled her to one side. "Now, do you need an overnight bag?"

*

Liam's house was on the outskirts of the village of Mawnan Smith, tucked away in a thicket of trees without much of a view or immediate neighbours. Contrary to the traditional Cornish cottage look of its exterior, the inside was surprisingly large and decorated in a cool white ultra modern style, which probably didn't conform to local building regulations, she mused.

The hall was bathed in early evening sunlight when she stepped inside, which gave a welcoming feel. He placed her overnight bag in the hallway and ushered her into the lounge. It was a split-level living room come kitchen diner, with a huge bay window to the front and French doors leading out to the small but perfectly manicured back garden. The front of the room housed two enormous white exquisitely comfortable looking sofas and a glass coffee table. A soft white rug lay in front of the open fire. To the rear left of the room, and up a level, the sparkling white and chrome kitchen emitted a warm smell of lamb and garlic roast vegetables. To the right, in the dining area, the glass dining table was set with crisp white tablecloth and matching napkins and in the centre stood a vase of unscented white roses. Everything looked lovely. He watched Faye's countenance as her eyes swept appreciatively across the room, and was relieved his housekeeper Mrs Milton had vacated the building before they arrived.

"Do you live here alone?" she asked anxiously,

registering a woman's touch in all she saw.

"It's my Cornish bolthole!" Liam nodded. Taking the coat from her back, he said, "Please take a seat and make yourself at home." He gestured to the sofas. "I'll fix us both a drink."

"No," she protested. "I'm on rather strong painkillers, maybe I shouldn't drink."

"Nonsense!" he said dismissively as he loosened the cork on the champagne. "After the ordeal you've been through, I think you deserve a glass of the old bubbly."

Very gingerly Faye perched on the edge of the sofa seat, unable to relax completely because of the pain. She was very grateful to Liam for his hospitality, and could see he had gone to a lot of trouble with the dinner, but in truth, she would have rather gone to bed with a cup of Horlicks and a hot water bottle. Eventually the pain eased and she began to breathe a little easier. "This is a lovely place Liam. Have you lived here long?"

He smiled inwardly, clicked the remote control of his CD and soft music began to play as the champagne cork popped. "A while," he said, handing the glass of bubbly to her. Settling down on the sofa beside her, they chinked glasses.

Feeling a little self conscious about the proximity of him, she cleared her throat nervously. "How did you hear about what happened?"

"Pippa rang me this morning."

"Oh, that was nice of her. I bet you thought I had stood you up yesterday?" She searched his face for any hint of annoyance.

He looked at her with dark serious eyes. "Well, nothing was set in stone was it?" He smiled.

*

Pippa knocked on the door of Faye's house only to be greeted by a man in white overalls. She smiled and looked beyond him. "Hi there, is Faye about?"

The man shrugged his shoulders. "If you mean the

woman who lives here, she's gone off with Mr Knight."

"Oh, when was that?"

The man sighed impatiently. "About……" He looked at his watch. "..Two and a half hours ago, I'd say."

Pippa furrowed her brow. "Did she say she was coming back?"

"No," he answered rudely.

Feeling quite put out that Faye hadn't bothered to tell her about the change of plan, she raised her eyebrows and said, "Oh, I see. And you are….?"

"I'm minding my own business like you should be!" He smirked revealing an uneven row of nicotine stained teeth.

Pippa bristled with indignation. "Don't be so rude! I want to know who you are and why you are in my friend's house, that's all."

The man threw his hands in the air. "What the bloody hell does it look like I'm doing?" He bent down and lifted the mop and bucket and shook it at her.

Pippa pursed her lips as she tipped her head to one side.

"Look love, I've got enough shit in here to deal with without getting any off you, so, if you don't mind, I need to get on." With that he pushed the door shut in her face.

Confused, angry and upset, Pippa knocked on Joe's door, only to find that he had been given the same short shrift by the cleaners. Reluctantly she made her way back to her own house, slammed a portion of the now congealed shepherd's pie she had made them both into the microwave and folded away the camp bed she was going to sleep on. "Well, I needn't have gone to all that bother," she spoke the words to the cat, which carried on sleeping in its basket. "She could have flipping well told me; I am supposed to be her best friend." She thumped her fists into her hips indignantly.

*

After a delicious meal, Faye and Liam took their coffees

back into the lounge. Conversation had been easy between them all evening, and Faye had learned a lot about Liam's work with the cosmetic company. It all sounded very exotic, very different to her office job. Faye didn't want the evening to end, but eventually tiredness prevailed, and at eleven-thirty Liam showed her to her room, kissed her tenderly on the cheek and said his goodnights.

As she lay in bed she felt very content and ever so slightly drunk. She had enjoyed Liam's company and for the first time had felt easy in a man's presence. She smiled at the thoughtfulness of her friend Pippa. How lovely of her to tell him what had happened. Without her intervention, her flat would still be in an awful mess and she wouldn't have had such a lovely evening.

7

Faye woke with a start as breakfast arrived on a tray at her bedside. "Wake up sleeping beauty," Liam said cheerily as he pulled the curtains wide open.

Dismayed at his presence in her bedroom, before she had a chance to wipe the sleep from her eyes, clean her teeth and other such ablutions, Faye dragged the bedcovers up to her neck in embarrassment.

Liam laughed. "Don't be so coy Faye." He sat on the chair opposite her bed. "I've been thinking," he said, stretching his long legs. "You are on the sick, and I'm sailing my yacht down the Helford at high tide today, so, why don't you come with me?"

She squirmed uncomfortably at his suggestion, causing a sharp pain to stab into her ribs. "Ouch. Thanks for the offer," she said, clutching her ribs. "But I really don't feel up to it."

"Rubbish," he answered dismissively. "It's just what you need to take your mind off what has happened to you."

"Well, it's not just that, I'm not a very good sailor. I'd rather not, if you don't mind."

"Well I do mind," he said smiling steadily. "I insist on taking you out for the day and I won't take no for an answer. You'll love it, just you see. Come on lazy bones, get that breakfast down you and get up. I'll run you back to your house and you can put some warm clothes on. It can get a bit chilly down on the river."

Faye sighed heavily. Too fatigued to argue, she glanced at the breakfast she had no appetite for.

*

Back at her house, which was restored to its former glory, and a good deal cleaner than she had ever seen it, she took a shower, a task she found excruciatingly painful. Her sore eye had begun to open but the socket area shone blackish purple and the look rather reminded her of a Dutch rabbit she once owned. Her complexion had taken on a grey pallor and no amount of blusher or lipstick could add colour. In the end, she gave it up as a hopeless job. It took every ounce of effort to muster up the energy to dress, but eventually she emerged, dressed in light blue jeans, a couple of T shirts, topped with a purple jumper.

Liam stood back and looked at her appreciatively. "You look lovely," he said tongue-in-cheek. "Maybe a little grey around the gills, but lovely all the same. Tell me, did the doctors say how long it would be until your face returns to its normal beautiful self?"

Faye blushed. "Two or three weeks they think."

"Good, now don't go all coy on me again, you know you are lovely. It's time to let people appreciate your beauty."

She frowned. "What do you mean?"

He looked at her with a half smile. "Nothing, come on." He beckoned her to the door.

Faye reached for the telephone. "Can I just call Pippa? She'll be worried about me?"

"Pippa knows you are with me. After all, she was the one who instigated all this, wasn't she?"

"I suppose so, it's just…."

"Later, come on or we shall miss high tide."

*

Thankfully the day was calm and sunny, with only a faint breeze blowing up the Helford. Faye gingerly stepped aboard with the help of Liam, and settled down in the cockpit as he started the engine and unleashed the mooring rope from the quay. Slowly he manoeuvred his yacht down past the other moored yachts and into the channel of the river. As they motored away, Amos stood and watched them with dark brooding eyes from the banks of the quay. "I thought you said you didn't like sailing Faye," he said sadly under his breath.

The trip down the river took forty minutes. Once in the basin of the Helford, Liam hooked up onto a mooring buoy and cut the engine.

"Right then." He rubbed his hands together gleefully. "Come, I'll show you around," he declared proudly as he ushered her down the galley steps. "Kitchen area here, all mod cons." He opened and closed the oven and fridge door. "Seating area to dine, and err, the small room with shower, and finally the sleeping area. Quite spacious isn't it?"

Faye nodded. "It's truly beautiful Liam," she said absorbing the splendour of the luxurious surroundings. It was evident that no expense had been spared.

Liam sat on one of the seats. "I actually don't sleep up in that part, it's too small and enclosed. All these seats here make a really spacious bed, big enough for two," he said, patting the upholstery. Faye nodded shyly but didn't comment. "Would you like a drink?" he enquired.

Faye glanced at her watch. "But it's only eleven-thirty!"

He laughed heartily. "I asked you if you wanted a drink, not what the time was. For goodness sake Faye, loosen up a little. We're having a day out, enjoy yourself."

She held her hand up in defeat. "All right, a small gin and tonic then."

A few minutes later he handed her a large gin and tonic which was filled to the brim with ice.

She thanked him, took an obligatory sip and looked for somewhere to place it.

Back on deck, the river was crystal clear, gleaming as the sun enamelled the surface. Neither of them spoke for several minutes as they took in the splendid view of their surroundings.

"How peaceful," Faye said relaxing slightly.

"I agree. After the hustle and bustle of London, this is sheer bliss." He gave a relaxed sigh as he folded his arms behind his head.

Faye was surprised how easy it felt to be in Liam's

company. "You know, I feel as though I've known you forever," she said smiling warmly.

"I know what you mean, it must be all those telephone conversations we've had over the winter. We've got to know each other quite well without meeting, haven't we?" He raised his glass. "So I propose a toast to us really getting to know each other." He winked mischievously. "Do you agree?"

Faye smiled shyly as they chinked glasses.

"Tell me, how long have you worked in the boatyard office? It can't be that long; you weren't there last summer were you?"

"No, it will be eight months now."

His mouth twisted into a smile. "And are you happy in your work?"

"Well, I work with some lovely people, but in truth, I'd rather be a full time artist," she said, her eyes glinting. "But all in all, it has its good points."

"Like people chatting you up on the telephone?"

Faye grinned broadly. "Only *you* do that."

"Good, let's keep it that way," he replied flatly. Faye frowned slightly at the implication, but he just grinned and said, "Okay, how about a spot of lunch?"

She nodded gratefully. "Can I do anything?"

"You can sit there and look pretty."

Faye pursed her lips, and then turned her face upwards to let the sun warm her.

Lunch consisted of cold chicken, tomatoes, cheese, paté and French bread, all washed down with a chilly Chablis.

Faye shook her head in disbelief when she looked at the tray. "My goodness, this is lovely, you shouldn't have gone to all this trouble for me!"

"It's no trouble honestly. Just a little something I rustled up from the Premier shop in Gweek." He raised his glass. "Here's to good wine, good food and splendid company. You know, I must say, for a little village in the back of beyond, your little shop is well stocked."

Faye bristled slightly. "Gweek is not the 'back of beyond'," she emphasised strongly. "It's a living, thriving, working village. It doesn't die in the winter, like a lot of the seaside villages you know."

He grinned in amusement. "Oops, I think I touched a nerve there didn't I?"

She regarded him for a moment. "I'm very proud of Gweek and all it achieves, that's all." She folded her arms to her chest, and then winced as she touched her sore ribs.

He laughed heartily. "Oh dear, we are sensitive today aren't we?" He moved closer and kissed her lightly on the cheek. "I'm only teasing you."

Faye was silenced by his gesture and eventually they settled down to spend an idyllic lazy afternoon on the river, before Liam hailed a water taxi to take them to shore.

"How about dinner tonight?" he asked as they waited for a cab to take them back to Gweek.

"Oh no sorry, I can't tonight. It's quiz night." She gave him a soft apologetic smile.

He quirked his eyebrows. "A quiz night! Are you telling me you would rather do a quiz than be wined and dined by me?" His mouth turned down like a petulant child.

She laughed lightly. "I'm afraid so."

"Huh, I'm deeply hurt. So, who do you do that with?"

"Pippa, Joe and Sid. You know Sid. He drives the crane in the boatyard."

He nodded. "Who is this Joe then?"

Faye smiled affectionately. "Joe's my neighbour; he was the one who saved me from that bloody awful bird."

Liam's mouth tightened. "He's always popping in your house is he, this Joe fellow?"

"Yes." Faye smiled happily. "He's a good neighbour. We have a good laugh on quiz night, and of course we all sing together in a group called 'Three Fold'. You should come and see us one evening." Faye saw the muscles in Liam's jaw tighten. "Oh don't worry, Joe isn't competition if that's what you think," she added playfully.

"Well come out to dinner with me tonight then, if he means nothing to you."

Faye shook her head. "No, I can't, I told you. We're doing the quiz. We always do the quiz. It's on every other Thursday. I don't want to let them down. I'm the one who answers the music questions," she added proudly.

"So, you would rather let me down." He feigned disappointment.

Faye reached out and touched him gently on the arm. "Of course I don't want to let you down, but…."

"Good, I'll pick you up at seven tonight." Faye opened her mouth to protest. "No arguing," he said placing his finger on her lips.

Resigned to the fact, Faye shrugged her shoulders in defeat as Liam helped her into the taxi.

Back at the boatyard, Liam watched her walk towards the offices; the sight of the sunlight on her auburn hair caught his breath. She turned to wave, smiling brilliantly back at him. He lifted his hand and smiled inwardly. Perfect, he breathed; she was going to be just perfect for the project. We just need to dye her hair blonde.

*

Amos skulked behind his boat at the far end of the yard and watched bitterly as Faye emerged from the taxi. He sank back on his haunches, and then threw the paintbrush he'd been holding to the floor in frustration.

*

"Hi Pippa," Faye said cheerily as she popped her head into the boatyard office. Pippa looked up and smiled thinly.

"What's the matter?" Faye asked.

"Well, thank you for finally turning up to tell me that you're okay. Did it not occur to you that I would be worried? You could have rung," she said crossly. "I thought we had arranged that you were to stay at mine last night." She tried to keep the whine from her voice, but failed miserably. "I had dinner all ready for you. I'd made up a bed and everything."

Faye was taken aback. "Gosh, I'm so sorry Pip; Liam said he'd arranged everything with you and you were okay with it!"

"Well he didn't!" she snapped.

"Oh?" She gave her a blank look.

"I came round to your house in the end, only to get short shrift from two ignoramuses who were apparently cleaning it. One of them was really rude to me!" she added indignantly.

Flustered now Faye said, "Liam arranged for them to come and clean up, he just sort of took charge last night. I really thought you knew what was happening otherwise I would have okayed it with you, you know I would!"

"Well, as I say, he didn't. But you could have rung me this morning, but apparently you went out on his yacht.....so Amos told me."

Faye stood silent and scratched her head. "I'm really, really sorry Pippa. There has obviously been a huge misunderstanding."

Not in her nature to be angry about anything for long, Pippa got up from her desk and moved to hug her friend. "Oh well, never mind, you're here now. Are you okay?"

Faye stepped back cautiously. "Careful Pippa, I'm still in a great deal of pain."

"You'll be okay for the quiz tonight though won't you? We thought we were going to have to get someone else if you didn't turn up."

"Ah, well, the thing is....." She bit on her lip.

Pippa pulled a face. "What now?"

"Liam wants me to have dinner with him tonight."

"But can't you go another night; we always do the quiz…"

"I know, I know," she tried to appease her. "It's just

that he is going to be away for a few days, and well, I'd rather like to go and have dinner with him, if you don't mind."

Pippa folded her arms and pursed her lips in mock annoyance. "Well, it's a sad day when your best friend passes you over for a man."

Faye looked crestfallen. "Oh Pippa, don't say that."

A cheeky smile passed over her lips. "Of course I don't mind. Who am I to stand in the path of true love?" She winked.

Faye's eyes shone. "Apologise to the boys for me if I don't see them."

"I will, have a good time."

She watched Faye walk across the boatyard and for some reason a great feeling of foreboding washed over her.

8

During the days which followed her funeral, Nathan became very aware that Elizabeth had gone from his life, so, so, gone. Additionally, having to attend the funeral of his goddaughter, Jasmine Quintana three days after Elizabeth's, had been more than his poor heart could undertake. He'd been mortified at his outburst at that funeral, and answered a phone call from Sarah Quintana that same evening with great trepidation.

"Nathan, it's Sarah, I'm phoning to see if you are okay?"

"Oh God, Sarah, please forgive me. That was a despicable thing to do….."

"Nathan?"

"I'll never forgive myself….." he said shaking his head.

"*Nathan?*"

"I just…I can't believe I did that…" His words were punctuated with stifled sobs.

"Nathan. Listen to me."

"I…"

"Will you *listen* to me?" Nathan fell silent. "I know exactly what you were laughing about, without you having to tell me."

He took a deep breath. "You do?"

"Of course I do! My God we've had some mileage over the story of her birth through the years. I'm right aren't I? That is what you were thinking?"

"Yes," he answered flatly, resting against the wall for support.

"I thought so. It's good that you could remember such a happy time. Please don't beat yourself up over this. We wanted the funeral to be a celebration of her life, and if you had stayed you would have heard us mention her entry into the world. In the end everyone was laughing."

"Thank you for being so understanding Sarah." He swallowed a sob as he spoke. "You sound so calm, I admire you for it. Elizabeth would not have got through her last few months if it wasn't for you. I'm just so sorry you…we, don't have her strength to get us all through the next painful months."

"I know Nathan; this is all too much for all of us. I fear for David, he is a man destroyed. As for me, well, I don't know how I'm holding myself together, but I truly believe that remembering the good times is the only way I can get through this. I am dying inside, as I am sure you are for the loss of Elizabeth, but we all need to gather strength from whatever we can." She could hear Nathan crying gently on the end of the phone and felt her own eyes fill with tears. "I'll say goodbye now Nathan, we'll meet up soon, take care of yourself and Greg."

"You take care too, my regards to David, tell him how sorry I am for…. you know."

"No need, goodnight Nathan."

*

A few days later Nathan was standing in the lane outside Gwithian Cottage to bid a farewell to Elizabeth's father. The sun was high, and soft clouds skittered across the pale blue sky, but rain was forecast for later. Elizabeth's garden was bursting into life, and Nathan bent down to pick a stem of pink thrift to put in his button hole, but as he wasn't wearing a jacket he pushed the flower through the knit of his jumper. Elizabeth had picked a flower every day for him to wear; he would continue the gesture in her memory.

"Well, goodbye son," Elizabeth's father said, giving a firm handshake. He sighed heavily. "We've been dealt a powerful blow, you and I. For me to lose a daughter and you a wife, one wonders how the poor heart can carry on at times like this." He shook his head sadly. "I remember that losing Elizabeth's mother all those years ago was almost too much to bear. But I had an obligation to

Elizabeth. I needed to stay strong, so as to ease her distress. She was so young when her mother died. I barely had time to grieve. And now, she too has gone." He put a fatherly hand on Nathan's shoulder. "It's going to be hard on you, believe me I know. But you need to find something to hold onto Nathan. Live your life to the full, like Elizabeth did and you will come through the other side. The words you said at the funeral, they were strong and honest, bide by them, they will stand you in good stead."

Nathan patted the hand on his shoulder and gazed into the tired red-rimmed eyes gazing back. "You take care too John. Phone me when you get back to Scotland, just so I know you are okay."

John nodded. "Give my regards to your parents."

"I will. Thank you. They were sorry not to have made the journey over, but Australia is such a long way away to come for a funeral, isn't it? I really didn't expect them to come."

Nathan watched as his father-in-law drove out of the village, and as he turned to go back inside he saw the postman approaching.

"Just one today." He smiled handing over the envelope.

Nathan sighed, his home was full of bereavement cards, he wasn't sure there was room for another. He pulled the card out and noted it was a copy of a hand painted watercolour of a sunrise. He sat on the bench to read it.

'Dear Mr Prior and family,

Please accept my sincere condolences for your loss.

Darkness will have descended on your life, but there will be light one day. A necessary thought to hold onto when one is left to live alone when love has died suddenly. Hold on to your memories, they alone will help you through.

Kindest regards, Faye Larson.'

The name meant nothing to him. He closed the card and held it to his heart. People were so kind.

*

Over the next few days, Greg feared for his father's emotional state, and dreaded the day he would have to leave him to deal with this empty house alone.

Nathan too worried about his son's departure. He knew Greg had his own life to lead; he had almost finished his Art degree at Falmouth and had made some good contacts. Soon he would be an established artist in his own right. So, when the dreaded day came, they were both understandably reluctant to say their goodbyes.

When Greg asked if he would be able to manage, Nathan insisted that he could. "A young woman from the village has offered to help me with the cooking and cleaning, so I won't be completely alone to fend for myself," he assured him.

As Greg finished packing his bag, Nathan took a walk up to the churchyard. He visited Elizabeth's grave, well, he called it a grave, but as yet, there was no headstone, nor in fact a body beneath it. Elizabeth couldn't bear the thought of being buried, but requested that a headstone be erected in her memory. So, at the moment, there was just a cross with her name on it stuck amongst the heady array of funeral flowers and a half buried vase in which he had placed a bunch of Elizabeth's favourite wild flowers. As he walked towards the back of the churchyard where the grave was, his heart flipped when he saw his wild flowers discarded and in their place was a dozen red roses. Dismayed, he dropped to his knees to gather the wilting blooms. True, they had no monetary value like the roses, but he was at a loss at whoever could had done this. Reluctantly he slotted a few of the wild flowers back in with the roses, but the action had upset him. Consequently when Nathan returned home to Greg, his mind was preoccupied.

Greg placed his holdall in the hallway, lifted his coat and scarf from the hook and sighed heavily.

"Did you by any chance put roses on your Mum's grave

Greg?" he asked hopefully.

"No, why?"

"No matter," he said, trying to push the mysterious roses to the back of his mind. Nathan smiled sadly. "Ready to go are you. Have you got everything?" He tried to sound cheerful, but in his heart he was dying.

Greg nodded. "I'm sorry Dad. I don't want to leave you like this, so soon after Mum. But I have to go now."

Nathan tried to shrug the dread from his heart and patted him on the shoulder. "I know son, I know. Don't fret about me; I'll be fine I promise. I know you need to get back." Nathan laughed gently forcing a smile. "Your mum said you have someone special in your life as well, you'll want to get back to her I should think. I'm glad you've found someone, both your Mum and I have wanted to see you settle with someone, I just hope you'll be as happy as we were."

Greg stood in the dark hall and shifted uneasily. Nathan reached out and patted his arm again. "Sorry son, look at me talking of you settling down. You've probably only known each other a few weeks. But when you're ready I would like to meet her."

"She is a he, dad," Greg blurted the words and instantly regretted them. He knew he needed to have this conversation with his Dad, but he wanted to wait until he was emotionally ready to listen.

Nathan let out a bewildered laugh. "What?"

Greg smiled and replied cautiously. "I live with Simon, we've been together some time now...as a couple." Greg watched as his father digested his words. He was shocked, he could see that. He watched him struggle with his emotions. His brow had furrowed and the colour seemed to drain from his face as the full force of Greg's disclosure appeared to age him instantly.

Nathan opened his mouth to speak, but no words came. He closed it again, and swallowed hard to disperse the lump growing in his throat. He looked down to inspect the carpet and chewed painfully on his lip. Presently his gaze lifted to meet Greg's eyes and he shook his head in confusion.

Greg held his gaze as his father moved towards him, but in the next step Nathan had turned to the front door and grasped the handle. A moment later Greg found himself alone, staring at the closed door in absolute stillness, scarcely venturing to breathe. His heart told him to follow him, but his head told him otherwise. He waited and waited, but his father did not return.

*

The pale blue slit in the cold steel-grey sky, heralded a turn for the better in the weather. Zennor, ragged and battered from the recent storms, began to brighten in the watery sunshine. But with the change in the weather came a sense of despair as Nathan sat on the cliff nursing a hangover, the consequence of a ten hour arduous session with a bottle of rum at the bar of the Tinners Arms. How could he face the coming spring and summer without his family to enjoy life with? His grief was solidly set in winter mode and sunshine had no part in his life anymore. What fool loses both of the people he loved more than life itself in the space of a week? What had possessed him to walk out on Greg yesterday, he had no idea. He was shocked, that was true, he had no inkling of Greg's sexual preferences, none whatsoever. It had been a complete bolt out of the blue. How could he not have known, how can you love someone and not know them? All these questions went round and round inside his head. He had no problem with homosexuality, so couldn't fathom why he had reacted so negatively. And to walk out and leave the lad standing there had been a despicable act of cruelty. He groaned and held his aching head in his hands in despair.

A slight cough alerted Nathan that he was no longer alone. He looked up through his bleary eyes. The woman who stood before him was a tall, slim hipped twenty-four-year-old, with short blond hair, hazel eyes and a sharp pointed nose.

"I've been waiting at the cottage Mr Prior," she said nervously. He stared at her blankly. "I'm Carrie Stockton, we spoke the other day .....about me coming to be your housekeeper." Unsure of Nathan's silence, she continued. "We agreed that if you were happy with my work, I was to come and live in. You said for me to come and see you today at eleven.....I've been waiting at the door for half an hour," she added, quite sulkily.

Nathan closed his eyes and sighed deeply. "I'm sorry, err?"

"Carrie," she said, giving her best smile an airing.

He forced a smile. "I'm sorry Carrie, I'm err..... I'm not feeling too good at the moment. Can we do this another time, say, maybe tomorrow?" He raised his eyebrows hopefully.

Not to be dismissed so easily, Carrie parried with a quick reply. "Well I'm here now, why don't I make you some breakfast? You'll feel so much better!"

"No." He shook his head at the thought of food. "No thank you".

"A drink then, let me make you a drink?"

Nathan groaned inwardly and stood up from where he was sitting; his head ached with all this talking. He staggered slightly, feeling faint and lightheaded and Carrie automatically grabbed his arm.

"Come on my lover. Let's get you a nice cup of black coffee."

He baulked at the thought of the drink, but being unable and unwilling to put up a fight, he gave in and she walked him towards Gwithian Cottage.

*

Later that evening, Nathan sat down to a dinner he did not want and could not stomach. He had no appetite for food, no matter what delights Carrie conjured up in the kitchen. Unperturbed she sat down at the table in the warm cosy kitchen and began to eat her own dinner. She smiled her sweet smile, biting her tongue, when she felt the need to scold him for not eating. He would eat eventually, she told herself, so she must let him be for the time being. Her role in life, she decided, was to make everything easy for him from now on. To scrub and clean his house until it shone like a new pin. To launder his clothes, build fires and make hearty meals for him, even if he didn't feel like eating them. It was the little things that would help him through these dark days. She was going to make herself indispensible.

As Nathan pushed the food around the plate with his fork, he sighed heavily. His mind was in turmoil over his son Greg. He stood up, scraping the chair across the stone floor. "Sorry." He gestured at the discarded meal. "Sorry, it looks lovely, it's just...."

Carrie shook her head. "No matter," she said, as he walked out of the kitchen. She heard him pause in the hallway, and then the front door opened and closed behind him quietly.

Outside, the early evening sun dappled the moss covered wall of the front garden, its red and amber rays bathed the bay in a magnificent sunset. Not long ago he would have rushed to his studio, squeezed his oil paints onto a pallet and painted the scene in all its glory. But he had no stomach for his art. The turpentine which normally stirred his senses into creating paintings now revolted him. His muse had gone, along with his passion for life and wonder of nature. He was very much afraid that it would never return.

9

Faye had heard nothing from Liam for the last two weeks. She couldn't understand if she was disappointed or angry at his silence. He had made it so clear to her when they had dinner that night that he was interested in her, but now she was unsure if she had read the situation wrong. She began to resign herself to the fact that the relationship was over before it began, and chalked it up as another failure.

Pippa watched as Faye crumpled at the rejection and did everything she could to help and comfort her friend, but although she would never admit it to Faye, she hoped with all her heart, that Liam wouldn't come back. Faye was a beautiful, talented woman and she was sure there was someone out there far more deserving of her.

*

"Hello my luvver," Gloria Barnes said as Faye entered the boatyard cafeteria.

"We are in desperate need of cake," Faye exclaimed, glancing at Amos who was nursing a coffee at the far end of the room.

"Oh those words warm my heart. I can't do with folks who don't like cake." She beamed a broad smile. "Coffee with that?"

She nodded. "Two cappuccinos please."

"And how is that young man of yours? The delectable Mr Knight? I haven't seen him about for a few days."

Faye swallowed hard to hide her disappointment. "No, he is very busy up in London I should think."

"My, but he is a dish, I've never seen a more handsome man. He's just the ticket for a pretty girl like you, and he smells wonderful," she said swooning. "I don't know what it is, but he always seems to smell of almonds, don't you think?"

Faye laughed softly. "It's Givenchy for Gentlemen."

"Is it now? I'd get some for my Owen if I thought he would use it."

"You should then," Faye said picking up the tray.

"Nay, he won't use the stuff. He says that perfume is for girls! Damn him. I shall just have to put up with the smell of engine oil." She grimaced.

As Faye left, Amos grinned to himself as an idea hit him.

"Two cappuccinos and cake accompaniment," Faye declared brightly, placing the tray on the desk. They both looked round as the door of the office opened.

"Delivery for Miss Faye Larson," said the man, carrying an enormous bouquet of flowers. The heady perfume filled the room as Faye read the note attached: 'Miss you my darling, I'll be back soon." With that Pippa's hopes were crushed and Faye's soared.

*

One of many vases of blooms now adorned her dressing table. Faye sat at her mirror, brushed her hair and smoothed on her lip gloss. Nearly all the bruising on her face had gone now thank goodness. There was just a slight purpling in her eye socket and a couple of scratches on her forehead but apart from that, her face was almost back to normal. Her ribs still hurt like hell though. She glanced at the clock; Joe would be along in a minute to walk with her to the quiz. A knock at the door was Faye's cue to grab her coat.

"Coming," she called, pausing for a moment, as her hand hovered at the door knob. There would always be a degree of anxiety associated with the back door, since the ostrich incident. Tentatively she opened the door. "Oh, it's you!" She stepped back in surprise.

"Charming welcome after two weeks," Liam said as he stepped through the threshold into the kitchen. Before he said anything else, he seemed to study her face intently. "I thought the doctors said your face would have recovered by now."

Tilting her head to the side, Faye laughed. "Is that all you can say to me after two weeks?"

He pulled her towards him and kissed her passionately. "Did you miss me then?" His mouth broke into a cheeky smile.

Faye feigned indifference. "Well, I hardly know you to miss you."

He laughed loudly. "You missed me, I can tell."

She looked at him with dark serious eyes. "I was just about to go out, Joe will be along soon. Do you want to come to the quiz?"

"No, and don't worry about Romeo, I've just sent him packing. Now, go and change into something more suitable for a candlelit dinner for two."

*

The Black Swan was buzzing with people when Joe opened the door. He fought his way through the crowds of people towards Pippa and Sid. "Gosh it's warm in here," he said glancing at the roaring fire.

Pippa looked over Joe's shoulder, then towards the bar. "Where's Faye?"

He tsked at her. "Oh, lover boy has just turned up."

"Oh no!" Pippa's face dropped.

The muscles in Joe's jaw tightened as he tried to control his temper. "Oh yes, and you know what? He told me to 'sling my hook'," he added indignantly.

Not normally one to make any comment on anyone, Sid said simply, "I don't like Liam Knight."

"You and me both," retorted Joe.

Pippa sighed heavily. "Unfortunately Faye does," she said, with a note of exasperation.

10

As April came to a close, the hills above Zennor were tinged purple with a carpet of bluebells. Luckily they would paint the landscape for several weeks over here on the west coast. But over in Helston, some twenty two miles away, the bluebells in the surrounding area would be picked bare to decorate Helston town, in readiness for their annual Flora Day, or Furry Dance, as the locals called it.

Helston Flora Day was one of the oldest surviving May customs which celebrated the end of winter and coming of spring. Nathan had attended almost every year; he had even danced in it as a boy. It was a time of celebration. Families, some of which were scattered far and wide throughout the country and the world, would travel back to Cornwall to enjoy food and drink and watch the series of dances which were performed throughout the day. The day would start at seven a.m. at the Guildhall with the Early Morning Dance, which in days gone by would have been for the servants to take part in. He and Elizabeth had joined hundreds of people along the high street in the cool of the early spring morning, waiting in anticipation for the invigorating boom of the first drum strike of the day. That was it, the dance commenced. Spring had officially arrived. By mid morning everyone would jostle for the traditional performance of the Hal-an-Tow, a moving boisterous street theatre with much shouting and singing. Elizabeth loved it, but always complained the noise gave her headache. He smiled to himself, remembering the headache was soon cleared by the sight of the Children's Dance, which caused many a spectator to sigh at the sweetness of it all. At noon the principal or Furry Dance took the form of a procession. This would consist of elegantly dressed ladies and gentlemen who would wind their way around town, even passing through houses and shops. Nathan and Elizabeth had danced this dance many times in the past few years and my goodness was it hard on the feet. By five p.m. the exhausted crowd, fuelled by copious amounts of Spingo beer from the Blue Anchor pub and a belly full of hearty Cornish pasties, would cheer the Final Dance through the town. All day long the same tune was played and by the end of the day everyone would be humming it.

Nathan stood quietly in the middle of the bluebells, listening to the birds singing in the gorse bushes, and sighed. He wouldn't be attending this year.

Life was no easier for him a month after losing Elizabeth. Someone had said to him 'you have to keep living until you feel alive again' and that was what he was doing…just living. He sighed again heavily. If he could have a pound for every sigh that had passed his lips he would be a millionaire, he mused.

Three weeks had passed since he and Greg had parted company and the expected hadn't happened. Nathan felt sure he would have received a return letter from Greg. After all, he had poured his heart out to his only son. But it was all in vain, for there had been no response and therefore all hope of reconciliation was diminishing. Greg, it seemed, would not forgive him for his behaviour.

He walked a little, found a stone to sit upon and opened the letter he had received that morning. His heart had soared when Jim the postman handed it to him, only to find it was from Lemon Hill Gallery in Truro requesting permission to hold a retrospective exhibition for Elizabeth. The exhibition was to include Nathan's work as well. If he had a choice, he would have declined, but the gallery had been good to him over the years and he felt an obligation to them. It was to be held in October, six months from now. He shook his head in despair. Would he, could he, stand in the crowd of friends and acquaintances and make small talk on the opening night? Of that he had no idea.

Elizabeth had always been at his side at opening nights, as he had with her. He sighed again and reached into his pocket and retrieved an orange. He turned it over several times in his hands, observing the pitted skin with his artist eyes. Digging his thumb nail into the soft flesh, the scent of citrus oil filled his nostrils making his mouth salivate in anticipation of the taste. He parted his dry lips and closed his eyes, savouring its sweetness, and it struck him, that maybe, slowly, his senses were opening up again.

*

"Nathaniel Prior, buy your own roses for your wife!"

The words cut through Nathan's fug of sadness like a knife in a wound. He turned from where he sat at the bar and placed his glass of beer down. After a couple of weeks of sympathetic pats on the back, kind words of condolence and kindness in abundance, harsh words from anyone were the last thing Nathan expected. Thomas Trevone stood before him with a face like thunder.

He shot Thomas a blank look. "Pardon?"

"I'm sick to death of you stealing the roses from my Ethel's grave to put on Elizabeth's. It's a despicable thing to do and I'm surprised at you."

Nathan sat open-mouth, as the crowd in the bar of the Tinners Arms fell silent. All eyes were upon him. He suddenly felt the special status that the bereaved held in the community dissolve in an instant.

Nathan stood to square him up. "You are mistaken Thomas."

"I am not!" Trevone stood his ground.

"I wouldn't do such a thing, you know I wouldn't."

"Oh yes you would and have. I put roses on my Ethel's grave every week because she loved them, and every week since your Elizabeth has died, my roses have found their way onto your wife's grave. Now, what do you say about that?"

"I…"

"And don't try to deny it Nathaniel Prior." He cut

Nathan short. "I marked the last lot with coloured tape on the stems, and guess what?....I found them on Elizabeth's grave this morning." He folded his arms in defiance, as the crowd murmured in shock.

Nathan felt the embarrassment of tears as they threatened to prick at his eyes. He cleared his throat and blinked hard. "I do know what you are talking about, but I am not the culprit."

Thomas twisted his mouth. "Oh yes, who is it then?" he snapped.

"I don't know, and that is the honest answer. I put wild flowers in the vase for Elizabeth every week, because that's what *she* loved. But every week my flowers are discarded and six red roses are put in their place."

Thomas Trevone's face twitched as he shifted awkwardly from where he stood. "Well, I'm not happy. If it isn't you, then who is it?"

"I don't know Thomas, and if it's any consolation to you, it's been upsetting me too. I thought at first it was one of Elizabeth's friends, perhaps someone who hadn't been able to come to the funeral, but as you say, this has happened every week since, and it's been puzzling me. I am truly sorry if someone is stealing your flowers Thomas, it is as you say a despicable thing to do, but I promise you, I am not the culprit."

Duggie Martin ceased from polishing a glass and said, "When do you put the flowers there Thomas?"

Thomas glanced at the landlord. "I've done it every Wednesday, without fail, for the last seven years," he added proudly.

Duggie looked at Nathan. "And when do they appear on Elizabeth's grave?"

"Thursday," he answered quietly.

"Well then, it should be easy enough to catch the bugger."

Thomas frowned. "Are you seriously suggesting that we sit in the graveyard all night?"

Duggie drummed his fingernails on the bar. "Well, if you want to catch the culprit, yes." He grinned.

Thomas looked to Nathan for guidance. "Well, I don't know, what do you think Nathan?"

Feeling more relaxed now, Nathan nodded. "Why not, I've nothing else to do."

*

In the thirteenth century west tower of the Church of Saint Senara, Thomas Trevone and Nathan Prior, wrapped in several layers of warm clothing, settled themselves down for a long uncomfortable night. Armed with flasks of hot tea and a selection of sandwiches, they stood and watched through the grills of the bell tower, as twilight fell on the graveyard.

Nathan surveyed his surroundings. Naturally he had been in the church many times over the years, though never perched up in the bell tower before. For all its beauty, he found the Church of Saint Senara darkly mysterious. It had stood here overlooking the sea since at least the sixth century AD and was reputedly founded by Saint Senara on her return from Ireland with her son, who was by then a bishop, when they founded the village of Zennor. The Tinners Arms public house, where in the past few weeks he had spent many hours wallowing in his own self pity, was situated only a few yards from the church steps, and had been built to accommodate the stonemasons who built the church. Visitors came from far and wide to this little church on the edge of Cornwall, to view one of only two remaining bench-ends in the church which portrays the Mermaid of Zennor; a beautiful carving depicting the mermaid admiring herself in a mirror.

Legend has it, that a beautiful richly dressed woman had attended the church regularly to hear the choir sing. The parishioners were enchanted by her beauty and her sweet melodic voice, but no one knew where she came from. One day she heard the voice of Mathey Trewella, the son of the churchwarden, and the best singer in the parish, and enticed him to come away with her - neither was ever seen again. The parishioners commemorated the story by having the ends of two benches carved in the shape of a mermaid.

A wind had got up that evening, and trees surrounding the graveyard creaked and groaned with every movement through them. By eight p.m. the graveyard was pitch black and the two men were straining to see any movement.

"This is ridiculous," Thomas said rubbing his aching back. "We should have got the police to do this."

"Shush, there's someone with a flash light."

Thomas pulled Nathan from the grill. "Where?"

"Over in the far corner, do you see?" Nathan whispered.

Nathan could hear Thomas breathing hard down his nostrils, the anger rising in him as he watched the torch light up Ethel's gravestone. "Right then come on, what are we waiting for? We can catch the bugger red-handed."

"Shush, just a moment, let's just see….." But Thomas was making his way down the tower steps, so Nathan quickly followed him. Once outside, Nathan pulled Thomas back by his sleeve to slow him down, and very quietly they padded along the soft grass towards the crouching figure that was now at Elizabeth's grave. As they approached, they could hear the man's voice as he emptied the wild flowers from the vase and replaced them with the roses.

"I see that husband of yours has adorned your grave with weeds again. He never did deserve you. This will show him how he should treat you."

"Not with my bloody flowers you won't you thieving bastard," Thomas yelled as he lurched forward and grabbed the crouching figure by the neck. Nathan quickly followed suit and grabbed the man by his coat. A struggle ensued, but a swift elbow in the ribs made Thomas loosen his grip and the man quickly relieved himself of his coat, causing Nathan to stagger backwards clutching the garment in his hands. Before they could catch him again the man had scrambled over the graveyard wall and out into the open fields. Thomas lurched forward towards the wall, but it was no use, he had disappeared into the night.

"The police will be waiting next time," Thomas shouted out into the darkness. "Did you know him?" Thomas turned and asked Nathan.

Nathan threw the coat to the floor. "No."

"Well, he seemed to know your Elizabeth!"

"I know," Nathan sighed anxiously.

Thomas walked back to Nathan and bent down to retrieve the discarded coat. "I'm taking this to the police." He sniffed the garment. "Whoever it is, he has an expensive taste in aftershave from the smell of this."

Thomas laid a hand on Nathan's shoulder. "I apologize for accusing you Nathan, you're a good man, I should have known better."

"Think nothing more of it my friend. I just wish we could have found out who it was."

"Well, whoever it was, I think we may have put a stop to his nocturnal activities. Come on, I'll buy you a pint."

11

Change when change happens, even when one expects it, and has indeed looked forward to its coming, can be extremely daunting when it does come.

Faye had longed for something exciting to happen in her life, though she had thought her change of circumstances would be because a major art gallery would take her on. But this, this was so unexpected and so diverse a career change. Her stomach churned with apprehension as she prepared to make the journey to London to meet the advertising executives at Lemmel's headquarters in London.

The invitation had come completely out of the blue. Liam had driven down from London, quite unexpectedly one Thursday evening and delivered the news to her just as she was getting ready to go out. He had told her that he would be arriving on Saturday morning, so when she heard his car pull up outside her cottage, a tiny part of her felt disappointed that another evening with her friends would be cancelled.

Her relationship with Liam was now in its second month, though she saw him only every other weekend, due to his work commitments. His position as the Advertising Executive for Lemmel kept him working long hours at their head office. Consequently time together was at a premium, so she found that she very rarely made it to the fortnightly quiz night nowadays. Liam always promised to come on Friday evening, but inevitably, he would drop in on her unexpectedly on Thursday, just as she was getting ready to go out, and as she hadn't seen him for days she felt obliged to cancel her plans to be with him.

He arrived that night with a bouquet of flowers in one hand and a bottle of Bollinger in the other.

He entered her house without knocking, as was his

way, and Faye began to take off her jacket. She sensed immediately that he was pumped with adrenalin. Probably from the drive she thought, though normally the drive took it out of him.

He placed the flowers and champagne on the table and scooped her into his arms. "Hello my lovely girl." He noted she was dressed and ready to go out. "Oh sorry, were you just about to go somewhere?"

"No." She sighed as her chin dropped slightly to her chest. "It doesn't matter." He knew very well where she was going to go, she thought.

"Never mind, I'm sure it wasn't anywhere important." He grinned. "We can have supper together now," he said placing the bottle in the freezer to chill down. He kissed her passionately on the lips. "Have you missed me?"

"Yes," she answered automatically.

"Good, now then, I'm famished. What can you rustle up that will go with Champagne? I've driven non-stop from London," he said, throwing his coat on the chair.

Faye retrieved it and hung it with her jacket on the coat stand. "What's the Champagne for?"

"Food first woman, then I'll tell you," he said playfully circling his arms around her waist.

As Faye searched through her cupboards, franticly concocting a meal from her jars of pasta and sauce mixes, Liam picked up her holiday brochure from the table. He pursed his lips. "You're not planning a trip are you?"

Faye took the brochure from his hand. "Yes, I walk a section of the South West coast path every year. I'm looking for guest houses to stay in."

"Well you can forget all walking trips this year if my plan comes to fruition."

Faye stared blankly at him. "I'm not with you. What plan?" He stood and grinned at her. "What plan? What's going on Liam?"

"Oh okay, okay I'll tell you, I was going to let you know after dinner, but.." He took the spoon she was waving in the air and placed it on the draining board. "You, my lovely girl, are coming to London with me on Sunday evening."

Faye listened to his proposition in stunned silence.

Liam watched her response. "Well, what do you think?"

"Why do they want to see me?" she asked innocently.

"Why the hell do you think?" Liam retorted crossly. God but she could be infuriating sometimes.

"But they don't know me!" Faye answered evenly.

He blew out an exaggerated sigh. "I know you! They've seen the photos. You know the photos I've taken of you these last two months."

Faye listened with dismay; sometimes he could be quite sarcastic, she thought to herself. She forced a smile. "Oh, silly me, and I thought you were taking photos because you liked me, I didn't realise there was another agenda." The moment she said the words she berated herself for responding in the same vein as his tone of voice.

He regarded her for a moment, moved towards her and pushed a wisp of hair away from her face. "What's the matter? I thought you'd be thrilled. Most girls would die for a chance to get their face on the covers of the glossies."

"Glossies?"

"Glossy magazines!" He laughed. "You really don't understand the enormity of what is on offer here, do you?" He took her by the shoulders. "You, my darling wonderful beautiful girl, will wow their socks off when they see you at Lemmel."

Discovering Faye was a 'dream come true' for Liam - the last few weeks had been quite tense to say the least. For weeks he had been compiling a portfolio of photos of Faye in preparation for the monthly meeting of the board of directors at Lemmel, London. This meeting was to discuss a new range of beauty products, which in reality was an attempt to rescue Lemmel.

Lemmel, London had been amongst the most popular cosmetics companies in the world. Established in the early 20th century, it was one of the major producers of perfumes, soaps, powders, hair pomades and other toiletries.

As the swinging sixties exploded, Lemmel knew it had to update its old-fashioned image to stay in the market and aimed their products at their younger customers. Young, vibrant, affordable perfumes were introduced to an appreciative consumer with great success.

Lemmel had rubbed along with its contemporaries since then, but in an ever-changing market, many of the perfume companies were setting their sights on the more discerning customers with expensive tastes.

Lemmel knew that to survive, they too must move with the times, so in 1994 Angus Fox had taken on the role of Managing Director and with him he brought the financial backing of several shareholders. Lemmel, London was now out to rival some of the leading cosmetic companies.

Their new fragrance 'Infinity' would have placed Lemmel alongside the other companies. Unfortunately with the death of Jasmine Quintana and the loss of revenue from the withdrawal of the massive advertising campaign they had built around her meant that Lemmel found itself and its two hundred plus workforce fighting for survival. They were insured of course for such an eventuality, but the company's reputation was at stake. They needed a new product and a new 'face' if it was to survive. Several cosmetic companies in Paris had made significant enquiries into a takeover of Lemmel, and Angus Fox the Managing Director was in no mood to let that happen.

"We need this new product to work, do you hear me Knight?" Angus Fox slammed his fist onto the conference table.

Liam swallowed hard. "And I have just the person to promote this," he said firmly, laying a selection of photos he had taken of Faye on the table.

Angus pulled the images toward him, "Mmm" he said mildly as his eyebrows rose appreciatively.

Spurred on now Liam said, "You have to agree, she's perfect for our new product 'Guinevere'," he said hopefully. "You said you wanted someone enchanting, beautiful and mystical, well, here she is."

The photos were passed around causing a buzz of approval in the room. "Who is she?" Frank Hardy the Quality Assurance Director asked.

Liam's eyes fell on Hardy. "Never mind who she is! She's young, fresh and vibrant, she's perfect."

"Is she with an agency?"

"No."

"So she has no experience then?"

Liam grimaced. "No, but..."

"I can do without buts Knight, we have a lot riding on this," Angus snapped. "I still think we should use someone famous," he said, pushing the photos away.

Liam cleared his throat. "Famous people cost money Angus! Trust me on this; I know we are onto a winner. She'll be perfect. As soon as I saw her I knew she would be just right for this project. She will turn our fortunes around."

"I hope you're not sleeping with her," Ronnie James the Purchasing Director said enviously.

Liam pursed his lips in disdain.

"Of that there is no doubt," Frank Hardy the Quality Assurance Director said crisply.

"Well he better keep her sweet, we don't want her running out on us," Ronnie added.

Exasperated, Liam addressed Angus. "Look! We're digressing here. I think she is perfect."

Silence ensued for what seemed like an age then Angus said, "Much as it pains me to agree with you Knight, she, whoever she is, *is* perfect."

Liam smiled knowingly; an agreement from Angus

would win the rest of them over.

"You had better bring her in on Monday," Angus growled. "But this advertising venture will be very different. If she is any good, there won't be the money to throw at her launch like the Quintana girl. There'll be no company car, no flash hotels this time. We are still suffering the financial deficit from that bloody stupid accident! She'll work hard, bloody hard, and you'll see to it. Got it?"

"Yes Angus," he answered meekly.

*

In the space of two days, Faye had found herself amidst a whirlwind of shopping, hairdressers and manicurists. Liam had arranged it all; she had been exfoliated, moisturised, buffed, blow-dried and polished to within an inch of her life, at the best salons Truro could offer. As she stood in front of her mirror, she hardly recognised herself as she smoothed down her new outfit.

*

On Monday morning Faye fidgeted nervously as she stood in front of Angus Fox. The room was hot and stuffy and the large balding man who sat before her perspired profusely. Angus gave her an unhurried look from head to toe and if he was impressed, he did not reveal this in his countenance.

"So Miss…?" He looked straight at her for confirmation.

"Larson," Faye answered, smiling nervously.

"This is quite an opportunity for someone like you." Faye's face remained neutral. "I do hope you appreciate how lucky you are. After all you are unknown!" Still Faye made no effort to answer.

Liam stepped in and said, "She does Angus."

Angus gave a jaded sigh. "I am told you have no previous modelling background."

"No," Faye answered shortly.

"What do you do then?"

Faye moistened her lips. "I'm a yacht broker at the moment, but first and foremost I am an artist," she answered proudly.

He gave a derisive snort. "Everyone is an artist nowadays my dear. We'll just stick to you being a pretty face who sells boats for now and forget about your attempts at daubing, eh?"

"I beg your pardon?" Faye prickled with indignation. She felt a sharp dig in the side of her ribs as Liam attempted to silence her.

Angus looked down his nose at Faye. "You can go now Miss err…" This time Faye didn't prompt him. She pushed her chair back with such force she nearly knocked it over. Liam quickly manoeuvred the chair neatly back to its place and followed Faye out of the door.

"Just a moment Knight," Angus shouted. Liam swallowed hard and returned to the room. "What have you brought me here?"

"I'm sorry she spoke back to you Angus, I…."

"She's trouble," he said, glowering at him.

"No, I promise you, she'll be no trouble." He could feel the sweat prickling down his back.

Angus swivelled his chair and looked out onto the London skyline. "She had better not be, otherwise she'll be out on her ear and so will you. Do I make myself clear?"

"Absolutely."

"Good, get out."

Incensed, he marched Faye out into the car park. "Are you completely mad?" His voice was low and full of rage.

"As a matter of fact, yes I am mad, I'm furious in fact. How dare he belittle me by calling me just a 'pretty face?'" she retorted as she walked away from him.

He grabbed her by the shoulders and shook her. "You are a pretty face you stupid woman. Why else would you have been picked for this advertising campaign?"

Trying without success to curb her anger, she turned on Liam. "I may have what you call a pretty face, but let me tell you, I am so much more than that. I'm no Einstein, but I'm not stupid either, and if that's what you think of me, then you can find someone else to pose for your bloody photographs." She turned on her heel and walked away.

Liam was completely taken aback. No one spoke to him like that, least of all a woman. "Faye," he snapped, but she kept on walking. He stood there incredulously for a moment, and then against his better judgement he ran after her. He caught her by the shoulder. "Faye look darling, I'm so sorry I called you stupid. You're not, of course you're not. I shouldn't have said it, it was very wrong of me and I apologise." In truth the apology almost choked him. She turned and looked into his handsome face as he smiled down at her. "Do you forgive me?"

She bit down on her lip and nodded slowly, but deep down she realised that a tiny bit of her love for him had died that day.

"Good." He held out his hand to her. "Come on, we need to go back to my office, we have some planning to do. I need to sort out your release from the boatyard and did I tell you I'm taking you to Paris on Friday on a tour of our perfume factory?"

Her heart lifted at the mention of Paris, but as for her release from work....? "I'll have to work one month's notice you know!"

He shook his head. "I don't think so," he answered confidently.

*

Before the Paris trip, Faye returned to Cornwall to collect what she needed from her house and to say her goodbyes to her friends.

Her first port of call was Owen Barnes' office, to apologise for not working her month's notice.

"Well my dear, Mr Knight was adamant when he rang me that your contract with Lemmel must start with immediate effect. So, I really had no option but to let you go. I must say it's left me in a bit of a predicament, but who am I to stand in the way of your new glittering career?" he said rather tongue-in-cheek. He walked around the desk and held out his arms to hug her. "There will always be a place for you here if you ever want to return. We shall all miss you terribly."

Faye hugged him tightly. "I shall miss you all as well. You've been wonderful to work for."

He gave her a fatherly smile. "I fear Pippa will wash us all away in the river of tears she's shed since learning of your departure. Off you go and see her, she's expecting you. Now, you take care of yourself won't you?" He watched her leave the office and shook his head. Deep down he feared for her, because try as he might, he couldn't warm to Liam Knight and he didn't trust him as far as he could throw him.

Before Faye could step through the door of the office, Pippa's eyes were full of great fat tears.

"Oh Faye." She sobbed into her arms. "I know it's a wonderful opportunity for you, and I'm so happy for you, you know I am!" She sobbed again and blew noisily into her handkerchief. "I just feel like I'm losing you bit by bit. Is this really what you want?"

Faye hugged her friend tightly. "No, it isn't what I really want, you know that, it's just…sometimes opportunities are presented to you in life, and if I choose not to take this one, then I will always wonder. Do you know what I mean?"

"I suppose so." She sniffed noisily.

"I don't want to leave you Pippa; you're the best friend anyone could ever want. But it might be good for me as a painter, you know to see new places and make new contacts."

"Are you giving up the house in Gweek?" she asked with a strained smile.

"Absolutely not, I shall be back in-between jobs, I promise, and I shall phone you all the time. Look, Liam's given me a mobile phone." She produced the Nokia from her handbag. "Though I'm damned if I can fathom out how to use it at the moment."

Pippa wiped her eyes and took the phone. "Well don't ask me. I can't see the point in them to tell you the truth. I mean, how desperately does anyone need to phone someone that you have to carry this contraption about with you all the time? It weighs a bloody tonne."

Faye smiled and slipped it back into her handbag and nodded. "Well, it might come in handy if there isn't a phone box about and I want to speak to you."

Pippa started to cry again.

"Oh Pippa don't cry, you're breaking my heart. Please be happy for me. I just can't turn something down like this can I?"

"I know. I'm sorry, I am happy for you," she wailed through the tears. "Oh God, I'll miss you so much Faye," she said, retrieving another tissue from the box.

As the girls embraced, Amos stepped into the office preceded by an overwhelming pong of strong sweet aftershave. Both girls gagged as the smell caught in the back of their throats.

"Amos! What the hell are you wearing?" Pippa choked, covering her nose with her hand.

"Givenchy for gentlemen," he answered proudly smiling at Faye.

Faye's shoulders fell sorrowfully.

"Good grief man, what have you done, washed in it?" She grabbed Faye by the sleeve and with watering eyes they both ran to the door for fresh air.

Owen passed them at the doorway as they stumbled into the yard coughing and choking. "What's the matter with you two?" he said as the smell hit him full face. "What the Hell! It smells like a tart's boudoir in here. Is it *you* boy?" he asked Amos, who stood awkwardly in the middle of the room.

Amos nodded slowly. "I'm wearing it for Faye. I

thought she liked it," he answered miserably.

"Well whatever it is, I don't like it." Owen sneezed violently and rubbed his nose with his hand. "I should think we'll smell this for the next month in here. Go on, be off with you," he said pushing the boy out of the office. "Pippa, come back in here and get some of these windows open. We need to get a through draught or we shall poison all our clients."

Amos and Faye stood in the yard together. "I'm sorry," Amos said. "I didn't know how much to put on."

"Don't worry Amos," Faye smiled and reached out and placed her hand on his arm tenderly. "You just need a little bit, after you have washed and shaved," she answered gently.

He lifted his deep brown eyes to meet hers. "Are you really going away with him?"

Faye nodded.

"Make sure he takes good care of you then," he said in earnest.

Faye smiled gratefully.

"If you ever need anything…." His eyes looked desperately at her.

"Thank you Amos," she answered softly.

She turned and blew a kiss to Pippa and Owen through the office windows then began to walk out of the boatyard away from her old life. She knew all eyes were watching her, but she had no idea how worried everyone was for her.

12

Elizabeth's gravestone was erected at the end of May and was a fitting tribute to a wonderful woman. Nathan polished the granite with his handkerchief, and stepped back to read the inscription once again.

In memory of Elizabeth Trent Prior.
Beloved wife of Nathan and loving mother of Greg.
An Artist of selfless integrity, whose quiet example and delightful sense of humour enriched our lives.
Resting in peace under a Cornish sky.

This wasn't entirely correct - at the moment her ashes were resting in peace next to his bed. She specifically wanted a headstone in the churchyard, but her ashes were to be scattered out on the cliffs that she loved. Unfortunately Nathan could not decide on the best place to do this at the moment.

The day was hot with a slight on-shore breeze, which made the soft crash of the surf at the foot of the cliffs more audible in the tiny churchyard. It was the sort of day Elizabeth loved. Armed with an easel, canvas and paint, she'd be out of the door as the birds began to sing, and he would find her on the cliffs later that morning, her nose pink with sunburn, and her eyes would be shining with delight at the day. He would bring her a flask of tea and make her wear a battered straw hat. She would stop painting only to kiss him, then he knew to leave her be, as she created her next masterpiece. That was how it was. On sunny days she painted, and on dull days she sat in her workshop and moulded clay, or chipped away at granite and marble. She was a prolific artist whatever she put her mind to. The art world and Nathan had lost someone very special.

"Oh Greg, you should be here with me today." The sadness Nathan felt at the loss of both wife and son was unfathomable. So, he stood alone, his bouquet of pink sea thrift, campion and bluebells, in his hand. "You are forever in my heart my darling Elizabeth," he said as he placed them in the vase, safe in the knowledge they would not be disturbed by any more nocturnal goings on.

The police had drawn a blank as to the owner of the coat they had stripped from the thief's back that night, as there was nothing in the pockets to reveal his identity. He seemed to have disappeared without trace.

*

It seemed that Cornwall, for all its peace and tranquillity, could not heal a grieving heart, so, in early June, Nathan took himself off to London and ensconced himself in the safety of the Chelsea Arts Club. There he could be himself, the bohemian artist, with his own type of people. He needed something to bring back his zest for life, to talk with his fellow artists and to not be what he had become, an empty shell, a boat without a rudder, and a man without reason.

Carrie was left to her own devices in Gwithian Cottage, and as she waited for his return she nursed her discontentment like an open wound.

13

When the taxi came to a halt in the busy Rue de Mansel, Paris, Faye alighted and gazed with delight at her surroundings. She had never been to Paris and was eager to experience everything about this bustling exciting city.

Liam paid the driver and put his hand to the small of her back. "Come on," he urged, as he moved her towards a dusty carved wooden door with the words 'La Parfumerie' etched into a brass plate. After Liam had pressed the bell several times, the door was opened by a disgruntled, albeit very stylish woman in her mid fifties.

Liam spoke quickly and fluently in French, but all Faye picked up was that the woman stood before them was called Madame Deponte. The woman hissed at him quite frenetically and for a moment Faye was unsure as to whether they would gain admittance. Presently she opened the door wider and watched cautiously as they both entered. Almost immediately she walked past Madame Deponte, Faye's nostrils picked up the odious smell of stale sweat and she unconsciously covered her nose with a hand. Liam glanced at Faye, furrowed his brow reproachfully, making her drop her hand to her side like a scolded child. Once again there was a quick interaction between Liam and Madam Deponte before she left the room.

Liam turned to Faye. "Do you have to act so childishly?" he hissed.

"She reeks of sweat," Faye answered in her defence.

"Shush," he snapped, as the door opened and Madame Deponte came back. She gestured for them to follow her. Once in the antechamber of the perfumery they were left alone again and Faye gazed at the glass cabinets filled with bottles of oils. A brief sharp expletive preceded the arrival of a younger woman.

Unruffled, Liam moved towards the woman and kissed her on each cheek, and then there was what sounded like a muffled angry conversation between them.

"Faye, this is my good friend Allett. Allett, this is Faye Larson!"

"Hello, Bonjour," Faye stammered, hoping she had said the right word in French.

The woman examined Faye cautiously, pursing her lips in distaste, and then looked blankly toward Liam. Faye watched the exchange curiously, and began to feel very uncomfortable. For all of this woman's beauty, and she was quite stunning in her appearance, Faye disliked her persona instantly. It was quite obvious the feeling was mutual. Faye watched as she smoothed her hands down her tight black dress, and then began to adjust an invisible wisp of hair from her coiffured head. She moistened her lips, cleared her throat and began to speak in perfect English. It took Faye several seconds before she realised the tour of the perfumery had begun.

"Perfume is a beautiful luxury; get it right and your scent suggests you have superior taste in all things, it gives you sophistication and allure," Allett said importantly. "Remember Miss Larson, it will become one of the most memorable things about you. Imagine you pass a woman in a corridor, for a split second you take in their appearance, style of dress, makeup, and then all that is left is their scent. Now you have to ask yourself, does the scent reflect the person. You must choose the perfume for the way you are. There is nothing nicer than someone saying, 'you smell so good,' it would make you feel gorgeous wouldn't it?" Allett paused for a moment and tilted her head awaiting her response.

Faye nodded obediently.

"Nothing captures the imagination like perfume, and nothing encapsulates the essence of you, the wearer, more than your scent. So if you are trailing clouds of scented glory, make it as luxurious as you can."

Allett began to walk through to the next room and Faye followed obediently. Inside there was a collection of large copper vats along the centre of the room and the aroma was quite overpowering. "So, Miss Larson," Allett resumed her spiel. "Let me tell you that there are many approaches to experiencing the art of perfumery. As a beginner, we are taught to experiment with fragrance oils. These oils are very easy for beginners to use. Fragrance oils are blends of various materials, both synthetic and natural, that are diluted so that they are easier to work with. The fragrance oils are not meant to be worn directly on the skin; they are meant to be used as ingredients in composing a blend. Many people prefer creating perfumes out of natural essential oils. These can be a little trickier, because many natural components in their pure form smell quite powerful. To evaluate their true scent, i.e. their aroma, in a perfume composition, you would need to dilute them, often to a one percent dilution. When you get to know their true character, then you can blend with them in their natural state with more confidence." She halted for a moment and looked towards Faye to see if she was listening.

Faye's eyes darted between Allett and Liam, wondering if she was meant to make some kind of response.

Allett pursed her lips and continued. "We then come to aroma chemicals. Aroma chemicals are the molecules that are the 'building blocks' of scent. For example, natural rose oil is composed of molecules such as geraniol and phenylethyl alcohol. Many of these molecules can be isolated from the complete oil by natural means such as fractional distillation. These aroma chemicals are very challenging, in that many of them have effects on a perfume composition that are not obvious when evaluating them separately. These are components that appear in the most valued classic perfumes, as well as popular modern fragrances.

Please remember that perfumery is an art Miss Larson,

as well as a science. Let me show you a few simple mixes." She walked towards a drawer of what looked like test tubes, and pulled from one of them a spatula of liquid for her to sample.

"If you want to smell unique, and want to symbolise independence and self confidence, then we mix a feminine scent of jasmine, honeysuckle and tuberose with vanilla, amber and musk." She offered up a second spatula. "Should you want to feel sexy we mix blackcurrant, chocolate and vanilla with a twist of musk, and for a more delicate feminine fragrance we base the perfume around flowers, namely the rose. These are the bases of the new fragrance 'Guinevere' which we have perfected for Lemmel. Aroma therapists say that the rose awakens feminine sexuality, it sooths, heals and restores. So the wearer can be graceful and refined but with a will of iron." Allett gave Faye an unhurried look up and down. "'Genevieve' is designed to appeal to a more discerning woman, seeking quality and rarity from her perfume."

As suddenly as the tour started, it was over, and Allett turned swiftly to leave the room without a by-your-leave. Almost in unison, Liam shouted, "Allett," as Faye called, "Merci Madame," but Allett continued to walk away without turning. As the door closed, Liam and Faye glanced at one another.

"Well, what was all that about, why was she so unfriendly?" Faye said with a laugh.

"No idea," he answered crossly. "Anyway, so now you know about perfume. Come on let's get out of here."

Relieved that the encounter was over, Faye's mood began to lift at the thought of a spot of sightseeing, but once outside, he hailed a taxi. "If we are quick we can catch the last flight back to Gatwick," he said and Faye's heart sank.

Once back in London, Faye was ensconced in a hotel near Covent Garden, where she and Liam shared a room service meal and a bottle of warm white wine. The next day she was to have her portfolio shot by the renowned photographer Calvin Romano.

Faye had never been to London before and if truth were known she wasn't too impressed. She hated the bustle of the crowds, the crammed streets, and the incessant noise from the volume of traffic on the roads. So it was with great relief that she and Liam finally arrived at Calvin's studio.

As they stepped into the studio, a small slim Chinese woman greeted them. She politely took their coats and offered refreshments and seated them on a luxurious sofa surrounded by high-class glossy magazines. Faye couldn't help feeling a little out of place in the high street garments she had quickly purchased for the trip. The slightly distasteful look Liam had given her when he saw what she was dressed in had added to her insecurity. She glanced at him as he flicked through a magazine; he was always dressed in an Armani suit and fine Italian leather shoes when working. Not for the first time she grimly thought that this was his world, not hers.

To Liam's annoyance, Calvin kept them waiting over two hours, and when eventually the photographer did emerge from the studio, he had a sleepy look in his eyes as if he had just woken, which added to Liam's annoyance.

Calvin was a small slim American Italian, handsome when he didn't sneer and a little creepy in his slow snake like persona. When he set eyes on Faye, her beauty overwhelmed him, as Liam knew it would. Calvin moved slowly around her, his eyes skimming her body, mentally assessing the proportions of her perfect size ten figure. As he stood behind her, he looked towards Liam and pointed at her hair.

"It's all in hand Calvin," Liam said confidently.

She could hear Calvin sigh on each breath and she shuddered inwardly as he moved his face in front of hers. He took a large intake of air. "Purr-fect," he breathed. "Provincial but perfect."

Faye's eyes darted nervously at Liam who winked at her.

"You can leave us now Mr Knight," he hissed. "Faye and I have work to do and she doesn't need her agent here," he added, glancing back at Faye from under his dark lashes.

Agent? Faye thought to herself. She had no idea Liam was acting as her agent, in fact she didn't realise that she needed an agent.

"Oh by the way, Allett has been on the phone for you. She didn't sound too happy, if you ask me." He smirked.

Liam flashed him a look of contempt. "Nobody asked you."

Faye watched with concern at the altercation. She didn't like all this bad feeling, it unnerved her.

As Calvin showed Liam out, he lifted a 'Do Not Disturb' sign from the hook on the door and placed it on the doorknob, and for some reason the gesture made Faye shudder. Calvin turned his head slightly to make eye contact with Faye and his mouth twisted into a smile. "Now to work," he said, rubbing his hands together slowly. "But first darling we need to get you changed out of these ...." he curled his lip in disdain, "....things you are wearing into something more, err, stylish."

Faye was the most photogenic woman Calvin had seen for a long time. Tall and slender, high cheekbones, flawless skin, beautiful emerald eyes which sparkled in the spotlights and an abundance of golden auburn hair the colour of sunset. When Faye walked out of his studio that day, her portfolio completed, he was immediately on the telephone to Lemmel, confirming there was no doubt in his mind, Faye Larson was the woman to save their company. She was the 'Face' of Guinevere.

Work for Faye started almost immediately, so Liam took himself off back to Head office, after he arranged for Faye to have a personal shopper to make sure she never turned up for a shoot again in 'high street' clothes.

She was to reside in London for the first few weeks for more photo shoots with Calvin, and her base was a small flat in Chelsea which she was to share with two other models, a girl named Alex, short for Alexandria and a man called Leo - no surnames were ever used nor given out freely.

When Faye arrived, Alex showed her around the apartment. "Well this is it. Drink darling? Champagne, whiskey, cognac! It's all there." She gestured to the cabinet. "Just help yourself, whatever you want." Faye put her bag down on one of the sofas as Alex said, "Be a darling Leo and give me a fix."

Faye watched horrified as Alex tied a rubber band around her own upper arm, patted her punctured arm for a vein and waited in anticipation as Leo prepared the needle.

"Hey honey, you want some of this?" Leo asked.

Faye shook her head violently. "I think I'll go to my room, we have a busy day tomorrow."

Leo shrugged his shoulders. "Suit yourself, we're going clubbing, you're very welcome to come."

Again Faye shook her head, this time adding a smile for politeness, picked up her bag and headed for her bedroom just as Alex moaned and fell back against the chair as though she had fainted.

An hour later when Faye heard the others leaving the flat, she emerged from her bedroom and picked up the telephone to call Liam. She listened to the ringing tone, then it clicked onto the answer machine and Faye reluctantly replaced the receiver without speaking. She sighed as she glanced down at the needle, lighter and spoon needed to heat the white substance that Leo had left her in case she changed her mind. She turned her nose up in disgust. So much for the glamorous world of beauty, she thought.

*

Within four months of Liam's suggestion, Faye's picture adorned every major magazine and billboard. 'The face of

Guinevere' became famous during prime time television adverts, and life was a far cry from the poorly paid job in the boatyard, but oh dear, she missed it so much.

As she inspected her appearance in the mirror she would not have recognised herself from her old life. Her beautiful auburn hair was now dyed white blonde, and the condition of it had suffered dramatically. Although she protested frantically at the hairdressers, the deed was done and her appearance had changed overnight. From that moment on, her alter ego was 'Cordelia Hart', her own name being deemed too ordinary. Apparently she did not own her hair now. Lemmel owned it, according to her contract, which was eight pages long and had dropped on her door mat along with a curt message from Liam: Read it, digest it, sign it and I'll pick it up later. She had done what he asked, except sign it! She needed to clarify a few things with Liam before she signed her life away.

She had worked non-stop for the last few months and was exhausted. For all its glamour, modelling was a business full of back stabbers and bitchiness. It was also a very lonely life for someone who didn't drink to excess, do drugs or club all night long. Faye was desperately unhappy and longed for the friendship she had shared with Pippa. Her days were full of photo shoots and fashion shows, and more often than not, her weekends were spent wandering around art galleries and museums. She longed for Liam's company, but all too often when she rang him, all she got was his answer phone. She had thought that with them both working in London, she would see a lot more of him, but he seemed to be always away on business, working to promote her, he would tell her. If it hadn't been for Pippa at the end of the phone, Faye felt she would not have survived.

14

It must have been fate for Nathan to attend the party that evening at the Chelsea Arts Club. It was mid August; the air in London was stifling, and under normal circumstances, Nathan would have taken himself off to bed early after an evening stroll around the grounds of the club.

"Come on old boy," Chester Coulson had said to him, "There's a party inside. It's full of lovely young nubile models. It's just the thing to get the old artistic juices flowing. What do you say?"

Nathan blew a sigh of resignation. When Chester got the bit between his teeth about something, there was no swaying him otherwise.

Once inside, Chester had his own agenda and quickly made his way towards a crowd of laughing girls on the other side of the room. Nathan ordered a brandy which he decided he would drink quickly and leave before Chester had noticed he had gone. It was then that he saw her. Her image came into view through the crowds of people and it caught his breath. Her face puzzled him, it was beautiful and he felt sure he had seen her before somewhere, but where he could not place. He had not looked at her more than a few moments when he was charged with the urge to pick up a paintbrush. My God, who is she to move me so, he contemplated.

Faye standing alone at the very edge of the room was quite unaware she was being watched as Nathan noted that she looked pale and unwell. She had a sadness that matched his own and he felt drawn to her. There was nothing else for it; he must go and introduce himself. He turned to place his empty glass on the bar and when he looked back, he could not locate her. He moved through the crowds scanning the periphery of the room for a sighting, but his muse had gone, though the image he held of her was sketched that night in his room. It was the first of many sketches and the beginnings of a body of work which he used as therapy. A body of work he called 'The Look'. This had been all he needed. He would pack his bags in the morning. Cornwall and his studio beckoned.

*

Faye, stifled by the heat of the party, bored with the company and exhausted from her latest assignment, stepped out of the club and into the noise of the London evening traffic. Her flat was three blocks away, sanctuary was her bed, and her pillow was her shoulder to cry on.

Back at the flat she flung her bag onto the sofa. Desperately needing to speak to someone, Faye keyed in Liam's number for what would be the fifth time that day; again she was forced to leave a message on Liam's voice mail. She sighed heavily and put the phone away. Suddenly she felt a chill, as though a door had opened causing a draught. Without turning around Faye recognised the voice behind her, a sound something between a sigh and a purr, a sound which always made her flesh crawl.

"Elusive isn't he?" Calvin breathed down her neck.

"He's busy that's all," she answered curtly without turning around.

"With whom though?"

Faye did not answer.

"Don't you think it's strange that he doesn't take you to his home in Richmond?"

Faye looked at him cautiously. "He has the builders in. He's been sleeping on a friend's couch."

Calvin gave a wicked smile. "Has he now?"

"What are you trying to say?" she snapped angrily.

"I'm not saying anything. But if you were mine, I would be a lot more attentive to you. How often does he come around, every other weekend? It seems to me that I would rather sleep in your bed than on some 'friend's couch'-

what do you think?"

There was no mistaking it. The statement hit a nerve with Faye, and Calvin could see the despondency in her eyes. Slowly he began to walk around her as Faye stared at him, watching his lips twitch lustfully. She felt completely naked in her clothes. His eyes travelled across her body. "So beautiful, so per-fect," he purred.

His hand stroked her arm and Faye flinched. "I can help you with your loneliness you know. I know what you need." He put his hand to her cheek and stroked it, and as his hand travelled down he brushed her breast intentionally. A sickness rose into Faye's throat as she pulled away from him in disgust. Unperturbed he moved closer and instantaneously Faye smacked him across the cheek. His eyes flashed dangerously as he grabbed her, pushing her against the lounge door.

"You keep your filthy hands off me," she hissed, averting her face as he bore down on her. He grabbed her face and pulled her round to face him and she felt herself go suddenly cold. The muscles in his jaw tightened as he tried to control his temper. He turned and grabbed at the glossy magazine on the table bearing Faye's image and pressed it against her face. "Just remember who I am. Just you remember who put you here." He pushed the magazine harder into her cheek. "I could end your career you know, just as quickly as I started it. I have the power."

Faye was trembling. "Let go of me." Her voice was high, her words checked.

Enjoying the power he held over her, he tightened his hold. He screwed the magazine in his hands and threw it to the floor. "If I refuse to work with you, no one else will take you on, don't forget that." His voice was low and threatening.

"Good, do it then, because I'm sick of it all," she snapped.

"You ungrateful bitch," he said, his voice low and filled with the bitterest contempt. He grabbed her by the shoulders and flung her to the floor. "You'll be sorry you said that."

Scrambling to her feet, she grabbed her coat and bag. "No, you'll be sorry when Liam hears about this." Her voice broke into a sob.

He looked at her scornfully. As he made to leave he said, "I don't think so." He slammed the door shut behind him.

Faye ran to her bedroom, locked her door and collapsed onto the floor in despair. She could still feel his hand on her breast and it made her skin crawl. She was sick to the pit of her stomach, sick with this business she had been projected into, sick of the loneliness and sick of the people who thought they owned her. The tears began to fall incessantly as she lay on her bedroom carpet. She cried like an injured animal, halted only by the ringing of her mobile phone.

She pulled it from her bag and pressed the talk button. "Hello," she whimpered.

"Faye?"

Faye's heart leapt at the sound of Liam's voice. "Oh Liam at last, I've been trying..."

He stopped her mid sentence. "What the hell are you playing at?"

"What?" she said, stunned for an instant.

"Calvin says you've been very rude to him. He's even threatening to blacklist you."

Faye was speechless for a moment.

"Have you completely lost your mind? The whole future of Lemmel depends on you. How could you be so rude to Calvin after all he has done for you?"

Faye felt the anger rising inside her. "He made a pass at me," she retorted.

"Don't be stupid Faye; you must have misunderstood what he said. Calvin would never make a pass at his models. He's far too professional. He simply said he was trying to be friendly and you turned on him like a wild cat."

Faye was stunned momentarily.

At length, Liam said, "Faye?"

She didn't answer.

"Faye, are you still there?"

"Yes," she snapped angrily. "I'm still here. I was just wondering, how was it that Calvin managed to get in touch with you on the telephone, whereas I have been unable to contact you for days."

"He was lucky that's all, he just caught me between meetings," he answered curtly. "Anyway, I have to go now, pressing business you know. Now behave yourself, you naughty girl," he said, his voice softening. "I've made arrangements for us to go down to Cornwall next weekend. Sorry, got to go now. Talk to you soon."

The line went dead in her hand, and she looked at the receiver incredulously. She quickly dialled the number again, but as always the voicemail clicked in.

15

Nathan stood at the gate of Gwithian Cottage in quiet contemplation. The front door was bright blue, framed with an abundance of spent wisteria, nothing had changed. He lifted the gate latch, stepped through, clicking it quietly behind him and then picked his way through the overgrown borders which spewed across the path. Elizabeth would turn in her grave if she saw her beautiful garden like this. He had been away too long.

As he stepped inside, the cottage seemed very still. Carrie must be still sleeping. He placed his suitcase in the hall and ran his hand along the top of the coat stand to where he kept the key to his studio. As soon as he retrieved it, he stepped back out into the sunlight.

A short walk took him down to the cove, where four fishing boats rested lazily on their sides and scraps of seaweed, intermingled with coils of greasy rope, were strewn across the pebble beach. He took the coast path up towards St Ives, a climb of many steps. At the top he stood and looked down the path he had just ascended - it was breathtakingly beautiful. The meadows inland were knee high with wild flowers; soon they would be cut and baled.

There was no doubt about it; the break from here had done him the power of good. He was itching now to get back to work, to smell the turpentine, and to feel the brush in his hands transferring his sketches to canvas.

His cliff top studio nestled deep into the scrubland, hidden from view, but perfectly placed to paint the surrounding coastline. At the door he had to push several times to make it open, as the damp Cornish air had made the door jamb swell. Once inside he felt a calmness descend upon him. He walked slowly through the studio, picking up scraps of driftwood and sea shells, his eyes skimming the faded sketches and photographs which covered the walls. His old wool jumper, which Elizabeth had knitted with all the colours of the rainbow, lay discarded across the worn velour armchair. Tubes of paint lay next to his mixing pallet along with jars of sable brushes gathering dust. At the French doors, he ran his hands down the peeling paint and picked at the cracked and broken putty. He smiled inwardly- no time for DIY, he had more pressing things to do. He pushed open the doors and stepped out onto his balcony. The sky was a sparkling blue and the glistening sea broke with turquoise luminescent waves.

"Home," he shouted up to the white fluffy clouds, startling the seagulls as they drifted gently on the breeze.

Back inside, he walked to his easel which held the painting of Elizabeth, titled 'Enduring Love', the fifth painting in the Love Chronicles. It was painted during her illness and though the ravages of cancer had altered her appearance, she never lost the vibrancy in her eyes and smile. He lifted it off the easel, kissed the smile he had painted and placed it carefully with the rows of stretched canvases which lay abandoned against the far wall. A new canvas was secured to his easel, and then he unscrewed and inhaled the pungent smell of turpentine. A smile crinkled the fine lines at his eyes as he started to work.

*

When Carrie woke and found Nathan's suitcase in the hall, she surmised that he must have driven down through the night and gone to bed. Her excitement was immense. She quickly ran to the kitchen, and ten minutes later she knocked on his bedroom door, carefully balancing a tray of scrambled eggs on toast and a steaming pot of tea. Without waiting, she turned the handle only to find his bed empty. Feeling slightly bewildered, she put the tray down and ran into every room shouting his name - to no avail. The local shop owner hadn't seen him and the coast path showed no signs of Nathan. So she waited. Lunch came and went, dinner was prepared and scraped into the waste bin. At eleven-thirty that evening Carrie's disappointment was intense. Where the hell was he? Why hadn't he come back to her? She locked the door, almost breaking the key in the latch, turned and walked to her bedroom, angrier than she had any right to be.

*

High up in the cliff studio, Nathan sat and looked out at the stars. He had eaten little that day, just the remains of a sandwich he had bought for the journey. The night was warm and tiredness prevailed. He pulled the rainbow jumper across him and closed his eyes. The painting of Faye on the easel had begun to take shape. A new dawn was coming.

16

The drive down to Cornwall that hot August evening had been strained to say the least. As Liam pulled onto the A30 he commented, "You're very quiet tonight."

Faye remained silent for a while then asked, "Why do you never answer my calls when I need you? This incident with Calvin really upset me you know?" she chided. But as always, Liam turned these problems back on Faye.

"For goodness sake Faye, I can't always be there at your beck and call. I don't think you appreciate how hard I'm working on your career. I think about you every moment of the day darling, you know I do." He patted her leg patronisingly. "You have to remember, everything I do, is for your benefit. This product 'Guinevere' is going to make us so rich; we will have so much money we won't know what to spend it on. As for Calvin, stop worrying, and act a little more professionally. It's all getting very tedious this ridiculous 'he made a pass at me' story you keep going on about."

She flashed her eyes angrily at him, and the worm of discontent wriggled, not for the first time, in Faye's stomach. "How's the house in Richmond coming along?" she asked sarcastically.

"Pardon?"

"The building work you're having done. I just wondered when it would be ready, because I'd like to see where you live."

He shifted uneasily in his seat. "I'm afraid you'll have a long wait." He scratched his nose unconsciously. "The whole roof is off and I'm having an extension built on the back. It's an absolute building site at the moment darling, and probably will be for months to come."

Faye turned her head to look out into the darkness and wondered why he was lying to her.

*

They arrived in Gweek late on Friday night. Faye quickly changed the sheets on the bed and they both slept fitfully without making love.

When Liam woke he was alone. He swung his legs quickly out of bed, pulled on his shorts and found Faye in the kitchen talking on the telephone. He shot her a swift sideways glance as he made for the coffee pot and poured himself a cup. He leant heavily against the kitchen sink and sighed impatiently. Sensing the atmosphere, Faye ended her phone call with a cheery, "See you later then."

An awkward silence ensued for a few moments until Faye said, "That was Pippa on the phone."

"Yes, I gathered that. I knew from the tone in your voice who you were talking to," he answered acerbically.

Faye gave him a quizzical look.

"Have you any idea how utterly ridiculous you sound when you are speaking to Pippa on the phone?"

"I beg your pardon?"

"You're like some demented schoolgirl with your childish giggling and squealing. I'd be careful if I was you that nobody ever hears you, otherwise they would think you are completely mad."

Faye felt her confidence crumble under his harsh words. "What a despicable thing to say to anyone."

Liam shrugged his shoulders nonchalantly. "Just stating a fact, that's all." He drained his cup and placed it in the sink. "Come on then, let's be off, a day on the yacht beckons." As he touched her arm she shrugged him violently away. "Oh come on Faye, you're just too sensitive. I'm only telling you for your own good. Just find a better telephone voice, that's all I'm saying. You have an image to keep up you know."

Trembling with indignity she stood rooted to the spot. "I'm spending the day with Pippa," she said defiantly.

"The devil you are, come on." He beckoned her to him with a snap of his fingers.

She shook her head at his audacity. "I said I'm spending the day with Pippa," she retorted firmly.

Visibly annoyed, he stared intently at her. "What are you seeing her for? I wouldn't have thought you'd have anything in common anymore."

Using everything in her power to keep her temper under control she answered, "Pippa is my best friend, and if it hadn't been for her on the end of the phone, I would have gone mad these past few months."

Liam stared at her intently. "Oh yes, talking of which, you do realise the mobile phone is for business use only don't you? It's been noted at head office that you're using too much credit calling friends."

Faye looked at him incredulously.

"Just passing on a comment that has been made that's all," he said holding his hands up. He sighed heavily. "Okay, have it your way. I'll pick you up here for dinner at seven then."

Faye tipped her head to one side. "I might have dinner with Pippa."

He gave her a stony look. "You'll have dinner with me. I haven't driven you all the way down here to spend my weekend alone. I'll see you at seven. Oh, and don't be acting like a silly school girl with her, you really show yourself up with your ridiculous antics."

Faye was livid. She picked up her bag and stormed out of her house, his words ringing in her head.

The morning air was warm and Gweek wore its usual peaceful charm, but as she walked the familiar path towards Pippa's house, her mind was preoccupied with self doubt. Did she really act like a child with Pippa? They certainly knew how to have a good time and they did laugh constantly, but that's just what friends do. She'd never given a thought to how she came across in other people's eyes. She paused for a moment at the crest of the bridge letting the scenery wrap its comforting arms around her. She glanced at her favourite tree, now in full leaf, shading the grassy ground in readiness for the girl who used to come and sit and paint and day-dream. Her heart buckled, where had that girl gone?

As she walked through the door of Pippa's house, all her worries began to drain away as she embraced her friend.

"Wow, look at your hair! I know I've seen it in the magazines, but now, in real life, wow, it's..."

"Oh Pippa, don't, I know it's awful isn't it?" She consciously patted her bottle blond hair.

"No, it's not awful, it's just, not you."

"Well I'm not me anymore. My name is Cordelia Hart apparently." Pippa sniggered. "Oh I know. It's terrible isn't it?"

Pippa took a long hard look at Faye and because she knew her so well, she could see all was not well. "Are you okay otherwise?" she asked gently.

"I've made my bed as they say," she answered flippantly.

Pippa rubbed her hand on Faye's arm. "Owen would have you back tomorrow, you know that."

"I know. It's just that I feel an obligation to complete this assignment."

Pippa gave her a gentle shove. "An assignment eh? Get you and your flashy ways." She grinned. "What does your Mum think of the transformation?"

"Oh don't....She doesn't know, I haven't told her, she still thinks I'm working at the boatyard. I do know that she wouldn't approve though, nor would my step-father. You know how set in their ways they are. Fortunately she doesn't read any of the women's magazines, so she won't have seen me, and even if she did, she wouldn't recognise me looking like this."

Faye thought back to her old life in the Larson household. The newspaper rack contained only The Guardian and an odd copy of the 'War Cry' whenever the Salvation Army knocked at their door. Entertainment came from Radio Three and Four, and the only cosmetic item on her mother's dressing table had been hairspray. 'Make-up is for whores' her step-father would pronounce and the most daring accessory her mother used was a paisley scarf. So, having their daughter fronting a huge cosmetic campaign would not go down well in the Larson household at all, she mused.

"Come on, let's go for a swim at Poldhu Cove, I think you need to wash that London grime out of your hair."

"I wish I could wash the colour out of it," Faye mumbled.

As they sat and chatted over a coffee at the Poldhu beach café after their swim, Pippa watched Faye visibly relax in front of her eyes. With her legs stretched out in front of her, her wet hair drying in the breeze and a smile back on her face, it was almost as though they hadn't been apart.

"God, but I've missed this." She glanced at the sparkling sea through the clumps of dune grass. "The number of times I could have driven down here just to sit here and drink coffee. This is heaven on earth. I have been to some lovely places these past few months Pippa, but nowhere can beat this."

"Well coffee sales have plummeted since you went away," Pippa joked. "Oh it's lovely to have you back. I thought when Amos saw Liam a fortnight ago you would have been with him. Couldn't you get away?"

Faye's eyes opened wide with interest. "Liam was down here a fortnight ago? Are you sure?"

Pippa nodded and cursed herself for making such a faux pas. "Amos said he saw him on deck when he was checking the buoys in Helford Passage. Oh Faye, I'm sorry if I've said anything out of turn."

Faye waved a hand of dismissal, but her mind went into overdrive. Presently she asked, "Was he on his own?" chiding herself immediately for asking the question. Of course he was on his own. Who else would he have been down here with?

Pippa reached over and patted her hand. "Amos said he only saw Liam," she assured her. "Come on let's go home for lunch, I'm famished."

Faye loved Pippa for her casualness, there were no airs and graces with her. Later, when they lunched at her house, the wine flowed as they sat at a table full of condiments and utensils, with various bowls of scrumptious food chucked into them to pick and share.

"I know you said you have this assignment to complete Faye, but I know for a fact that Owen would welcome you back with open arms if you wanted it," she said hopefully.

Faye smiled wistfully. "I know this sounds avaricious, but I'm on an awful lot of money Pippa. If I can stick it out for a couple of years, which is the length of my contract, I could put a deposit down on my own beach café somewhere."

Pippa sighed and smiled sadly, then reached for the bottle of wine, filled their glasses and made a toast. 'Here's to your beach café then.'

Faye was quite merry by the time Liam collected her at seven in the evening, which annoyed him immensely. Dinner that night was a rather stiff affair in a new French restaurant in Truro, then much to her disappointment she was expected to spend the night on the yacht. She was never very comfortable sleeping on the 'Ina'. The constant swell of the water caused a movement in the boat that made her feel quite queasy. She also disliked the fact that he insisted they make love as soon as they returned from dinner, which on a full stomach just added to her nausea.

As she lay awake in the sticky confines of the hot yacht, she tossed the same two questions about in her head. Why hadn't Liam told her that he had been down to Cornwall two weeks ago, and why hadn't he asked her to join him? He knew her weekends were normally free.

Sunday on the River Helford wore its usual late August appearance, as crowds of holidaymakers littered the banks and swarms of boisterous children played by the waters edge. The traffic on the river had been frenzied earlier in the day, but now, in the heat of the afternoon, the water had a perfect stillness about it.

Faye spent a lazy day on board the yacht with Liam. They lunched at the Shipwrights Arms in Helford village, and then returned to doze on deck.

Try as she might she could not stop from asking him the question which burned within her. "Pippa said you were down here a fortnight ago. You never told me. I would have come with you if I'd known." She tried to keep her voice light.

He made a gesture of irritation. "Pippa's obviously lying. I didn't come down here a fortnight ago, so you can tell her that, and tell her to stop trying to cause trouble."

Faye bristled. "She's not trying to cause trouble, she wouldn't do that."

He looked at her coldly. "Well, she's upset you with her lies, hasn't she? You now seem to think I have been down here without you. If that's not causing trouble I don't know what is."

"Pippa said Amos had seen you on the yacht."

"Well, he's lying as well then."

"Don't be daft, why would Amos make something like that up?"

Liam got to his feet. "Oh for Christ's sake Faye, use your brain for once. That greasy little toe-rag is sweet on you. Of course he's going to make up stories to damage my reputation. Now shut up about all this nonsense, I'm trying to relax," he said pouring himself another gin.

Faye watched as Liam settled himself down on deck. He'd had one too many gins again, which meant he was in no fit state to drive home. She would have to drive all the way back to London with him snoring beside her. With every moment that passed and every beat of her heart she could feel what little love and regard she still felt for him diminish. Presently, her thoughts turned to work. This was the last weekend she would have off for some time, and although her next assignment was in Cornwall, it was over on the North coast at Tintagel. She wasn't sure if she would get time to pop back to Gweek. They were using the ruins of the castle of the legendary King Arthur for the photo shoot to launch the next spring range of 'Guinevere' products. This was an assignment she was looking forward to. It was just the thought of working with Calvin which marred the situation. Her working relationship with him had become notably strained as he treated her with icy insolence. He would bully and shout at her for not holding her head still. He would throw tantrums if she was a moment late for the shoot, and then would turn his anger onto the rest of the crew, which they despised Faye for.

As Liam snoozed she took herself down to the galley kitchen to clear the remnants of the breakfast cups. She plumped up the cushions and straightened a few books on the shelf. They were mostly sailing books, but as her eyes skirted the shelf unit, they settled on a large plain black leather-bound book, pushed in behind the other books. On closer inspection she realised it was a Filofax with the initials JQ embossed in gold lettering on the front cover. Furrowing her brow, she glanced out of the galley to check that Liam was still sleeping on deck. Quickly she unclasped and opened the book, and flicked through the pages. All the entries were written with great care, in beautiful handwriting. The pages were full of engagements and reminded her of her very own Filofax, though hers was full of scribbles. She made a mental note to write more carefully. There were appointments and dinner engagements, photo shoots and such like. She flicked to the end entry which was the 25th March 1995. Why did that date sound familiar? Then, there it was, Liam's name jumped out at her. She flicked through several pages and noticed many, many times his name was written down. The first entry was in September last year. Her heart lurched when she recognised Liam's spidery handwriting:

Friday 2nd September. *Have dinner with me tonight. I'll pick you up. 7p.m.*

P.S if all goes well, you will need this Filofax. Liam x

From then on, the entries were made by another hand and in diary form.

Wednesday 7th September. *Lunch date with Liam, 1.30 p.m.*

Friday 9th September. *Weekend on Liam's yacht in Cornwall! Lovely.*

Monday 19th September. *Meeting with Lemmel, London 2.00p.m.*

Tuesday 20th September. *I got the job!*

Thursday 22nd September. *Three glorious days in Paris with Liam, including a tour of the Perfume Factory. I'm in love.*

Monday 26th September. *Shooting my Portfolio with Calvin 10 a.m.*

The rest of the entries that year and through to the beginning of 1995 were full of photo shoots, trips to exotic places, endless parties, and dinner and lunch dates with friends.

Engrossed in the Filofax, which bore an uncanny resemblance to her own Filofax, excluding the parties, Faye glanced again to check whether Liam was still sleeping on deck. The end of January and start of February saw a change in the entries. It seemed to Faye that whoever this book belonged to, she was becoming heartily sick of Liam.

Friday 27th January *Cancel dinner with the girls. Dinner with Liam now 7 p.m. – Damn him, he didn't turn up!*

Friday 3rd February. *Dinner with Liam – he cancelled again, (at least he rang me this time)*

Wednesday 8th February. *Book restaurant for dinner with the girls on Friday night. Booked.*

Friday 10th February. *Dinner with the girls.* The words were scribbled out and replaced with *Dinner with Liam.*

Wednesday 15th February *Must pick up tickets today for*

New York with the girls this weekend. Note to myself. Must cancel trip to Cornwall with Liam on Friday.

Friday 17th February. *Shopping trip to New York with the girls.* This entry was violently scribbled out and replaced with *Cornwall with bloody Liam!*

Faye could see a pattern emerging. JQ? Faye tossed the initials about in her head. She flicked to the beginning of the book to find the owner had written 'if found please return to Jasmine Quintana. The address supplied was Carbis Bay, Cornwall. Jasmine! Oh my God, the penny dropped. Jasmine, the Lemmel model that died in that freak accident in March! But didn't Liam say to her, on their first meeting, that he didn't really know her? Why would he lie to her about that? She quickly flicked forward to March to read the last entries.

Friday 24th March. *2 p.m. Pick up my new company car from the Mercedes Garage in Reading! Drive down to Cornwall for a celebration Dinner with Mum and Dad tonight at home 8 p.m.* Then she had written quickly scribbled in pencil below. *Last minute Lemmel meeting called at Andover Country House Hotel in Hampshire with Liam and the team at 3 p.m !?*

The last entry was written on the next page

Saturday 25th March. *Infinity Launch day! Major television advertisement to be aired on Saturday night prime time! Note to myself - Speak to HR about Liam!*

Faye heard Liam moving about on the deck and quickly stuffed the Filofax back behind the books.

"Oh there you are," he said yawning as he descended the galley steps. "What's wrong with you? You look like you've seen a ghost."

Not trusting her voice to speak, she forced a smile.

17

Nathan took a bite of his toast as he read the letter from Lemon Hill Gallery, but suddenly lost his appetite. He knew the date was drawing near for the exhibition, but he had conveniently pushed it to the back of his mind.

They wanted to arrange a visit to Gwithian Cottage to select pieces of sculpture from Elizabeth's own collection. A few choice pieces of her work were displayed proudly within the walls of the cottage, but the lion's share was locked in Elizabeth's studio, a place he had not ventured into since her death.

Carrie watched with concern as Nathan pushed his breakfast away. "Bad news?"

"Huh?"

"The letter." She nodded at the envelope. "Not bad news I hope."

"No, no." He rose from the table and walked out into the garden without enlightening her on its contents.

She watched him pace the back garden several times. He looked troubled and agitated. She wished with all her heart that he would open up to her sometimes. She wanted to ease his pain and loneliness, but try as she might, she seemed invisible to him at the moment. At least he was painting again, that was a good sign. She would have to be patient. One day he would heal, one day he would notice her, and one day he would realise she was just what he needed. Carrie lived for that day.

The morning was hot, and after several minutes pacing the garden he could feel the sun burning his scalp. It was no good, he had to do this. He stopped at the door of Elizabeth's studio which was situated in one of the outhouses slightly to the left of the cottage. With his fingers, he felt above the door for the key, cursing when he caught a splinter in his finger. He took a deep breath before turning it in the lock. The door was stuck, swollen with damp and it took several shoves with his shoulder to gain entry. The momentum of the force meant that he ended up colliding with a half finished statue which stood in the middle of the room. He cursed loudly as he landed on the dusty floor cradling the shape of a half formed woman in clay. Dusting himself down, he stared silently at the room. He closed his eyes to see if he could feel her presence, but opened them again when he couldn't. The room was covered in a film of white dust. The window, which looked down towards the coast, was opaque with grime, and the tools she used were scattered where she had left them, the day she had taken to her bed. Against the back wall, shelves of sculptures sat ready for her next exhibition. Her bin of clay sat waiting for the scoop of a hand. Bunches of wicker, some of which had spilled across the floor, stood in military precision, waiting to be contorted and woven into fabulous garden sculptures. Everything was there except the expert hand from which the magic was produced. He walked back to the window and leaned heavily on the chair back. He picked up a cloth and wiped a perfect circle in the dirt. On the chair was Elizabeth's hat and scarf. Carefully he lifted the scarf to his face and drank in her perfume. So faint, but so powerful was the emotion which swept over him. Suddenly she was there, right by his side, infusing his senses with her essence. Her vibrancy, her lust, her love, her warmth wrapped around his body, and warmed the very core of his being. For a few perfect seconds Elizabeth had returned and Nathan wept with happiness.

"Oh, was this Elizabeth's studio?"

Carrie's voice pulled him through a vortex away from his utopia, leaving him confused and breathless. At first he couldn't recognise the figure standing in the brightness of the doorway, then with panic in his voice he said sharply, "Please, stay there, don't come in."

Carrie stepped back into the garden and watched as

Nathan closed the door on her. Stunned into silence, her lip trembled as she turned back towards the cottage.

18

Rain and high winds hampered the photo shoots at Tintagel. Dark racing clouds brought with it heavy downpours, drenching Faye through to the skin on more than one occasion. It was a shame to see the summer moving to a close as it had been hot and dry for most of August and September. An October shoot in Cornwall had been chosen simply because the vast amount of holiday makers would have gone home for the winter. Calvin was being insufferable, his temper was frequently frayed and his venom was constantly directed at Faye. He even blamed her for the bad weather!

On Friday morning, after watching the weekend weather forecast, Calvin called a halt to the shoot until Monday and everyone except Faye set off back to London. Come rain or shine, Cornwall was the only place she wanted to be. Watching the others load up the van from her hotel bedroom, Faye rang down and arranged a hire car. This was an ideal opportunity to get away for the weekend, maybe go home to Gweek, but first she needed to walk by the sea and she knew just where to go.

It had rained as predicted for the duration of her drive down to the Lizard. Her windscreen wipers were kept going constantly and only when she pulled into the gravel car park high above Kynance Cove did the clouds break and the sun peep through. Faye smiled to herself - she knew the Cornish weather could be like this. The whole of the county could be covered in cloud but occasionally the toe of England would catch a different weather band.

Donning her waterproof clothes, she began her descent towards the tiny café at the foot of an impressive granite rock. Seagulls screamed above her as they spiralled down to settle on 'Asparagus Island'. Kynance Cove considered one of the most beautiful beaches in the world, and Faye could not dispute that fact as she sat in the pale watery sunlight drinking a cup of coffee. It felt good to be free, albeit for a couple of days. To be wrapped up and hidden from the constant flash of a camera was all she longed for.

She picked up a 'Galleries in Cornwall' brochure from the café and flicked through the pages. Dark clouds had gathered again and Faye decided it would be a day to take in the local art. After exhausting the galleries in Falmouth, Faye moved on to Truro. After enjoying a light meal of pasta she took a stroll along Lemon Street.

Despite the inclement weather, the city was crammed with people moving from one public house to another. Dull yellow lights shone through restaurants, and cars and buses made their way slowly through the town centre to take shop workers home to their families. Outside Lemon Gallery, Faye noted a crowd gathered inside. She moved up and peeped through the corridor to see who was showing. The sign read:

Elizabeth Trent-Prior
A retrospective.
Celebrating the life and works of a renowned Artist and Sculptress.
With Nathaniel Prior

Faye could see it was a private view, but a crowd of people came up the steps behind her and she was ushered in along with them. The main reception Gallery was packed with art lovers and clients. The walls were hung with various paintings by both Elizabeth and Nathaniel, but it was the ones hung at the back of the gallery which took Faye's attention. There hung a collection of four works called 'Love Chronicles'. They were all oil paintings of Elizabeth by Nathaniel. Faye noted how beautiful she was and how dreadful it must have been for Nathaniel to have lost her. The first painting, 'Love Letter', showed her in a cream shift dress reading a letter. The accompanying note stated: On loan from a private collection. The second,

'Love Divine' was a painting of Elizabeth in a wedding dress, sat at her dressing table, adjusting her headdress in the reflection of the mirror. Note: From the artist's own collection. In the third, 'Infinite Love', Elizabeth was resting on a bed, on her side, one arm above her head the other cradling the baby growing inside her swollen stomach. Again the note said: From the artist's private collection. The fourth and final painting in the series was 'Mother's love'; Elizabeth was painted asleep on a bed with a child protected in the crook of her arm, also asleep. Each one of the paintings had a luminescence about them. Nathaniel knew about light and how to capture it. The room was a love story told in oils.

As she moved around she could see Nathaniel talking to a great crowd of people, so Faye took herself off to the lower gallery which housed a collection of Elizabeth's sculptures. She worked in all different mediums, from marble to steel, wicker to cast bronze. They were mainly figures and all very beautiful. It was such a shame that all that talent was now buried in the ground, but oh, what a wonderful body of work to be remembered by.

En route to the top gallery she stopped to pick up a glass of orange juice in the main reception, in the hope that Nathaniel would be free to have a quick word with her, but alas, he was still surrounded by crowds of people. She stood and watched him for a moment. His smile seemed strained at times and she noted a quiet sadness in his eyes. His eyes flickered towards her for a second, but again his attention was pulled away and Faye turned and made her way upstairs to view Nathaniel's work.

Again the room was full of people and Faye began to make her way around. Here hung a selection of Seascapes, all of places she loved to walk. There were dramatic cliffs and turquoise luminescent seas, which were either pounding the rocks or glistening under timeless skies. They were all wondrous, and then she saw it, the original oil painting of the photo she kept in her handbag. The painting was called 'View from Blue Bay Café'. Measuring at five foot by three foot the work was outstanding; you could almost walk into the painting and sit down. She studied it, but it was nowhere Faye could recognise and as far as she could recall she had never sat in a café with that view in front of her. She was intrigued. As she lifted her head and turned towards the far wall, she was stunned at the sight that greeted her.

She opened her mouth with an O of surprise. "Oh my goodness," she murmured, suddenly feeling very faint and lightheaded, as her eyes scanned the paintings of her own image, accurate in every way except that her hair was its natural colour of auburn. Very quickly the people who stood around her began to recognise her face from the paintings. In a panic she swiftly made her way toward the stairs, ran along the corridor and out into the wet street. She had no idea what had caused her to take flight. She was deeply flattered that Nathaniel Prior had painted her, though goodness knows where he had picked up her image from. The magazines and TV adverts depicted a false and untrue representation of her, but upstairs in that gallery, it was as though he had reached through and found the true Faye Larson. It frightened her, to think she was losing her real identity. Maybe the time was coming for her to shed this unnatural skin and find her way back to herself.

*

As the last of the champagne bottles were loaded into the boxes, Nathan shook hands with the last of the guests. There were several red dots on his paintings in the upper gallery and Nathan felt a little uncomfortable about selling at his beloved wife's retrospective. He was just about to pick up his coat and say his last farewells when a fellow artist congratulated him on the new body of work called, 'The Look'.

"I see she was here tonight!" he said jovially.

"Who was?"

"The girl you used for..." He stuck his hands in the air

and wagged each of his index fingers, "…'The Look' paintings."

"Was she?" he answered in astonishment.

"Yes. Do you think you can get her to sit for me? She really is something else! Though you know, I've seen her face before somewhere, but I'm damned if I can recall where."

"To tell you the truth, I don't know who she is. I just saw her across a room in the Chelsea Arts club, and like you I thought she looked familiar. She didn't sit for me or anything. I just painted her from memory."

He laughed lightly. "There speaks the words of a true artist. Well, she certainly woke your imagination up. You captured her image perfectly."

19

The first Christmas without Elizabeth was unimaginably hard to contemplate. Even with Carrie in the house, Nathan felt like an empty vessel. Carrie, to her credit, had cheered Gwithian Cottage up with festive holly, and a small tree stood in the front room adorned with garish tinsel, baubles and flashing lights, which Nathan switched off whenever he entered the room.

Christmas Eve was spent at the Tinners Arms with Carrie, who was excited at the prospect at making her first Christmas dinner, though Nathan didn't relish the idea of the celebratory meal.

The next morning he woke to the strange silence that only belongs to Christmas morning. Last year he and Elizabeth enjoyed a champagne breakfast in bed with scrambled eggs and smoked salmon. A church service preceded a drink in the Tinners Arms, then home for dinner and presents. Elizabeth loved Christmas. Today he could barely muster up the energy to get up. The day was grey and misty and unusually temperate for December. He could hear Carrie busy in the kitchen and wished with all his heart that she wasn't in the house today. All he wanted to do was curl up and let the day pass by. A soft knock on his bedroom door roused him from his misery.

"Nathan, may I come in? I've made you some breakfast."

"Of course," he said groaning inwardly.

As the tray was presented triumphantly, she wished him a happy Christmas. He looked at the glass of orange juice, a bowl of porridge and a mug of tea and smiled at her kindness. "Thank you Carrie, this is lovely."

A smile beamed across her face. "Christmas dinner will be at four, if that's okay?"

"That will be lovely, thank you." He smiled gratefully.

An hour later, he returned the breakfast tray to the

chaos of the kitchen. As he scanned the worktops to find somewhere to place the tray, he enquired if there was anything he could do.

"No, everything is under control," Carrie answered, wiping the perspiration from her face with her sleeve.

"Okay if you're sure, I'm going to visit Elizabeth's grave, then nipping over to Will Mather's place. We always pop in on Christmas morning for a hot toddy." Carrie nodded, but he could see she was deeply involved with wrapping rashers of bacon round a pile of fat sausages.

It had rained all night but the day was clearing now and ribbons of mist were lifting above the cliffs of Zennor Head. Nathan turned and made his way to Will's cottage which was situated to the south of the village. Hardly a day went by when Nathan didn't see Will and his dog Jasper on their travels. Elizabeth had a real soft spot for the brown and white pointer and always had a doggie treat in her pocket for him. Since her death, Nathan carried on this tradition. As he approached the cottage he could see an ambulance outside and quickened his pace in time to catch them carrying Will out of the door on a stretcher.

"Oh Nathan," Will gasped, clutching at his chest.

"Try not to speak Mr Mather," the paramedic urged.

"What's happened," Nathan said standing at the doors of the ambulance.

"Mr Mather has suffered a heart attack. He's concerned about his dog."

"May I speak to him? I'm a friend of his." The paramedic nodded and Nathan stepped up into the ambulance. He took Will's hand in his. "You'll be fine my friend, I'll take Jasper home with me, don't worry about a thing." He looked at the paramedic. "Is he going to be okay?"

"We need to get him to hospital as soon as possible."

Seeing the urgency in his face Nathan said, "I'll follow you then."

As the ambulance drove off at high speed, Nathan

entered the house, found Jasper's lead and fastened it to the dog. He collected his bed, bowls and a tin of dog food from the cupboard, and walked the confused and distressed dog back to Gwithian Cottage. Carrie was busy preparing the potatoes as Nathan rushed in.

"Carrie, you might have to put the dinner on hold for a while."

Visibly cross, she looked up at him then down at the dog. "Why and what is that dog doing in the kitchen?"

"Will's had a heart attack, so I'm going to the hospital with him. Poor old lad doesn't really have anybody else. I don't know how long I will be - I'll phone from the hospital. Just hold off with the dinner for a while will you, and be an angel, take Jasper out for a walk if he needs to go. Sorry, got to rush, see you later." He tied the dog to the table leg and left.

Carrie threw her hands in the air in exasperation. The dinner would be ruined. She looked down at the dog who was whining pitifully. "And you can shut up as well," she shouted, throwing the potato peeler into the sink.

*

Will Mather passed from this world to the next at four-fifteen that very day. Nathan sat with him to the end. It was only when he was driving into Zennor later that evening did he realise he had forgotten to inform Carrie that he was coming back home. The poor girl would have been waiting all day to cook the Christmas dinner.

As he opened the door, Jasper barked loudly and ran towards him, swiftly followed by a very frosty faced Carrie.

"Carrie, what can I say, I'm so sorry, Will died this afternoon and I clean forgot to phone you."

"That bloody dog has whined all day long," she snapped.

He scratched the dog's ears and smiled thinly. "Oh dear, he'll be missing his master I would think, won't you boy?"

"Do you want me to make the dinner now?" she asked

crisply.

He shook his head. "I don't think I could stomach a full dinner. If you cooked the turkey, a sandwich would suffice."

Without speaking, Carrie turned on her heel and marched into the kitchen. "We'll have your lovely dinner tomorrow," he called after her, but she did not answer. He looked down at the dog and pulled a face. "I think we're in trouble boy."

20

Faye replaced the receiver and walked miserably from the hotel foyer. It was the twenty-ninth of December and she had been on a photo shoot at Lake Bled in Yugoslavia for the past three days and felt thoroughly wretched.

Christmas had been an absolute washout for her, what with her preparing to fly out on Boxing Day and Liam cancelling his plans to spend Christmas Day with her at the last minute. Some problem with his father being ill, he had told her. His father! Faye had no idea that his parents were still alive, he had never spoken of them to her before. He was such an enigma. It puzzled her as to why he was so secretive with everything. Her friend Pippa was away skiing, so in the end she had rung home on Christmas Day and spoken to her mother. That had been a brief and strained affair, probably because her step-father was hovering in the background as she spoke.

Christmas at her parents' house was not something she really missed, due to her step-father's domineering ways. He certainly wasn't someone who knew how to have fun. Carl her step-father was the main reason she had not been back to Yorkshire these last four years. Faye's upbringing had been particularly strict after her own darling father had died in a car crash when she was four. Her mother had married Carl two years later and life at home became very difficult under his authoritarian ways. The only person who helped her through her difficult childhood was her older step-sister Gayle. She had always got on well with Gayle; she was a sunny happy girl who had grown into a sunny happy woman. She had settled down with a lovely man and produced two lovely children on whom they doted. It never ceased to amaze Faye that Gayle was Carl's real daughter, they were so different. Fortunately for Faye, Gayle, her husband Ryan and their two children had been there when she had rung, so she had chatted happily with them all for ten minutes. She finished her telephone conversation with her usual promise of a visit to Yorkshire, though both parties knew the event was quite unlikely.

Faye could get no coverage on her mobile phone in Yugoslavia and all attempts to contact Liam from the hotel phone had been unsuccessful. She decided a walk was what she needed. Outside, the driving rain of the previous night had left ribbons of grey mist intertwined through the trees. The damp air hung musty as she zipped up her waterproof and began to walk around the lake's edge. An hour later she found an old wooden seat almost hidden in the undergrowth and sat down, ignoring the soft rain which now fell. The lake of Bled, some fifty kilometres north of Ljubljana, was like something out of a fairytale, which was why it had been chosen as a location for the photo shoot.

She gazed at the lake with its castle perched on a cliff above the lake shore. Her eyes travelled towards the tiny island with a church built over a pagan shrine, and then to the towering Julian Alps which surrounded her. It would be hard to find a more romantic spot, but Faye had never felt so alone in her life. Her relationship with Liam had been strained for the last few months. The discovery of Jasmine's Filofax and its contents troubled her. Why had he denied knowledge of her that very first day she had spoken to Liam when he clearly knew her intimately? And how come he was in possession of the book when her family were so desperate for information about the night she had died?

The mist curled up from the lake and into the trees like smoke. Faye sat for a long time, a sad song playing in her mind - a melancholic tune that she used to sing so sweetly with 'Three Fold', the group she belonged to with Joe and Sid. Oh how she missed everybody. Chilled to the bone, she stood and shivered, rubbing the numbness from her hands, and stamping her feet to the hard ground to regain some feeling in them. Sighing miserably she began to collect her belongings to make her way back to her soulless empty room at her hotel.

Thunder rumbled in the distance and as Faye looked up, a small wooden boat covered with a colourful awning emerged through the vapours of mist. The oarsman dressed in oilskins appeared to be stood rowing with two oars. Slowly he made his way to the shore coming to a halt on the beach. Once his oars were secured he stepped ashore.

"Pozdravljeni," he said, pulling off his hat. Faye glanced about her, to see who he was addressing. He spoke again as he approached, "Hello?"

Realising he was speaking to her, she nodded. "Hello."

"Ah, you are English! You are here filming?"

"I am yes."

"I am Branek, I take visitors to the castle. I'll take you? I'll take you for free. I think you need to go to the tower to ring the 'wishing bell' to make a wish. Yes?"

Faye looked puzzled. "A wish, why?"

"Ah, you do not know the legend of a young widow Poliksena who once lived at the Bled Castle?"

Faye shook her head.

"Ah well, I'll tell you. It was she who had a bell cast for the chapel on the island in memory of her husband. During the transport of the bell, a terrible storm struck the boat and sank it together with the crew and the bell, which to this day is said to ring from the depths of the lake." He gestured his hand towards the lake. "After the widow died, the Pope consecrated a new bell and sent it to the Bled Island. It is said that whoever rings this bell and thereby gives honour to the Virgin Mary, gets their wish come true. I think you need to go and make a wish. I think you are not happy. Maybe you need to ask the 'wishing bell' for a change. Yes?" He watched as her face began to contort and she looked as though she was about to burst into tears. "Please, do not be distressed. You come with Branek." He gestured her to follow.

Without a moment's thought for her safety, her sadness and a want for a change in her life urged her to follow the stranger.

At the edge of the lake he took her hand and escorted her onto a flat bottomed boat. "This is my Pletna boat," he said proudly. "It has been in my family for many years." Faye moved towards the awning and sat near the pointed bow. Her teeth chattered with cold, and she blew furiously into her hands to warm them. "Here, wrap this around you. It will keep you warm." Branek handed her a wool blanket which she took appreciatively.

The thunder continued to rumble as Branek swiftly and skilfully rowed the boat across the emerald lake surrounded by Alpine peaks, and out towards the gothic church nestled on the centre of a tiny island. As they drew nearer, Faye could see the many steps which climbed towards the medieval castle, looming above from its rocky perch. It truly was a fairytale setting.

At the foot of the ninety-nine steps, Branek helped her ashore and walked with her to the bell tower. The view across the lake was magnificent, even on such a thunderous day. She turned to Branek. His face was old and leathery, but his eyes were kind. She smiled. "How do you know I need to change my life?"

"I see such sadness in your beautiful face, you have been here for a few days and I have not yet seen you smile."

"Have you been watching me?"

"But of course! A beautiful woman like you should be admired. But a beautiful woman without a smile is like a summer day without the sunshine. Go, ring the bell and you shall be filled with peace and new hope," he urged.

21

Faye had had enough! The New Year came and passed, again without the presence of Liam. His contact with her had been sparse and unapologetic when it came, but the growing feeling of discontent unsettled her and her sadness turned to anger, an emotion she was not familiar or comfortable with.

She had stumbled into this new and unfamiliar world quite unwittingly, and it bore no resemblance to her old life. She no longer knew who she really was.

The trip to Lake Bled had unsettled her. If she was visibly showing her unhappiness as Branek had said she was, then things had to change. She had rung the 'wishing bell' as Branek had told her to do; now she was going to make her wish come true one way or another. Of all the things she could have wished for, all she wanted, was to sit in the very spot where Nathaniel Prior had painted the picture 'View from Blue Bay Café'. There she would order a coffee and plan the rest of her life, which would not feature Lemmel.

She had four weeks leave before her next assignment, and when Liam rang her mobile, all he received was a message that said: 'Faye is away.'

Liam's face darkened with rage when the same message came up the eighth time he phoned her. How dare she do this to him? He had taken a week off to spend some quality time with Faye in bed, and this was all the thanks he got. He felt the anger rising in him. He searched out Calvin in the hope he knew her whereabouts.

"Gone missing has she?" A malicious gleam entered his dark eyes.

"No! The stupid woman has turned her phone off that's all."

Calvin bared his teeth in a stark grin. "Well, Leo said

she packed her bags yesterday and left without a by-your-leave. If she's turned her phone off, I'd say she doesn't want to talk to you," he jeered, enjoying Liam's humiliation.

"Go to Hell," Liam snapped as he left the studio.

"See you there," Calvin hissed after him.

*

The view from the holiday cottage at Kynance Cove was stunning as Faye stood in the front garden warming her hands on her mug of tea. A monstrous sea crashed and pummelled the cliffs of 'Asparagus Island' and she savoured with relish the glorious salty tang in the wind. It had been a stormy first night in the cottage. The rain and hail had battered incessantly at the windows and it filled Faye with an exhilarating feeling of being alive and free. She could hardly wait for the dawn to come, to step out into the wild invigorating elements. Here she was alone, but not lonely, as she watched the wind pushing heavy grey clouds across the darkening sky. Occasionally, strips of bright sunlight would wink periodically through the racing clouds, teasing her with a promise of sunshine. She closed her eyes, took a deep breath and smiled broadly. Though the weather was wild and unsettled, Faye felt a deep calmness within herself.

*

Pippa woke to the persistent ringing of her phone. Bleary eyed she lifted the receiver.

"Yep?" she said yawningly.

"I'm looking for Faye," Liam said evenly.

"Pardon?"

"Faye, I'm looking for her."

"Why the hell are you ringing me then?" She could hear him sigh angrily which brought her to full consciousness.

"She's not at home. She's not answering her phone, so I assumed she is with you."

Pippa smiled broadly as she answered, "Nope, I haven't seen her."

"Where the hell is she then?" he shouted.

Pippa loved this. At last Faye was seeing sense and playing him at his own game. "I have absolutely no idea where she is and if you don't mind I would very much like to get back to my lie-in. You have just ruined the only one I will get all week."

"I want to know where she is!"

"Sorry, can't help you. Goodbye Liam," Pippa said as she put the phone down on him. She sat up in bed and punched the air in celebration. Her dislike for Liam was intense for the way he treated Faye. Yes he had given her this fantastic opportunity, but he'd left her to flounder in a world which was completely alien to her. Why would he do that? There was definitely something dodgy about him and she didn't trust him as far as she could throw him.

*

Liam looked incredulously at his phone as it went dead and he threw it angrily across the room.

22

Faye turned on her mobile phone in readiness for the journey home to find she had twenty-four missed calls from Liam and one from Pippa. She immediately returned Pippa's call.

"Hi, it's me," she said cagily when Pippa answered.

Pippa sighed with relief at the sound of her voice. "Are you okay?"

"I'm better than I have been for a while I have to say."

"Where are you?"

"I'm on my way home to Gweek."

Pippa laughed. "Brilliant, I'll come round at lunchtime."

"No sorry Pippa, I can't stay long, I just wanted to know if Liam is in the boatyard?"

"Well, he was last week, albeit briefly. I don't think he believed me when he rang and I said I didn't know where you were."

"Oh, so he rang you then?"

"He did…he…. oh just a moment, someone's coming." The office door opened and Amos walked in. "Don't worry, it's okay, it's only Amos," she whispered.

"Was Liam angry?"

Pippa's voice stayed low, "I'll say. He was absolutely fuming! He still was, when he came down last weekend. "

Faye fell silent.

"So, what's going on? Do you need to talk?"

"Not at the moment Pippa, if you don't mind. I just need to find my way again, but I do need you to be there for me."

"Always, you know that."

"Look Pippa, I'll have to go, I need to go home to collect some warm clothes for the next assignment."

Pippa detected the tedium in her voice. "Where're you going to this time?"

"Switzerland," she answered nonchalantly.

"Go and enjoy Switzerland Faye. Do your job, but enjoy the surroundings if you can. Take your paints with you. Things will turn out okay, I'm sure they will. I'm here when you need me."

"Thanks Pippa," she said, her voice wavering. "I'll pop in the office before I leave. See you soon."

Pippa put the phone down and sighed heavily. Amos moved towards the counter and said, "Has she found out?"

Pippa frowned. "Has she found out what?"

Amos held her gaze for a moment then turned to leave. "Nothing, it doesn't matter," he said as he stepped out of the office.

*

She had been back in her London flat only two hours before Liam arrived. Obviously the spies had been at work.

Thin grey drizzle smeared the windows. It was strange how rain looked in different locations. She had seen her fair share of rainy days in Cornwall during the last three weeks. There had been watery sunshine too on several days, but it didn't matter. She spent every single day walking the coast in her waterproof clothes trying, but failing, to find the elusive 'Blue Bay Café. She had had a glorious time.

She didn't relish this meeting with Liam and the adrenalin began to pump furiously through her veins as he walked into her flat and stood before her. He was visibly angry but very calm.

"So, you decided to come back then did you? Have you any idea how worried I've been? Have you?" His face was pinched and his mouth set hard.

Faye looked at him with dumb insolence.

"Where the hell have you been?"

Refusing to be perturbed, she answered calmly, "On holiday."

He looked aghast. "On holiday! Is that the only explanation I am going to get? Why did you do it so

142

secretly? Who have you been with? You had better not have been with anyone."

"Don't you dare accuse me of that!" she spat the words venomously.

"Well tell me woman, where the hell have you been and why did you switch your bloody phone off, you know I need to be able to contact you. I am your agent after all."

Faye tipped her head to one side. "Oh I thought you were my lover, silly me."

"Don't be a bloody fool," he said exasperated. "Of course I'm your lover, first and foremost, but I need to be able to contact you."

Faye laughed ironically. "Just as I need to contact you, but you are never there when I need you, are you?" She looked at him questionably. "Have you any idea how lonely it is here alone in London? Well, I'm sick to the back teeth of spending lonely hours in this soulless place, in fact I'm sick to the back teeth of it all."

"I see," he breathed, glancing at her suitcase, which was almost packed. "You seem to forget, if it hadn't been for me you would still be working in a dead end job in that boatyard with the other no hopers, but now you have the world at your feet. You'll have wealth beyond belief coming your way, you should be thanking me not moaning at me," he scolded. "But no, it's not enough is it?"

"No," she yelled. "It's not enough. I fell in love with you, not this faux lifestyle you have projected me into. I hate it I tell you, and I hate being with this lot, they're not my sort of people." Her face began to contort and she looked as though she was about to burst into tears, but her resolve held them back and she continued, "And stop being so derogatory about my friends. They are the most honest, hardworking, reliable people you could ever meet and I'd go back there tomorrow if I could." Her face was flushed with emotion.

It crossed his mind that she was about to walk out on him, so he softened his demeanour and folded his arms about her. "Faye, this is such a marvellous opportunity for you. Enjoy it, live the life. I know I've been preoccupied of late, but I'm constantly working and promoting you. In April you'll be given four months leave. I've got some time off too, so, we can spend the first week or so together, just you and me on the yacht, and everything will be back to normal."

Faye pulled away and didn't speak, she just stared at him.

He lifted her hand to his lips and kissed it tenderly. "So, off you go to Switzerland. Have a drink with the crew, join in with the parties, they're a good bunch of people when you get to know them." He cocked his head and smiled. "Okay?"

She looked back with empty eyes but did not reciprocate the smile.

He gave a short derisive laugh. "Look, I'll have to go. I'll call you later, okay, and don't turn your phone off this time."

"Just a moment Liam, how is your father?"

"My father?" He looked puzzled.

She smiled knowingly. "You remember; he was the reason why you cancelled Christmas with me?"

He coloured slightly. "Oh yes, he's fine thanks, on the mend as they say." A moment later he was gone and Faye felt as though the life had been drained from her.

*

Liam called into the studio as Calvin was packing the last of the photographic equipment into the metal containers.

"Found her then?" Calvin asked.

Liam threw him a look of contempt. "Where's Leo?"

"He's in the back." He smirked.

Liam walked into the gloomy room which smelt of sweat and stale tobacco. He called out his name. There was a scuffle and Leo emerged from behind a curtain, quickly rolling his sleeve down. "Oh, it's you! Been to see her then?"

Liam nodded and handed him a roll of banknotes. "I want to know who she sees, and everything she does, have you got that?"

Leo sniffed, nodded and snatched the money from his hand, stuffing it quickly into his back pocket as Liam turned to leave. He turned and pulled the curtain to one side, he had no intention of spying on Faye.

23

Cold air flowed through the open window as dawn reluctantly arrived. Nathan had lain awake all night but his sleepless night had not left him fatigued, he felt renewed by spending the night reliving the memories of past and happier days. He put his arm behind his head and sighed as he stared at the ceiling. Twelve months had passed since his lovely Elizabeth had died in his arms in this very bed, twelve lonely empty months. He could feel the sadness sweep over him now, replacing the happy memories with painful ones. The anguish of those last few hours of Elizabeth's life coming now to the foreground. A lone bird began to sing to break the dawn, its sweet voice filtering through the room. For a moment, Nathan left all memories behind to listen to its song. Elizabeth loved to hear the dawn chorus; she said it made her feel good to be alive. Nathan smiled to himself, pushed the bedcovers from his body, and made for the shower.

It was an unusually bitterly cold day for March in Cornwall, the frost clung sharp and crisp to ground and tree alike. The sun shone long and low without warmth from the pale cloudless sky. Nathan walked briskly up from the beach, swiftly followed by his dog Jasper, noisily snuffling at the stick his master carried, urging him into a last throw and chase game, but Nathan had somewhere to go that day; he had something very special to do and was keen to get home.

He breakfasted swiftly and then packed his rucksack with his special cargo. Jasper jumped from his basket as Nathan turned the latch on the front door, but was sent back with a firm, "No, back to your bed," which the dog obediently did.

Once outside, Nathan climbed the steep coast path high above Zennor. He stopped at the top of the hill to catch his breath, and leant heavily against a stile scarred yellow with lichen to look down the path he had just ascended. The sea was calm, and the sunlight, a little warmer now as the day progressed, winked periodically through misty clouds. Seagulls drifted and cried gently on the breeze high above him. He smiled and closed his eyes, breathing in the cool salty air as though it were a life-giving elixir. Summer would not be far away; it always came early in Cornwall. He walked for about an hour, not aimlessly, but with direction, until finally he came to the place. It had been Elizabeth's wish to have a headstone in Zennor Graveyard, but her ashes were to be scattered on the coast path overlooking the sea. She hadn't specified exactly where this place should be, but had been so confident that Nathan would find somewhere beautiful for her, she had left the final decision to him. So after many walks and much heart searching, he finally found the perfect place. Nestled away from the mighty sea and gusty winds, slightly off the beaten coast path, amongst the bright yellow gauze and freshly budding pink thrift, he had found a clearing in the undergrowth. He sat quite still for a moment and looked out towards Pendeen Watch in the far distance. Below him, an empty rocky shingle cove embraced the gently lapping waves as they rose and fell against it. The sun glinted now on the vast turquoise sea, gulls screamed high up in the blue sky, and there was a strong salty tang in the breeze which blew like a whisper on his face. It was indeed a truly beautiful place for a truly wonderful person.

Slowly he undid the lid on the crimson container, which bizarrely resembled a sweet shop jar, and he stared at the soft ash remains inside. Very carefully he shook the contents out into the clearing and thankfully they remained where they lay, the deed was done, she was free forever.

He closed his eyes and remembered kissing her beautiful lips, burying his face into her soft fragrant hair, feeling his arms around her tiny waist. He could hear her laughter and see her smile. The image was powerful even now, twelve months since she had died. "Oh Beth, my darling Beth, I miss you so much, the loneliness is unbearable," he spoke the words into the breeze.

He recalled the week after Elizabeth had died, everyone had been so kind. He was so busy, with so many things to arrange, so many procedures to follow, so many people to inform, that his grief had been almost on hold. He'd received cards and letters from people he didn't even know. He smiled to himself; one especially had struck a chord in his heart. In it was written: 'Darkness will have descended on your life, but there will be light one day. A necessary thought to hold onto when one is left to live alone when love has died suddenly. Hold on to your memories, they alone will help you through'. It was signed 'Faye Larson'. He still had the card, and looked at it often, but oh, when would the light come? When would this darkness lift?

Nathan looked down at his wife's ashes. "Oh Beth, what shall I do about Greg?" He looked to the sky and hoped for an answer, but his wife's voice did not come into his head. He recalled that awful last conversation they'd had, the memory of that day, reverberating in his head. When his letter to Greg had gone unanswered, he drove to Falmouth to try and find him, only to be told he had moved away and no one had a forwarding address. It seemed he was lost to him forever. Hot tears began to fall upon the ashes he had just scattered, disappearing on impact as though Elizabeth was absorbing them. He shook his head, the loss of his beautiful wife and his only child was too much for one man to bear, and it seemed he could do nothing about either. He wished with all his heart that something could take this loneliness away.

*

Carrie was preparing the dinner when Nathan finally arrived home. Carrie had been working for Nathan for almost a year now and they had become good friends. She lived in, which in itself had caused a stir in the village, but the rumours were unfounded and Nathan kept their working relationship friendly, but professional. It didn't stop the gossips of course, but then nothing ever could. One particular woman in the local pub had broached the subject one day while Nathan drank his pint of beer.

"How's Carrie?" she had asked, raising her eyebrows to her friend next to her.

Nathan observed her with mild curiosity. "Fine," he replied.

"She must be a great comfort to you, since, well you know," she said crinkling her nose.

Nathan rolled his eyes and turned away from her.

The woman moistened her lips before proceeding, "There are rumours you know, you might be thinking of marrying again." She paused hopefully. Duggie, the landlord, shot her a steely look. "What are you looking at me like that for Duggie Martin? I know you've heard the rumours as well. There's no smoke without fire," she said with a nod of the head.

"And there's no bloody gossip without malice," Nathan shouted at her, angrily slamming his unfinished pint on the bar before walking out.

The gossipers kept their thoughts to themselves after that and as far as Nathan knew, he had put a stop to it.

Carrie remembered he'd been visibly shaken by the incident in the pub and he had even boycotted the pub for a month in protest. Carrie knew he had not been ready for a new relationship then, it had been too soon after the death of his wife, but today, she thought to herself as she prepared a dinner of lemon chicken with roast vegetables, today was a milestone. She knew, without him telling her, where he had been today. She had noticed, when changing the sheets on Nathan's bed, that the crimson casket, which had sat next to his bed for the last year, had gone. She hoped this would be a turning point in his life. She hoped that he would now begin to live again. She sighed. Whatever happened now, she would be here for him.

At dinner that night he was quiet while he ate, distant in his thoughts. From time to time he looked at Carrie and smiled. "Nice meal," he said for the third time. As she cleared the dishes, he pushed the chair back and stretched. "I'm going to the studio for a while, don't wait up."

Later, when he opened his bedroom door just after midnight, Carrie was in his room, naked and waiting.

24

London wore its usual steely grey coat in the rain, as Faye stepped out of her flat. Throwing everything she would need for the summer into her old and trusty Sierra, she set off with great joy down the motorway. The journey to Cornwall, her spiritual home, was tiring and hazardous. Spray pelted her windscreen as driving rain had laid pools like liquid silver on the busy carriageways. As she neared the end of her long journey, the rain ceased and the western sky was drenched in a blazing sunset. Cornwall seemed to beckon her like an old friend, lifting the heavy burden of the last seven months from her shoulders.

The night was drawing in as she pulled up outside her cottage. Inside, the familiarity of the cosy front room embraced her. 'Home for the summer' she murmured, as her eyes filled with emotion.

Liam had arranged for her to meet him in the boatyard in the morning, but tonight, she had a much needed get-together arranged with Pippa and the boys, where no doubt copious glasses of white wine would be consumed. She turned her phone off just in case Liam decided to spoil her plans.

As morning dawned, Faye cautiously walked her hangover from Pippa's house to her own. The previous evening had been a joyous affair. Sid and Joe had joined them for dinner and the evening had been full of laughter and singing, until all of them had crashed out in a happy state of slumber on the sofas.

Gweek, as always, looked green and peaceful as she stood on the rise of the bridge. The tide was out, exposing the vast mudflats, but the stream, swollen from the recent rains, rushed out from under the bridge, cutting a gash in the slimy mud as it made its way down the two sides of the central bank of the river. A white egret waded long-legged in the stream, picking and dabbing at his aquatic meal. The boatyard looked busy as yachts were being washed and prepped in readiness for the high tide at two thirty. It was a full moon tonight, so those of a certain draft had to go down river on this tide, otherwise the depth of water rendered it impossible to negotiate the narrow channel down to the Helford. Liam's yacht 'Ina' would be on that tide. She could see him onboard it now from where she stood, as it sat on its bilge keels alongside the river bank. He was busy checking the sheets and cleats on deck; the sail will have been raised and lowered again and was now tied securely to the boom. She really was a magnificent vessel, even though it was not her preferred mode of transport. Thankfully he was too busy to notice her watching him, so she stretched the stiffness out of her back and with a couple more hours to herself she made her way home to soak in a hot bath.

Just after lunch Faye popped her head round the office door to say her hellos. She grinned at Pippa who too was nursing a monumental headache.

Faye grinned broadly. "Oh dear, are you still suffering?"

Pippa looked up and moaned, "How come you still look so flipping perfect? You and I drank the same last night. I feel like death warmed up."

"I rather think a large black coffee and a long soak helped to tell you the truth. But I'm not looking forward to the voyage I can tell you that. But don't tell Liam that. He's already cross that I turned my phone off last night and he couldn't find me at home." A wry smile flickered across Faye's face as she spoke.

"Well, you're only going down to the mouth of the Helford aren't you?"

"I should think so. I bloody hope so anyway," she said biting the inside of her cheek nervously.

Pippa looked at her pensively. "Does he ever put the sails up and take it for a spin?"

"No, thank God. I don't want him to either. I'm not like you Pippa; I have no desire to sail on the high seas."

Pippa laughed heartily. "You don't know what you are missing."

"I think I do."

"So, you just sit on a mooring in the Helford?"

"Yep, if you ask me I don't think he knows how to sail the thing. I'm absolutely sure that if it didn't have a motor, he wouldn't take it anywhere." She grinned.

Suddenly an overwhelming smell of sweat and engine oil preceded the appearance of Amos at the door.

"Hello Faye," he said eagerly, moving into her personal space.

Faye moved back a step for comfort and acknowledged him with a smile.

"It's nice to see you back, isn't it Pippa?" he said excitedly.

Pippa raised her eyebrows. "Yes it is."

"How long are you staying?" He looked at her hopefully.

Faye moved further away from him. "For the whole summer," she answered with relish.

"And are you all right?" He looked at her intently and she looked back and smiled.

"I'm fine Amos, thanks for asking, and you, are you okay?" she added.

Amos nodded and fidgeted for a moment, took a deep breath and said, "Faye, if you need anything, I'm your man." He looked at her in earnest.

Faye glanced at Pippa who shrugged her shoulders. "Thank you Amos, I'll bear that in mind."

"Good," he replied smiling brilliantly. "Good." He turned swiftly as Owen Barnes walked into the office.

"Amos, you're needed out there. Come on move it. The tide's at its fullest now."

He cast an unhurried look at Faye. "Liam Knight is looking for you."

Faye sighed and nodded. "Okay." She quickly hugged Pippa. "I'll be back in a week, and then hopefully we will have the whole summer together."

"At least the weather is good for you," Pippa said, not wanting to let her go.

As she stepped on board the 'Ina' she noted Liam was noticeably irritated with her.

"Now what's wrong?" Faye asked crossly.

"Where have you been? We nearly missed the tide," he snapped.

"With Pippa," she retorted.

"I would have thought you'd had enough of each other last night!" he said sarcastically.

Owen and Amos exchanged glances at the altercation as they untied the yacht from the bank.

Faye moved out of his way and down into the cabin to empty the food into the ice box, as Liam cast off and the vessel began to move slowly down into the channel.

Amos watched as the yacht disappeared, and with nothing else to do, he stood aimlessly kicking at the gravel underfoot until the tide ebbed away.

There wasn't a lot of conversation between Faye and Liam as they made their way down the Helford. But once moored, and all was secured, Liam's mood changed. His face softened and the look in his eyes was one of animal desire. The next two hours were spent in the cabin.

As Liam snored gently beside Faye, she contemplated the last few months, and in truth, dreaded the next few. Lemmel was re-launching 'Infinity' at the end of the year and Faye was to head the campaign. The Switzerland shoot had been for the Christmas advertisements and she had studio shoots and TV appearances lined up in the autumn. A trip to Lake Garda was on the cards in January to shoot the advertisement for the Easter editions of the glossies- it was all go. She sighed heavily and tried to push the negative thoughts to the back of her mind. She cast a sidelong glance at Liam. She knew in her heart she didn't love him, in fact she didn't really like him anymore. At first Liam had made life so exciting, she had fallen head over heels in love with him, but, as the months had gone by, it was obvious to Faye, this relationship was very one-sided and going nowhere.

After dinner at the 'Ferry Boat', they made their way back to the yacht in the dinghy and turned in at ten-thirty. It was always strange, the first night spent on the yacht. The constant movement always unsettled her balance, causing her head to swim slightly. She would have longed to stay in the house at Mawnan Smith again, but there was always some building work going on there, so Liam told her. Faye had listened to the lick and slap of the water on the hull, until finally sleep came.

Unexpectedly a voice woke her. She glanced at her watch it was twelve-thirty. The voice called out again, "Liam Knight, are you out there?"

Faye nudged Liam gently.

"What is it?" he said gruffly.

"I don't know, listen, I think someone's calling you."

"Mr Knight. Are you there?" The voice punctured through the night.

Liam's eyes flashed wide open and he jumped out of the bed. "Stay there." It was an order rather than a request.

Faye was a little taken aback by his manner but stayed put while Liam swiftly pulled his trousers on and ran up the galley steps. As soon as he was out of sight she scrambled out of bed, pulled the sheets around her nakedness and stood silently at the bottom of the steps.

Once on deck, Liam shouted into the darkness. "Who's there? Who's shouting?"

"Mr Knight is that you?"

"Yes, yes, who are you and what the hell do you want?" he said crossly.

"It's Owen, Owen Barnes from the boatyard. I've had your wife on the phone. She's been trying to get in touch with you. Your son's been injured in an accident; he's been taken to Richmond General. Your wife said she's been trying to get hold of you all evening."

Liam quickly kicked the galley doors shut with his foot, rendering any further conversation inaudible, but Faye had heard enough to make her feel suddenly very ill.

A sudden movement on deck caused Faye to jump, the galley doors were yanked open again, and Faye scurried quickly back to the bed. She watched in despair as Liam grabbed the rest of his clothes and dressed hastily.

"Where are you going? What's happened?" Faye said, her voice wavering slightly.

"It's nothing, go back to sleep, just a little trouble at work. I need to make some phone calls. I'll be back as quick as I can." And then he was gone.

She waited a few moments then slowly crept up the galley steps onto the deck. The night was still, and a lamp from the river bank lit the way for Liam as he negotiated the dinghy between the other moored yachts.

"Hurry, I'll drive you back to Gweek. Your wife Ina is going frantic," Owen said, as Liam approached the bank.

"Be quiet man, do you want to wake the whole river?" Faye heard him say irritably.

Under the cover of darkness, Owen smiled to himself. The only person he wanted to hear him was Faye. It was about time she knew the truth about Liam Knight.

Faye gasped, had she heard correctly, did Owen call Liam's wife Ina? She cast her eyes around the yacht she was standing on. Oh my God this yacht was named after her. "You bloody fool Faye, you should have realised", she cursed herself as tears of humiliation streamed down her face. Faye felt sick to the pit of her stomach. She had become quite unintentionally the one thing she abhorred, the 'other woman'.

She stumbled clumsily down the galley steps. She glanced painfully at the bed she had shared with Liam occasionally over the last year; why hadn't she realised he was married? All those excuses for not seeing her, only spending every other weekend with her, and Christmas, of course, it all made sense now, she should have known! "You fool, you bloody fool," she cried bitterly. She collapsed on the bed as feelings of worthlessness washed over her.

She sat for a very long time in dazed silence, forcing herself to re-assess her life. How dare he deceive her for all these months? She began to collect her belongings, cramming them into her holdall. She knew Liam had taken the dinghy, but even if she had to swim to the shore, she was determined not to be here when he returned. She scooped her toiletries into a bag and checked the shelves for her books. She would leave nothing behind, because she would never return, and if she ever saw Liam Knight again, it would be too soon. As she moved swiftly about the cabin, she noticed that Liam had left his overnight bag. In the front pocket, a mobile phone was clearly visible. This panicked her, if he had left his mobile, he would be back sooner rather than later. She picked up the phone and studied it. It was similar to her phone, but different to the one Liam normally used. She quickly turned it on and to her horror a list of text messages, all from women and all quite intimate rolled down before her eyes. She moved to the contact list only to find it was full of women's names. Allett being the first entry, hers being further down the list. It was no wonder she could never get him on the phone, he obviously had a separate phone for business and pleasure. Faye was sickened to the very core of her being. She threw the phone back into the bag as though it burnt her fingers. As she pulled her novels from the bookshelf, her hand settled on the black filofax. She pulled it from its slot and made the decision that this belonged to Jasmine Quintana's family.

A large rapping sound on the hull stopped Faye in her tracks and made every nerve in her body stand on end.

"Faye, are you in there?"

Faye held her breath and listened intently.

"Faye, it's me, Amos."

She scrambled up on deck. Amos was tying up alongside in the boatyard rib. "Amos? What the devil are you doing here?"

"I thought you might need a lift to Gweek," he whispered. "I saw Owen after he had taken the phone call from Liam's wife. I thought you might need some help."

"Give me a moment." Sharp hot tears pricked at Faye's eyes as she slammed the galley doors shut. "Oh Amos, I can't thank you enough," she said swinging her bag over the side and lowering it down to him.

"Don't even think about it, now put your coat on, it's going to be a chilly ride up to Gweek."

*

It was Sunday evening when Liam returned to the yacht. Even though it was four days since he had left, he was slightly irritated that she wasn't still there waiting for him. He supposed she must have taken a water taxi back to shore the morning after he left. There was no note, which was reassuring in a way. He had wondered if she heard that fool Barnes mouthing off about his wife. But if she'd have heard, he suspected she would have let him know by now. He must be more careful in the future. He sat down heavily in the cabin, exhausted from the drive. The last few days had been taxing to say the least. Otis his son had stupidly fallen off his skateboard, no doubt doing some ridiculous manoeuvre down some steps. The idiot had broken his collar bone, given himself mild concussion and twisted both his ankles. Ina had insisted that he stayed up in Richmond until the boy was discharged from hospital. She'd been furious with him for not being contactable, but it wasn't his fault that the mobile phone coverage was rubbish on the Helford. Once the boy was home, he could take no more of her griping. He packed his bags on the pretence of an important meeting in New York and drove himself back down the motorway to the peace and quiet of his yacht.

He unscrewed the top of a whisky bottle and poured a

generous measure. He couldn't be bothered to drive all the way back to Gweek tonight; he'd go and fetch Faye back in the morning. As he flicked through the Subaru brochure he had collected from the Subaru dealer that morning, he smiled self-satisfied, and looked forward to the day he would take delivery of his brand new company car.

25

It was Monday afternoon. Angus was dozing at his desk after his substantial lunch, when suddenly David Quintana burst into his office, brushing aside his personal assistant as she tried to stop him. He slammed the black filofax down onto Angus's desk.

"Where is Liam Knight? I want to see him, right now," he demanded.

Angus pushed his executive chair back slightly, but kept his cool. "He's not here. Why, what do you want him for, Mr err?"

His face was flushed and there was a cold anger in his eyes. "You don't even know me do you? I'm Jasmine's father." He raised his eyebrows. "You know, the woman your company killed last year." David pushed the filofax towards him. "It's all in there, read it, I hope it sickens you, like it sickened me. What sort of place are you running here? You employ that bastard Liam Knight and he is the reason my beautiful daughter of nineteen years is buried in the cold earth."

A look of puzzlement crossed Angus's face.

"He lured her to that hotel, and I want to know why!" He thumped the table violently.

Angus moistened his lips. "Mr Quintana, please take a seat, I'll get Sue to make us some tea, I'm sure this is all a misunderstanding." Angus pressed the intercom, but David reached forward and swiped Angus's hand from the phone.

"To hell with your bloody tea, this is no misunderstanding. Now, where is he?"

"He's not here. He's on holiday with his family I believe."

David straightened his back. "Is he now?" His lip curled as he dropped his voice to a low hiss.

Unable to control his aggressor, Angus felt his own anger rising. When he got hold of Liam, he'd personally kill him himself. He took a deep breath as he tried to control his emotions. "If you would like to leave this with me," he said calmly placing his hand on the Filofax. "You will appreciate that I need to read its contents."

"Yes, you do that. You read and digest it and you'll see he was the cause of my daughter's death. If he hadn't lured her to that bloody hotel, her car would never have been in that car park." His voice broke as he choked on the words. He paused to recover, but his face turned from scarlet to purple. He winced slightly as a sharp pain shot down his left arm. He felt his chest tighten with anger as he lent forward towards Angus. "Then you tell him, you tell that bastard, that I'll have him for this."

As David turned and wrenched the office door open, he stopped dead in his tracks and clutched his arms to his chest, a moment later he was down on his knees.

After the paramedics had taken David Quintana away in an ambulance, Angus pressed the intercom. "Sue, get me Knight on the phone, now!"

*

As Liam drove towards Gweek on Monday afternoon his mobile phone began to bleep incessantly at him. He pulled over onto the grass verge and noted the twenty four missed calls from work.

Five minutes later Liam hung up the call and sat in stunned silence on the quiet country lane. His ears were ringing from the wrath of Angus, whose anger knew no bounds and his retribution was sharp and severe to say the least. Blaming Liam for the financial loss Lemmel suffered at the cancellation of Jasmine's 'Infinity' launch, Angus promptly cancelled Liam's new company car and his end of financial year bonus. He was immediately stripped of his executive position and relegated to general manager of advertising. In short he was lucky to still have a job.

*

It was quiet in the office, as it always was between eleven and midday. Most of the yard workers had returned to work after their morning break and this short break in the morning meant that Pippa could catch up on all her paperwork.

Pippa sighed at the loss of her friend. She had known how unhappy Faye's life had become, and it seemed her suspicions of Liam's character had been justified. The first she knew of her disappearance was when Amos gave her a note from Faye. It was a quickly scrawled message of few words:

Liam's married, I need to leave Gweek for a while. I will call you at eleven-thirty on Monday to explain. Love Faye xx.

How the hell Amos had got hold of the letter she had no idea, and he was keeping very tight lipped about it.

The boatyard crane rumbled slowly past the office with a twenty-two foot yacht cradled in its straps bound for its launch into the river. Pippa glanced at the clock; it was eleven-twenty-eight. Her eyes turned to the telephone and waited for Faye to phone.

The office door was pushed open with such violence Pippa's first thought was that the crane had crashed the yacht into the office door. A moment later Pippa registered Liam as he thrust his whole weight towards her. His face was purple with fury.

"Where the hell is she?" he demanded, slamming his hands on the counter.

Pippa recoiled in fright as her whole body began to tremble.

He locked eyes with her. "You will tell me where that bitch is, because I know you know. Now tell me, where is she?"

Pippa's face paled, chilled by the intensity of his anger, her heart was thumping. "I don't know where she is," she stammered, unconsciously glancing at the clock.

"Liar," he yelled.

The phone began to ring; Pippa glanced at the phone

and again at the clock. Pippa felt sick to the stomach and her face turned puce with guilt. Oh God, stop ringing, oh please stop ringing she prayed. The phone stopped, and the answer machine clicked in. Pippa closed her eyes willing Faye not to speak. "Hi Pippa, it's me! You're obviously busy I'll….." On hearing Faye's voice, Liam vaulted the counter and wrenched the phone off the hook while she was mid sentence.

"Where the hell are you?" he yelled at her. "Don't think I won't find you, because I will. You can't hide forever. My God I'll make you pay for what you have done. Do you hear me? Don't think you can just walk away from this because you can't. You sly bitch, I know what you did with that Filofax. Have you any idea the trouble you have caused?" He laughed ironically. "Of course you bloody well know what you've done. Nobody crosses me, do you hear me? You can't stay away forever, you have a contract to fulfil and when I get my hands on you, I shall not be responsible for my actions. You have made an enemy of me today young lady."

Faye ended the call abruptly and Liam slammed the phone down with such ferocity it smashed into smithereens. He grabbed Pippa by the sleeve of her jacket and yanked her towards him, baring his strong white teeth at her. "Where has she gone?"

"I honestly don't know," she said swallowing the tears which immediately bubbled up. "All she left me was a note to say she would phone me today. I've no idea where she is, I promise." She began to shake with fear as Liam's grip on her jacket tightened.

"Hey, what the hell is going on in here?" Owen Barnes stepped into the office swiftly followed by a very anxious looking Amos.

Liam released his grip on Pippa and as he made to leave the office he put his hand on Owen Barnes face and pushed him so violently he fell backwards onto Amos, who in turn crashed into a pyramid of paint tins.

*

In Burndale, North Yorkshire, Faye stood with her back to the telephone box door, her trembling hand clamped to her mouth as she digested Liam's venomous words. His onslaught had shocked her to the core. The hatred in his voice had been appalling. Yes, she had sent the Filofax to the Quintanas, and yes she knew it would implicate him on the night she died. But what was he worried about? He didn't kill her; he was just the one she was meeting. Faye fully believed that it would give the poor girl's family some closure as to why she was at the hotel that night. As far as she was concerned she had done nothing wrong in sending the Filofax to them.

She swallowed hard and screwed her eyes tight shut. Oh Pippa, why did you tell Liam I was going to phone you? The words screamed silently in her head. Or was it Amos who had betrayed her? She shook her head. No, why would he do that, he had been the one who came out to the yacht that night to rescue her. He had been so sweet to her and she was so grateful to him. It gave her a head start to get away before Liam returned.

She began to walk away from the phone box and made her way down to the River Wharfe. She sat quietly on a bench as the tranquil view calmed her frazzled nerves. He would never find her; she'd make sure of that. In all the months she had known him, he had never once asked her about her family or where she had come from. It had always been about him, what he had done, who he had met. He was such a self-centred individual. She laughed ironically. It was funny how he failed to tell me about his wife and family. She cursed herself for being so gullible, to be so taken in by his charm. What a fool to think of all those days she had waited for him to phone, and all those times she had tried to phone him and only got his answer phone. And only ever seeing him every other weekend! She should have known there was someone else somewhere baying for his attention. To think she had bemoaned the fact that he never seemed interested in who she had been, it was all about whom she had become. She was his prodigy, just like Jasmine Quintana had been. She shivered at the thought of what had happened to her! Well, Cordelia Hart had gone forever.

After Amos had dropped her off at Gweek, she had kissed him lightly on the cheek for his help and kindness. It turned out that Amos had found out some time ago that Liam was married, but hadn't the heart or the nerve to expose him. He confessed to seeing Liam wearing a wedding ring on the day he came looking for Faye in the boatyard back in January, and his suspicions were roused from then on.

Amos had waited while she scribbled a quick note for Pippa, then she had packed all her belongings and set off, albeit reluctantly, back to her parents' house in Yorkshire. The only stop she made on the four hundred mile journey was in Bristol, and that was to find a hair salon to restore her hair to its normal auburn colour. From there she posted the Filofax to the Quintana's home in St Ives. The other parcel she sent to her flat in London marked 'For the attention of Liam'. In it, she put her mobile phone, and my, was she glad to see the back of it. On the latter part of her journey, she had felt like a butterfly emerging from its chrysalis, as her worries lifted. The future she had planned with Liam had gone forever and it would take quite a while for her humiliation to subside. But time, she knew, was a great healer.

26

It had been eighteen months since his beloved Elizabeth died. Nathan's work had ground to a halt again, after the fleeting surge of inspiration Faye had given him. He pondered a moment as he remembered seeing her face through the crowd at the Chelsea Arts Club. She had something he had never seen in a woman before. A transient, almost transparent look, as though she didn't belong on this earth. He knew now who she was, after seeing her image in Vogue. He had made several enquiries to her agent, a rather abrupt and unpleasant character called Knight, as to whether she could work as a private model for him, but it seemed Cordelia Hart was exclusive to Lemmel, which was a great shame. His cliff top studio was locked up, and he seemed now to spend his days walking Jasper, the dog he had inherited on Christmas day when old Will Mather had passed away. He laughed to himself - he never really wanted a dog, but now he wouldn't be parted from it. Jasper gave him something to get up for in the morning. He wasn't a young dog, but over the past months he had retrained Jasper to walk to heel without need of a lead, and would sit for hours by his side, occasionally lifting one eager eye in anticipation of a walk, should Nathan move just a fraction. Yes he was a good companion, just like Carrie wanted to be.

Carrie, oh Carrie, she was a problem to him. He recalled the day he had found her in his bed. He was shocked, and the image of someone on Elizabeth's side of the bed repulsed him momentarily, it had been the first anniversary of Beth's death. The sight of her had stopped him in his tracks. "My God Carrie, what the devil are you doing?" he'd spluttered.

"I want you Nathan," she'd replied softly. "I want you to be happy again. I want to make you happy again."

He'd forced a smile. "Carrie I..." His voice caught his breath, but he couldn't finish the sentence.

She'd climbed out of bed and moved towards him. Placing her fingers on his lips, she whispered, "Don't say anything, just come to bed."

Nathan had shaken his head in denial. "Carrie, this is not a good idea," he'd whispered, as she slowly unbuttoned his shirt. It was wrong, it felt wrong, but had he not prayed for something, someone to help him begin to live again. Was it to be Carrie who would save him? Maybe if he closed his eyes he could make believe it was Beth. It had been so long since he'd held a naked woman, and against his better judgment he'd taken her in his arms. But as he laid her on his bed, all he could think of was Beth. He knew then he could not respond to the woman who was whispering love in his ear. He knew his body would not respond to her caresses. It was no good; he'd jumped swiftly off the bed. "Sorry, I'm sorry, I can't," he'd said running from the room. Lifting his coat from the hook by the door he'd run like the wind to spend a miserable night in his studio.

The next morning at breakfast Nathan broke the awkward silence. "Carrie, about last night..."

Carrie lifted her hand to silence him. "I apologise for last night Nathan, it was very wrong of me," she'd answered casually.

He'd laid his spoon down in his porridge. "No, I'm sorry, I'm sorry for you; it's just that I'm not ready for..." he'd paused for a moment looking for the right words. "I'm just not ready. It's too soon."

She reached over and placed a hand on his arm. "It's okay Nathan, I'll wait," she'd said smiling, as she cleared the breakfast plates.

Nathan looked out at the ocean and sighed. It wasn't right, he knew that, he knew it was spoiling Carrie's chances of meeting a young man of her own. Something must be done to discourage her from waiting for him, and it must be done soon. He turned and looked at the surf which was crashing against the shoreline. Several surfers were out far beyond the breaking waves, waiting and hoping for the ride of their life.

He walked over to the next cove, which was more secluded, then stripped off his clothes, leaving them in a pile on the sand. Jasper, eager to swim, waited for the command to go in. Once in the sea, Jasper was a puppy again, leaping and crashing into the shallows, and this made Nathan smile. The icy water stung his thighs as he waded purposely through the foaming surf and with a sharp intake of breath he plunged into the icy water and swam to forget.

27

All was not well at Lemmel. Faye had been missing for five months now, and Liam was again reeling from Angus Fox's wrath.

"Where the hell is she Knight? Calvin tells me she didn't come back to work after her summer break? She should have been back in the studio in September, it's now October, so where the hell is she?"

Liam baulked slightly; he had hoped Calvin would have kept his mouth shut. After all, they had enough photo shots to see them through to Christmas.

"Err, she's on compassionate leave," he lied. "Her father is terminally ill."

"Damn. How long has he got?"

"I'm not sure."

"Well is it a month, two months, a bloody year," he dropped his voice to a low hiss.

Liam's face paled. "I don't honestly know. It's not something one likes to ask."

Angus cocked his head and regarded Liam with contempt. "Well, I'm asking. She is an employee of ours, and you are her so called agent. I think we have a right to know, no matter how bloody delicate you think the question is." Angus buzzed through to his secretary. "Get me Faye Larson on the phone." He locked eyes with Liam and watched him squirm. A silence ensued, and then Sue came back on the line. "I'm sorry sir, Miss Larson's mobile seems to be dead, and her home phone number in Cornwall has been disconnected."

"Well there must be a next of kin contact number,

phone that," he barked.

Unruffled she answered, "I've already done that. She put her ex-employer Owen Barnes at the boatyard down as next of kin, but he doesn't know where she is either."

Angus sat back and folded his arms. "So, she doesn't seem to be contactable eh? Highly irregular don't you think? So, where is she Knight? Where is she nursing her 'terminally ill' father?"

"I'm not sure," he stammered. And in all honesty he didn't know. He had never really bothered asking her about her past life, where she was born, where her parents lived etc, and she for her part had never offered up the information. He had to think on his feet. "I believe it is somewhere abroad, she was always very secretive about her family." He watched intently as Angus digested his words.

"I see." He breathed heavily. "Well, what the hell do you plan to do without her? This product will go down the drain if we don't keep the punters interested."

"Everything will be okay I promise, we can cancel all her TV appearances, I'm sure they will understand…under the circumstances." Liam swallowed nervously. "As for future publications, Calvin did enough photos to see us through the Christmas promotions." He paused for a moment. " ..and if Faye is still unable to return to work after Christmas, I'll have found her replacement. Someone younger and prettier." He grinned weakly.

"Bullshit, if you think for one moment I am ever going to listen to you again, you, who obviously conduct business via your trousers, if the Jasmine Quintana fiasco was anything to go by - well you must think I am mad. Now get out of my sight and make sure you get her back, I want her back to work in January, dead father or not. Do I make myself clear?"

"Yes Angus." Liam walked out of the MD's room shaking with rage. There was nothing else for it; he had to find her, but where? He had searched everywhere for her and every place he looked he had drawn a blank. Even Pippa, her so called best friend denied any knowledge of her whereabouts. This vexed him greatly for he was sure she was lying and knew exactly where she was. But he had been warned by Owen Barnes against entering the boatyard office, and that if he showed any more threatening behaviour towards Pippa or anyone else connected with Faye, he would have to find somewhere else to lay his boat up for the winter. Without doubt, he would kill Faye Larson if he got his hands on her.

28

It was a cold, damp, November afternoon, when Faye turned the key and pushed open the front door to her rented terraced cottage, deep in the heart of Burndale, Yorkshire.

Faye had been born in Cornwall but brought up in Burndale after her father had died. It was a small village a few miles from the larger market town of Skipton. In the summer it was a thriving place, situated on the River Wharf. It was a place set in the past, only the gossiping Joanne Tubbs, who lived at the far end of the village, kept everyone up to date with goings on, and Faye's residence in Riverside Cottage would no doubt be the topic of today's news.

Faye shivered as she stepped into the uninviting hall. The place smelt damp and musty and the décor hung pitifully off the walls from years of neglect. It wasn't a patch on her lovely cottage on Post Office Row in Gweek. She sighed heavily; it had broken her heart to give that place up. But she had no option. She didn't want Liam to find her and she still felt she needed to lay low for a while, just until the dust had settled. She stood and surveyed the room. Well, it would do for a while; she told herself.

"Oh my God Faye!" Her half sister Gayle gasped in disbelief. She huddled closer to Faye bringing the cold air in with her. Gayle's eyes moved around the room. Words failed her as she plunged her hands deep into her coat pockets as though she was afraid of touching something horrible. She walked from room to room, her eyes betraying disdain, and her nose screwed up at the smell of stale cigarettes.

Faye looked at her elder half sister and laughed heartily. "You like it then?"

Before Gayle could answer, Ryan, her brother-in-law

pushed the front door open with his foot and staggered into the hall with a large cardboard box in his arms.

"Where do you want this.... oh my God!" His mouth fell open aghast, as his eyes skimmed the room.

"My sentiments exactly," Gayle said.

Ryan stood open-mouthed. "What the hell is this place? It's not a house, it's a pigsty. Are you completely mad Faye? This place is completely uninhabitable!" He placed the box on the kitchen drainer. "Well it's no good, you can't possibly stay here. You'll catch pneumonia or something. Tell her Gayle, tell her she doesn't have to move out, tell her she must stay with us a while longer."

Faye smiled thankfully at her brother-in-law, and then shook her head to decline. "I'll be fine here, I promise. It just wants cleaning that's all. A bit of elbow grease and this place will be spick and span in no time."

Gayle and Ryan exchanged dubious glances.

"Anyway," Faye added, "I think I've probably outstayed my welcome."

"Nonsense," said Ryan adamantly. "You've only been with us a couple of months."

"Eight to be exact," her sister Gayle announced. "And yes, she has outstayed her welcome," she added, winking at Faye.

Faye laughed. "I'm so grateful to you both for taking me in. I could not have stayed with my parents a moment longer. It was as though I had never been away. I know he is your real dad and all that Gayle, but he still treats me like a wayward child. I couldn't do anything while I was there; he always wanted to know where I was going and what time I would be back."

Gayle screwed her nose up affectionately. "He just worries about you."

Faye forced herself not to roll her eyes at this comment.

"Well Ben and Lucy are going to miss you. Aren't you kids?" Ryan asked as the children ran in to the house clutching a pot plant each. The children both nodded and ran back out to the car to collect more of Faye's belongings. If the truth were known, Ryan would miss her as well, probably more than he should.

Gayle studied her husband for a moment and smiled inwardly. "He doesn't want you to go you know, because he fancies you," she said to Faye.

"Excuse me dear wife, but I do not fancy your sister. Well.... I may do a bit. Yes okay I admit it, I fancy her to bits."

Gayle threw her hands in the air. "See, I knew it, he's been on a big ego trip since you joined us. It's always been his fantasy to get both sisters in bed."

"I see," Faye murmured. She moved towards Ryan, smiled seductively and plucked at his jumper. He was an athletically lean muscular man, who kept himself in peak physical condition. Her eyes twinkled mischievously as she saw the look of anticipation in his grey eyes. "Well," she said huskily. "That's just tough isn't it, 'cause you're not going to get your fantasy, so get back out there and help me to move in."

He feigned dejection. "You're nothing but a tease. All I can say is that you don't know what you are missing."

The sisters exchanged amused glances. "You're not missing anything Faye, believe me," Gayle shouted over her shoulder as she followed Ryan out to the car.

When Faye was alone later that night, she sat in her freshly scrubbed lounge in front of a blazing fire, opened a bottle of wine, and raised her glass to toast to a new start. Her life had been in tatters when she arrived at Burndale the day after learning of Liam's secret family. She had left behind her friends, her home and her lucrative job. Her pride was bruised but not beaten, she would find her way again, but for now, she would sit it out in the bosom of her family.

After leaving Lemmel, she found to her amazement that her bank account showed up a huge amount of money which had been deposited as an end of year financial bonus. This money she felt sure would be claimed back from her when they realised she had defaulted on her contract. So, she quickly invested the money in a high interest Isa and left it until it was claimed back. That way she might at least get some of it for all the work she had done. She had been frugal with her money during her time with Lemmel, and saved a great deal over the last seven months. But this was to go towards buying her much coveted beach side café one day, and she was adamant she would not touch it. Fortunately Ryan had found her a job as a Customer Service representative at 'Stationery Express' in Skipton, the local stationery firm where he worked as a manager, so she was able to pay rent on this cottage.

She had explained to her family that a relationship had gone wrong for her and she needed to get away from Cornwall for a while. She didn't elaborate and they never asked. As for her job, they still believed she had worked at the boatyard and fortunately no one had made the connection with Cordelia Hart, the 'face of Guinevere', and she had no intention of telling anyone about Lemmel. There had been the odd comment in the village about how much she looked like the woman on the TV perfume ads, but Faye just laughed it off. That life was gone now; she must look to the future.

*

It had been a busy morning at work for Faye; the telephone hadn't stopped ringing since she arrived at nine. She was just about to take a drink of coffee when the telephone rang again. Faye swallowed quickly, took a deep breath and as she had been trained, smiled as she answered the telephone: "Hello Customer Service, Faye speaking, how can I help."

"You can start by dropping whatever you are doing tonight, to come to dinner," Ryan said.

"Dinner? Mmm, well let me see, what have I in my

social diary for tonight. Oh silly me, I don't have a social life do I? What's the occasion?"

"Lyndon Maunders the MD has a delegation over from the States and I'm hosting a dinner party for them at home, and we need you to make up the numbers."

"Oh, charming, so it's not my wit and sparkling conversation you need then?"

He laughed. "No it's purely to make up numbers darling."

"Then how can I decline?"

"You can't. Dinner is at eight, can you come at seven? Gayle needs you to help. See you there." The line went dead.

Gayle and Ryan Farrington lived in a converted barn at the edge of the pretty village of Burndale, about fifty yards from Faye's cottage and a quarter of a mile from Faye's parent's house. Faye walked along the path beside the river which was situated at the bottom of the Farringtons' driveway and took in the splendour of their garden as she approached the front door. Gayle was a keen gardener and though this was late winter, Gayle still managed to fill her garden with colour and structural plants.

"Thank God you are here," Ryan said, as he opened the door to Faye. "Gayle's having a crisis in the kitchen!" he added, rolling his eyes.

"I wouldn't be having a crisis if you had told me earlier about this dinner," Gayle yelled angrily from the kitchen.

Ryan smiled grimly and kissed Faye on the cheek. "Go and help her will you?"

Actually, Gayle as always had everything under control, so was just making Ryan suffer for springing this on her.

When the guests arrived at seven thirty, there was an air of serene calmness about the house. The table was set with the finest crystal and china. Soft music played on the stereo and the children were packed off to their grandparents' house for the night.

"Do I look okay?" Gayle said, as she checked her

reflection in the mirror. Gayle was dressed in a stunning cream cocktail dress, her dark brown hair was carefully tucked into a chic chignon, and her fair complexion glowed with a slight blush to the cheeks accentuating her dark brown eyes.

"You look lovely," Faye answered.

The dinner was a huge success. The Americans enjoyed fine food and wine and for some strange and unknown reason, Faye found herself the centre of Lyndon Maunders' attention. Not that she minded being engaged in conversation with this tall fair-haired man with handsome features. He was the first man she had felt comfortable with since Liam, apart from Ryan of course, but he didn't count.

As the guests prepared to take their leave later that night, Lyndon held back a little so as to speak with Faye. "It's been a real pleasure to meet you Miss Larson, I hope this will not be the last time I have this pleasure."

Faye smiled warmly. "I hope not too," she heard herself saying. As she waved Lyndon goodbye at the door, she was unaware of the reproachful look Ryan had shot her.

The next morning Faye received a large bouquet of flowers from Lyndon, and was happily arranging them when Ryan knocked at the door.

"Oh I see you got some too." He nodded towards the flowers. "I've just left Gayle arranging hers as well. Lyndon always sends flowers as a thank you."

Faye felt suddenly deflated, but managed to hide the emotion from Ryan.

Ryan picked up the card which came with the flowers and skimmed his eyes over it. "You seemed to be engaged in conversation with Lyndon for most of last night. What were you talking about? He practically ignored his American guests for you," he added lightly.

Faye picked up the vase of flowers and placed them in the window, cocking her head slightly to admire them.

"Oh you know, nothing much, this and that," she said, smiling at Ryan.

Ryan opened his mouth to say something, and then closed it again. He picked up an old newspaper, then dropped it again without reading anything, and then scratched the back of his head in a most agitated way.

Faye watched curiously but said nothing. He moved over to the window and gently sniffed at the flowers. "Did you like him?" he asked the question quietly without looking at her.

Faye frowned slightly. "He was very entertaining yes," she answered cautiously.

Ryan moved towards her and reached for her hand. "Don't rush into another relationship Faye," he blurted out. "You've only just got over being hurt."

Faye pulled her hand sharply from his. "Who said I'd got over it?" she answered sharply.

"I'm sorry; it's none of my business. It's just that I don't want you to get hurt again that's all."

Faye paused for a fraction of a second, switching her thoughts around, searching for the right way to convey her feelings. "Thank you for your concern Ryan, it's very kind of you, but, I think I can make my own decisions about men."

Ryan bit down on his bottom lip. "Sorry, I can't help it. You are just so very dear to me."

Faye's eyes softened. "Ryan, you are a very dear brother-in-law to me too, but you're getting ahead of yourself. I've only chatted to him for a couple of hours; I'm not buying a wedding dress yet!"

Ryan sighed and hung his head low. "Sorry, but just remember you are just recovering from a love affair. Go gently."

Faye smiled brilliantly to lighten the mood. "Well, I'd hardly call it a love affair, but thanks anyway. Now if you'll excuse me, I have a large pot of white emulsion paint waiting to be applied to these drab walls, so if you're doing nothing you can pick up that roller and help."

He smiled thinly, shook his head. "Sorry, no can do. I'm due to meet Gayle in..." He checked his watch and panicked. "Oh my God, ten minutes ago, she'll kill me."

Faye watched as he ran quickly down the path and a sense of uneasiness washed over her.

29

Without doubt Lyndon Maunders' mind was elsewhere today, Lyndon's secretary Elaine Elmer surmised. Normally so meticulous in his work, Elaine found his desk in disarray when she brought his morning coffee. He hadn't signed any of the documents she had placed there that morning, and the tea she had brought him first thing stood congealed and cold where she had put it.

"Is everything all right Mr Maunders?"

Disturbed from his reverie, he looked up at Elaine. "Pardon?"

"Your tea, you haven't drunk the tea I brought you this morning Was there something wrong with it?"

"No, I just forgot to drink it that's all." He picked up the cup and thrust it towards her, gesturing for her to take it away.

Elaine cleared her throat. "I need to get these papers off to accounts." She pointed to the pile on his desk.

"Yes, yes, I'll do them in a minute. I'm busy at the moment."

Elaine regarded him for a moment. "Is there something I can help you with?"

He didn't answer her, so she turned to leave, and Lyndon returned to his thoughts. He could not get Faye Larson out of his mind. It was quite an unusual dilemma he found himself in. He wasn't the sort of man who found it easy to be with a woman; in fact at thirty-six he had resigned himself to bachelorhood. He had a brief relationship with Natalie Dankworth from the accounts department, but that finished a couple of years ago, and since then there had been no one, until now. Faye had enchanted him, and he was eager to become more acquainted.

He lifted the phone and buzzed Elaine. "Get me Ryan

Farrington on the line please."

"Hello Ryan. Lyndon Maunders here."

Ryan sighed inwardly. Lyndon never rang him in person. "Morning Lyndon, what can I do for you?" As if he didn't know.

"Well, first to thank you for Friday night, it was a real success. The Americans were impressed with our hospitality, but apart from that I was just wondering..." He laughed in a slightly embarrassed way. "Is Faye involved with anybody?"

"Faye?" Ryan replied cautiously. He felt a cold chill run through him.

"Yes, Faye, your sister-in-law, you remember her? Is she involved with anyone?"

"Not sure," he mumbled.

"Well she lived with you for months, surely you must know if she is seeing someone."

Ryan detected a slight irritation in his voice. "Well there is, was, someone, but I'm really not sure how things stand now."

"Oh, I see." He breathed heavily.

"Sorry I can't help you Lyndon."

"No matter," Lyndon said and put the phone down.

*

When Faye arrived home that evening a bouquet of flowers awaited her in the porch. The accompanying card read: *Would you care to have dinner with me tonight? Lyndon.*

Lyndon was a gift from heaven to Faye. He was kind, considerate, charming and romantic. Faye was so glad she accepted his dinner invitation.

Over the course of the next few weeks they took to having dinner together each Saturday, normally at some small exclusive restaurant, far away from the prying eyes of his work colleagues, in the rural idyll of the beautiful Yorkshire dales. Life was looking up.

*

Liam was called into the office on Monday the

thirteenth of January. He knew this meeting was imminent and he knew it would not be pleasant.

"Right, where is Miss Larson?" Angus's voice was quietly angry.

"In all honesty I don't know." Liam shifted nervously where he stood.

Angus shot him a sharp look. "You are her agent, but you don't know where your client is?"

"No." His answer was almost inaudible.

Regarding him reproachfully, Angus barked, "Is that all you can say?"

Liam felt his heart begin to pound. "Yes Angus, I'm so sorry."

Angus sighed heavily, and looked down at his diary. "She has been missing without leave for the last ten months!" Liam nodded. "I've been told you were in a relationship with her."

"No."

"Liar!" Angus flashed him a look of contempt. "You take me to be a fool," he said raising his eyebrows. "It is a well known fact that you conduct most of your business via your trousers. What did you do to her to make her leave?"

"Nothing, she just left to look after her father that's all I know."

He laughed sarcastically. "Ah yes, her ailing father, well, what about our ailing company? She doesn't seem to give two hoots for that does she?"

Liam remained silent.

"Ten months absent without leave, I'd say she was in breach of contract wouldn't you?"

"Yes I do." Liam's lip twisted into a half smile. "I think you should take her to court."

"Do you?" Angus stood up and Liam stepped back slightly. "Bring me the contract she signed."

"The contract?" Liam's mind raced as he tried to recall what he had done with the document.

182

Angus leant towards him. "Now."

Liam turned and ran into his office; he pulled violently at the filing cabinet drawers and searched through the L's. With enormous relief his fingers pulled out Faye's file and he made his way triumphantly back to the MD's office. This would teach her, he mused, Lemmel would take her for every penny she had. "One contract," he said triumphantly, as he placed the file on Angus's desk.

Angus flipped the document to the last page, and lifted his eyes to meet Liam's. "It isn't signed," he said evenly.

Liam opened his mouth to speak then shut it again in despair.

"Get out, you incompetent idiot." Angus snapped.

*

Faye and Lyndon had been seeing each other for a couple of months when Lyndon invited Faye to his country retreat 'Orchard Hills' near Bolton Abbey for the weekend.

Faye had first thought that she was going to 'Orchard Hills' to meet Lyndon's parents, but instead found herself quite alone with Lyndon. It turned out that 'Orchard Hills' belonged to Lyndon himself.

The house was well off the beaten track; buried deep away from prying eyes, through a thicket of woodland, but when they emerged from the darkness of the trees the drive opened up to a grand old country mansion which took Faye's breath away.

Lyndon observed the look in Faye's eyes as she took in the surroundings appreciatively.

"This is beautiful Lyndon, I had no idea it was going to be this grand," she said, as she stepped out of the car onto the gravel drive. Once inside Faye could see that Lyndon had gone to a lot of time and trouble to welcome her into his home. Flowers were placed in every room, and a cold meat buffet was laid out on the south facing sun terrace overlooking the formal gardens to the rear of the house. It was nearing the end of February, but the sun, though pale in the sky, warmed the terrace enough for them to lunch there. With a glass of champagne in her hand, listening to the peacocks, whose cries could be heard from their roosts in far off trees, it seemed that happiness had returned to Faye's life.

After dinner in the opulent surroundings of the mahogany panelled dining room, they sat before a roaring fire, sipping brandy and talking long into the night.

When the time came for them to retire, Lyndon walked Faye to her room and kissed her gently on the lips. "I'll be next door, if you need me," he said casually.

Faye smiled as he turned to go. "Lyndon?" she whispered softly.

"Yes my love?"

"I need you."

Lyndon was a tender lover, there was no urgency about him, no animal wanting, just a gentle sensual need to love and be loved.

When Faye rang in sick to work on Monday morning, Ryan called round to see her that evening.

He knocked and without waiting, walked in. "Faye, where are you," Ryan shouted, as he glanced into the empty lounge. "How was your weekend in the famous 'Orchard Hills'", he added, unable to hide the hint of sarcasm in his voice. He spun around when he heard a groan come from behind the kitchen door.

"Oh God, I can't walk!" Faye moaned as she crawled on all fours from out of the kitchen.

He looked at her with alarm and prickled with indignation. "Oh for Christ's sake Faye, what the hell did he do to you?"

She laughed at his assumption. "Oh put your duelling pistols away, this is with horse riding yesterday. I haven't ridden for over ten years, and I can tell you now, I won't be riding for another ten years. In fact I don't think I'll ever be able to walk again!" She winced as she tried to climb onto the sofa.

After helping her into a seated position, he sat beside

her and asked gently, "How was it then?"

"It was wonderful actually," she answered dreamily.

Ryan nodded unhappily.

30

Faye was aware her departure from Lemmel had caused the company financial trouble, and she was truly sorry for what was happening. It had been Lyndon who had alerted her to the fact as he read the Financial Times one morning early in March.

She had watched with interest as he frowned and cursed over breakfast.

"Is everything all right Lyndon?" she had enquired.

"Damn shares in Lemmel have fallen dramatically that's all."

Faye's mouth went suddenly dry. "Do you have a lot of shares with them?" she asked nervously.

"Enough to hurt, if it goes down, and after speaking with my financial adviser last week, I think that they are going to struggle to stay afloat. Apparently some bimbo they employed to front their perfume advertisement has gone AWOL, leaving them in big trouble."

"Oh," Faye said, suddenly losing her appetite.

*

Faye had spent the day in Leeds shopping with Gayle, and on her return Faye found a letter waiting for her. It had been a long day and she was fatigued from the journey. Gayle made for Faye's small kitchen to put the kettle on, while Faye eased her shoes off and slumped down on the sofa. She picked up the letter and turned it over, studied the handwriting, which looked like Lyndon's, then ripped it open, frowning at the contents as she did.

You are cordially invited to the grand christening of 'Digby' on Sunday March 29th at Orchard Hills. I'll send a car for you at ten a.m. Lyndon x

Faye frowned.

"What is it?" Gayle said placing a much needed cup of tea in front of Faye.

"Lyndon's invited me to Digby's christening on Sunday!"

"A christening - so a family get together is on the cards. He must be serious about you."

"Yes but who the hell is Digby?"

"Who cares, he obviously wants you to be there to meet the family! I do believe I will need to buy a new hat soon."

*

Faye emerged from the car that sunny afternoon, conscious of being inappropriately dressed for the occasion. Twice she had phoned Lyndon for more information about the christening, but was told he was away on business.

The drive was littered with expensive cars and as she walked to the entrance, she could hear a strange roaring sound, almost like a jet engine firing up, coming from the back of the house.

She was greeted at the door by a woman she had never seen before with a 'no nonsense' face, who took her coat and raised an eyebrow at Faye's attire.

"Faye my darling there you are, how are you?" Lyndon said as he swept towards her. He kissed her warmly. "Come, we are all outside." He swept his eyes over her. "You look.... very nice. Come and meet Lucinda, my oldest friend, I'm sure you'll get on like a house on fire." Faye was thrust into a huge crowd of people, who smiled and nodded at her as she made a path through them.

"Lucinda, meet Faye."

"Faye, this is Lucinda Hervey, be a darling and arrange some refreshments for Faye. I think I am needed elsewhere."

Faye heard another loud blast coming from behind a thicket of great oak trees as she handed a card she had brought with her to Lucinda.

"Oh what's this darling?" She ripped open the envelope and pulled the christening card out. She studied it for a second with great amusement. "Baby boy!" she exclaimed. "Oh God darling." She laughed loudly. "Silly you, it's not that sort of christening. Oh look everybody, how sweet, Faye thought we were christening a baby today. Well that certainly explains the outfit." The crowd around them smiled into their drinks.

Embarrassed beyond belief, Faye could gladly have strangled Lucinda. It wasn't in her nature to dislike people, but the resentment towards this woman was instant and enduring.

"We are christening an envelope, don't you know."

"What the hell do you mean christening an envelope? I have no idea what you are talking about," Faye snapped irritably.

"You know, an envelope, for a hot air balloon! My goodness, this will not do. We shall have to educate you in the finer things in life." She stopped at a white linen draped trestle table, scooped up two glasses of champagne and thrust one into Faye's hand. "Come on darling; let me introduce you to Digby."

As they passed underneath several age old oak trees, a flurry of activity was going on in front of her. Lyndon, holding a bottle of Bollinger, beckoned them over to the balloon. Crowds of people had followed Faye and Lucinda through the thicket of trees and after making sure everyone had a full glass of champagne, Lyndon raised his glass in the air.

"I name this envelope Digby. May God bless him and all who fly him!"

Everyone raised their glass, to a chorus of, "Digby." Then took one sip and threw the rest on the envelope. The gesture shocked Faye, simply for the waste of good champagne, and cradled her still full glass protectively at her breast.

Lucinda stepped in, took the glass from her and threw the contents out and returned the glass to her with a self-satisfied smile. "Don't look so worried darling, there is plenty more where that came from."

Almost instantly her glass was exchanged for a full one and everyone stepped back as the balloon crew gathered round the end of the wet balloon. In unison they opened up the edge to allow a powerful fan at the base of the envelope to inflate it.

A large wicker basket, housing three propane tanks and navigational equipment, lay on its side and when there was enough air in the balloon, Faye watched a member of the crew blast the burner flame into the envelope mouth. Suddenly the balloon was inflated enough to begin to lift off the ground. Forgetting her irritation with Lucinda, Faye stood in awe at the massive structure inflated before her. The balloon was rugby ball shaped with a huge dog's face printed on the silk and enormous ears which flapped in the breeze.

There was a flurry of activity and all the ground crew members ran to hold the basket down. Without warning her glass was once again taken from her and a white boiler suit was thrust at her. "Lyndon wants you to put this on quickly. Lyndon needs your help in holding the basket down."

Faye held the garment out for inspection. "Whatever for?"

"Hurry up darling put it on, don't keep Lyndon waiting," Lucinda said quickly.

Slightly bewildered, Faye reluctantly stepped into the suit as Lucinda fastened her into it. With great trepidation Faye moved towards the wicker basket. Lyndon was aboard along with another pilot.

"What do you think of Digby?" Lyndon asked, as Faye joined the other members of the crew holding down the suede edge of the basket.

"It's wonderful, I've never seen one close up before," she replied.

"Fancy a ride?"

Faye let go and stepped back. "No, I don't."

"Don't let go," he barked at her. She quickly moved forward again and hooked her arms over the top. "Don't let go until I tell you okay?"

She nodded like a scolded child.

"Right then everybody ready? After three, let go. One, two…"

On the count of three Faye was picked up by two of the crew and unceremoniously tipped into the basket just as the pilot fired a steady flame from the burner lifting the balloon off the ground.

Lyndon bent down to help Faye to her feet. "Sorry about that darling, but I really think you should experience this. But first we need to get rid of these," he said, pulling her new shoes off her feet and tossing them over the edge of the basket.

"Hey, don't do that," she squealed with indignation.

There wasn't a single emotion Faye didn't experience on that maiden flight. She was overwhelmingly scared at the thought of being in the balloon, and couldn't bring herself to look over the side. She angrily batted Lyndon's hand away as he tried to pull her to her feet, irritated that he had ignored her and that he'd thrown away her best shoes. She sat defiantly hugging her knees, fighting back the tears which threatened to bubble up and spill down her cheeks.

After exchanging a few words with the pilot, Lyndon left Faye alone for a while. Presently, he said to her, "You know, if you actually need to get somewhere, a hot air balloon is a fairly impractical vehicle. You can't really steer it, and it only travels as fast as the wind blows. But if you simply want to enjoy the experience of flying, there's nothing quite like it. Most people who take their first flight think it's the most serene enjoyable activity they've ever experienced. Please stand up Faye; I really want you to see this. I'm sorry I bulldozed you into it, but come and look, you'll be amazed."

Slowly she stood and cautiously she looked over the

side of the basket. Without warning a smile crossed her face. "Oh my goodness, it doesn't feel the same as standing on the edge of a cliff or being in an aeroplane, there is no sensation of height," she exclaimed.

"I know isn't it lovely?" he answered softly, aware he was treading on eggshells. "The balloon doesn't so much leave the ground as the ground leaves the balloon! You're floating gently along with the breeze, so there's no sensation of movement either."

Faye felt an enormous feeling of wellbeing fill her body; this was the most wonderful experience she had ever had.

The day was clear, though a little chilly and Lyndon held Faye close to him as the beautiful Yorkshire dales spread out before them, following the River Wharf as it meandered down away from Bolton Abbey.

Lyndon gestured for the pilot to look away as he fumbled in his pocket for the tiny box he had hidden there. He knelt down on one knee and took Faye's hand.

"I know it's only been a few months, but I love you Faye, and I want you to be my wife." He held out the box containing a beautiful antique ring.

Faye was speechless, as Lyndon placed the ring on her finger. "We can have it altered to fit. It was my grandmother's ring. I think she would approve of you having it."

Holding her hand out to admire the unexpected gift, she pulled Lyndon to his feet and sealed her love for him with a kiss. Silently and weightlessly, they floated through the sky towards their future.

*

Ryan appeared at her desk first thing Monday morning. "How did the christening go? Did you meet his family?"

Faye could hardly contain herself. "He wants to marry me Ryan!" she said softly.

There was a pause as Ryan's face turned ashen. "Well you can't."

She laughed incredulously. "What do you mean I

can't? I can do whatever I like."

"But you haven't known him two minutes."

"Well sometimes you just know when you've met the right person," she said firmly, resenting his opposition to the match.

Faye watched as Ryan stood motionless for a moment as he mulled his next response. His disappointment was intense.

Faye's phone began to ring. She smiled thinly. "I need to......" she reached for the telephone. The conversation was halted as she answered the call, and Ryan threw his hands in the air in defeat.

"Well there is no accounting for taste, that's all I can say," he said curtly, before marching out of the office, slamming the door behind him.

"Ryan?" Faye called out, covering the receiver with her hand. Faye sat and watched the door gloomily. He'll get over it, she sighed. She hoped with all her heart that he would, as she valued his friendship more than he would ever know.

The caller on the line interrupted her thoughts. "Hello, are you still there? Hello?"

*

Ryan wasn't the only person opposed to Faye's attachment with Lyndon, as Faye found out when she breezed into Lyndon's office just before lunchtime.

"Hello Elaine, is Lyndon free?" Faye said gaily.

Lyndon's secretary Elaine Elmer shot her a frosty look. "It's Mr Maunders to you, if you don't mind."

Faye raised her eyebrows slightly. "Well could you tell Mr Maunders I'm here?" Faye replied, smiling through her irritation.

Elaine flicked through the pages of her desk diary. "I'm sorry but he has asked me to keep the rest of the day free, so if you would like to make an appointment to see him, I'm sure I can fit you in somewhere next week."

Faye smiled and chose to ignore this mild chastisement.

"No I don't think I'll make an appointment, I think I'll just wait here for him, if you don't mind."

Elaine prickled with indignation. "Well I do mind actually, Mr Maunders doesn't like cold callers, so you'll be wasting your...."

Just at that minute Lyndon opened his office door. "Faye darling, I didn't know you were here. Have you been waiting long? Elaine, why didn't you tell me Faye was here?"

"Well I err..." Elaine blustered, blushing profusely.

"Oh never mind. I hope you've cancelled my appointments this afternoon."

"Yes sir, I......"

"Good because my fiancée and I are going to have her engagement ring altered. Oh and would you book a table for two at the Abbey Restaurant? See you tomorrow."

Elaine's mouth gaped open in astonishment and Faye couldn't help but notice the cold hatred in her eyes as Lyndon ushered her out of the office. Elaine was so obviously in love with him too.

31

In Gweek, Faye's house on Post Office Row was still up for let. With a paper under her arm and a bottle of milk in her hand, Pippa stood on tip toes and peered through the window to look inside.

Sid emerged from his liquid lunch at the Black Swan and joined her at the window.

"I always hope that I'll look through the window and all her things will be back one day," she said unhappily.

"Well if you ask me it doesn't look like she will ever return."

"I know," Pippa answered sadly.

"Still no word?"

"Not a peep, it's been over a year now. I think she thinks I told Liam she was going to phone that day you know!"

"Have you no idea where she might have gone to? Doesn't she have family somewhere in Yorkshire?"

"Yes she does, in Burndale I think she said, but she never really got on with her step-father. I'd be surprised if she went back there."

"Well, sometimes people are where you least expect them to be, so why don't you send a letter via the Post Office there saying you're looking for her. You never know, it might just get to her or her family."

"Well I did that ages ago and it just came back, return to sender addressee unknown."

"Well, I'd give it another go, she might be there now."

*

The letter duly arrived at Burndale Post Office on May the tenth. Sara Baker the post mistress picked it up.

"What's that you've got there then?" Jim Baker asked his wife.

"It's another letter for someone called Faye Larson, but

I have no idea who she is. I know a Carl and Marjory Larson but not a Faye."

"You do, she's the one who lived with the Farringtons for a while. She lives at No. 3 River cottage now."

"Oh."

"What?"

"I didn't know that. I sent the last letter that came for her back to sender."

Jim laughed. "Oh never mind it probably won't be anything important, give it here, I'll pop it through her letter box."

*

Tears of joy poured down Faye's face as she read the letter from Pippa. Everything seemed to be coming together nicely now. Life was back on track, and after an emotional phone call, Faye had her Chief Bridesmaid.

32

The wedding date was set for the sixth of September. It was to have been August bank holiday but Gayle was due to undergo a hysterectomy at the beginning of August, so the date was put back in order for her to recuperate enough to be able to attend the wedding.

It had taken a couple of months, but Ryan had finally become resigned to the fact that Faye was getting married, and slowly their friendship was back on its proper footing.

Gayle was due out of hospital on the fourteenth of August. Faye made sure all her essential wedding shopping would be done in good time so that she could devote her time to helping Gayle with the children.

She had picked up her wedding dress that morning, but the traffic had been horrendous on the way home from Leeds so she was late arriving back. She hung the dress on the doorjamb, glanced at the clock and picked up the telephone to call Ryan.

Ryan was in the drive outside his house trying to get the children settled in the back seat of the car when Faye rang.

"Come on Ben, get in the car, so we can go and fetch mummy from the hospital," Ryan said impatiently, as he secured Lucy into the child seat. Looking after the children full time had been a little bit of an ordeal for Ryan. Thank goodness he'd had Faye's help, for without her he would have floundered.

"Daddy, the telephone's ringing in the house," Ben exclaimed.

Ryan lifted his head to listen, bumping it on the car roof. He rubbed his head furiously. "That could be your mummy phoning again, I'll just go and answer it. Ben, put your seat belt on and sit quietly, I'll only be a moment."

He slammed the car door shut and ran up the drive,

fumbled with the key and cursed when it wouldn't go in. Suddenly the key worked and the door gave. "I'm coming, I'm coming," he shouted to the telephone, willing it to keep ringing.

Ben watched his daddy enter the house. When he was out of sight he released his seat belt and climbed over to the driver's seat. Just as Daddy always did, he pulled the seatbelt across him, snapping it in place, then he pressed the central locking down, released the handbrake and grabbed the steering wheel and pretended to steer.

Faye listened to the telephone ring about eight times, then cursed. Damn, she must be too late; she had hoped to look after the children for him while he went to pick up Gayle. He must have left early. She was just about to replace the receiver when Ryan answered.

"Yes hello," he said slightly out of breath.

"Hello it's just me."

"Faye darling, hi how are you?" Ryan said warmly. "I was just setting off for Gayle, she's climbing the wall in that hospital she's so bored."

"Oh dear, poor thing, I was just phoning to see if you would like me to take the kids off your hands for an hour or two, while you fetch her home."

"Thanks, but they are dying to go and pick her up. Anyway, what are your plans for tonight? Come over if you want, I'll cook, as I don't think Gayle will be up to it for a while."

"That's great, see you later then. Send Gayle my love."

"I will darling, thank you."

Ryan put the receiver down, picked his keys up and tossed them into the air. He glanced out of the hall window and stopped short in surprise. The car had gone! As he rushed to the front door, he could hear shouting and screaming and several people running to the river.

"Ryan, Ryan, your car's in the river, you must have left the handbrake off!" a neighbour shouted.

"Oh no! For Christ's sake, the children are in the car!

I left them in the car!" he yelled, ripping off his jacket as he ran down the river bank. Several people followed him into the swollen river, but the car had already completely submerged.

The police and paramedics arrived within minutes, divers had been called in immediately, and Ryan was dragged, kicking and flaying out of the water to stop him hindering the rescue team.

He stood on the path, shivering with shock and fear, filled with a dread such as he had never ever known before. His neighbour stood with a comforting arm around him, not knowing what to say or do and a small group of onlookers stood silently as the police divers plunged into the cold depths of death.

*

After waiting for an age and phoning the house several times and getting no answer, Gayle finally phoned her father to come and collect his very disgruntled daughter from the hospital.

*

It seemed to take an age to winch the car out of the river. As soon as it was free of the water the locked car was released and the children were pulled from their watery grave.

Ryan gazed in stunned silence at his children's tiny bodies on the river bank. Their innocent smiling faces and shrill joyous laughter had ceased forever, as they lay inanimate in their black polythene body bags.

He closed his eyes, his lips moving as if in silent prayer, while shock waves ran through his body. He fell to his knees, covering his face with his trembling hands. All he could hear was the thud, thud, thud of his heart.

The crowd looked on in shocked disbelief, some were weeping, some murmuring, others just stood and held each other, it was all too shocking to comprehend. The sound of Carl Larson's car as it pulled into the drive drew their attention away from the scene, and they all watched silently as Gayle stepped gingerly out of the car.

Gayle felt her scalp prickle with fright as her eyes swept across the scene before her. She noted the ambulance and the police car, and then she looked at her husband, kneeling on the ground, his anguished face staring back at her, then at the two tiny bodies of her children. She began to shake her head slowly; her mind could not comprehend what her eyes clearly saw. Her legs buckled under her and she sank back on her haunches, her head began to spin and very suddenly her world went black.

33

Lucy and Ben Farrington were buried together on August the twenty-third. The rain fell from the sky like a veil of tears, emulating the grief felt by all who attended that day; and there were many.

The service was a simple affair. It wasn't a service to celebrate their lives; it was a poignant, moving, shockingly emotional service of loss, regret and the waste of two such lovely children who hadn't even started to live.

As Gayle and Ryan emerged from the church, Ryan broke down. The sight of hundreds of people overflowing from the church, standing silently in the churchyard in the pouring rain, was quite overwhelming.

Almost every inhabitant of Burndale had come to pay their last respects and offer their condolences to Gayle and Ryan. There were some people who were only passing acquaintances, but each and every person felt their pain. It was the single most dreadful day Faye had ever witnessed.

As the tiny coffins were lowered into the sodden earth, Faye observed her sister's countenance; it was expressionless, void now of any emotion. It was as though Gayle had totally detached herself from the world. Faye glanced at Ryan, dressed in his long black coat, the rain dripping from his hair, congealing with the river of tears which streamed incessantly down his face; he was a man destroyed. She watched with heartfelt sorrow as he reached out to touch Gayle for comfort and be comforted, only to be rebuffed by her. The gesture forced him to hang his head in shame and weep uncontrollably. Faye knew only too well the reason for the estrangement.

The night of the tragedy Faye had called at Gayle and Ryan's house, to offer her help and whatever comfort she could. Ryan had just returned from the police station where he had given a statement and Gayle was in bed having been sedated.

There was a strange unrealness following the hours after the deaths, a feeling of bewilderment, emptiness, and denial. It was as though the family were strangely detached from the outside world. Faye sat on the sofa opposite Ryan, but he didn't look up. He was staring blankly into the empty fire hearth. He held a glass of whiskey in his hand which rested precariously on his thigh. From his inebriated state, Faye knew it was not his first drink and certainly would not be his last.

Faye leaned her head back on the sofa and closed her eyes and recalled the shocking call she had received from her mother earlier that day. How would the family cope with this she thought to herself, how do you recover from such a tragedy? Faye was heartbroken for Gayle and Ryan; there was no hope for them now. The hysterectomy operation meant there would be no more future children to help Gayle and Ryan ease the void left by Ben and Lucy, if that was even possible.

Faye sighed and opened her eyes to find Ryan standing over her.

"Drink?" he said, thrusting a glass of amber liquid at her.

"I don't like whiskey."

"Neither do I," he said gravely and downed the rest of his glass.

They sat for a long time, not speaking, just thinking, but trying not to think. They both turned when they heard footsteps on the stairs.

"Have you nothing to say to each other?" Gayle asked calmly. Her face was in the shadows, but her voice was cold and hollow. She stepped into the light of the sitting room and looked at them with cold haunted eyes. "You do surprise me, you two are normally chattering away together, I can't normally get a word in edgeways," she said icily.

Ryan placed his glass on the floor and jumped up from

the chair. "Gayle darling, oh Gayle," Ryan whispered, as he moved towards her.

She held out her hand to halt his approach. "Don't. Don't you touch me," she hissed.

Ryan stopped short at the harshness in her voice. "Please come and sit down my love. Let me get you something, a drink, something to eat perhaps?"

Gayle stared at her husband, ignoring his efforts to appease her. At this moment in time she hated him so intensely it frightened her. Presently she walked over to the telephone and touched it briefly.

Ryan and Faye exchanged anxious glances.

Then she turned to him, her eyes blazing with fury. "Why?" Her anger rendered her voice almost inaudible. "Why did you have to answer the telephone Ryan?"

Ryan furrowed his brow. "Sorry?"

"Why couldn't you just let it ring? Why Ryan, why did you answer the bloody telephone?" Her voice was almost a scream.

He moistened his lips slightly. "Well I... I thought it was you calling," he answered meekly.

She threw her hands in the air and laughed incredulously. "Why would I be calling you? I knew you were picking me up, we'd made the arrangement only an hour before; there was no reason for me to call you again."

"Well I just thought..."

"No Ryan, you didn't think, that's the problem. You just left my children unattended in the car, to answer the telephone," she shrieked. "You just couldn't resist answering in case it was Faye calling for a little tete-á-tete, could you? Well I hope you're happy with yourselves." She glanced at both Faye and Ryan reproachfully. "You have managed to kill my children between you."

"Gayle. Please." Faye was on her feet now, moving swiftly towards her sister.

"You," Gayle answered, placing her hands together and pointing for emphasis. "..can leave, now. I don't want you here in my house."

Ryan saw Faye's face begin to contort as great tears welled up in her eyes, but Gayle remained stony faced. Ryan watched helplessly as Faye picked up her coat and made to leave. Faye glanced miserably at Ryan then took a deep breath before addressing her sister.

"I'll call round in the morning Gayle," she said tentatively. But Faye knew from the look in Gayle's eyes she would not be welcome.

That was ten days ago, and the gulf between them all had grown extensively. From the information she had gleaned from her parents, Faye learned that Gayle had not shed a single tear, but her emotions were that of raw anger, which, for the last few days had been vented against Ryan. There was no reasoning with her. As far as Gayle was concerned, there was no other reason for the death of her children. Ryan and Faye had killed them.

After the funeral service, family and close friends returned to the house for refreshments, but Gayle took herself off to her room and locked the door, leaving Ryan, Faye and her parents to see to the mourners. An hour later, when they had all gone, Faye sat beside Ryan, put her hand on his for comfort and he fell into her arms and wept. A little while later, they were all sat drinking tea and talking in hushed tones. "I've spoken to Lyndon about the wedding Mum," Faye began. "We're going to postpone it for a while. We just don't think it would be appropriate to go ahead with it at the moment."

Suddenly a voice from the back of the room made them all jump as if electrified. "No!" said Gayle furiously, as she emerged from the stairs. "I want to see you married."

They all stopped short and turned in surprise at the sound of the unexpected voice. Gayle's pale and fragile figure stood trembling before them.

"I'd rather wait for a while Gayle," Faye explained as she got up from the chair.

"Why? Do you think I'm going to get over this in a few weeks? Because I'm not," she answered acidly. "I'll never get over this, not even if you postpone the wedding for a hundred years. I want it to go ahead as planned, the sooner you are married the better it will be for all parties," she snapped, glowering at Ryan.

"Oh Gayle, Gayle," her mother said, as she wrapped her arms around her step-daughter. "My poor darling," she crooned. "We know how dreadful this is for you and Ryan. Faye just feels that a postponement would be the right thing to do."

Gayle pulled herself away from her mother's embrace.

"No, the wedding goes ahead," she said firmly. "Now if you would all be kind enough to leave, I need to talk to Ryan."

Faye observed the look of hope which flickered in Ryan's eyes.

Without further ado her mother picked up her handbag and coat and said, "We'll go right away darling. Come on, Carl, Faye." She beckoned them to follow.

Ryan saw them to the door, thanked them for their help, but when he returned to the lounge, Gayle had gone. When he heard the click of the lock on the bedroom door upstairs, Ryan knew there would be no talking.

34

September the first would have been Lucy Farrington's fourth birthday. As the occasion was too painful to bear, Faye's parents made arrangements to take Gayle and Ryan away from Burndale for a few days.

Faye's cottage was but a short walk to the churchyard. The rain had eased slightly, so with an armful of flowers and being the only member of the family left behind, Faye set off to place them on Lucy's grave.

As she approached the church, dedicated to St. Andrew, she stopped briefly to admire the building. It was an ancient structure built in the thirteen hundreds on the ruins of an existing church, which, according to local history was built in the early eleven hundreds. It had a magnificent clock tower, which was damaged during the Civil War, but was restored and again damaged in 1853, this time from lightning. Faye wondered how many people had passed through this churchyard en route to their worship, christening, or weddings, and indeed who had been laid to rest there. What stories these old buildings could tell if they could talk.

She was on the path which skirted the church and led to the graveyard, when a voice called out from the church porch.

"Excuse me? Miss, excuse me?"

Faye turned to greet the church minister.

"It's Miss Larson isn't it?" he enquired quietly, his hands clasped together as though in prayer.

"Yes it is."

"Oh thank goodness. I've been trying to contact your sister and your parents for the last few hours."

"Oh, well there is no one home I'm afraid, they're all away."

"Oh dear," he said unhappily.

"Why, what is it?"

"It's Mr Farrington. I'm extremely worried about him."

She looked at him, her eyes widening. "Ryan! Why?"

"Well my dear," he said, taking her by the arm. "He's been at his daughter's grave all day, he won't come away and the weather has been so inclement, I fear he will catch a chill if someone doesn't intervene." They walked around the church to the graveyard beyond. "There, see. Oh dear, he seems to be laying down now."

"Oh my goodness," she exclaimed in alarm. "Leave him to me." She gestured for the minister to stay put.

Ryan was lying prostrate amongst the masses of decaying flowers and muddy soil, his arms embracing the mound where soon a headstone would be placed.

Faye dropped to her knees and touched him gently on his back. "Ryan my love, Ryan what are you doing here? I thought you'd gone away," she said softly. "Come on Ryan you must get up,"

"No!" He sobbed uncontrollably, his shoulders heaving as he dug his hands deeper into the sodden earth.

"Ryan, you must get up, please get up," Faye pleaded.

"I want to stay with my children. It's my Lucy's birthday and I'm staying with her," he moaned pitifully.

It was beginning to rain again and Faye knew she must get him to move. "Ryan darling, come on, it's me Faye. Come home with me. This is doing no one any good. Lucy would not want her daddy to lay in a graveyard getting soaked to the skin. She'd think you had gone mad."

Ryan fell quiet for a moment, sighed deeply, lifted his head and turned to look at her. "Faye?"

"Yes it's me. Come on now, get up."

He reached out his hand for help. He'd been drinking, the stench of alcohol made Faye nauseous and she could feel him trembling as she put her arms around him and helped him to his feet.

"Can you manage to walk?"

He nodded sorrowfully and placed his muddy arm around her neck for support. It was a struggle, but Faye managed to get him out of the churchyard, along the main road, which passed by the Post Office, then down the street to her house. She saw no one en route, but she had been observed. Joanne Tubbs almost cricked her chubby neck straining to watch as they went by.

When Faye got Ryan indoors, she quickly covered her sofa with a waterproof coat and sat him down and she stood back with her fists dug firmly into her hips. She shook her head at how shocking his appearance was. He was unshaved and unwashed, his face was gaunt and his eyes were blood red and tortured with guilt. It was plain to see he had not eaten for days, but had consumed copious amounts of whisky.

A few minutes later she knelt at his feet, and offered him a steaming cup of coffee and a slice of toast.

"My poor darling Ryan, look at the state of you," Faye said, gently stroking his muddy hair. "Get this down you and then go upstairs and take a hot shower. I'll make you something warm to eat when you've finished."

He drank thirstily at the coffee, but the toast was left uneaten. Presently she led him upstairs to the bathroom, turned on the shower and began to take his dirty wet clothes off. When he was down to his underwear, she moved him towards the steaming shower. "I'll leave you to it. There's a towel on the rail, I'll be back in a while."

She ran down the stairs, picked up the phone and dialled Lyndon's phone number.

Lyndon was at his desk going through a couple of reports when the phone rang. He ignored it for a moment, and then answered it gruffly. "Lyndon Maunders".

"Hi it's me, sorry am I disturbing you?"

"No, not at all." his voice softened at the sound of Faye's voice.

"Listen darling, do you mind terribly if we don't go out

tonight? It's been a bit upsetting today what with it being Lucy's birthday."

"No, no I understand, to tell you the truth, I'm a bit busy myself so that's fine by me. I'll see you tomorrow then."

"I shall look forward to it. I love you."

"Love you too," he answered mouthing a kiss.

Faye put the receiver down and sighed deeply. She wasn't sure why she hadn't told Lyndon the truth about Ryan; maybe it was to save Ryan from any embarrassment.

Just as Lyndon placed the receiver down, he remembered that he had to pick some work up from Faye's, which he had left there the previous evening and he needed for a meeting tomorrow. He picked up the phone and rang back, but Faye was upstairs and didn't hear it ring. He let it ring several times, frowned then placed the receiver back down. He sat at his desk, tapping his pen on the ink blotter for a moment; glanced out of the window at the rain laden sky, put down his pen, grabbed his car keys and set off to Faye's.

Faye knocked quietly on the bathroom door and walked in - it was empty. She glanced in the mirror and was appalled at the sight of herself, her face was streaked with dirt and her damp hair hung limp against her face. She quickly decided to strip and take a quick shower. Five minutes later, she wrapped a towel around her wet hair, pulled her bathrobe about her and walked out onto the landing. She found Ryan lying on the bed in her spare bedroom. He had a towel wrapped around his waist and was crying into the pillow.

Faye turned to leave but as she grasped the door handle, Ryan cried out to her: "Faye... please will you hold me? I need someone to hold me."

She walked over to the bed and lay down beside him, slipping her arms gently around him. He buried his head deep into her embrace and sobbed noisily. Eventually the convulsions eased and he lifted his head and cleared his throat.

"Gayle won't speak to me Faye. She won't eat or sleep with me. If she comes into a room and I'm there she just looks at me with loathing then turns and walks back out. She was adamant that I was not to accompany her when she went away with your parents. I can't take much more. I'm hurting too. How can she begin to forgive me if she won't speak to me?" He choked back a sob. "I didn't mean to kill them. I didn't do it on purpose." He stared searchingly into Faye's eyes, looking for solace, seeking absolution for his part in the accidental death of his children.

"Hush now Ryan," she said gently to comfort him, as tears drizzled miserably down her own face. "There is nothing to forgive. It wasn't your fault. You must believe that Ryan. You answered an innocent phone call from me, which lasted no more than twenty seconds. We did not kill your children. You could have gone back in for anything, your wallet, your coat, anything. It was an accident Ryan, a tragic, terrible accident."

Lyndon stood outside Faye's cottage and tapped lightly on the front door. There was no response.

"She's in there," Joanne Tubbs announced as she walked past the front gate.

Lyndon spun round. "I beg your pardon?"

"I saw her go in with her brother-in-law about half an hour ago," she said smiling. "They looked drunk to me," she added.

Lyndon bristled slightly, tapped again then opened the door and walked in. He scanned the lounge and glanced into the kitchen. Everywhere was deserted. Then he heard voices upstairs. He paused for a moment at the foot of the stairs before climbing them very quietly.

Ryan was crying softly, and Faye held him closer. The more he cried the closer she held him to her, at one with their grief, seeking solace in each others arms. Ryan held onto Faye as though his life depended on it.

Lyndon stood motionless at the doorway to the spare room, unable to believe his own eyes. Ashen-faced he turned, stumbled blindly down the stairs, picked up the folder he had come for and slipped quietly out of the front door. He paused outside the door and sucked up great gulps of air. A moment later he glanced up and down the street, cleared his throat to compose himself and made his way to the car.

A little way down the street, slightly obscured from view, Joanne Tubbs strained her neck to observe Lyndon as he left the house. She noticed his pained countenance and a malicious gleam entered her piggy eyes.

Faye felt Ryan move at her side, but when she looked down at him, he was sleeping soundly. She carefully slipped out of the bed and left him to sleep it off.

35

Lyndon arrived early at work the next day, and his secretary Elaine knew instantly that something was amiss. When she took him his tea, she found him staring out of the window.

"There is a Mr Paul Lister on line one for you Mr Maunders. I told him you were busy, but he said he was an old friend and it was regarding the wedding."

Lyndon gave a brief dismissive sigh at the thought of the wedding then shuddered as though to rid himself of horrible thoughts. "Put him through."

"Hello old chap," Paul spoke breezily. "Sorry it's short notice and all that, but Bridget and I can't make the wedding now. Bridget's fallen and broken her hip, poor girl, she can't get about and I can't really leave her. I must say, I never thought you'd do it though. I thought you would be a bachelor all your life and I was surprised at your choice of bride. Phew, don't get me wrong she is something else, well done and all that, but I must say you must be a forgiving sort of chap."

Lyndon pursed his lips. "What do you mean forgiving?"

"Well, you know, after the dramatic fall in shares with Lemmel?"

"What about it?"

"Well, I should think you lost a deal of money, just as I did and many more I could name."

"Yes, but what has that got to do with my wedding?"

There was a long pause in the conversation. "You are marrying Faye Larson are you not?"

Lyndon sucked in a great gulp of air. "That was the plan," he answered stiffly.

"Correct me if I'm wrong, but Faye Larson is the woman who fronted Lemmel's massive perfume advertisement before she just upped sticks and disappeared. She went under the pseudonym of Cordelia Hart of course. It is the same girl I take it."

Lyndon sat in stony silence.

"I was talking to Frank Hardy from Lemmel last week, and he said she just appeared one day, brought in by Liam Knight, some young upstart in the company, and landed herself the top job. There was no rising up the ranks of the modelling ladder for her, like her predecessors. Frank insinuated….." he paused cursing himself for his own indiscretion. "….well, you know Frank and his insinuations. I don't believe a word of it. This Liam Knight fellow is a married man with three children. But what is a work place without gossip eh?" he said lightly. "Anyway, there is no doubt about it that her disappearance has caused no amount of problems for the company. What with her and the Quintana girl's accident a couple of years ago, I'm not sure they can weather this storm. Who would have believed that she had fetched up in the depths of Yorkshire and stolen the heart of a committed bachelor eh? I don't blame you though old chap, she's a real catch, well done, but you're a more forgiving man than I am, I'll tell you that. Anyway, all the best, we'll catch up sometime soon. I hope all goes well. Bye for now."

The line went dead and red mist clouded Lyndon's eyes rendering him blind with anger. It took him a full half an hour before he knew what to do. He buzzed through to Elaine. "Drop whatever you are doing and come to my office. I need you to take an extremely confidential letter," he snapped angrily.

*

Pippa arrived two days before the wedding and the reunion at Skipton railway station between the girls was a glorious affair. Tears were shed, but this time they were tears of joy. The past few weeks had been the most appalling time for everyone, and although the thought of her wedding seemed so wrong, she was urged by all to go ahead with it. How wonderful it was to sit and chat with Pippa about things other than the terrible accident which everyone else wanted to talk about. They chatted incessantly on the journey back to Burndale, as though they had never been apart these past eighteen months. Once home they quickly fell into that happy, cosy intimate position they had always shared. Pippa was dying to meet Lyndon; she had heard so much about his kind gentle ways and had almost fallen in love with him herself. Unfortunately Lyndon was on an unexpected business trip, which would keep him away until the eve of the wedding, so she resigned herself to not meeting him until the day he took her best friend to be his wife. And so they spent a blissful forty eight hours alone catching up on all the boatyard gossip, except for a brief visit from Ryan. He came embarrassed and apologetic, bearing a huge bunch of flowers, to thank Faye for her kindness. He stayed but ten minutes and was introduced to Pippa, who for once seemed very shy and quiet. When he left, Pippa watched him walk down the street until he was out of view, then she turned and said, "Flippin' 'eck Faye, he is gorgeous."

*

Lyndon rang Faye a couple of times each day while he was away, a far cry from the last relationship she had with Liam, who had barely spoken to her from one week to the next. She marvelled at the interest he was taking in the wedding arrangements. He told her he had hired the chef from their favourite restaurant to cook all the food, and that he was worried there wouldn't be enough champagne. He told her he wanted no expense spared on this wedding. Faye listened with quiet apprehension; the more champagne they ordered, the more cost her parents would have to bear. Because Faye's parents were not wealthy, they would not be able to pay for the lavish wedding befitting a local landowner, but they did want to contribute something, well, her mother did anyway. So, it was decided that they would pay for the flowers, the cars and champagne, and Lyndon would foot the bill for the rest.

The day before the wedding, Faye was in the Post Office, buying a birthday card for her Mum. Joanne Tubbs was in the Post Office and watched intently as Faye studied the poor choice of cards on offer, then when she came to pay for the one she'd chosen, Tubbs asked brightly, "Are your wedding plans coming along okay?"

"Fine thank you," Faye replied guardedly.

"Oh good," she said, forcing a smile. She almost wanted to ask Faye how her brother-in-law was, but checked herself before she did. "My son is covering the wedding for one of the national newspapers you know. He is the top reporter for the Echo," she said proudly.

Faye balked. "Reporting on my wedding?" Her heart sank. If she was to be splattered all over some seedy newspaper, then Liam would surely learn of her whereabouts. She had hoped that she'd put all that worry of him finding her behind her.

"Oh yes, this is the biggest event the Dales has seen for a long time. Mr Maunders is Yorkshire Royalty around here you know, you're a very lucky woman; everyone thought he was a confirmed bachelor. But then, most men are suckers for a pretty face," she smirked. "Oh yes this will be a big scoop for my son," she said, with a gleam in her eyes, conscious that the information was upsetting Faye. "He started as a reporter with the Dales Telegraph you know, and then went onto the Yorkshireman and naturally the Echo picked him up." She bared her small white teeth as she awaited a response.

Faye regarded her cautiously. For some reason she didn't trust Mrs Tubbs. Someone had once said to Faye about her, 'There are people in this world who will do you a good turn; then there are people like her.' Putting on her sweetest sickliest smile Faye said, "Oh well, never mind, I'm sure your son will rise back up to the ranks of a decent newspaper one day." She picked up her card and left without saying goodbye, leaving Joanne Tubbs seething with indignation.

"Well, of all the cheek!" Tubbs exclaimed, glancing at Sara Baker the postmistress.

"You asked for that," Sara answered turning her back on her.

36

September the sixth dawned bright and sunny; Faye had woken early with a mixture of excited anticipation. She and Pippa had spent the previous evening catching up and drinking white wine, whilst sat amongst the piles of boxes ready to be moved up to Orchard Hills during the wedding ceremony. The removal firm had promised to take care of everything, so she didn't have to worry about a thing.

As she lay sleepily in bed, she recalled the previous evening, their so called 'Hen night' as Pippa had called it.

"I'm so excited to meet Lyndon. From the sound of it he is perfect for you. Especially after, you know who."

Faye's face paled.

"You're not still bothered about him are you?"

"Well, I would have liked to continue keeping a low profile. I don't want to risk him coming up here to cause trouble, but unfortunately I've just learned that a newspaper reporter is going to be at the wedding."

"Oh it'll only be for the local rag won't it?"

"No, it's the Echo, and you know how they like to exaggerate the truth."

"I shouldn't worry Faye. Once you are married to Lyndon, he's not going to let a toe-rag like Liam Knight bother his wife. He does know about Liam and Lemmel, I take it?"

Faye twisted her mouth. "No."

"Oh!" Pippa's shoulders sagged. "Why not?"

"Oh Pip it's a long story, I was going to tell him, truly I was, but I found out that he had shares in Lemmel and I sort of chickened out at the last minute."

Pippa considered her for a moment and then plastered on a smile and slapped her playfully. "Oh it'll be fine. If he loves you, he'll forgive you anything."

"I hope so," she answered chinking her glass against

Faye's.

"I take it you've given up your dream of opening a café on a beach? Don't get me wrong, it's lovely up here in the Yorkshire Dales, but you are a flipping long way from the beach you know."

"I know," she sighed heavily. "I'm a long way from my beloved Cornwall as well. Oh Pippa, maybe it was just a pipe dream. One consolation though, by marrying Lyndon, I will have the time and freedom to pursue my painting career if I want. I can of course keep working at Stationery Express, but Lyndon is quite happy for me to do what I want to do. So, there is no reason why I can't still try to sell my paintings down in Cornwall. I could even have a gallery somewhere in the Yorkshire Dales." She smiled thinly. "It just won't have a beach view that's all," she added forlornly.

Pippa regarded her for a moment. "Well, as long as you are happy, and I believe you are."

Faye nodded. "I feel happy and safe here."

"Good, that is all that matters. You do realise though that you have left a trail of broken hearts behind you."

"What do you mean?"

"Well, there is Joe for a start; you know he always had a soft spot for you."

"Oh dear, poor Joe, I loved him too, but he was like a brother to me.

"And Amos, of course, he will be inconsolable when he finds out."

Faye lowered her eyes. "So you didn't tell him?"

"No, we thought we would keep it quiet, just in case Liam got wind of your wedding. I'll tell you what though, you would not recognise Amos if you saw him now. He has really cleaned up his act, and I mean clean. He showers every day, I see him walking across the boatyard to the shower block every evening after work. His clothes are fresh off the peg of Henry Lloyd and Helly Hansen. He actually looks like he's stolen Liam's wardrobe of clothes. Not only that," she emphasised. "He has only gone and bought a Range Rover, just like Liam's! I hate to admit it but he actually looks quite handsome now, I could even fancy him myself." She grinned.

Faye widened her eyes in amazement. "Where has he got his money from?"

"Well." Pippa moved closer as though to tell a secret. "He seems to have a lucrative job, on the side, if you know what I mean. He disappears on a Friday afternoon and doesn't come back until Sunday. But he's not letting on where he goes to anyone. Whatever he is doing, he is making a lot of money doing it." Pippa sighed. I think he is trying to be like Liam. He has high hopes that you will come back one day. I am dreading breaking the news to him about you and Lyndon."

Faye looked at the floor; she hated the thought of his wasted efforts. Presently she looked up and smiled at Pippa. "What about you then Pip? When are you going to settle with Mr Right?"

"Me? Oh God, I'm a lost cause, I shall probably die an old maid."

"No you won't, you will probably meet someone at my wedding and be completely swept off your feet. I shall introduce you to all the eligible bachelors I know."

"Good, I'll keep you to that."

*

Faye lay on her bed, watching the sun filter through the fine voile curtains; she could hear Pippa moving about, which was her cue to get up. She glanced at her wedding dress hung on her wardrobe door, and thought how lucky she was to have found happiness. This was a new start and she couldn't wait for it to begin.

Pippa had brewed a pot of tea by the time she entered the kitchen and together they ate a little breakfast. They both showered before making the trip to the hairdresser.

An hour before the wedding Faye sat before her dressing table to apply her make up and even though

Pippa was on hand to help, she wished with all her heart that Gayle was here to help her dress, but their estrangement seemed irrevocable. In fact Faye was amazed to learn that Gayle would be attending the wedding with Ryan. The break she had taken with her parents seemed to have calmed her nerves, but she was still not ready to forgive Ryan, and according to her mother, her brother-in-law still felt the full force of Gayle's resentment and her scathing accusations of negligence. Faye wondered if they would ever be able to repair their marriage.

"Your Mum and Dad have just arrived Faye," Pippa called up, as Marjory climbed the stairs to join her daughter.

"How are you doing darling?" Faye's mother asked, as she entered the bedroom.

"I'm ready," Faye answered turning around to face her.

"Oh my, you look beautiful my dear," she said, kissing her cheek. "The car is here. I'm leaving now with Pippa. Do you have everything you need?"

Faye smiled. "I will have in an hour."

As her mother stood at the door she smiled and cocked her head slightly.

Faye looked at her quizzically. "What is it?" she asked.

Her mother laughed slightly and shook her head. "I was flicking through an old magazine at the hairdressers and there was a girl who looked just like you in one of the advertisements. She was a brassy blond though, obviously came out of a bottle, I can tell a mile off you know. But she looked remarkably like you facially, it was uncanny. Oh now what did they call her? It was Colette or something, no Cordelia that's it. Have you seen it?"

Faye swallowed the lump which had formed in her throat and laughed nervously. "No, I haven't," she said quickly.

"Well you are without doubt as beautiful as her, if not more so. I'll see you at the ceremony," she said blowing a kiss.

A quarter of an hour later, to Faye's astonishment a horse drawn carriage arrived to pick up Faye and her stepfather.

"I hope I'm not paying for this Faye. I said I would pay for the taxis - I didn't think you were going to this expense," he said stiffly.

"I'm sure you're not, Lyndon must have ordered it as a surprise."

He grumbled unconvincingly. "Come on then, let's get going." He gave her a look of disapproval as she adjusted her headdress. "Did you have to plaster all that muck on your face? You look like a painted wh…" He stopped before he said the word.

Faye looked up at him unable to keep the hurt from her eyes. No matter what the occasion, he always tried to spoil the day with his unpleasantness.

The wedding was to be held in the grounds of Orchard Hills, where two huge marquees had been erected; one for the ceremony and the other for the reception. As she waited for the photographer to take a few shots before the ceremony, Faye glanced into the reception marquee and was stunned at the grandeur of the place. In the far corner a string quartet rehearsed quietly, while waiters placed trays of glasses on a trestle table ready to fill with expensive champagne. The room was huge, and housed sixty tables dressed in pure white table linen and cut-glass crystal. Garlands of flowers draped the walls of the marquee with matching table decorations which filled the air with a sumptuous sweet fragrance.

Lyndon's favourite chef, Cecil Dakin, had been brought in at enormous expense to cook the wedding breakfast, which consisted of consommé, seafood and avocado platter, followed by a choice of fresh salmon, or seared beef, and lemon syllabub to finish.

This all felt too much for Faye, she had only wanted a simple wedding, but Lyndon had insisted on a much grander affair, but she had no idea it would be this grand.

At the entrance to the ceremony marquee, she was again overwhelmed by the scent of flowers.

Carl yanked Faye's arm. "Just a minute young lady, when I offered to pay for the flowers, I meant the bouquets you know. I hope I'm not paying for all this lot?" her father asked anxiously as his eyes scanned the inside of the marquee.

"Shush, please stop worrying," Faye answered uneasily. She looked towards Pippa. "Look at all these flowers," she mouthed.

Pippa nodded. "I know; people are sneezing like mad in there. Have you seen the reception marquee, there are twice as many in there, the smell is almost overpowering," she whispered.

The music started and very slowly Faye moved towards her husband-to-be, trying to ignore the sneezing and sniffles as she passed by the hundred or so guests.

At the Altar she looked up at Lyndon, but he did not turn to look back. A very small niggle in the pit of her stomach began to manifest itself. Faye nervously turned and handed her bouquet to Pippa who smiled warmly back.

The vicar stood before them and the ceremony began.

"Dearly beloved, we are gathered together here in the sight of God, and in the face of this congregation, to join together this Man and this Woman in holy matrimony."

As the words were spoken, Faye continued to glance at Lyndon, but he remained stony faced, looking out over the vicar's shoulder. Something was wrong, she knew it. She began to tremble and her mouth felt dry as the adrenalin began to pump round her veins.

"Faye Larson, will you take Lyndon William Maunders to be your lawful wedded husband? Will you cherish and respect him, and be loving, faithful and loyal to him throughout your marriage?"

Faye looked anxiously at Lyndon, but still their eyes did

not meet. "I, I will," she stammered.

"Lyndon William Maunders, will you take Faye Larson to be your lawful wedded wife? Will you cherish and respect her, and be loving, faithful and loyal to her throughout your marriage?"

"I'm afraid not, no," he said.

Faye's eyes darted between Lyndon and the vicar as a gasp travelled amongst the guests seated.

The vicar looked up. "I beg your pardon?"

"I said no, I'm afraid not," he answered, and then turned to address the congregation. "You see, this woman, completely and utterly stole my heart when I fully believed I would never marry. I believed I would spend my life with this beautiful and intelligent woman, I also believed that she would have my children. But, Faye has a secret ladies and gentlemen, that I would like to share with you all."

Faye swallowed hard and a feeling of dread began to sweep through her body.

"Faye Larson is the face of 'Guinevere', from the Lemmel advertisements. Aren't you darling? Sorry should that be Cordelia Hart? That's your working name isn't it? I believe quite a lot of the congregation will have lost a deal of money after you walked out on Lemmel."

There was a buzz of chatter between the women guests and Faye bit down on her lip until she could taste blood.

Lyndon smiled down at Faye and seemed to enjoy her embarrassment. "Anyway, after that little revelation ladies and gentlemen, I have to tell you that Faye has another little secret, a dirty little secret at that, haven't you Faye?"

Faye began to feel sick to the pit of her stomach as she turned her head to look up at Lyndon and a hush fell on the wedding guests.

"Would you like to tell your family and all our guests about your grubby little affair with your brother-in-law?"

"What?" Faye said incredulously.

"Oh come, come dear girl, you can hardly deny it. I saw

you and Ryan only a few days ago with my own eyes, tucked up in bed, all very cosy. Tell me I'm not wrong? " He cocked his head to one side as though to wait for a response as Faye stood open- mouthed. "I thought not," he said with a wry smile. "Oh, I would just like to say thank you for the gifts, I'm sure Faye will endeavour to return them all to you soonest. That's the least she can do. I bid you all good day. I shall send you the bills for the wedding Faye, via your solicitor and as for all your *things*, you'll find them back at the removal depot," he said with a crooked smile. He walked out of the marquee, nodding acknowledgments to his stunned friends. Lucinda Hervey quickly followed.

Faye looked at the guests; they were all staring back at her in astonishment. She glanced at Gayle and could feel the hatred oozing out of her eyes, then at Ryan's stunned expression and closed her eyes. There was a slight murmur amongst the guests, but Faye could not bring herself to open her eyes again. She heard rather than saw Gayle alight from her chair, then felt a stinging blow as Gayle smacked her resoundingly across her face. The guests started to leave in a hurried fashion, and the waiters who had gathered by the door stood in military precision with their mouths gaping wide open.

Faye turned to her step-father as he began to speak.

"You will pay for every penny of this wedding, do you hear me girl? You have brought such shame on your family. You are a liar and a cheat, you're despicable. I never want to lay eyes on you again. Do I make myself clear? How could you do this to your sister? After all she has been through. How could you be so evil? I'm finished with you. Come on Marjory," he said, dragging his shocked wife to her feet.

For the second time in her life, Faye felt as though she had stepped out of the real world into a nightmare. She tugged at her veil and dropped it on the floor, as one by one everybody disappeared from the marquee, leaving only

Pippa and a shell-shocked Ryan, sitting amongst the debris of her wedding day.

"Blimey," Pippa said putting a comforting arm around Faye's shoulder. "What was all that about?"

"Faye, I'm so sorry," Ryan's voice wavered.

The soft summer breeze flapped lazily at the marquee and Faye sat down on the altar steps and closed her eyes as if trying to clear her mind of the demons which haunted her. Presently she cleared her throat and in a low husky voice she said, "You must tell Lyndon it isn't true Ryan, you must tell him what really happened."

"I will, but I doubt he'll believe me!" He buried his face in his hands.

Faye swallowed hard and cleared her throat. "It was so innocent, I was only comforting you." Her voice was almost inaudible.

They sat in silence for a long time, both trying to come to terms with what was left of their lives.

Presently Ryan said, "You never told me you were that woman on the Guinevere ads."

Faye looked at him incredulously. "Oh shut up," she snapped. With a rustle of silk taffeta, Faye rose from where she sat, and walked into the reception marquee to the table of unopened wedding presents. Aware that many eyes were upon her, she fingered the cards and ribbons which bound them. Once again her life was in ruins.

Ryan came to stand beside her, placing his hand on her shoulder. "Come on Faye, I'll take you home," he said just as a camera flash went off behind them. "What the bloody hell…" They both turned and the camera flashed again, momentarily blinding them both. The spotty faced reporter beamed with glee as he turned and ran from the marquee.

Faye's knees crumpled underneath and she knelt into a cloud of silk taffeta. Ryan crouched down to help her back on her feet, but she brushed him away. "Just go Ryan, just leave me alone, please," she said trembling.

*

Faye and Pippa arrived back at her house by taxi. She walked wearily through the front door and bent to pick up the four letters which lay on the doormat. Three were invoices for the wedding, addressed to her father, which he had wasted no time in pushing through her letter box. The other letter puzzled her; it was obviously from work as she recognised the stationery. She flipped it over in her fingers a couple of times and then opened it. It was dated September the second and read:

Miss Faye Larson
Riverside Cottage, Burndale
North Yorkshire.

Dear Miss Larson,

Due to the delicate nature of recent events, I think it would be advisable for you to relinquish your post with our company forthwith. I would of course welcome your resignation and will endeavour to supply any future employers with good references regarding your work with us here, but should you contest my request I will not hesitate to terminate your employment with us.

Yours sincerely
Lyndon Maunders
Managing Director
Dictated, and signed by

Faye could not believe her eyes. She could imagine Elaine Elmer's elation at being asked to type this letter, as she surely must have, as Lyndon could hardly turn the computer on, never mind type anything on it. Oh how she must have relished every word she typed.

It all made sense now, why Lyndon had suddenly taken an interest in the wedding preparations. That is why he had insisted on bringing in a top chef for the reception and why he had ordered all those extra flowers and bottles of champagne! He knew exactly what he was doing; he was going to make her pay financially for her so called indiscretion. Well she'd see about that. She would see her solicitor on Monday and see if she could make some sort of counter claim towards him.

Pippa and Faye spent the night mulling over the dreadful day. Faye had explained what had happened with Ryan, and Pippa had been a tower of strength to Faye. Without her she would have surely floundered.

"I don't want to leave you tomorrow Faye," Pippa said in earnest before they went to bed.

"I'll be okay Pip, don't worry. I'll drop you off at the station in the morning and then make a decision as to what to do."

"Why don't you come back with me?" Pippa pleaded. "You can stay at mine for as long as you want."

"No, I have things to sort out."

She slept fitfully that night. Sleep was punctuated with long spells of wakefulness as she pondered her future. The house was re-let now, and she had no idea where she was going to live after the house keys were handed over on Monday, and she wondered briefly if she should call a halt to the Let, but the thought of living in this village now was intolerable. Everybody would know by the morning, so she knew she could not stay.

So it was that very reluctantly Pippa left the next morning. Faye drove her to Skipton railway station to catch the early train back to Cornwall. After an emotional farewell, she drove back to the house and was shocked to find a group of reporters milling around her front garden. Parking her car out of the way she sneaked through the back gate to the rear of River Cottage. Once inside she began to silently gather her belongings together. Thankfully she hadn't opened her curtains, so was able to move about quite freely. Occasionally her letterbox would be pushed open and one of the reporters shouted her name. On one occasion a tabloid newspaper was thrust through, causing Faye to leap back out of view. Carefully she bent to retrieve the paper from her doormat, and a cold shiver ran through her body as she read the headline.

CAMELOT COMES TO BURNDALE
But this is no fairytale

In a modern day twist of the Arthurian legend, the lavish wedding of Faye Larson, a top cosmetic model, who fronts the highly successful beauty advertisement 'GUINEVERE', for 'Lemmel, London,' to her 'KING ARTHUR', Lyndon Maunders the Yorkshire entrepreneur, was halted yesterday, when her affair with her own brother-in-law, a modern day 'LANCELOT' Ryan Farrington was exposed at the Altar.

Miss Larson, who works under the pseudonym of 'Cordelia Hart,' met Lyndon Maunders, the Managing Director of Stationery Express, shortly after her departure from the cosmetic company Lemmel, London. A reliable source informed reporter Kevin Tubbs of the Echo, that Miss Larson arrived back at her family home at Burndale, North Yorkshire, after tiring of a year long affair with Lemmel's Advertising director, Liam Knight, a married man with three children.

It was also reported that sources at Lemmel, London headquarters were very interested to learn about the whereabouts of Miss Larson, who is in breach of contract with them.

The alleged affair between Miss Larson and Mr Farrington came as shocking news to the residents of the small Yorkshire village, as Ryan Farrington and his wife Gayle (Faye Larson's step-sister) had very recently suffered the terrible tragedy of losing both of their children in a drowning accident. A resident, who would like to remain anonymous, hinted that the accident happened whilst Mr Farrington and Miss Larson were chatting on the telephone. It was thought the affair had been going on for some time.

The article continued onto the second and third pages but Faye was too shocked to carry on reading. This was dreadful. This was the ultimate violation of her privacy as headlines all across the country proclaimed her guilt. Overnight Faye had become a monster. She quickly gathered her belongings together, threw them into the backyard, locked the door and stumbled down the back street. As she approached the back gate, she heard her neighbour's voice calling her a bitch, and then felt herself being pelted with eggs. By the time she reached the car she was covered in yellow slime. She threw her bags into the back seat, jumped behind the wheel and started the car. Another egg hit and smeared the windscreen, but there was no time to stop and clean it, as her rear-view mirror caught the group of reporters running in hot pursuit behind her. Breaking the thirty mile an hour speed limit, she drove quickly away from the life she knew, once again.

She checked into a motel on the outskirts of Skipton and sat motionless in the soulless room as she took stock of her life. Outside in the motel car park, a black Audi stood in quiet vigil, its occupant settled down to a long night, watching and waiting.

37

Liam Knight woke with a start to the sound of his mobile phone ringing incessantly.

He glanced first at the clock then at his wife lying beside him. "Who the hell is phoning me at seven on a Sunday morning?" he grumbled, as he flicked the sheets away from his naked body. "Hello," he said trying to keep the anger from his voice.

"Knight. Get your arse to the office now!"

"What?" Liam said, trying to distinguish the voice on the other end.

"Now!" the voice barked again and the phone went dead.

Liam stared at the phone still trying to register why Angus Fox the MD wanted to see him in the office on a Sunday. He blew out an angry sigh, pulled on his black jeans and pullover and picked up the keys for his Range Rover.

*

After an uneventful journey across London, Liam walked into Angus Fox's office only to have a copy of the Sunday Echo newspaper thrust into his hands. He glanced down at the paper and saw the picture of Faye on the front page.

"We're ruined," Angus said, trying to control his temper. "You and your slut have ruined us."

Liam scanned the story, hardly able to take on board what he was reading.

"Have you nothing to say for yourself?" Angus snapped.

"Well, I can't be responsible for what she gets up to. This isn't my fault; you can't blame me for what she does."

"Oh but I can. I don't care what she does in her spare time. I don't care how many children she drowns or how many lives she ruins by her indiscretion, but when my company is brought into disrepute by some no good bit of skirt that you just happened to be jumping, then I'm afraid I can't trust your judgment anymore. I've been onto our financial advisors and they expect the shares to plummet even further first thing tomorrow. We pinned all our hopes on this product and now we are finished, as are you my friend. You can clear your desk now. You're fired."

"But, but surely we can do something," he pleaded. "Let me see what I can do. Now we know where she is, I'm sure...."

Angus stopped him mid sentence as he banged his fist on the table. "I've told you what to do; I want you out of my sight."

Liam sat in the car park and glanced again at the damning article in the sleazy tabloid, and it was on his second reading that he saw his name mentioned. His eyes narrowed.

"Oh my God, you bitch!" he spat angrily. It was all there, every detail of how Faye had become the face of 'Guinevere'. "How could you do this to me? After all I did for you!" he yelled.

When he pulled onto his drive, he saw the figure of his wife's best friend Pat Jennings, scurrying down the driveway. She was a sour faced woman at the best of times and she always seemed to hold Liam in contempt, and today was no exception. The look she flashed him alerted him to the fact that his wife now knew about his affair with Faye. He took a deep breath and walked into the war zone.

Georgina was weeping in the sitting room; the children were sat to the side of her comforting her. "I want a divorce." She sniffed through the tears.

"Do you now?" he answered arrogantly, as he walked casually up the stairs.

"Yes I do." She got up from the sofa and yelled at him from the foot of the stairs. "And I want you out of this house." He made no reply. "Do you hear me?" she sobbed again.

Liam appeared at the head of the stairs. "I should think the whole street heard you," he said calmly, as he descended the stairs.

She brushed away her tears sniffing noisily. "Are you leaving?"

"Briefly," he smiled wryly. "But I'll be back."

"Well I don't want you back," she screamed furiously.

"Tough," he said, as he left the house.

"Go, go on. Go to your whore," she screamed from behind the front door.

Liam unlocked the car, wrenched the door open, and jammed the keys into the ignition. He glanced again at the newspaper, slammed the car into gear and headed towards Yorkshire.

*

When Joe collected Pippa from the train station it was clear that everyone in Gweek knew what had happened as he showed her the front page headlines. When he dropped her off, Amos was waiting for her.

"Is it true?"

"Which part of it are you referring to Amos?" she answered curtly.

He bristled. "Well, I'm sure most of what they said in the paper is a lie. But is it true that she was dumped at the altar?"

"If you must know, yes, and that bastard is going to take her to the cleaners." She stopped, when she realised she was saying too much and turned to walk away.

Amos stood for a moment, and then he decided what he must do.

*

Burndale was a hive of gossip that Sunday. The media interest had escalated and the village saw hundreds of on-lookers trying to catch a glimpse of the scarlet woman.

The Red Lion along with the Post Office had been doing a roaring trade all day. Joanne Tubbs had just sat down outside her cottage with a cup of tea, and had just taken a large bite of chocolate cake when yet another stranger walked up to her.

"Yes," she muffled trying desperately to swallow the contents of her mouth.

The man looked at her with disdain and said in a deadpan voice, "I'm looking for Faye Larson."

"You and hundreds of other people," Tubbs replied giving a throaty laugh.

He scowled arrogantly. "Where can I find her?" he said flatly.

Indignant she answered, "How the hell should I know, I'm not her keeper. She's probably skulked off somewhere by now. She certainly hasn't been at her house since early morning." The stranger blew an angry sigh and turned to leave. "Err just a moment." Tubbs liked the look of this man; he looked a little sinister. He was just the sort of person Faye Larson deserved to be pursued by. "I don't think she is at home at the moment, but you could try Mr and Mrs Larson's house - it's just over there, up the hill, number nine, and if she's not there, try the Farringtons' house, just up there to your left." She gave a wry smile, knowing full well he wouldn't be welcome at either of the places. "Oh and if you want to leave me your name and number, I'll be more than happy to let you know when she surfaces again. She can't have gone far, she lives here, she has nowhere else to go," she said, with a glint in her piggy eyes.

The man shot a steely look at the woman, took a pen out of the inside pocket of his jacket and scribbled a mobile phone number on a piece of paper.

"If she turns up, you can phone me on this number," he said, flicking the paper towards her, as he walked away.

She glanced at the number and shouted out to him, "And you are?"

But the stranger left without revealing his name.

*

Faye was tired and drawn as she sat silently in the soulless solicitor's office on Monday morning. She could barely focus on what her solicitor was saying due to lack of sleep.

"I'll need some kind of contact address for you Miss Larson," he was saying. "Miss Larson? Miss Larson?"

She shook the weariness from her head. "Sorry, you were saying?" she said sleepily.

"I'll need a contact address," he said softly.

Faye nodded. "I'll be in touch as soon as I know."

"Good. Well, leave everything with me Miss Larson. I'll see if we can recover some of the money towards the reception. I'll write to your father and get him to forward all accounts to me. I think with this letter you received from Mr Maunders, and because of the date on it, we can prove he ordered more flowers etcetera for the wedding, after he found out about….after what he thought he had seen," he corrected himself. "Then we may be able to recoup some of the money owing from him. If not, well, do you have any capital?"

She nodded unhappily at the thought of her 'Café' nest egg. "I have some money of my own yes, but I'm not sure it will be enough, the wedding was a grand affair."

"Well, let's see how it goes. There is always bankruptcy."

"Oh what a happy thought," Faye said tearfully.

"I'm sorry." He smiled thinly.

Faye stood up. "Well, thank you so much for your time, you have been very kind."

The solicitor observed her carefully. She certainly didn't come across as the cold heartless monster the tabloids were reporting. Still, you never know what people are really like. "My pleasure," he replied, holding his hand out to shake.

Faye sighed heavily and as she approached the door the solicitor said casually, "What are you going to do now?"

Faye shook her head. "I really don't know," she

answered with all honesty. What could she do? She was hounded by the press, fired from her job, deprived of all public freedom, she had no choice but to go and hide somewhere again.

With no plan and nowhere to go, she headed to the nearest petrol station and filled her car. She glanced at the boxes in the back of the car that she had picked up from the removal people. Once again her life had reverted to a car full of possessions and nowhere to put them. Would she ever settle somewhere permanently she wondered? As she pulled out of the service station, the Black Audi was only moments behind.

38

It was mid morning. The clear blue September sky winked periodically through the dense branches of the trees which flanked the road, which itself had become uneven and carpeted in a thick layer of fallen leaves. Faye brought her car to a halt just outside the tiny hamlet of Castallack, a few miles west of Penzance. She slumped forward onto the steering wheel and sighed with relief; she was physically, emotionally and mentally exhausted.

When she left Yorkshire, Faye had no idea where she was going; she just knew she had to get away, far away. With a tank full of petrol she headed for the M6 motorway. On the services on the M5 she spoke briefly to her mother. A short, curt, strained conversation ensued where she tried to explain what had really happened that day. Her mother was terse initially, but seemed to soften as she said her goodbyes to her daughter. She didn't say where she was going, for she didn't really know herself. But knowing how persistent the gutter press could be in hounding a person, Faye knew she would have to melt into the background for a very long time.

After another sleepless night in a motel just outside Exeter, Faye rose early and pulled up in Penzance car park at seven-thirty. The sea was calm and an array of boats bobbed gently in the harbour. She selected three hours in the parking machine and headed for the nearest café where she devoured a bacon sandwich and a creamy cappuccino.

Somehow the very fact she was back in Cornwall eased her troubled mind. Her cares and worries of the last couple of days seemed to peel away with the sound of gulls and the gentle lap of the sea against the harbour wall. She needed to rent somewhere and she needed it quick. She checked her watch: eight twenty-five. Hopefully she could find a letting agent in town open.

The events of the last few days and the long drive were taking their toll on Faye, but her journey wasn't over yet. She managed to rent a small cottage, well away from the main road, snuggled into lush green woodland, about half a mile from Lamorna cove. The agent had said the cottage was a 'little tired' and hadn't been lived in for some time, and seemed delighted that Faye agreed to the tenancy and took it without seeing it. At a tiny hamlet called Drift, she pulled over, checked her map then drove a little further, stopping when she saw the sign for Lamorna. Reaching over to the passenger seat she picked up the house details, and traced her finger across the directions she had followed. She sighed in relief, if she wasn't mistaken it must be around here somewhere. She got out, stretched her legs, and set off in search of a wooden plaque which bore the house name 'Willow End', which, the details said, should locate the entrance to the drive of her cottage.

"Good afternoon. Can I be of some assistance?"

Faye jumped, and spun around to find a tall handsome fair-haired man, standing behind her.

His kind face smiled. "I'm so sorry; I didn't mean to startle you." He hesitated for a moment, noting the fear in her eyes, and then said softly, "Oh dear. Are you all right?"

Faye flushed violently. "Yes err.. Yes I'm fine." She stumbled over her words. "I was just looking for something. I hadn't realised there was anyone about." She took a deep breath, cleared her throat to regain her composure. "I was looking for 'Willow End'."

"I see," he murmured. "Well then I think I can help you. This is 'Willow End'." He gestured towards the run down cottage at the end of an unkempt drive, then leaned forward and picked the mossy plaque off the top of the wall to show her.

Faye's heart sank momentarily. Well what did she expect for the price she was paying? She turned back towards the stranger and gave him a rather gloomy smile. "Thank you," she whispered.

He nodded courteously. "My pleasure," he replied and then he was gone.

Faye parked the car with some caution on the slippery moss covered driveway. At the front door she struggled for a moment with the lock, pulling and pushing the handle as instructed by the letting agency until the key clicked into position and the front door swung open. The front room was cold and uninviting, the air hung dank and musty and Faye crinkled her nose disdainfully. She stood silently for a moment as tears pricked her eyes, then shook the emotion away and began to gather her belongings from the car.

Three hours later, she had thrown open all the windows and aired the place. She'd lit a fire with wood and coal she had found in the shed and cleaned the house from top to bottom. Once again she stood in the front room, hands resting on her hips while she observed her surroundings. She gave a deep satisfied sigh; there was just one more thing to do now. She grabbed the chemist bag from the sofa and made for the bathroom. Slowly and methodically she cut her rich auburn waist length hair to her shoulders, and smothered it with a very dark brown hair dye. An hour later, her dark hair hung in two unflattering stumpy bunches, and she was dressed in a pair of faded jeans, trainers and an overlarge sweatshirt. Faye studied her reflection in the pitted mirror at the back of the bathroom door. Would the hair cut and dye disguise the fact that she was Faye Larson the face of 'Guinevere'? Would anyone recognise her from the newspaper? Hopefully she would be just a five day wonder and people would forget all about her.

39

A week after the wedding, Pippa received a rather unexpected phone call. The office was quiet and Pippa had just walked back from the cafeteria with a coffee and slice of home made lemon drizzle cake. She had just taken a bite when the call came through.

"Hello," she muffled.

The gentleman asked, "May I speak to Pippa please?"

With one last gulp she answered, "Speaking. How can I help you?"

There was a pause for a moment then the caller cleared his voice. "Pippa, hello it's Ryan Farrington here, forgive the intrusion, but I wondered if you knew where Faye was."

Pippa remained silent, unsure of what to say. She did know, but she was under strict instructions not to reveal her whereabouts to anyone.

"It's just that I want to know that she is safe and well......that's all." There was a desperate plea in his voice.

"As far as I know Ryan, she is okay, but I can't tell you anymore, I'm sorry."

Ryan sighed with relief. "That's fine I just needed to know that she was okay."

Pippa recalled his handsome good looks and couldn't resist asking, "What about you Ryan, how are you bearing up?"

He gave a short sharp laugh. "Things have been better, I must say. I was sacked from my job. I received the same letter Faye had received from Lyndon." He laughed again. "At least it's made me change career direction."

"What are you doing now?" For some reason she wanted him to stay on the line. She loved the sound of his voice, even though it was punctuated with sadness.

"Well, I'm a marine mechanic by trade, so I am back

mending barges on the Leeds-Liverpool canal temporarily. It's not too bad. I'm based in Skipton, in the canal basin. It's not a bad place to work."

"Did you try to explain to Lyndon what had really happened?"

"Yes, I sent him a letter when he wouldn't take my calls. He probably ripped it up, because I haven't heard from him."

"And what about Gaye?"

"Gayle," he corrected.

"Sorry, what about her, did you explain?"

"I tried. I told her through the closed door of our bedroom." He remembered standing with his face against the cold painted door, his cheeks hot with emotion as he poured his heart out to her.

"And…?"

"I'm still awaiting a response," he answered sadly.

"I am so sorry Ryan. I hope everything works out for you."

Her words were sincere and they tugged at his aching heart. He sighed heavily. "Thank you."

"I'm always on the end of the phone Ryan you know, if you need a chat." She had no idea why she had said that, but as soon as she had she was pleased with herself.

"Thank you Pippa, I appreciate that. Look, if you see Faye or speak to her, tell her…." He paused. "Just tell her, I'm so very sorry."

"I'll tell her Ryan, I'll tell her."

As she put the phone down Owen breezed into the office.

"Just to warn you Pippa, Liam Knight will be a live-aboard now."

Pippa's face dropped. "No."

"It seems so. Between you and me, I think his wife has thrown him out. What with all that nonsense in the newspaper last week. He's lost his job as well from what I can gather."

Pippa was aghast.

"He asked me if there was any work going. He said he'd do anything, sweep the yard, general labouring, that sort of thing."

"Really?" she said in wide-eyed astonishment.

"Yes," he answered with a gleam in his eye. "Oh how the mighty have fallen, eh?"

"You're not going to give him a job are you?" Pippa asked incredulously.

"What do you think? I don't even want him in the boatyard to tell you the truth."

"You and me both," she declared. "Oh dear," she fiddled with her pen. "Faye will never come and visit now he is back in the village."

"What is the news on Faye?"

"It's not good. She's had to leave Burndale because of reporters and that bloody wedding is literally going to bankrupt her."

"You're kidding?"

"I'm not. Lyndon Maunders has taken her to the cleaners over this."

Owen shook his head knowingly. "She should never have left us, I told her at the time. Where is she now?"

Pippa shook her head, walls had ears and she daren't tell anyone where Faye was. She had promised her faithfully. "I don't know," she lied. "I think she is keeping a low profile somewhere."

"Well, there is always a job for her here, tell her that won't you?"

"Huh, that's not going to happen with Liam Knight in residence is it?"

"Well, he might not be here for long. He is on a warning already."

As Pippa walked out of the boatyard that evening, Liam stopped her at the gate.

"What do you want?" she snapped.

"Come, come Pippa, that isn't very friendly is it?" He

gave a sardonic smile.

Pippa could feel the adrenalin begin to pump and she hated this feeling. This was her village, the place where she had been born, it annoyed her that he was making her feel uncomfortable. "You are no friend of mine," she snapped viciously.

"No, I never was, was I? You never really liked me did you, Pippa?" He bared his teeth slightly.

Finding an inner courage, she hissed, "And with good reason don't you think."

He laughed in her face.

Twilight was falling now but she could see the cool anger in Liam's eyes. Pippa stepped around him and made to walk away but he caught her sleeve.

"Where is she?" he growled.

Pippa wrenched free of his grip.

"She owes me."

"She owes you *nothing*!" Pippa spat the words venomously at him.

"I'll bloody find her you know, I'll bloody well make her pay for ruining my life."

Pippa's eyes narrowed. "You've got a bloody nerve." Her voice was high and filled with rage. "If your life is ruined, it's your doing and nothing to do with Faye. You deserve everything you get you despicable bastard. I'm going to make sure everyone in this boatyard knows about you. I'm going to tell them what you did, and, what you have just said. You have no friends here." She could hear him laughing at her as she stormed out of the gate.

40

For the first couple of weeks Faye enjoyed the solitude of 'Willow End'. Most days, come rain or shine she took the footpath up Lamorna Valley and out on the coast path until she came to Boscawen Point far above the boulder-strewn beach of St Loy, where she could watch the soft crash of the surf upon the rocks. She really didn't mind being alone, no one could hurt her here, she felt safe and very content as a recluse.

Faye shared the wooded valley with a couple of artists. Greg and Simon had a large airy studio about fifty yards from Faye's house. Simon, Faye learned, was the handsome stranger she'd met the day she moved in. He and Greg had called at 'Willow End' later that same evening, to introduce themselves briefly and offered to help with her unpacking, which Faye thanked them for, but refused gratefully. They gave her a couple of weeks in which to settle down in her new home before they knocked on the door again, this time bearing a couple of bottles of wine.

Reluctantly Faye invited them in, but to her delight found them both to be extremely amiable company.

Faye learned that Greg and Simon were a couple and had been together for almost three years.

They told her that they had met at Falmouth Art School then lived for a short time up country and though they never did anything to offend anyone, they had suddenly found themselves outed and ridiculed for their sexuality, which they both found hurtful and offensive. They uprooted their life and headed back to the bohemian lifestyle of Cornwall, where Greg had been born and where they could be very private and live quietly in peace, without prejudice. Faye had never felt more comfortable with anyone in her whole life as she felt with Greg and

Simon. She instantly adored them both.

As they chatted, Faye observed her guests with great interest. Greg was tall and dark, with a proud bone structure, sharp nose and grey eyes. He had an abundance of dark curls, which he constantly twisted around his long bony fingers, possibly a nervous tendency Faye thought.

Simon was equally as tall, but more muscular. He had fair-haired handsome features, blue eyes, a kind mouth and a soft melodious voice, which Faye felt she could listen to all day long.

Both Greg and Simon equally enjoyed Faye's company and as they left that evening in a flurry of kisses and hugs, she was invited to come and look around their studio the next day, which Faye accepted with relish.

To say she was amazed at how beautiful the studio apartment was would have been an understatement. The image she had conjured up in her mind of two artists living together was not what was before her as she walked through the door into the kitchen.

All around her shone of white marble and highly polished granite worktops. The room then led off into a large spacious living room, which had a cool, calm feel about it, as light flooded in from large south facing windows and skylights. The walls were white and high, on which hung huge colourful canvases. In contrast, a rough granite shelf ran the full length of the living room, providing a hearth for the fire, and there was a display space which housed several fine pieces of sculpture. Two large sofas flanked the open fire, and the sanded floorboards were dressed with large cream rugs throughout. Faye noticed there was no clutter and everything was 'magazine shoot' perfect.

To the far side of the living room were two bedrooms, and a working studio overlooked the sea.

"Wow! This place is fabulous," Faye exclaimed, as she placed her handbag on one of the sofas. "Wow. It's just fabulous!" she reiterated.

The men smiled at each other as Faye began to study the paintings on display. In the studio there was a mixture of both Simon and Greg's paintings exhibited. Greg's work was bold and fresh and had a vibrancy about them that grasped attention. Simon on the other hand had a fragile confidence about his work, which in Faye's view was beautiful and feminine. There was no doubt about it; their work matched their personas perfectly.

As Faye moved to inspect the paintings in the living room, she stopped short when she came to a familiar painting.

"Oh my goodness, I don't believe it!" She clasped her hands to her face. "This one is by Nathaniel Prior. I love his work," she exclaimed passionately as she examined the painting of a beautiful woman sitting in a window seat, reading a letter. She felt she knew this painting intimately. She glanced at Greg, beaming with delight. "It's called 'Love Letter' isn't it?"

Greg nodded that it was.

Faye turned back to the painting. "Whenever I see this painting it makes me believe that the woman in the picture is so profoundly in love with the person who wrote the letter she is reading. It's as though you can feel her happiness emitting from the painting. It's so real, don't you think?"

She turned to Greg, eager for his agreement. Greg smiled and nodded in response.

"Oh listen to me, going on," she said, slightly embarrassed at her passionate outburst. "I'm no art buff, but Nathaniel Prior is one of my favourite artists, apart from you two of course." She winked cheekily. Her eyes fell upon the painting again. "Oh but this painting in particular is my favourite, and of course the one called, 'Mother's Love', that one is truly lovely - have you seen it?"

Greg, clearly amused, glanced swiftly at Simon then took Faye by the hand and led her to the far wall. There he presented the painting, 'Mother's Love'. Faye was astounded. The painting depicted an elegant woman asleep on a bed with a child protected in the crook of her arm, also asleep.

"I can't believe it!" She gasped. "This is so bizarre, to actually find myself here with someone who has these two paintings in one room. Just a moment," she said, examining the painting close up, "..this is an original." She quickly walked back to the first painting. "So is this! When I saw these paintings in a Truro gallery some time back, it stated that they weren't for sale. How come you managed to buy them?"

Greg laughed. "I didn't, Nathaniel gave them to me."

Faye looked both astonished and envious. "Wow," she said incredulously. "Why did he do that?"

Greg moistened his lips slightly. "The woman in both of the paintings is my mother," Greg said calmly. "I am the child in 'Mother's Love'!"

Faye paused for a moment. "So, Nathaniel Prior is...."

"My father, yes," Greg answered, finishing her sentence.

Faye clapped her hands together joyfully. "I can't believe my luck. I make two new friends and find that Nathaniel Prior is the father of one of them!"

The smile fell from Greg's face. "Well don't get too excited, I'm afraid my father and I are estranged," he answered sadly.

Her hands flew to her mouth. "Oh, I'm so sorry, that was very insensitive of me."

He shook his head slowly. "It doesn't matter; it was a while ago now. I've sort of got used to it," he said evenly.

Faye looked deep into his eyes; they held a sad emptiness within them. "And there is no hope that relations can be mended?" she inquired softly.

"Not unless I stop being gay, and I don't think that's an option," he answered with a shrug of his shoulders. "I haven't seen him for over two years; in fact it was just after

Mum died when we quarrelled. I feel terrible about the estrangement, but it was his doing, not mine. But I can't help wondering if he is all right living alone in Zennor. I'm not even sure if he still paints. Mum was his inspiration."

"That's terrible, have you tried to speak to him?"

Greg smiled thinly. "Yes, I sent a letter a few months after our initial estrangement, but never received a reply. I had hoped to see him at the exhibition Lemon Gallery held, but in the end I thought it was better that I stayed away. Anyway, there is no point in dwelling on things that can't be fixed." Greg glanced back at the painting again and smiled. "These paintings are part of a set of five you know? Dad has the other three; they are part of a collection he called, 'Love Chronicles'. This is the first one," he said, pointing to 'Love Letter'. "The second is 'Love Divine'. The third was 'Infinite Love'. This one is the fourth 'Mother's Love'," he nodded to the painting on the wall. "And the fifth and final one was called 'Enduring Love'." Greg sighed deeply. "Dad painted that one when Mum was diagnosed with cancer. It's never been shown."

Faye touched Greg's arm to comfort him. "I actually went to that exhibition, you know."

"Was father there?"

"Yes, he looked tired, I thought."

Greg lowered his eyes. "Had he done anything new do you know?"

Faye regarded his question for a moment. "Well, funnily enough, there were three new paintings…."

"And?"

"Well." She lowered her eyes slightly. "They were of me actually!"

"Why, do you know him personally?"

"No, I've met him only once," she laughed lightly. "He came to my aid once, while I was out walking near Zennor. I had stumbled and grazed my knee. He very kindly helped me back to the village."

Greg's lip curled into a smile. "Dad never forgets a pretty face. I do believe, my dear, you must have inspired him." He smiled softly.

"I don't know." She paused momentarily. "The paintings had a touch of melancholy about them."

Greg nodded knowingly. "Like the air you give off now?"

She clasped her hands to her face. "Oh God, do I come across as a misery?"

"No, but something troubles you, that's for sure."

She smiled gently. "I'm sorry you are estranged from your father."

"Yes so am I. I can't tell you how much I miss him, and mum of course. Anyway, enough of this melancholia, where are my manners. Would you like a drink? You'll stay for dinner of course?"

Faye smiled warmly. "I'd like that very much."

The weather turned wild and stormy as they sat down to eat later that evening. By the time they had finished, the spray from the sea lashed against the window and they huddled around a roaring fire, talking and drinking wine. Inevitably the question, which Faye dreaded, was brought up.

"So, what's your story Faye?" Greg asked softly.

Faye grimaced and cleared her throat. "What makes you think I have a story to tell?" she answered lightly, trying to keep her voice calm.

Greg smiled kindly. "Well you don't get many beautiful women hiding away in the back of beyond. You seem to be a very lonely person, you don't seem to have anyone, no friends, family, and...." He paused for a moment. "Forgive me for saying, but you don't look like the sort of woman who normally has her hair cut and dyed so unprofessionally."

Faye quickly touched her hair and lowered her eyes to hide her distress.

Greg was quickly at her side. "Oh I'm sorry Faye that

was very rude of me. I didn't mean to upset you. You don't have to tell us anything, it's none of our business," he said softly.

She looked intently at them and something inside told her she could trust them both. "It's okay, I'll tell you." Her voice was filled with sadness as she recalled the sad and sorry tale. When she neared the end of her story she looked up tearfully and said, "What could I do? I had no choice, but to run away."

"Well your secret's safe with us my love," Greg said, putting a comforting arm around her shoulders. "But you really must go and have your hair cut and dyed properly dear; it really is in a shocking mess. I know just the person to send you to." He grinned mischievously.

Over the next few weeks Faye became a regular visitor to their studio. And although it was October, all three of them took a bracing swim in the cove each morning, long before the walkers began tramping the well-worn coast paths. Afterwards they would wrap themselves in bath robes and run up the woodland path through the fallen leaves, which in spring time, Greg assured her would be carpeted with bluebells. They would arrive at the studio damp and exhilarated, to be greeted noisily by their two golden retrievers, who would lay idly by the fire until they heard the click of the door, then bounded excitedly around their feet. When they got back, it was Simon's job to prepare breakfast and steaming coffee - he didn't allow anyone else in 'his' kitchen - while Greg built up the fire and Faye took the first hot shower.

Faye found life idyllic and free of worries for the first time in an age.

41

November the first which was a Saturday, dawned cold and damp, and for three days in succession driving mists shrouded Lamorna valley.

The crumbling walls of 'Willow End' ran wet with condensation. Great patches of black mildew grew in the darkest corners of the rooms, seeping into wardrobe and drawers alike, rendering Faye's clothes smelly and unusable. All around was the stench of decay and mould. She rose early that morning as always, stood at the mirror and ran her hands through her newly styled hair. This house depressed her - she had to get herself out of this place. She needed a job - what little spare money she had was fast running out. Faye had never been the type to sit about all day and idleness did not become her.

When Greg called later that morning, he could see she was in poor spirits. He took a look around the tiny lounge, turning his nose up at the musty smell. The cottage was clean and tidy, but was situated deep in a dell of trees, rendering it impossible for the sun and light to reach it during the winter months, hence the dampness. He sat her down in front of the fire which struggled to warm the room and put his arm around her. "Faye, you can't stay in this place, it's so damp. I swear you could grow mushrooms as a cottage industry quite successfully here. In fact, Simon and I were discussing this very matter when we woke this morning. It's a wonder that you haven't come down with double pneumonia living here."

"I can't afford anything else Greg."

"I know, so, you're to come and live with us in the studio for the time being."

Faye opened her mouth to protest, but Greg put his finger to her lips. "We absolutely insist."

Faye settled in comfortably with Greg and Simon and

within a week of her moving in, Greg, who taught art at the local college, arrived home one evening with an unusual work proposition for Faye. They need a life model at the college, he explained tentatively, adding that he thought it would be a perfect way for Faye to earn some easy money, if it was something she felt comfortable about.

"Nude work?" She asked wide eyed.

"It's more money if you do. We really struggle to get young women to pose nude. It would really help the up and coming artists to be able to study the real female form."

This was a gift from God and Faye instantly agreed to the proposal. So, it was without hesitation or embarrassment that Faye happily posed nude for four one-hour stints everyday. That was until the secretary of the college, Irene Woods, began to take an interest in where Faye had come from.

"Is something wrong?" Greg asked one evening on the way home. "You seem very quiet, you're not ill are you?"

Faye smiled and sighed. "No I'm fine. I was just thinking though, I'm not sure how long I can continue working at the college."

Greg glanced at her. "But I thought you were enjoying the work."

"I am. I love it." She sighed again. "It's Irene at work; I think she is going to make trouble for me," Faye exclaimed unhappily. "She looks down her nose at me whenever I pass her in the corridor, and yesterday I heard her chatting to the cleaner about me. Apparently she is 'totally disgusted' that I am allowed to flaunt my body for money. She said I was no better than a common prostitute. But the most disturbing thing is that she said she recognises me from somewhere. I am really worried in case she makes the link with Lemmel."

Greg drew a deep breath as he felt the anger rising in him. "She's a real prude. She was opposed to you posing in the nude right from the start. And, she's cross that I won't enlighten her as to who you are. That damn woman wants to know everybody's business and is more than happy to share it with anyone who will listen." Greg snapped indignantly. Then a smile suddenly came over his face and he lent over and patted her hand. "You leave Irene Woods to me!" he exclaimed with a wink.

The next day, Irene emerged from the Principal's office, her face scarlet with rage, having just received a reprimand for 'inciting unrest amongst the students'. Her reprimand was the outcome of a rather disturbing morning the Principal had encountered, when her office had been besieged with furious students, who felt Irene Woods was out to deprive them of a unique opportunity to draw the female form. Faye too was called into the same office that evening to be told that her presence in the college was invaluable and if she were willing to continue, the college would be happy to increase her pay.

On hearing the news, Greg smiled inwardly; the subtle hint he had dropped to one of his students that Faye might leave because of Irene Woods prudish tendencies, had obviously spread like wild fire around the life painting class.

When Faye walked across the car park to Greg's waiting car that evening she looked at him knowingly. "All right, what did you do?" she said, as she jumped into the passenger seat.

He raised his eyebrows and clasped his hand to his chest. "Moi?"

"Yes you."

"God's honour, I hardly did anything," he said, his mouth twisting into a wry smile.

Faye smiled, but couldn't help the niggling feeling that she had made an enemy out of Irene. People scorned normally found some way of retribution.

42

On Saturday the thirteenth of December, Faye drove into Penzance to meet Pippa for a spot of lunch and Christmas shopping. They had met regularly in secret over the past couple of months and it was glorious for Faye to catch up on all the news from Gweek. Because Liam had taken up residence in the boatyard, it was impossible to visit her friends there, which made her incredibly angry. And as Liam's threats against Faye worried Pippa, she had kept her shopping visits secret, even from Sid and Joe.

"You look like the worries of the world have been lifted today," Pippa commented as she embraced her friend warmly.

Faye smiled happily. "I think my luck is changing at last Pip. I have a job. I have a bit of money and look." She waved an envelope at her. "This came through the post today, it's from my solicitor."

Pippa raised an inquisitive eyebrow.

"It's about the cost of the wedding."

"Oh dear, are you bankrupt? Am I buying lunch?" she said to lighten the blow which was inevitably coming.

Faye shook her head. "No, I'm not going to be bankrupt after all. The solicitor managed to recoup some of the costs that Lyndon incurred in his rash spending spree between the so called 'incident' and the wedding date. Thankfully, the letter Elaine Elmer typed so efficiently clearly stated the date it was dictated, which was a few days before the wedding fiasco, when it should have been post dated." Faye could not resist a wry smile. "I bet she was in trouble for that. So, it proves that Lyndon tried to make me pay dearly for his humiliation. As for the rest of the cost, well…" She sat back in her chair and blew a mystified sigh. "Someone has paid it in full."

"No way!" Pippa exclaimed wide eyed.

Faye nodded. "Yes, every last penny of it."

"Do you have to pay it back?"

"Apparently not, the matter is closed."

"Do you think Lyndon paid up for it all in the end?"

"I have no idea, absolutely none, and my solicitor said the benefactor wishes to remain anonymous."

"How much was it in the end?"

"After making Lyndon pay his fair share, the final cost to me was fifteen thousand pounds!"

"How much?" she said almost spilling her coffee.

"I know, it's an awful lot of money, but Lyndon wanted the best."

Pippa gave a snort of indignation. "Well he had the best, when he had you, but the idiot lost you. ..... I'm glad you didn't marry him in the end, I didn't like him anyway," she added tossing her hair.

Faye smiled at her friend.

"So, someone has paid out all that money? That is just wonderful, isn't it?" She looked at Faye whose eyes began to cloud over. "What's the matter, I would have thought you'd be relieved?"

Faye waved her hand in dismissal. "I am, really I am, it's a real weight off my mind, but who would do such a thing? Who would spend all that money to get me out of trouble? To whom am I indebted?"

Pippa studied her friend for a moment. "Look Faye, this is a gift, this is the new start you were looking for. Someone somewhere has your best interests at heart. I say, be grateful, stop worrying, go and buy that café you so want. Then I won't have to pay the extortionate prices this place is asking for cappuccinos," she grinned cheekily.

As Faye and Pippa hugged each other in the harbour car park, they quickly made arrangements for Pippa to come and stay for a few days over Christmas. Greg and Simon had expressed a wish to meet her friend, and so it was, she would visit on Boxing Day and would stay on until the weekend. As Faye waved Pippa off with blown kisses she glanced at the Black Audi parked next to her own battered Sierra. She gave the car a swift appreciative once over, then jumped into her trusty old car to drive back to Lamorna.

*

Christmas was a happy affair for Faye with her friends about her, and so it was she entered the New Year with a sense of hope and vitality, until something began to unsettle her.

As it was early January, it was unusual to see any parked cars on the roadside leading to Lamorna, so when Faye had seen the same black Audi five times, parked in various locations, her senses moved to high alert.

The first time she'd seen it was in the car park in Penzance; then it was parked next to her car in the supermarket, which in itself was strange, as the car park was virtually empty. Then in a lay-by near the Merry Maidens stone circle, a route she walked most days with the Labradors. She'd seen it again in the college car park and today more worryingly along the road leading to the studio. She knew it was the same car because the registration was not dissimilar to a car she had once owned. There was never anybody in the car when she spotted it, but unconsciously she began to get the feeling that she was being followed.

At eight-thirty that night Faye parted the blinds to check that the car was still there. It was a clear, cold moonlit night and although the Audi was parked slightly obscured from sight at the bottom of the road, Faye could see a faint glimmer of light coming from its interior. She sighed heavily.

Simon looked up from his painting. "Is something the matter Faye?"

"No, no, just looking at the night," she lied. For a few days now she had had an uneasy feeling that she had been found. She'd seen Irene Woods flicking through an old copy of Bella, which Faye knew, carried a four page article on the rise of Cordelia Hart to the dizzy heights of becoming the face of 'Guinevere'. She remembered quite categorically that Irene seemed to have made some sort of connection between her and Cordelia. If someone was following her, she knew it wouldn't be long before the gutter press would be at her door. She didn't want to bring that on her friends. She lifted the blinds again and knew it was time to leave.

Later that night, she wrote them a letter, thanking them for their kindness, explaining that something had happened and she needed to get away. She told them not to worry and that as soon as she was able, she would contact them. She then packed her bag, blew a silent kiss to Greg and Simon as they slept and took a last nostalgic look around the studio where she had been happy. She carefully opened the fire escape door, where she knew she could climb down and sneak away from the studio without alerting the driver of the Audi who was still parked in the lane. She glanced at the painting called 'Love Letter' and knew at once where she was heading for, then slipped out into the cold night air.

43

It was a long, cold walk to Pasco's garage, which was situated in the centre of the hamlet of Drift, a couple of miles north of Lamorna. It had taken Faye almost an hour to negotiate the narrow lanes under the moonlit sky; all Cornish roads look the same in the daytime, never mind at four in the morning. An owl flitted amongst the branches of trees, and small animals stirred in the hedgerows as she walked, all of which made the journey a little more eerie.

She had dropped her car off at Pasco's garage the previous morning for its MOT, but as she and Greg were late coming home last night, she hadn't had time to pick it up. She had rung Sinclair Pasco, the proprietor, paid for the MOT over the phone, and asked him to leave the car on the forecourt with the key on the rear tyre. She told him she would collect the car first thing in the morning, though when she had spoken to him she hadn't envisaged she would be so early.

Half of an hour later, Faye found herself totally lost on the moorland road. She pulled her car onto a soft verge and resigned herself to wait until daylight before continuing. She yawned and closed her eyes. She was exhausted - she'd had precious little sleep and the early morning walk was beginning to take its toll. Before she knew it, she was fast asleep.

She was woken with a start by a loud rap on the driver's window. She squinted as the sun streamed down on her, obscuring her view. She opened the window and took a deep breath of fresh air.

"You can't sleep there my luvver," a kindly voice was saying. "I need to get my tractor out of the yard."

"Oh goodness, I'm so sorry," she said wiping the sleep from her eyes. "I must have dozed off." She fumbled for the ignition key, smiled apologetically at the farmer and started the car. She glanced at the car clock, and was shocked to find that it was almost ten o clock; she had slept solidly for five hours.

"Are you lost my luvver?"

"I'm heading to Zennor."

"Well then, it's just over that hill," he nodded toward the west. "Turn right at the end of this lane and you'll see it in the distance."

"Thank you and ….sorry for blocking your yard."

"Don't you worry my lover, no 'arm done."

As she drove over the brow of the moor, the view before her was breathtaking. She pulled onto the verge, this time making sure that she didn't block anyone's way, and got out to stretch her stiff legs.

It was a clear crisp day and the turquoise sea glistened in the winter sunshine. The air was bitterly cold against Faye's face as she stood in stunned silence at its beauty. Zennor lay nestled in the valley, as though it was waiting to be discovered by the modern age. She had no idea why she decided to go to Zennor or what she was going to do when she got there, but something urged her to go to the place where Nathaniel Prior gathered his inspiration for his beautiful paintings.

The last part of her journey took her along a twisty road, flanked on each side by high Cornish hedges that restricted her view. Finally it widened slightly and Zennor beckoned her down the steep lane, past the watermill into the heart of the village. She parked her car next to a dilapidated caravan in the Tinners Arms pub car park, checked her watch and waited for the pub to open.

At eleven, Faye checked her appearance in the rear view mirror, brushed her hair and stepped boldly into the pub. It was a wondrous sight, almost like stepping into another world; the pub looked like it hadn't changed since it opened in 1271. It had low ceilings, and a glorious open log fire burned welcomingly in the hearth. As she made her way towards the bar, she was very conscious of her shoes as they made a clip clop sound against the stone floors.

"Hello my lovely," the landlord greeted her smoothing his unkempt hair down. "What can I get you?"

Faye licked her lips as she scanned the bar for her choices. "I don't suppose you do coffee do you?"

"Coffee is it? Well, let me see what I can do." He disappeared into the kitchen and a couple of minutes later emerged with her drink. Faye had settled herself at the bar and he set the cup down in front of her. "On holiday are you?" He cocked his head and asked quizzically.

"No, I'm looking for work," she answered without thinking.

"Well my dear, what sort of work are you looking for?"

"I'll turn my hand to anything really. Shop work, waitressing, whatever."

"Well, I could do with a pretty waitress, if you've a mind."

"Really?" Faye smiled brilliantly. "When can I start?"

"Just as soon as you've finished your coffee if you wish."

Faye laughed happily. "Thank you, I will," she said, astonished at her good fortune.

"Duggie Martin's the name," he said, holding his hand out to Faye. "And you are..?"

"Faye Larson," she said, making to shake his hand, but instead he took her hand to his mouth and kissed it, then winked and grinned at her.

Just then a young family, who had settled themselves by the fireside to study the menu, approached the bar to order food.

"If you take a seat sir, my pretty waitress will take your order." He winked again at Faye. "You will find an apron in the kitchen."

Faye looked at her untouched coffee and slid quickly off her bar stool into her new role as a waitress.

The pub had been open all day and there had been a

steady flow of customers right up to nine-thirty when the kitchen closed. As she bid Duggie goodnight, he caught her by the hand and asked, "Do you have somewhere to stay?"

Faye nodded quickly and hurried to the door. In the cold night air she quickly ran to her car and drove to the far end of the back packer's café car park. She glanced at the car park sign where she pulled the car to a halt, which clearly stated: 'No Overnight Sleeping', then pulled a woolly hat down low on her head, wrapped a large scarf around her face and pulled the tartan travel blanket around her and settled down to a very uncomfortable night. She would look for somewhere to stay in the morning. But for now, she was content to have found work.

Uncomfortable was an understatement; first there was the cold, and then the wind got up about one a.m., blowing the sea into a frenzy. Salty rain and foam lashed the car, rocking it so violently Faye thought she would be sick. At four a.m. she noticed a light from the bottom of the car park. As it came closer she realised it was from a torch and was resigned herself to being arrested for flouting the car park rules.

A large figure in a dark coat and wide brimmed hat rapped on the window of the car. "Open the door," he said in a soft voice.

Faye pulled the blanket from around her, unlocked the door and eased herself out of the driver's seat.

"Lock up your car and come with me," he said, touching her arm lightly.

Faye followed him happily down the car park; the thought of a warm police cell was extremely appealing to her stiff and frozen limbs. As she looked about her for the waiting police car, the man in the dark coat beckoned her through a gate towards a small cottage. In normal circumstances, Faye would have been wary at entering a stranger's house in the middle of the night. But she was cold and tired to a point of not caring anymore.

He opened the door to the cottage and ushered her in. "Have a seat." He gestured to a rocking chair next to the blazing fire. "I'll bring you a drink to warm you up."

Faye immediately felt the warmth tingle her cold cheeks and she rubbed her face with exhausted relief. As she waited for the man to return she looked around at the small dark room in which she was seated. Heavy brown velvet drapes hung at the windows to keep out the cold. Apart from the rocking chair Faye sat in, there was a sofa and easy chair flanking the great fireplace, both covered in a variety of colourful throws and cushions. Behind her was a large mahogany sideboard on which a clock melodiously ticked the minutes away, making Faye feel very sleepy.

"Feeling better?" A voice roused her from her snooze.

She cleared her throat. "Yes thank you." Faye replied, and looked up at the man standing in the doorway with a cup of hot milky cocoa in one hand and an arm full of bedding. Her heart jumped at the sight of him.

"You best sleep on the sofa tonight, the spare room will be damp I reckon. It hasn't been slept in for a while. Here you go," he said, placing the pillows and duvet beside her. "The bathroom is at the top of the stairs if you need it. I'll be about if you need anything else. Just shout, okay?"

Faye nodded thankfully for his kindness.

"Well I'll bid you goodnight. Oh, I nearly forgot, Nathaniel Prior at your service ma'am," he said, bowing low as he left the room.

Faye had known before he introduced himself that she was in the presence of her favourite artist. She couldn't get over the fact that he also possessed the same warm friendly smiling eyes, softly spoken voice and dark unruly curls as his estranged son.

Faye slept heavily that night and became vaguely aware that she was not alone in the room the moment she woke from her warm slumber. She pulled the duvet from her face to meet the gaze of a young woman eyeing her suspiciously.

"Ah Carrie, there you are," Nathan said to the young woman, as he brought an armful of logs to the fire. "Do you mind starting on the spare room first? As you see, we have a house guest. It needs cleaning, and fresh linen on the bed. I'll be through later to light a fire in the grate."

The young woman said nothing, but held her gaze on Faye for a few more uncomfortable seconds before turning on her heel to get on with her work.

Nathan witnessed the look on Carrie's face and smiled wryly at Faye. "Well then, my unexpected house guest, did you sleep well?"

Faye swung her legs off the sofa. "The second half of the night was a vast improvement on the first, I must admit, thanks to you and your kindness."

Nathan gestured that it was nothing.

"No really, I can't thank you enough," she added rubbing the sleep from her eyes. "I don't think I would have survived the night if you hadn't rescued me. I don't know what to say."

"Well you can start by telling me why Cordelia Hart, or whatever your real name is, came to be sleeping rough in a car park?"

Faye smiled gently. She felt an overwhelming feeling of trust with this man. "It's Faye Larson," she said confidently, "….and this is the second time you have rescued me!"

He smiled knowingly. "I know. How is your knee?"

Her face was radiant as she turned her smiling eyes onto him.

"And you're sleeping rough because?" he asked quirking his eyebrow.

The light in her eyes flickered briefly. "It's a long story."

"I have all day," he answered with his soft Cornish accent.

Without hesitation, Faye relayed her story to him,

though studiously omitting the names of Greg and Simon. Nathan listened intently as she spoke. When she had finished her story he nodded knowingly, and set about building the fire back up. Eventually he stood up, stretched his long legs and gazed out of the window. He was a lean, muscular man, who obviously kept himself in peak physical condition; he had dark good looks, a mop of curly hair which was peppered slightly with grey and a kind strong mouth. Faye felt an enormous sense of relief at the telling of her tale, and felt strangely attracted to him.

"Well," he said at length. "You'll stay here I hope. The spare room's yours for as long as you need it."

"You're very kind Mr Prior but I can't possibly impose on you like this. Once the press find out I'm here you won't get any peace."

"Nathan, please call me Nathan. You are not imposing yourself on me. You'll be doing me a favour staying here. I'm in desperate need of some stimulating company and I suspect you, my dear, will fill that position perfectly. As for the press, well, we'll cross that bridge when we come to it. As for your contract with Lemmel, well, there is nothing that can't be sorted, I'm sure. I'll get my lawyers onto it, should it rear its ugly head again. So, you'll stay then, that is settled." Faye nodded thankfully. "Good, I've been too long on my own, well except for Jasper here," he said, patting the dog, "...and of course there is Carrie my housekeeper. But it will be nice to have someone else in the house."

44

Gwithian Cottage was a sturdy house, built of granite to withstand the wild Cornish weather. The gales in December had tested its structure to the extreme and as always the little house had emerged from the tempest unscathed. By the time the festive season had passed, the storms had blown themselves out and the January weather was calm and bathed in chilly watery sunshine.

Dawn had barely broken by the time Faye slipped out of the front door into the chill of the morning. Wearing white jeans, a chunky jumper and an oilskin she had borrowed from Nathan, she pulled on her walking boots, checked the pockets of her coat for her hat and gloves and set out down the garden path.

She always felt a little easier outside the confines of the cottage. That was not to say she hadn't settled comfortably into life at Gwithian Cottage, she had, it was almost as though Faye had found her niche in life at last. She considered herself extremely fortunate to have found such a lovely place to stay and that she was earning her keep with her job at the local pub. Nathan had been her saviour, and she would be eternally grateful to him for offering this safety net he had invisibly wrapped around her. Carrie, on the other hand, was the only fly in the ointment in her otherwise idyllic life.

She had made no attempt to welcome Faye into the household, and whenever they found themselves in the same room, Faye would smile and try to make conversation with her, but Carrie's answers were short sharp and one syllable, followed by long periods of icy silence. Faye knew this woman would be a threat to her life at Gwithian Cottage and that her days of happiness were probably numbered.

Ann E Brockbank

Faye climbed the cliff path up to Zennor head and stopped to sit on one of the granite rocks which overlooked the jagged outcrop called Gurnard's Head. She waited, so as to catch her breath for a moment and looked down the path she had just ascended to the peaceful cove below. Looking over towards Pendeen, the sea was ruffled and the waves were blown out as they pounded the cliffs. Above her, seabirds circled and cried on the breeze as the sun began to rise between the racing clouds from the east. After sitting a while she took the coast path back from where she had come, walking briskly to keep the cold at bay. As she carefully negotiated the steep path to the rocky beach, she noticed a figure purposefully striding out over the rocks towards the surf. She stopped when she realised that the figure was a man, a naked one at that. She smiled at his resolve, as he failed to waiver as the icy water washed over his body. He had a fine lean body whoever he was, and Faye felt not a pang of embarrassment for watching him, though she did shiver involuntarily as she watched him dive into the surf. He swam relentlessly for over a quarter of an hour, before he made for the shore. It was then that she noticed Jasper, as he bounded into the surf to greet Nathan as he emerged dripping from the icy ocean. Unaware of her presence, he dried his hair and rubbed his body vigorously with his towel. Turning quickly on her heel, Faye began to ascend the path back up from the beach, only to have her presence exposed when Jasper spotted her and began to bark.

"Faye? Is that you Faye?" he called out.

Faye turned and waved.

"Hang on. I'm coming up in a moment." Nathan pulled his clothes over his cold damp body and struggled to put his shoes on.

Jasper arrived at Faye's feet, first jumping and lolloping, and without any hint of embarrassment, Nathan approached soon after. Faye looked up into his handsome face, his sparkling eyes made brighter by the exhilaration

264

of the swim. His hair was wet and windswept and he hadn't shaved that morning, giving him a wild unkempt look.

"Hi. This is a surprise. I don't normally see you this early in the cove."

She laughed. "I'm surprised to see you too. Do you swim every morning? I can't believe you have just been in there," she said, pulling her wind blown hair away from her face.

His face wrinkled slightly. "No, not normally, I had a few too many whiskeys with Duggie last night, so I was trying to blow a few cobwebs off."

"Did it work?"

He nodded vigorously. "Come on." He put his arm around Faye's shoulder. "Let's go and find some breakfast, I'm ravenous."

*

After a hearty breakfast, Faye was working the lunchtime shift at the Tinners Arms. It was unusually busy at the pub for early January, and Faye was kept on her toes serving food and washing up occasionally. She loved her little job. Duggie was a pleasant, easy going landlord and it was lovely to get her wage packet at the end of the week, even though the amount was a pittance. But her needs were few, albeit a few toiletries and the odd paperback. Nathan categorically refused to accept anything from her for her board and lodgings, much to Carrie's annoyance.

At four that afternoon, Faye finished her shift and stepped out into the darkness of the early evening. The weather had turned damp since the morning. Drifting rain had moved over the land during the day and the drizzle penetrated her jeans as she ran home to Gwithian Cottage.

The house was warm and quiet as she shed her outer clothes in the hall. The front lounge had a fire in the grate and looked welcoming, and, as usual, all the lights were on in the other rooms of the house during the evening. She had a mind to sit and sketch for a while; there were lots of interesting objects placed on the shelves of the lounge, and a bowl of seasonal fruit was always on display on the sideboard. Nathan had offered her the use of drawing materials should she need them, and told her she could find them in his study.

Nathan looked up from his book, his concentration broken as Faye slipped silently through the open doorway to his study. She clearly hadn't seen him sitting there; he smiled to himself and watched as she moved silently around the room.

She noted it was quite small for a study and certainly not large enough for a studio, and couldn't believe an artist of Nathan's calibre didn't have some huge airy studio in which to create his beautiful paintings. The room was a collection of dusty easels and picture frames. Faded sketches and photographs covered the walls from one end of the room to the other. There was a wooden chair with a raffia seat in the very corner of the room, and the fire grate stood unlit, but ready with kindle and paper to take a lighted match. She moved towards a table and inspected the cardboard boxes full of paint. Along the walls stood various dusty lumps of marble and granite in all shapes and sizes. She had been so engrossed in her surroundings that she jumped when Nathan cleared his throat.

"Oh Nathan, I'm so sorry; I didn't mean to disturb you. I thought you were out, you were so quiet. I'll go, I'm sorry, I'll go."

"No, please no, you're not disturbing me. Please feel free to look around." He gestured to her.

She hesitated for a moment. "Well if you're sure."

"Be my guest," he answered happily. He watched as she walked over to the row of paintings leant against the wall, untouched since they had arrived back from Lemon Gallery. She was dressed in a blue chunky jumper, tight white jeans and trainers. For all her casualness, she was the most beautiful woman he had seen for a long while, or maybe she was just the first beautiful woman he had noticed in a long while. She so reminded him of his late wife, not so much in looks, as his wife had not possessed Faye's luxurious auburn hair, or the emerald eyes which at this moment were absorbing the images of his paintings with joy and appreciation. But he saw in her that same serene composure, which had inspired him to paint with such vivacity so many years ago.

"Do you like my work?" he asked softly.

"Oh I love your work. I've always admired your paintings. They are so real," she said, pulling the standing canvasses from the wall one by one and resting them against her thigh as she examined them.

Nathan put his book down and folded his arms. "Of course you know this work don't you. I believe you came to the retrospective for Elizabeth in Truro."

She smiled as she glanced at him. "Yes I did, I'm afraid I gate-crashed."

He laughed lightly. "I take it you saw the paintings I did of you then?" he asked.

She bit her lip and nodded. "It was quite a shock to tell you the truth. All of a sudden, there I was on the wall. I can't tell you how surprised I was."

"I hope you will forgive me for stealing your image."

"There is nothing to forgive. I am honoured that you should do such a thing. Did you get my picture from a magazine?"

"No, I saw you once at the Chelsea Arts Club. There was some party going on there. You were standing quite alone, at the other side of the room. I remember your disposition seemed to reflect my own that night; I suspect neither of us wanted to be there. You inspired me that night Faye, I had no idea who you were, but your countenance that day was so heavy with emotion; I couldn't get you out of my mind. You made me want to come home, and open the studio, to smell the turpentine, and to squeeze the paints on my pallet again. I thank you for that."

She looked at him and smiled. "It's my pleasure. Tell me though, why did you paint me with dark hair? I would have had blonde hair when you saw me."

"I wanted the real you, not some false media image. I only paint things that are real."

Faye pulled the rest of the canvasses away from the wall, and selected the group of paintings collectively known as 'Love Chronicles.' She cast a sidelong glance at Nathan and saw the sadness in his eyes; he appeared to drift away to another time. His memory took him back to a time when his beautiful wife was alive, a time of great happiness, of love and of hope.

Faye watched him for a moment and on realising that he was lost deep in his thoughts, she smiled then turned to leave.

The movement broke his concentration. "Don't go," he said softly, almost pleadingly. "Stay, I'm just going to make coffee if you want to join me?" he said getting up from his seat.

Faye nodded in agreement. "Coffee would be nice."

As Nathan filled the kettle he kept in the far corner of the study, Faye moved back towards the paintings.

He moved to her side and handed her a mug of steaming coffee and looked at the painting depicting a woman in a wedding dress, sat at her dressing table, adjusting her headdress in the reflection of the mirror. Faye knew this was the painting, 'Love Divine' the second in the collection of 'Love Chronicles'.

Faye turned to Nathan, looked into his eyes and smiled. "Your wife was very beautiful."

Nathan sighed deeply. "Yes she was. I painted this shortly after our wedding." His face lit up with a warm smile. "I remember her laughing about this dress. She said, 'most wedding dresses are only worn for one day'; she sat for me in it every day for twelve weeks while I painted her. It was worn out and slightly grubby when we finished."

Faye smiled at the story and thought of her own wedding dress, which had only been worn for a couple of hours.

"I admit I find it hard to look at the painting, that's why it's against the wall. I know it's a waste, but it hurts so."

Faye placed her hand tenderly on Nathan's shoulder. "I'm sorry, I didn't want to cause you any hurt. I'll put them back."

"No please carry on. I perhaps need to talk about it. In fact, just telling you the stories behind 'Love Chronicles' feels strangely liberating, it's what I need I think."

Faye watched as Nathan moved eagerly towards the painting entitled 'Infinite Love'. He stood back and absorbed the scene before him. Elizabeth was resting on a bed. She was laying on her side, one arm above her head the other cradling the baby growing inside her swollen stomach.

Nathan's eyes crinkled. "Beth was so tired towards the end of her pregnancy; she slept like this every afternoon. She was a perfect model. These were the second and third of the collection 'Love Chronicles'. I don't have the first or the fourth of course. My..., my son has those." His voice trailed off.

"Your son?" Faye's heart began to beat faster as she waited to hear more.

"I'm sorry Faye, I can't speak about him at the moment, forgive me. It's a sad tale." Nathan's eyes clouded, so changing the subject, Faye asked, "Are you painting anything at the moment?"

He sighed and began to place the paintings back against the wall. "No, when I lost Beth, I lost my muse, my inspiration and my way I suppose."

"Not lost Nathan; mislaid for a while perhaps," Faye said comfortingly.

He forced a smile. "Perhaps, but it's been a struggle these last years to paint with any enthusiasm." His eyes filled with fat tears.

"I can only imagine," she answered, gently touching his arm.

The tenderness of her voice triggered an emotion so strong in Nathan, that suddenly the flood gates were open, so that he could contain his grief no longer. Like a tidal wave, he began to pour his heart out to her. "It's been so hard you know. You really believe that when someone is terminally ill, even when the inevitable happens, your love for each other will always keep you together. You truly believe that the person you love will always be by your side, not in body, but in spirit. You hope that you will always feel them near you, so you can speak to them, and never let them go. But when the time comes and death takes them from you.." The tears spilled from Nathan's eyes as his voice faltered. A moment later he swallowed hard and continued. "It's such a shock to realise that they have gone.... and believe me, they are so, so gone!" He closed his eyes to contain his emotions, and Faye felt her heart break for him. He blinked the tears away. "I'm sorry." He looked at her apologetically. "It's just that you can't conjure them up to speak to them. You don't feel their presence like you thought you would, you're no longer part of a couple. You're absolutely alone in the world." He threw back his head in desperation and put his hands to his face. "Oh God, people want you to be happy again," he said, wiping his tears roughly from his face. "They want you to pull through the grief, and they do all sorts to 'snap' you out of it, but it takes a long time to work through grief. There is no magic cure, it takes time and you never really get over the loss of someone you love, because they are here." He beat his fist to his chest. "They are alive in your memory and your emotions are so raw." He hung his head and laughed scornfully. "You try to get on with life, try to go out and see people, and sometimes you need to speak to someone. But, woe betide you if that someone is of the opposite sex. You're quickly perceived to be starting another relationship, and thought on as unfeeling so soon after bereavement to seek the company of the opposite sex. When really, starting a new relationship is the last thing on your mind! You simply crave the company of someone the same sex as the person you lost." Nathan hung his head. "People want you to be well again, but they put obstacles in your way, it's a bloody minefield."

Without thought or agenda Faye placed her arms around Nathan to comfort him and he did not pull away. Eventually his emotions eased and he dried his eyes.

"I'm sorry Faye, I don't know what came over me, it's just that memories are so painful," he whispered.

Without hesitation Faye gently touched Nathan's face, it seemed the most natural thing to do at that moment. "No Nathan," she said quietly. "Memories are not painful, they are a necessity. Use them to comfort yourself. That is how grief works; it fills your days with treasured memories. Without them your future would be unbelievably empty; instead your life will always be full of love because of your memories. Keep them forever, never forget them and be grateful for them, because they will help you through your lifetime."

Nathan lifted his head sharply and looked deep into Faye's eyes. "You sent me that card didn't you? That sympathy card when Beth died. The one that said: 'Darkness will have descended on your life, but there will be light one day."

Faye nodded apologetically. "I'm sorry, I thought it would help."

"No, no don't apologize; it was the one card which stood out from all the hundreds of cards I received. You seemed to know what I was going through and it was as though you were giving me guidance through what was to be the rest of my life. I still have the card, look." He pointed to the card on the shelf. "What made you send it to a complete stranger?"

She shrugged her shoulders. "I suppose I just never thought of you as a complete stranger. I just felt that I knew you because of your paintings and of course you were my saviour that day you rescued me, remember."

He lifted Faye's hand to his lips and kissed it tenderly. "Thank you for your kindness. Do you know this is the first time I have spoken to anyone so openly about my loss? You're a good listener Faye, and I thank you for that also."

"Anytime," she answered softly.

Nathan smiled and took the coffee cups off her and a moment later the door to the study opened and Carrie breezed in.

She took one look at Faye and hissed, "I thought I heard something in here. What the hell are you doing, you have no right to be poking about here. This is Nathan's private room!"

Faye cast a glance at Nathan as he spun around and said, "There is nowhere private to Faye in this house."

Carrie's face paled. "Sorry Nathan, I didn't realise you were there. I ...I was just saying, that's all," she spluttered.

"Faye is welcome in any of the rooms, is that clear?"

Carrie pursed her lips. "Crystal," she muttered, casting a distinctly frosty look towards Faye. "I only came to find you to tell you that dinner's ready," she said and flounced out of the room.

Nathan and Faye exchanged amused glances. "I think we had better go to dinner," he said stiffly.

*

That evening, Carrie noted that Nathan was in exceptionally good spirits. Their once quiet dinners had changed into joyous occasions. Nathan no longer picked at his food; he seemed to have found his appetite and now ate with relish. Carrie seethed as she watched him chatting animatedly to Faye, and she in turn seemed enthralled by his charm and charisma. It seemed to Carrie that Nathan had conveniently forgotten the grief of losing his beloved wife; it also seemed that she was, in turn, losing her hold on Nathan.

45

Faye glanced at the clock, it was five-thirty. Unable to get back to sleep after a restless night, Faye got up and dressed quickly. She wasn't due to start work at the pub until ten, so that gave her time to take a long walk across the cliffs and down to the beach.

It was a ritual she had done often since moving into Gwithian Cottage. She walked about half a mile along the path before making her way down to the rocky beach. The day was damp and breezy, but warm and the surf was about two foot and clean. She walked towards the surf and took in the salty air. Her eye caught another person scaling down the path towards her. She turned and smiled as Nathan approached.

"Hello early bird," Nathan called out when he recognised her. She noted he was unshaven and still in the clothes he wore to dinner the previous evening.

"I could say the same about you. Have you been out all night?"

His face was pink with the fresh air. "In the studio actually, I slept on the chaise-longue, and jolly uncomfortable it was as well."

"What was wrong with your bed?"

"Too far away," he said quickly, not wishing to reveal the fact that he had found Carrie there again and wanting.

"Too far away? Why, it's only up the stairs!"

He laughed heartily. "I don't work in the cottage, that's just a study come storeroom. I have a studio up on the cliffs over there." He pointed towards Zennor Head.

"Oh I see." It all made sense now.

"I was just thinking of taking a swim; do you want to join me?"

Faye glanced at the wild Atlantic waves as they pounded the beach. "In that?" She looked aghast.

"It's good for the soul you know? It makes you feel alive."

She rubbed her neck and considered the invitation. "But I don't have my suit with me."

He crinkled his nose. "Neither do I. Are you tempted?"

She saw the glint in his eyes, smiled and nodded.

Suddenly his face straightened. "Pardon me for asking, but are you wearing underclothes?"

Faye grinned. "That is a very personal question Nathaniel Prior, but yes I am. Why?"

"Well, I'm going to swim in my underwear, you could do the same."

Her eyes twinkled. "Okay," she said undressing.

Quickly Nathan pulled his T-shirt over his head revealing the tanned skin on his back. She watched the muscles ripple on his arms and shoulders as he tossed the items of clothing to one side. He had a good strong body and sturdy legs which were covered in dark silky hairs.

The sea was ice cold as they plunged into the surf, Faye's body stung with the cold. Nathan was a much stronger swimmer than Faye, but the exhilaration she felt set a fire in her belly that eliminated the cold. With strong powerful strokes Nathan swam towards her. "Too cold to stay in for long, eh?" he said.

"Oh my goodness it's fantastic though," Faye enthused as they trod water.

"Can you body surf?"

"Never tried it, I've only ever used a board."

"Come on, swim nearer the shore," he urged. When they could feel the sand beneath their feet he held onto her hand. "Listen for the surge behind you, as it begins to pick you up, leap onto the crest of the wave and let it take you in, it's simple," he said. "Watch me, and then I'll come back to you.

A moment later a wave carried him towards the shore with such speed it took Faye's breath away. She tried desperately to keep her feet as the waves surged behind her. Nathan powered back to where she stood.

"Okay. Do you want to have a go?" Faye nodded, and Nathan revelled in her enthusiasm. "I'll be right with you."

Standing in the cold surf, Faye felt her heart begin to thump, she could hear the surge of water behind her, but try as she might she could not let herself go. The wave hit her with such force it forced her down into the swirling foam. She was winded momentarily as she flayed about to find her feet again. Nathan was at her side - she felt his hand grab her arm and instantly drag her upright.

"You okay?" His face was full of concern.

She nodded then choked as the sea water ran down the back of her throat and then rather unpleasantly poured out of her nose.

"Don't do it if you're frightened," he said, flicking his wet hair away from his eyes.

"No, I want to do it, it's just a case of persuading my body to do it as well," she laughed.

The sand beneath her feet shifted making her lose her footing. Another wave was coming, she felt her breath quicken as the fear engulfed her. Nathan was by her side, she could do this.

"Ready?" he said. "Point your arms and.....go," he shouted.

They both launched into the crest of the wave and sailed towards the beach. As the white water bubbled and foamed around her, Faye caught her hand on the shingle causing an involuntary somersault. Disorientated with the pounding surf she spluttered to the surface and was dumped unceremoniously onto the beach. Wiping the salt from her eyes she tried to scramble to her knees only to be hit by another breaking wave. Nathan stumbled towards her and pulled her from the sea and they collapsed together laughing on the beach.

There was a moment of innocent intimacy as they embraced each other, before Jasper pounced on them making them part.

"My God, I know what it's like to be in a washing machine now," Faye said, as she laid gasping and panting on the sand.

Pushing Jasper away, Nathan lifted himself onto one elbow and smiled down at her. She may have been tumbled and tossed in the surf, and her hair and body covered in sand and seaweed, but still she looked more beautiful than ever. "Well done you. I'm so impressed."

She smiled back at him and her eyes shone with joy.

They quickly dressed and began the ascent up the coast path passing a derelict building almost towards the summit. Faye stopped and stared as she often did when she passed by the building. The walls were covered in ivy and the roof was missing most of the tiles. Cows happily grazed in what would have been the front garden and most of the windows were rotten and broken.

"What a shame this building is in such a bad state of repair. It has the most beautiful outlook. Don't you think it would make a wonderful house come café?"

Nathan had passed the ruined building so many times, he hardly noticed it anymore, but he nodded in agreement.

"Oh what it would be to live here Nathan! I'd make it so cosy inside, and when the storms came in the winter, I would close the shutters and sit around my own fireside. How wonderful it would be to be able to look out at this wonderful view everyday. I would have a little café attached to the house and I would serve cream teas on the front lawn in the summer. Inside the café I would cover the walls with paintings from local artists, and perhaps a few of my own" she grinned. "I would bake homemade cakes and live in blissful happiness until I grow old."

Nathan looked again at the building, then out at the view. He was lucky, he had the studio to take in the view, but he often wished that Gwithian Cottage had a better outlook than it had. He looked back again at the ruined building. "It would take a deal of work though."

"And money, I don't think my little nest egg would cover the repairs." She turned and looked back at the sea view and sighed softly. "I can but dream," she said casting a last glance at it as they continued on their way. "How long has it been unoccupied?"

"For as long as I remember," he answered.

She gave a frustrated tut. "Well it's such a shame." She shivered with the cold.

"Come on let's get a move on before we catch our death of cold." They ran breathlessly into the village and raced towards the house. Stumbling and laughing through the door of Gwithian Cottage, they raced each other up the stairs to see who could get to the bathroom first to shower. With the ensuing joviality, Carrie emerged stony faced from the kitchen and stood at the foot of the stairs listening to the slamming of doors and whoops of laughter from above with cold resentment.

*

Faye had left for work and Nathan now occupied the bathroom. The morning swim had invigorated and energised him. He smiled at the warm feeling he felt whenever he thought of Faye. Nathan finished shaving, splashed cold water onto his face and patted it with a soft towel. Not usually one for vanity, he studied his reflection for a moment. The usual grief and bitterness that had etched lines prematurely on his face seemed to be diminishing. His mouth revealed a ghost of a smile; there was no doubt about it, Faye's presence in his life had altered his outlook. Could he love again? Was there room in his heart for love? He still missed Elizabeth with every beat of his heart, but Faye seemed to ease the pain of his loneliness. He laughed to himself at his optimism. If only he fifteen years younger, he may have had a chance to make a new life for himself. But not with Faye, no, he knew there would be no hope of an intimate relationship with her; he was far too old for her, more's the pity. But nevertheless, she had opened his eyes, and showed him that he could live again and for that he was thankful.

He closed his eyes and thought of Carrie, lying in wait in his bed again last night. Whatever sort of life was opening up for him, he just could not see Carrie as an intimate part of it. He liked her a lot and she had been a good and true friend to him over the last three years. But she didn't light that fire in his belly. He was truly sorry for her, but that was just how he felt. When he found her in his room last night, he had said nothing, he had just turned on his heels and left. He dreaded meeting her this morning, as again, he was at a loss as to what to say to her.

46

Spring had begun in earnest. The grass verges were adrift with golden daffodils, peaking a few weeks later than the mass produced commercial fields of daffodils which had painted a patchwork of yellow across the south west of Cornwall. The air was warm and filled with the scent of the sea, lines of washing flapped in the breeze and new foliage was beginning to show tender green on the apple trees in the orchard behind Gwithian Cottage.

Faye, much to Carrie's annoyance, was busy spring-cleaning. She had washed all the cushion covers and throws which adorned the sofa and chairs, brushed and vacuumed the dust from the velvet curtains and scrubbed the paintwork down throughout the lower part of the house. Nathan knew she would breeze into his study any moment, and sure enough the door opened and in she came with a pot of steaming hot coffee.

"How on earth can you find anything in all this mess Nathan?" Faye grumbled as she tripped over a pile of cardboard, the remnants of some newly delivered canvasses.

"It's not a mess, it's organised chaos. Anyway, it's just a store room really," Nathan answered, studiously searching through a box of sable brushes.

"It might be organised chaos to you, but to a potential buyer coming to look at your paintings, this place is a mess."

He scratched his head with the end of the paintbrush he was inspecting. "Ah, so you're my PR girl now are you? Anyway, creativity is a messy business, and first and foremost, I haven't got any new paintings to sell."

She smiled broadly. "You will have soon," she answered confidently. "Just let me tidy it up a bit. You know, paint the walls, get rid of the cobwebs and spiders," she said grimacing.

He cocked his head and frowned. "I like my spiders, they keep me company." Faye raised her eyebrows.

"Okay, you win. I'll let you tidy up, if you'll do something for me?"

"Name it."

"Sit for me?" he enquired hopefully.

Faye was deeply flattered. "Oh Nathan, I'd love to," she answered softly. "If you're sure that is what you want?"

"I never thought I would find anyone to paint after Elizabeth died. She was my muse for so many years." His eyes filled with unexpected tears. He shook his head and cleared his throat. "But now I find that I'd like to paint your image more than anything else," he exclaimed. "I didn't like to ask, as I know how much you have been exploited in the past. I know I have painted you before, but that was purely from memory, and all I captured was a split second image of you. This time I could really study you, if you would do me the honour." He looked at her and she looked back and smiled at his thoughtfulness.

"I take it I get to visit the famously secretive cliff top studio then?"

Nathan nodded. Only Elizabeth had set foot in his studio before. This was a giant step for Nathan.

"Well I hope there are no spiders up there." Her eyes glistened mischievously.

"I shall personally make sure there aren't any."

"Perfect. When do you want me?"

Nathan smiled inwardly at her unintentional innuendo. "When you finally stop spring cleaning my house!" he grinned.

Faye laughed and turned to leave. "Oh, I nearly forgot," she produced an envelope from her back pocket. "I pulled the hat stand out in the hall to sweep behind it and found this, along with three pens, a scarf and an old Vogue magazine," she added. "The franking date on it says nineteen-ninety-five. I hope it wasn't anything important!"

As she passed the envelope to Nathan and left, his heart flipped at the familiar handwriting.

*

As Faye emptied her bucket into the kitchen sink, she heard the front door slam shut. She stood up, stretched her aching back, pushed a stray wisp of hair from her face and washed her hands.

A moment later Carrie stormed into the kitchen and snapped at her, "What the hell have you just said to Nathan?"

Faye turned as she wiped her hands. "Pardon?"

"You must have said something to upset him! I could see in his face he was distressed, he practically pushed me aside, he was in such a hurry to get out of this house."

Dismayed, Faye pleaded, "I haven't said anything to upset him, I promise. He was talking about his wife. Maybe that stirred up his emotions?"

"Oh brilliant," she said throwing her arms in the air. "We'll be back to square one again now. Don't you know it's taken him three years to get over his wife's death? He was just getting himself together and what happens? You come poking your nose into his business and stirring the grief up again, you insensitive bitch."

Shocked at her outburst Faye retaliated. "I beg your pardon, but Nathan volunteered to speak about his wife to me. Sometimes it's good to talk about grief; it doesn't go away you know. And, if you think he has got over his wife's death, you are very much mistaken. You don't get over something like that; you just learn to live a different sort of life."

"Oh hark at you! What are you, some kind of grief counsellor?"

"No, I'm just somebody who listened to him. Look Carrie, there really is no need for all this animosity."

"Oh you think not do you?" Carrie spat her words out as though they would poison her. "I know all about you,

you know. I know you are the face of 'Guinevere'!" she laughed mockingly. "I read the papers, I'm not stupid. I know how you ruin relationships. From what I've read, everyone who has ever come into contact with you, have had their lives destroyed, and I'm supposed to sit back and watch you destroy Nathan's life am I? Well you're very much mistaken lady."

Faye recoiled in shock at her harsh words. "Carrie, please listen. Don't believe what you read in the newspapers, they lie about things."

Carrie snorted disdainfully. "I don't think so. Nathan and I were all right until you turned up. We were practically living together as man and wife, but all that changed when you moved in. I love him and he loves me, but you are coming between us. You might be able to pull the wool over his eyes, but I can see right through you, you're nothing but a whore, who steels other people's partners...... and murders their children!" she added with venom.

With sheer hatred in her eyes Carrie stormed out of the kitchen leaving Faye reeling in shock.

Gripping the sink for stability, Faye squeezed her eyes tight shut as a wave of nausea enveloped her. Gulping huge breaths of air she tried in vain to calm her jangled nerves, but the walls of the kitchen felt as though they were closing in on her. She needed some air. Dragging her coat from the stand by the door she stumbled out of the house and ran blindly through the village and up onto the coast path, ignoring the prickly gauze which ripped the skin on her legs. She ran until she stumbled against a granite rock, grazing her knee as she fell, then lay on the soft grassy headland and sobbed uncontrollably as the soft Cornish sun in the pale blue sky comforted her with its embrace. Carrie's words spun in her head. It wasn't the allegations Carrie had thrown at her about ruining relationships and killing children, she had heard all that before, and much worse. It was the realisation that Carrie and Nathan were in a relationship. A tiny little pain grew in her heart, because quite unintentionally, Faye had begun to fall a little bit in love with Nathan, and she knew it would be difficult to suppress that love now.

*

The letter Faye had given him had been from Greg, and Nathan was in deep despair. It had been sent to him nearly three years ago, and somehow it had been lost down the back of the coat stand for all that time. It wasn't a reply to the letter Nathan had sent him; it was a heartbreaking plea from a desperate son to his stupid father. It read:

109 Pulteney Crescent

Bath,

BA2 9YZ

Dear Dad,

I write this letter in earnest. We can't go on like this. I miss you terribly. You have always been my rock, my inspiration and my life. I'm so sorry my news shook you so. Maybe because you and Mum were so bohemian, I thought you would have had a more open mind about such things. I can imagine it was a shock, but there is no going back, I am what I am, and for what it is worth I am extremely happy with my life.

I understand that there is to be an exhibition on Mum's work at Lemon Gallery. They have requested the loan of the 'Love Chronicles' paintings for it. If there is no reconciliation between us, I will not attend on the night; I will leave it in your hands. I hope and pray that we can put this behind us.

I am as always, your affectionate son.

Greg

P.S You will see that I have moved from Falmouth to Bath. My new address is at the top of this letter. I hope with all my heart that we can work through this. xx

High above the cliffs of Zennor, Nathan sat in the studio in despair. He had read and re-read the letter until he thought he would wear the letters off the page. The address at the top was not the address he had sent his letter to. The last he knew, Greg was residing in Falmouth and that was probably why the mix up happened. 'God what a mess', he moaned as he held his head in his hands. Only the sound of another person weeping dragged him from his despair. He stood and looked down towards the cliff path. A moment later he was by Faye's side.

"This is getting to be a habit," he said, touching her arm gently. She lifted her head and brushed away her tears, as he inspected her grazed knee. "We really will have to stop meeting like this. Come on, can you get up?"

Holding her hand, he led the way up the hidden path towards his studio. He sat her down on the seat by the door and very gently cleaned the wound with warm water and lint.

"Thank you," she said softly as she gazed down into his blue eyes, which were watery and dulled with an unseen pain.

"It's my pleasure," he said, easing himself off his knees.

She watched as he walked to the open door and looked out over the bay. "So, this is where the magic happens then?"

He turned and frowned. "Magic?" he questioned.

"I have finally got to see your famous studio?" She smiled warmly.

"Oh I see, yes." He nodded.

Her eyes followed him as he turned to gaze again out of the window.

She studied him for a moment. "Are you okay Nathan?"

He sighed and shook his head, his shoulders hung as though age had suddenly crept up on him.

"I'm sorry if I upset you back at the house. I didn't mean to open up old wounds. It must be terribly hard for you to speak of Elizabeth," she said unsteadily.

He turned and looked puzzled. "You haven't upset me at all Faye. Whatever gave you that impression?"

Faye furrowed her brow. "Well Carrie…" She paused

for a moment. "I heard you left the house visibly upset. I thought it was because I had stirred up old memories."

He moved towards her and bent down cupping her hands with his. "Faye, your presence in my home has lifted my spirits more than you will ever know. You are the first person I feel I can really talk to. My distress is caused by my own stupidity. The letter you gave me this morning was from my estranged son," he choked slightly as he spoke.

Faye blushed faintly at the mention of Greg. "Oh!"

"It seems it had lain there these past three years. My poor boy has been waiting for my response all these years." His blue eyes intensified in colour as they watered.

Faye leant towards him and tenderly touched the side of his face. The gesture caused a new wave of emotion to sweep over him. He bent his head to her knee and as she stroked his hair calmness ensued. "You must phone him Nathan," she said presently.

He lifted his head and shook it. "It's too late now, too much time has past. He must hate me for the silence."

She shook her head. "It's not too late Nathan, trust me."

"You don't know him; he will have taken my rebuff hard."

Faye swallowed hard. "Nathan, I do know Greg! In fact I know him very well."

Nathan's eyes darkened. "What are you saying?"

"I'm sorry that I have kept this from you, but before I came here I lodged with Greg and his partner. They were very kind to me. I know for a fact, this estrangement is breaking his heart. He doesn't understand why it has happened. I know he wants it to end more than anything in the world."

Nathan got to his feet as he digested her confession. He gave a short confused laugh and regarded her with suspicion, then shook his head in disbelief. "I can't understand why you haven't told me this before. How could you keep this information from me Faye?" He tried without success to keep the hurt from his voice.

Faye gathered her thoughts and pulled her lips into a tight embarrassed smile. "I did want to Nathan, honestly. But you seemed closed to all discussion about your son. In all truthfulness, as time went on, I didn't know how to broach the subject." As she spoke, Nathan's face coloured. "Oh please don't be angry with me Nathan, I couldn't bear that." Her voice was loaded with anguish.

Nathan closed his eyes, threw his head back and let out a long painful groan. There was a long pause and Faye's heart buckled at the consequences of her confession. At length, he opened his eyes, looked at her and shook his head. "I'm not angry with you Faye, I'm angry with myself. You're right; I have closed all thoughts of Greg from my mind because they are too painful to endure. Oh what a mess I've made of things."

Relief swept over Faye like a cold mist as she walked to him and very tentatively took him in her arms to comfort him.

Uncomfortably aware of the close proximity of Faye's body to his, Nathan pulled gently away from her. "What did he say to you about me?"

Realising it was not her place to hold him so intimately, she let him move away. "Not a great deal. Just that the estrangement between you was very hard on him and he missed you terribly."

"And you say you stayed with him and his partner?"

Faye nodded. "They live in Lamorna now."

Nathan's shoulders sagged. "Lamorna, but that is only a few miles away!" He shook his head. "How long did you stay with them?"

"For three months, they rescued me from the dark stinking hovel I called home." She smiled gently. "It seems all the members of the Prior family have come to my aid one way or another."

Nathan cleared his throat. "Is he happy?"

"He'd be happier with his Dad in his life again."

Nathan moved towards the studio doors and looked out to sea. "Are you sure about that?"

Faye moved towards him and this time placed a friendly hand on his shoulder. "I'm absolutely, one hundred percent, sure!"

He chewed his lip nervously for a moment before pronouncing, "Well then, I had better phone him, if you are one hundred percent sure. I take it you have a phone number for him?"

As he moved away from the studio doors, Faye gasped in astonishment as she looked out at the view.

"What is it?" Nathan enquired.

"That view. I have a photo of that view in my purse. It's the view I've been searching for along these cliffs all these years. But the painting was called 'View from Blue Bay Café' and this clearly isn't a café! Why would it be called that?"

Nathan paled momentarily. "You say you have a photo of the painting?"

"Yes, look!" She fished in her bag for the battered photo and handed it to Nathan."

He took the photo and flipped it over and blanched when he read the inscription on the back. *Meet me at noon at the Blue Bay Café 14.06.75.* "Where did you get this?"

"It belonged to my father. I found it in a book called 'Elizabeth Trent, A life in Sculpture.' It's a book about your wife," she added unnecessarily. "They are the only things I have left that belonged to him."

Nathan's mouth went dry. "What is your father called?"

"Philip Morton."

Nathan gasped in astonishment. "Your father is Philip Morton?"

Faye noted a slight tremor in his voice and nodded. "Did you know him? He was a photographer."

"Yes, I know of him." He moistened his lips. "Goodness what a small world this is. How is your father?"

"Oh, he died when I was four."

"Died?" Nathan was taken aback by this.

"Yes, he died in a car crash. Mum and I moved up to Yorkshire after it happened and as I say, this photo and the book are the only things I have left of him." She watched Nathan's face contort with emotion. "Sorry, didn't you know? Was he a good friend to you?"

"Yes my wife and I knew him."

"Oh how wonderful. Maybe you could tell me a little bit about him, as I know absolutely nothing, except that he lived in Cornwall and worked as a photographer."

Not knowing where to start with this unexpected scenario, he smiled and said, "Well, he was my wife's friend before I knew him."

"Gosh isn't this wonderful, who would have thought eh? But hey, this is not as important as you going to phone your Greg, so go on, we'll talk later."

"Well, as I said, I know of him, but I don't think I can enlighten you with anymore information than you already know. I'm sorry."

Faye sighed; she got the impression that Nathan didn't really like her father. "Oh, never mind then," she said as brightly as she could.

As they walked back to Gwithian Cottage, Nathan's mind was in turmoil, and not only because he was about to build bridges with his son.

47

Leaving Nathan in the hall beside the phone, Faye walked into the kitchen to give him some privacy. Carrie was peeling potatoes at the sink and as she glanced at Faye, her eyes turned cold, her mouth set hard and she gave a sigh of annoyance. If the atmosphere had been icy before, it was positively arctic now.

"Nathan?" Carrie called out, as she wiped her hands on a towel.

"Oh he's just making a phone call."

Carrie ignored her and began to walk out of the kitchen.

"I think he needs some privacy," Faye said.

Carrie shot her a look of contempt. "There is nothing private between Nathan and myself," she answered haughtily.

She walked out of the kitchen, bristling with indignation. She had no intention of ever speaking to Faye again. She had seethed quietly all afternoon after having said her piece to Faye, but she was glad that she had made it quite clear what she thought of her. Now, somehow, she had to get rid of this cuckoo in the nest. A few days of being cold-shouldered and she would soon get the message and leave.

Passing through the hall, she put on the brightest smile for Nathan as she stood by the telephone. His fingers instantly stopped dialling the number.

"Sorry Carrie, I need to make a phone call."

"Oh don't mind me," she trilled, fiddling with the vase of flowers on the hall table.

"It's a private phone call," he said firmly.

Her smile melted away. "Fine," she said sullenly, and holding her head high she turned and walked up the stairs.

*

The phone call Nathan had made had been a rollercoaster of emotion for both father and son, and when Faye found Nathan in the garden shortly after, he was drained both physically and emotionally. He reached out and took her hand as though it was the most natural thing to do. "Oh Faye," he sighed, squeezing her hand tightly, "what a mountain I have just climbed."

"And now, are you safely back on level ground?" she asked hopefully.

He nodded. "Yes, the relief is enormous."

"I can imagine. I'm so happy for you both."

"Greg has been desperately worried about you, you know. He was so glad you were safe and well and with me."

Faye's heart sank. "Oh dear, I didn't mean to cause him any distress, but I just couldn't tell him I was leaving."

"Don't worry, he understands the reasoning. The morning you left, their studio was surrounded by reporters."

The colour drained from her face, so she was right after all, Irene Woods had made the connection with Lemmel. "Oh God, I didn't want to bring all that nonsense to their door. That is the last thing I wanted." She turned away and bit nervously at her lip.

"Faye?"

"Oh Nathan, sure as eggs is eggs, they will find me here one day. Maybe I should go now, before they catch up with me."

Nathan pulled her round so as to face him and placed his hands on her arms. "Listen, I want no more talk of you going, do you hear me? So what if they do come? They are just looking for a quick story that's all. Let them come I say. Let's finish this once and for all."

Faye looked up into his eyes and began to tremble uncontrollably. "But if they find me, Liam will be right behind them and Lemmel with a law suit."

291

He gave her arms a reassuring squeeze. "Well maybe it's time we sorted that little problem out once and for all. I don't want you to worry about anything anymore." He pulled her into a friendly embrace, but the gesture did not go unnoticed by Carrie, as she stood at her bedroom window.

Conscious that they may be being watched, Faye pulled away from him. "Are you going over to see Greg?"

"Not yet, no, I just caught him as they were setting off for the airport. They're off to Australia for eight weeks, so our reunion will take a little longer I'm afraid. So, back to normal life, when are you going to sit for me? I'm itching to make a start."

"Oh, if you are sure, will tomorrow do? It's my day off."

"Splendid, tomorrow it is. Oh Faye, I'm so happy about Greg I could burst. Come on, let's tell Carrie the happy news," he said pulling her indoors.

*

After selecting a dress for Faye to wear from her wardrobe, Nathan told Carrie they wouldn't be back until supper and they set off together back up to the studio. Carrie stood in the kitchen as they slammed the front door shut after them. She recalled the animated dinner the previous night. It was all 'Faye stayed with Greg before she came to us, how amazing is that?' and 'Faye urged me to phone him when I read the letter,' and 'thank goodness Faye found the letter' and then there was the bombshell when Nathan said, 'Faye is going to sit for me, so I can start to paint again properly.'

She had sat through dinner in stunned silence, forcing a smile whenever it was called for, all the time thinking 'this woman is stealing my life'.

She stood for a moment motionless and inhaled deeply, listening to the enormity of the silence in the kitchen. Unconsciously her teeth dug deep into her lower lip to stop them trembling, but nothing could stop the hot tears as they tumbled down her cheeks.

*

Thankfully the studio was spider free and warmed by a log burner, though the late April sunshine filtering through the windows gave an extra boost to the ambient temperature.

Faye was dressed in a simple shift dress made of white linen trimmed at the neckline and cuff with a delicate green thread. Her hair was loosely pulled back into a ponytail, and Nathan requested that her make-up was kept to a minimum. He wanted the image to be pure and simple, and in the end, it was Faye who set the scene and the composition was complete.

She stood motionless at the studio window, one hand gently leaning against the glass. Her eyes looked out as though in search of someone, her lips were parted slightly as she was lost in concentration.

Nathan had seen this stance several times since Faye moved in with them. If ever there was a window, Faye would stand and stare out for a good few moments. The image summed up the fact that someday, someone would come and change her life, and the uncertainty in Faye's eyes predicted that it may not be for the better. As he painted, he was overwhelmed by the melancholia which surrounded her, and his heart ached for her, as it was a feeling he knew so well.

As the morning wore on, Nathan worked methodically, using the paint sparingly, so hardly a splash touched his clothes or the floor. Occasionally he would say 'Rest for a moment' but Faye hardly dared to move a muscle, for chance she would spoil the moment.

Presently he stopped and stretched, stood back from the painting and smiled. "You can relax for a moment," he said. He walked to the studio doors and looked out, as though in search of the person Faye was waiting for. "You make a good subject. Not many people can keep still for as long as you did."

She turned and the smile she gave him warmed his

heart. "Thank you, I did my best. I suppose it's all that posing for the camera while I was with Lemmel." She thought of Calvin and his vicious tongue if she ever moved while a shot was being taken. Her eyes clouded at the thought of him.

Nathan watched her countenance change. "Hey now, no more thoughts of Lemmel, okay? That is all in the past now. I spoke to my solicitor this morning, and he said that if you didn't sign a contract, like you said you didn't, then they have no claim on you at all, so you can rest assured that there will be no law suit, okay? As for Liam Knight, I've instructed my solicitor to send a letter to him, care of the boatyard, warning him that if you receive any more threats, directly or indirectly, then the police will be informed and action will be taken against him."

The smile on her face returned and he saw her visibly relax at this news as Faye felt the weight of the world lift from her shoulders. "Thank you," she mouthed softly.

He glanced again out to sea; the turquoise water was utterly becalmed making the rocks and sand beneath luminously visible. "The sea is perfect today. I think I might take the boat out for a spot of mackerel fishing later," he said casually. "Would you like to come with me?"

She grimaced slightly. "I'd love to Nathan, but I'm not the best sailor in the world. I fear I may lose my breakfast."

He laughed softly. "Well, the trick is to not look down when you're in the boat, keep your head up and look at the wonderful view. Why don't you come and try. I promise the instant you feel your breakfast making an unwelcome return I shall bring you straight back to shore."

Faye glanced out to sea and nodded. "Okay, I'll give it a try. It does look rather wonderful out there." Faye's eyes sparkled in anticipation.

The eagerness in her face warmed his heart. "Good, a fishing trip it is then, but only if you keep still for another ten minutes."

Her head snapped back into position, but the melancholia had gone and the composition of the painting changed completely.

Because she was unsuitably dressed for a fishing expedition, Faye was wrapped in a warm coat belonging to Nathan, a pair of waterproof trousers, long fishing socks and wellingtons which were three sizes too big for her. He marvelled at how she could still look so lovely even in oversized men's clothes. Together they pushed the vessel across the beach until the foamy surf lapped at the hull. Faye quickly climbed aboard and covered her legs with a tartan blanket and sat waiting for Nathan to give it a last push before he too clambered aboard. As they drifted away from the beach, Nathan pulled the engine cord several times, swearing under his breath at each failure to start. A slight adjustment was made, which immediately made it jump into life. Soon they were motoring out to sea. They didn't go far, just enough to skirt the mountainous cliffs so that Gurnard's Head was in sight, and as instructed Faye kept her head up to keep the nausea at bay.

Nathan unravelled one of the two lines he had brought. There were six tiny feathers and a small lead weight attached to the end of yards of line wrapped around a wooden handle. He passed the first one to Faye and told her to let the line out until she could feel the sea bed. He quickly set up the other line and once they were both ready, he told her to lift and dip to attract the fish. After a quarter of an hour, Nathan proclaimed that the fish were not biting, as he pulled his line from the sea. Faye slowly raised her own line only to find three silvery mackerel attached, which she almost dropped in alarm.

"Hey, hey," he laughed grabbing the line off her before she dropped it back in the sea. "Well done you! You've just caught our lunch," Nathan announced dragging the slippery creatures from the flies. "Couldn't you feel them on the line?"

Faye nodded. "I felt something, but I thought I had

caught it on some seaweed."

She squealed and pulled her feet away as the fish thrashed against the hull covering her feet with silvery scales. Nathan quickly dealt with them with a short sharp bang on the head, and Faye watched in queasy fascination, as he cut and gutted them. Within the space of five minutes, the beautiful iridescent creatures had gone from swimming in the mighty ocean to being prepped and ready to cook.

"We'll have to cook these up at the studio BBQ; Carrie doesn't like the smell in the house," he said rolling his eyes. "I have to admit, there is nothing like the taste of fresh mackerel straight out of the sea."

They made their way back to the beach, dragged the vessel free of the surf and ran laughing up the coast path towards the studio. Nathan stopped en route to pull wild garlic from the hedgerow, and they stumbled into the studio, breathless and elated from their fishing trip.

With the soft spring breeze rustling through the foliage surrounding the studio doors, they lunched on the delicious savoury white fleshy fish, bathed in its own oil with just a hint of garlic to make it a mouth-watering delicacy. Licking her oily fingers in appreciation, a bottle of white wine was produced from his store cupboard, dusted down and poured into cracked mugs so they could toast their catch with joyous delight.

"Here's to your first meal at the 'Blue Bay Café'" Nathan raised his glass. "You see Faye, anywhere can be a 'Blue Bay Café' when you walk and sit on the beautiful Cornish coast. All you need is a packed lunch and a flask, or a bottle of wine." He winked. "…and Bob's your uncle, you have your very own beach side café. This one just happened to be the one Elizabeth and I chose as ours. But you are very welcome to share it."

*

The Gweek boatyard had been busy all day and Pippa was late taking her lunch-break. The day was warm and an hour under the shade of the chestnut tree on the village green was a welcome respite to the incessant ringing of the phone. Gathering her belongings together after lunch, she heard Owen calling her name.

"I haven't finished my lunch yet!" she shouted back at him crossly.

"I know, sorry, it's just that there is a phone call for you. Someone named Ryan?"

Lifting her hand to gesture that she was coming, she wondered with excitement why he was phoning her.

*

Slightly intoxicated, they stumbled their way back down to the village, parting when they approached the shop as Nathan needed firelighters. The phone rang just as Faye walked through the front door. She waited for a moment, knowing full well that Carrie, in her role as housekeeper, insisted on answering all calls. When no one appeared she lifted the receiver. "Zennor 601941" she said. The call caused her world to stop spinning.

As she replaced the receiver, Carrie appeared at the kitchen door and thumped her fists into her hips. "I answer the house phone," she barked angrily, just as Nathan came through the front door. "Nathan, would you please tell her that it's my job to answer the house phone, not hers!"

Nathan gave an exasperated sigh, but as he glanced at Faye he could see she was visibly shaken. "Is everything okay Faye?"

"My Mum's died," she whispered. "If you'll excuse me, I need to go to my room." She ran up the stairs as quickly as her legs would carry her. Nathan cast a sidelong glance at Carrie, regarding her reproachfully. "Perhaps you might apologise to Faye when you see her next," he said quietly. "Oh, and the phone belongs to everyone," he added as Carrie's heart broke further.

It was dark when a soft knock came on Faye's bedroom door. When she didn't answer, Nathan opened the door bearing a mug of tea and a couple of biscuits.

Faye lay quite still atop the eiderdown. Her tears had dried, but her eyes were red rimmed and puffy.

"When is the funeral?"

Faye cleared her throat. "It's already been and gone. My step-father didn't want me there. Apparently I'm an embarrassment to the family." She lowered her eyes and licked her dry lips.

Nathan's heart went out to her. "Who rang you?"

"Pippa did. Ryan, my brother-in-law was very angry that I hadn't been informed, so he contacted Pippa to see if she knew where I was."

He sat at the foot of her bed and his heart went out to her. "I'm so sorry Faye. Is there anything I can do?"

Faye shook her head. "I was having such a lovely day as well."

Nathan nodded, and offered his arms open for a hug, which she snuggled into without hesitation.

*

Faye had pondered for over a week before she made the decision to make the journey up to Yorkshire. Her relationship with her mother had not been an easy one, because of Carl. Her step-father had, with his domineering ways, pushed a wedge between mother and daughter, but all the same, Faye felt the need to lay flowers on her grave and say her own goodbyes. Nathan was bereft at her impending departure, though he tried hard to hide his feelings. "Are you sure you are going to be all right?" he asked softly, as he put her bag onto the train at Truro station.

"I'll be fine. Pippa is with me. I just want to pay my respects at her grave. I'll be gone no more than two days I promise, I should be back on Saturday."

"Well, I shall miss you," he declared sincerely. "As a friend," he added.

She smiled warmly. "And I you Nathan," she answered, kissing him lightly on the cheeks.

Once they were settled in their seats and waved their goodbyes, Pippa nudged Faye in the ribs.

"What?"

"He's lovely," she said gleefully.

Faye smiled and looked at her reflection in the window. Yes he is, she said to herself.

*

Liam watched with mild curiosity as Amos drove his brand new Range Rover out of the boatyard that same Thursday evening. Amos was a creature of habit and Liam could set his watch by Amos's movements. He knew Amos would drive to Helston, fill his car up with petrol, pick up a few groceries and be back in his own boat within the hour. Then on Friday afternoon, he would fling a large holdall into the passenger seat and leave the boatyard at three p.m. He left at the same time, every Friday and as far as Liam was aware, he was gone for a good forty eight hours. It occurred to Liam that Amos was up to something illegal. How else could he afford such luxuries? It wasn't just the car; it was the clothes he wore. He would often be dressed in expensive sailing attire, and when he wasn't working, his feet were shod with fine Italian leather shoes.

He watched Amos's Range Rover disappear from view, and sighed angrily. His own Range Rover had been the only other item apart from the yacht which Liam managed to salvage from the debris of his marriage, and that was only because he loaded it up and drove off in it, leaving his wife with the Volvo, which she complained of bitterly to her solicitor. I mean for Christ's sake, what else did she want? She had got the house because of the kids. The holiday home in Mawnan Smith was sold, and the proceeds of that went to her via the Child Support Agency, because Liam was out of work. In short he was left with nothing, except the yacht and vehicle and he was in no doubt that she would be after those before long.

Heavy rain had begun to sweep up the Helford when Liam climbed down the ladder of his yacht, pulled his coat over his head and walked swiftly towards Amos's yacht 'Odessa'. He looked up at the tarpaulin which covered the boat and was thankful that the ropes were not secured. With a swift glance about him to check the coast was clear, he climbed the ladder and stepped onto the deck. Casting his eyes over the scruffy deck, he walked over to the galley doors, lifted the catch and opened them up. "Good God," he said, reeling back from the overpowering smell of heavy aftershave which emitted from the galley below. He pulled a handkerchief from his pocket, pressed it to his nose, then turned and walked backwards down the steps. The rain was drumming violently on deck as he cast his eyes over the mess before him. What he saw disgusted him; for all his fine clothes, Amos lived like a pig down here.

He moved around the piles of junk and noticed a calendar hung above the galley sink. Every Friday was circled in red, and within the circle was written a different man's name, a make of van, and a registration number.

Liam grimaced. 'Well, well Amos, what the devil are you up to, with all these men?"

He kicked a pair of shoes which were discarded on the floor, picked one of them up and laughed. They were made of the finest Italian black leather, identical to the ones Liam wore; only these were size eleven, whereas Liam was a more petit size nine. He dropped the shoe back on the floor and opened up the makeshift wardrobe. It was full of clothes bearing the brand names of 'Helly Hanson', 'Musto' and 'Armani'. Liam laughed; he could have been looking at his own wardrobe.

"Oh dear Amos, this lot doesn't come cheap, what do you do to get your money, you sad, sad little man," Liam murmured.

He looked down at his own clothes and sighed. The way his divorce was going, Georgina would have the clothes off his back soon, and he would be dressed in rags. I wonder if you'll copy me then Amos Peel, he mused. As he turned to leave, he stopped short at a cork pin-board on the wall which was filled with pictures of Faye cut out of newspapers and magazines. The sudden sight of Faye's face angered him and he pulled out a spare pin and stabbed it into the eye of one of the photos. Finding nothing else in the boat, Liam climbed back down the ladder and had just about made it back to his own yacht when Amos drove back into the boatyard.

"What are you up to Amos Peel?" he said as he watched him drive past.

48

Disguised in dark glasses and a large floppy hat, Faye stood motionless in the warm sunshine of Burndale churchyard beside her mother's grave. At length she placed the spray of lilies on the mound of earth and moved over to where Ben and Lucy were buried. The grave was well tended and this being early summer the ground was a blaze of colour, with an array of yellow and purple irises, pink dianthus, and sumptuous clematis, which scrambled over the headstone. Faye's thoughts took her back to the day she had found Ryan drunk and bereft at his children's grave and how she'd played the Good Samaritan and took him home with dreadful consequences.

The church bells began to peal and she glanced at the church clock before realising that they were pealing not to announce the time, but for a wedding. She caught a glimpse of the crowd of people emerging from the church and shrank back when she saw Lyndon Maunders step out into the sunshine with his new bride on his arm, none other than Lyndon's posh friend Lucinda Hervey.

Lyndon was the last person she wanted to meet, so she lowered her head and moved swiftly back to where Pippa was waiting for her, only to find her talking to Ryan.

"Hello Faye," Ryan said softly. "Long time no see. I hardly recognised you under that disguise."

She grimaced. "Needs must and all that," she said embracing him warmly. "Thanks for letting me know about Mum."

He shook his head crossly. "I was so angry at the funeral, when I realised they hadn't informed you."

"Well, I really do appreciate it. Tell me, how did you know I was here?"

He laughed shortly. "Oh the jungle drums are doing their work. I don't think you had been in the village a minute, before Joanne Tubbs had spread the word."

"Oh that bloody woman. I could hit her."

Ryan laughed softly. "I think you need to get in a queue."

A lone blackbird sang sweetly in the tree above them and they all looked up towards it and felt settled by its song. Presently Faye turned her attention back to Ryan. "And how are you Ryan?" she asked softly.

Ryan shrugged his shoulders and shook his head. His life was miserable; an empty shell of unhappiness. He grieved constantly and silently at the loss of his children, without help or comfort from Gayle, who herself was bereft, but suffered her loss in cold resentment. She had made it quite clear that she would never forgive him, and spoke to him only when necessary. He lifted his haunted eyes to meet Faye's.

Faye knitted her brows together. "Are things no better?"

He closed his eyes and his mouth twitched sorrowfully. "In my sham of a marriage you mean?"

Faye stared at him for a moment.

"We have a sham marriage Faye, things never improved. Our marriage is just for show. It's all a big front now, so we can adopt children. Gayle wants another child. " His voice trailed off and he turned away to hide his emotion.

"Oh Ryan, is that what you want to do?"

He shrugged his shoulders and glanced towards his children's grave. "What does it matter what I want? My life is over."

Pippa gently put her hand on his arm. "It's none of my business, but my policy in life is to live it like you want to live it, not like someone else wants to live it for you."

He looked down into Pippa's eyes. "You're absolutely right, but...."

"No buts," she said with a wink.

"She's right Ryan, maybe it's time to move on. Talking

of moving on, I think we had better go before I'm recognised." She hugged him tightly and kissed him gently on the cheek.

Not wanting them to leave, he asked, "Where are you staying?"

"Over at Appletreewick. I didn't really want to stay in Burndale for obvious reasons. We arrived last night and are leaving first thing tomorrow."

He nodded. "It's so lovely to see you both. I've missed you a lot," he said sadly.

Faye felt his unhappiness keenly. "Pippa tells me you have a new job. Is everything going okay there?"

Ryan nodded despondently. "It's okay, I suppose. Beggars can't be choosers as they say." He gave them a weak smile.

Faye put her hand gently on his arm. "I'm sorry Ryan."

Ryan shrugged.

Faye took one last look at her mother's grave. "Did she suffer?"

"I don't know really. She had a heart attack at home and I saw them take her into the ambulance. I rushed over and when she saw me she said, 'Ryan, please tell Faye that I am sorry'."

Faye was puzzled. "What was she sorry for?"

"I don't know. That is all she said. I never saw her again because she had another heart attack on the way to hospital and died."

Faye swallowed the tears which immediately bubbled up, and Pippa put her arm around her. "Come on let's go," she said softly.

As they made to leave the churchyard, Joanne Tubbs was carefully drying the last of the Polaroid prints she had taken of Faye and Ryan's encounter.

Within an hour of Joanne Tubbs returning home, the Echo had their next morning's front-page scoop, and Gayle Farrington was in possession of three photographs of her husband and Faye. As she boiled the kettle for a cup of tea, Joanne Tubbs quickly dialled the mobile phone number on the card, which the tall dark stranger had left her all those months ago, and informed him of Faye's return to Burndale.

*

Liam screwed the letter up that he'd received that morning from Nathan's solicitor and threw it with force into his waste bin. He cursed loudly. He needed to be somewhere and he had no petrol in his own Range Rover and no spare money to fill it up with. Damn Georgina, she was milking him dry. How he hated having no money. He sighed angrily, and then suddenly a happy thought popped into his mind and he laughed out loud.

He scrambled up the galley steps into the fresh damp air. Five minutes later he was back in his own yacht pushing a few items into an overnight bag.

At three p.m. Liam cocked his head when he heard Amos trying to start his vehicle. He listened for a couple more minutes, then climbed off his yacht and made his way towards him.

Liam pushed his hands deep into his pockets. "Is something wrong?" he asked casually.

Amos's face was flushed and he was clearly agitated. "The damn thing won't start and I haven't time to mess with it. I have to be somewhere in...." He checked his watch. "Soon," he said in anguish.

"Oh dear, let me take a look. I know a thing or two about cars." He lifted the bonnet, scanned his eyes over the engine, tapped a few things and said, "Mmm, it's probably the alternator, I think I could mend it, but not until tomorrow."

Amos was beside himself. "I have got to be somewhere tonight. What the hell am I going to do?"

"Calm down mate, here you go, take mine," Liam said, throwing him the ignition keys to his own Range Rover. "It's the same as yours, so you'll be okay in it," he said sarcastically. "But mind, it'll need some petrol because it's empty." He grinned.

"But I won't be back until Sunday evening at the earliest," Amos added, handing over his own keys.

"It's okay. I won't need it over the weekend. The alternator will be about a hundred quid," he said, holding out his hand.

"Oh, right." Amos pulled his wallet out and peeled off two fifty pound notes and handed them over to Liam. "Thanks a lot, you're a real mate." He glanced at his watch. "I'll have to go," he said running towards Liam's vehicle with his holdall.

"No problem, I'll have this mended by the time you get back," he shouted.

As Liam watched Amos speed away, his mouth twisted into a wry smile. He opened the driver's door, pulled the fuse box open and replaced the fuses he had in his pocket. What good fortune it was that he found out that Amos always left his car unlocked. Within a quarter of an hour Liam too was driving out of Gweek.

*

At ten-thirty that evening Faye rubbed her head to ease the ache that had been with her most of the day. Pain killers hadn't worked so she told Pippa she was going out for some fresh air.

"Do you want me to come with you?" Pippa offered sleepily.

Faye shook her head as she buttoned her coat to keep out the evening chill. They were staying in the New Inn, a small country pub just outside the village of Burndale and not far from where Orchard Hills her marital home would have been. She knew they couldn't safely stay in Burndale without risk of reporters finding her, so she and Pippa had checked in as sisters under Pippa's surname.

Outside the pub she inhaled a deep breath of evening air and turned to walk briskly across the bridge. Almost all the lights in the village were out and Faye thought that either everyone had gone to bed early or they were all at

Lyndon's wedding reception. A slight prickle of apprehension made Faye aware of a movement behind her. She turned and heard a crunching sound like tyres freewheeling. Faye looked up towards the noise but the night was dark and moonless. The hairs on the back of her neck stood on end and she tried to step off the road. She heard the car engine rev up, smelt the hot oily fumes and then felt metal slamming into her body. The impact flung her into the air and she somersaulted right over the vehicle, landing on the road with a thud. The vehicle was swiftly put into reverse then accelerated towards her again. Faye felt her ribs crack with sickening agony. She tried to scream but nothing emerged from her mouth. She heard the vehicle coming towards her again and felt her leg crush under the weight, and then Faye lost consciousness and the pain faded away.

Pippa glanced at the clock and wondered where Faye had got too. She got up out of bed and pulled the curtains aside, but it was too dark to see anything. Parkinson had just started on the TV and Billy Connelly was one of his guests, so she got back into bed to watch for a moment. An hour later she woke from her sleep to find an old black and white movie on the TV. She glanced at the clock and quickly pulled her coat over her pyjamas and ran out into the village.

"Faye," she called softly, not wanting to raise the other guests.

"She's over here I think," a man's voice called out.

Pippa ran up the road towards a group of people gathered around the mangled body of her best friend. "Oh my God," Pippa cried cradling her. "Faye, oh my goodness, is she alive?" she screamed up at the group of people who had crowded around.

"She's breathing yes. The ambulance is on its way," a voice answered.

*

Ryan stepped out of the front door and sucked in the cool

night air. He was exhausted after the evening he'd just had! Gayle had arrived home an hour ago, from God knows where, and threw the damning photos at him. She had been beside herself with rage, ranting and raving at him about them rekindling their affair. He had just spent the last hour ducking and diving from all manner of ornaments Gayle had thrown at him, while he had tried to pacify her that their meeting had been quite innocent and in full view of the public. It was clear that Gayle was teetering on the edge of another breakdown. She had screamed at him that if the adoption authorities got wind of his latest indiscretion, it could seriously damage their application. He gave a short derisory laugh. Adoption, what the hell were they thinking about? Their marriage wasn't a fitting environment to bring up children. Maybe it would be a good thing for them to get wind of these stupid rumours. Then they could forget all about staying together. In truth, he had thought about nothing else, but what Pippa had said to him that morning. 'Live it like you want to live it, not like someone else wants to live it for you,' she had said, and as every moment passed, he was beginning to agree with her.

He leant against the door and took a drag of his cigarette, a habit he had kicked some years ago, but had recently taken up again. He looked up as Gayle's bedroom light suddenly illuminated down into the garden. He hoped she had gone to bed at last. He threw the butt of the cigarette down and twisted the toe of his shoe on it. As he turned to go inside, the flashing light from an ambulance blinded him as it sped into the village. He walked slowly down the drive to see where it was going and as the siren faded in the distance he returned to the house and the spare bedroom.

It was only when he arrived at the New Inn the next morning to say his last farewells to Faye, that he was confronted with the awful truth of what had happened the previous evening.

*

Pippa was distraught when Ryan arrived at Airedale Hospital. Faye had sustained multiple injuries, and Pippa had sat in vigil all night in the hospital as surgeons battled to mend her broken body. She had just been taken to intensive care when he arrived. He was told her condition was critical, but stable. Because of her injuries, she was in a drug induced coma for the time being. Now, both Ryan and Pippa sat in vigil hoping and praying that Faye would come back to them soon.

Ryan glanced up at the clock; it was almost lunchtime. "I'm going to see if I can get a bite to eat, do you want anything Pippa?" he said, getting up from his chair to stretch.

"Oh I couldn't eat a thing, but I'd like a drink please," Pippa answered, without taking her eyes off her friend.

As Ryan stood in the queue at the kiosk with his sandwiches and drinks, his mouth went suddenly dry as his gaze fell upon the front headline of the Echo.

'CAMELOT LOVE RAT' KEEPS IT IN THE FAMILY.

In a new twist to the Burndale 'Camelot' love triangle scandal, the infamous love rat Ryan Farrington, who six months ago was revealed as the lover of Lemmel's top model Faye Larson, aka the face of 'Guinevere', appears to have dealt another cruel blow to his long-suffering wife, as his ongoing affair with his sister-in-law is rekindled.

When Ryan noticed the picture of himself and Faye in the churchyard under the headline, he snatched a copy of the newspaper from the stand and scanned the page with disbelief. "Oh no," he muttered.

"Are you going to buy that paper?" the cashier asked acidly.

Ryan fished some money out of his pocket, slapped it on the counter and didn't wait for his change.

As he walked slowly back up the corridor reading the paper, a figure suddenly appeared before him.

A thin wheezing voice said, "Oh Mr Farrington? I wonder if I could just have a word with you."

Ryan glared at the young greasy haired journalist dressed in a long fawn Mac who had jumped out at him and was now stabbing a tape recorder to his mouth. He pushed him aside and walked on.

"I'm from the Echo," the journalist persisted, as he ran after Ryan. "I understand Faye Larson was admitted here last night."

Ryan came to an abrupt halt and glared at the man with disgust. "I know exactly who you are Tubbs, now get lost," he snapped, shoving him unceremoniously out of his way.

The journalist stumbled over a hospital trolley, but quickly got back onto his feet and set off in hot pursuit down the corridor after Ryan.

"How does your wife feel about your rekindled affair with her sister? Has she been to visit her in hospital? Is there any truth in the story that you are going to leave your wife for Faye Larson? Don't you think what you are doing is a bit cruel so soon after the death of her children?"

With every word the journalist uttered, Ryan's anger grew more intense. As he approached the intensive care ward he suddenly turned and stopped the journalist dead in his tracks as he threw a punch into his face with such force, Ryan felt as though he had broken his own hand with the blow. As he entered the ward doors, the journalist was flat on his back, out for the count.

From that moment on, the media interest in the Farrington/Larson affair escalated beyond belief. Crowds of journalists gathered outside the hospital doors for a glimpse of Ryan Farrington, but Ryan had been unceremoniously bundled into a police car on a charge of grievous bodily harm. He was under strict instructions from the police to keep away from the hospital and avoid any more conflict. So it was, that what the journalists couldn't find out, they made up.

Although Faye was unconscious and thus unable to give any answers to questions, it was clear from the evidence of tyre marks on her body that she had been run over by a large four-wheeled drive vehicle. As Gayle Farrington drove a four-wheel drive, and had a motive, she was first to be questioned about the incident.

When the police patrol car pulled up outside Ryan's house, they found him cleaning the vehicle whilst he tried to ignore the smattering of journalists at the end of his road. The officers glanced at each other knowingly.

Ryan picked up the bucket, straightened his back and watched the police officers walk up the drive.

"Now what do you want," Ryan asked irritably. "I've only just come away from the station."

"Just a word please, if that's okay," one of the officers said.

Gayle stood behind the curtains in the lounge watching the exchange of words and when they looked as though they were coming in, she swiftly ran upstairs.

As Ryan showed the officers through the front door, his eye caught a flash of Gayle's skirt as she moved along the landing.

The officer pulled his notebook from his pocket and with a pen poised he said, "Can we ask why you are cleaning your vehicle Mr Farrington?"

Ryan laughed incredulously. "It's dirty, why else would I clean it?" he answered caustically.

"Well, maybe to remove evidence perhaps?" The smaller of the two officers said dryly.

"What evidence? What on earth are you talking about? Hey wait a minute; you're not suggesting I had anything to do with Faye's accident. I don't even drive this thing. It belongs to my wife."

"Attempted murder."

"Huh?" Ryan scowled.

"It was attempted murder, not an accident."

Ryan gestured wildly with his hands. "Whatever."

There was a creak on the ceiling as Gayle moved involuntarily.

One of the officers looked up. "Is your wife in? We'd like to speak to her."

Ryan's mind was in turmoil. Surely Gayle hadn't tried to kill Faye? Then he remembered that she had been out last night in the vehicle.

"Mr Farrington, is your wife in?"

Ryan furrowed his brow. "Yes but she has a very delicate disposition at the moment. You can't just go in and accuse her of attempted murder."

"We want to talk to her that's all. Jim, arrange for this vehicle to be taken into the compound will you? With a bit of luck he'll have left something for forensics."

Ryan pulled on the sleeve of one of the officers. "No wait a minute, wait a minute. This is absurd."

"I'm sorry Mr Farrington; we are just doing our job. Now, if you would like to tell your wife we are here. The sooner we speak to her the better."

*

On Monday morning Amos sat and read the newspaper report of Faye's accident with horror. "Bloody Hell!" he exclaimed.

Owen Barnes looked up from his desk. "Huh?" When he didn't reply, he cocked his head and watched his face pale with shock. "What the hell are you reading Amos?" he asked.

He passed him the newspaper. "Look."

He skimmed rather than read the article and gasped, "Well there you are Amos. I've said all along that if she'd have stayed working here, none of this would have happened."

*

Pippa woke with a start, and scolded herself for dozing off. It was five thirty five in the morning when she checked the clock. She stood up, tidied the covers and stroked Faye's pale lifeless face. It was then she realised that no one had informed Nathan of Faye's accident.

49

For Nathan, Faye's absence seemed as endless as the mist which had rolled in from the sea the day she went away. He'd been worried sick about her and wondered why she hadn't phoned as she'd promised. He checked himself - why should she, it's not as if they were in a relationship or anything. She was probably just having a good time catching up with her friend Pippa. But still, it didn't stop him worrying. She should have been back on Saturday, but she must have decided to stay on a little longer in Yorkshire. He just wished she would phone and let him know. In truth, he needed her here with him. He smiled inwardly. She inspired him.

He was woken from his dreams at six that morning, by the shrill ring of the telephone.

Ashen-faced he replaced the receiver and walked slowly to the lounge and sat heavily on the chair by the window. The day was grey, and squally showers pelted the windows as Nathan sat in disbelief at what Pippa had just told him. He felt chilled to the bone. Presently he knelt by the hearth and began to build a fire and as he reached for the newspaper he saw the headline glaring out at him.

ACCIDENT OR RETRIBUTION?

Faye Larson, the infamous face of 'Guinevere' has been left for dead on the roadside in Appletreewick, near Burndale, North Yorkshire. A local woman has been taken in for questioning.

Nathan read on in disbelief.

The police are trying to identify the cause of the hit and run incident in which Faye Larson, aka the 'face of Guinevere' of the failed cosmetic giant Lemmel, sustained extensive and life threatening injuries.

Emotions have been running high in the nearby village of Burndale, as the police continue their search for witnesses. In a village already shocked at a previous incident involving Miss Larson's family, the residents are speculating whether this recent incident has anything to do with retribution for incidents which occurred last year.

Many of the villagers seemed reluctant to speak to the police, or to come forward with any information, which could help them with their enquiries. Only Mrs Joanne Tubbs had this to say: 'There seems to be an unsympathetic view amongst the villagers towards Miss Larson. There's a feeling of great empathy for Ryan Farrington's long suffering wife Gayle, who only last year lost both her children in a tragic accident while she was in hospital having a hysterectomy. It's no secret that Miss Larson's wedding was called off when her husband-to-be Lyndon Maunders found out about her affair with someone from the village. I'm not too sure who she had an affair with, but all I know is it upset the Larson and Farrington family greatly; especially Gayle Farrington. I feel so sorry for that poor family. They had just put the whole sorry incident behind them and had begun to build their life again, when that Larson woman arrived back to 'allegedly' rekindle her affair. I can tell you, Faye Larson is not thought well of here,' Miss Tubbs added. 'It seems to me, someone, somewhere, took great exception to her being back.'

Nathan gasped in disbelief. When he turned round, Carrie was standing by the door.

"I thought I heard you up and about," she said cheerily. "Do you want some breakfast?"

"No, I'm going away for a few days. Will you look after Jasper for me?"

"Of course I will, but where are you going?"

Nathan threw the paper on the sofa. "Read that!" he

said.

Carrie glanced at the paper. "Oh that!" she exclaimed indifferently.

Nathan stared at her in astonishment. "Did you know about this?" he snapped.

"The whole village knows about it. Yes."

Nathan felt the bile rise in his throat. "And you didn't think to tell me?"

She shrugged her shoulders nonchalantly. "No, why?"

He stood up from where he knelt as anger welled up in him. "For god's sake woman, why didn't you tell me?"

Carrie bristled with indignation. "What's it to do with us what she gets up to? She obviously just flits in and out of people's lives, ruining relationships. I thought you would be better off not knowing what sort of a bitch she's been," she said folding her arms defiantly.

Nathan's mouth tightened. "What the hell do you know about anything?"

"I know what I read," Carrie shouted indignantly.

"Well you read rubbish. This is rubbish," he raged, shaking the paper in front of her before he stuffed it into the fire grate. "Faye could have been dead by now for all I knew."

Carrie swallowed hard. "She may have bewitched you with her sob story, but I can see right through her. Why can't you see her for what she is Nathan?" she said, her words choking in her throat.

Nathan shook his head as he tried to control his anger. "You really don't know her at all Carrie, Faye is a wonderful person, who has been badly treated. I'm very disappointed in you, I would have thought you had more charity, but it seems you are no better than the gutter press. I'm ashamed of you."

Carrie's eyes filled with tears at the harshness of his words. He had never raised his voice to her before and she was deeply upset, but he was too angry to notice her distress as he went about the house gathering his belongings for his journey.

"I don't know how long I will be gone," he said to Carrie before he left. There was a marked coolness in his voice. "I'll phone you when I know what I'm doing, okay?"

Carrie nodded unhappily as he turned and left.

*

Faye had been in intensive care for two days, and it was decided to bring her out of her induced coma, but as yet she had shown no signs of regaining consciousness. Pippa was exhausted; she had spent every waking hour at her friend's bedside and whether it was the hospital's atmosphere or just exhaustion, she had begun to feel a little unwell herself.

The media interest had died down now and only a lone journalist nursing a broken nose, stood in vigil at the hospital doors, and security were keeping a close eye on him. Consequently security checks on visitors to the intensive care ward could at last be relaxed slightly.

It was seven forty-five that evening when Nathan arrived at the hospital. The car journey had tired him considerably, but he knew he must see Faye as soon as possible.

He gave his name at the desk and the nurse rang through to the ward.

"Sister, I have Nathaniel Prior here, he wishes to visit Faye Larson. He said that he is a good friend of hers."

"Nathaniel Prior the artist?" the ward sister asked curiously.

"Oh, I don't know. Just a minute, I'll ask." The nurse put her hand over the mouthpiece and said, "Are you by any chance an artist?"

He furrowed his brows. "Yes, why, is that the criteria for visitors?"

She smiled and shook her head in amusement as she returned to her phone call. "Yes it is Sister."

"That's fine send him through, we were expecting a call

317

or a visit from him."

As he entered the room, Pippa fell into his arms with relief.

"How is she?"

"Not good Nathan," Pippa said, as she stepped aside and watched his horrified face as he looked down at Faye. There were tubes up her nose, a drip attached to her arm, bandages on her head, a plaster cast on her right leg and left arm, her face was a bruised swollen pulp and stitches laced her forehead.

Nathan sat on the bed and carefully stroked her swollen fingers. "Oh my poor Faye, what have they done to you? It's me Nathan. I've come to help you get better." The words caught in his throat.

The Sister watched with interest and said, "Sadly, Miss Larson hasn't responded to anything since we stopped the drugs, Mr Prior."

Nathan sighed heavily. "Faye, come on love, I need you to wake up. Faye, please wake up."

Faye's eyelids fluttered slightly at the sound of his voice.

"She moved! Did you see it? She moved," he said animatedly.

The nurse moved closer, but saw nothing and smiled kindly at Nathan.

"She moved her eyelids, I saw her."

The Sister nodded. "Call me if she does it again."

Nathan glanced at Pippa. "Did you see her move?" Pippa rubbed her tired eyes and shook her head. "God you looked wacked, I'll take over for a while if you want to go and get some sleep."

"I've nowhere to go," she added wearily. "I had to check out of the New Inn. We had only booked for two nights and I can't really afford to stay anywhere else. I've managed to grab a couple of hours here and there, on this chair."

Nathan opened his wallet and passed a fifty pound note

to her. "Here, I'm booked in at the Stirton House Hotel, go and book yourself a room and have a good night's sleep." He smiled weakly, and as she made to leave he asked, "Pippa, who would do this to her?"

"I don't know, she's had a lot of bad press, and none of it is true you know. The bloody papers, they keep dragging up this cock and bull story about her having an affair and it is all lies. She never had an affair with her brother-in-law. Faye wouldn't do that. She even dropped Liam Knight like a stone, when she found out he was married."

Nathan bristled at the mention of Liam's name. "Do you think this has anything to do with him?"

"God knows. I do know they are questioning Faye's step-sister though."

Nathan nodded knowingly. "I saw that they were questioning a woman, I wondered who it was."

Pippa began to feel quite lightheaded and had to steady herself. "I'm sorry Nathan I think I need to go and lie down."

"Well get yourself a taxi and I'll see you later."

When she had gone, Nathan looked down at Faye and shook his head. "Faye?" he whispered gently into her ear. "My lovely Faye, open your eyes. Let me see you open those beautiful eyes of yours. Do it for me, once more. Come on, you can do it." He watched intently, but she lay still and deathly silent. He glanced around at the equipment attached to her. There were tubes in her arm, her stomach and her nose, the heart monitor flashed constantly and the oxygen hissed quietly. He looked at the sign above the bed, 'Nil by mouth' and shook his head in disbelief. He picked up her pale hand and kissed it gently. Faye's eyelids flickered again then ever so slowly she parted her eyelashes and turned to look at Nathan.

He gasped, and shouted joyously, "Nurse, nurse, please can you come here quickly."

The nurse moved swiftly down the ward. "Mr Prior, please keep your voice down, there are other patients in this ward you know," she bristled indignantly.

He lowered his voice to a whisper, "I'm so sorry, but she's awake, Faye is awake, look!"

Faye had finally broken through the barrier that held her back from the outside world. But all she could hear was a long drawn out never ending moan, as though some animal was in great distress. Then she realised she was in terrible pain, and that it was she who was emitting the terrible noise. She felt her hand being squeezed and Nathan was at her side. Confusion blurred her senses and her brain couldn't unscramble what was happening to her. All she was really aware of was the pain, the terrible unbearable pain.

The doctor was called and her morphine was upped, and Faye lapsed back into sleep. Nathan gave up a silent prayer of thanks and Faye began her long road to recovery.

50

With the knowledge that Faye was recovering, Pippa set off on the train back to Cornwall. With no pressing need to return home himself, Nathan had promised Pippa he would stay until Faye was well enough to be transferred to the Royal Cornwall Hospital.

As the days passed, Faye's medication was reduced and she was able to converse with Nathan.

Hardly leaving her side, he watched as her bruised face turned from red to blue to yellow and finally to flesh coloured. The drip in her stomach was removed and finally she began to eat, albeit a morsel. On questioning, she couldn't shed any light on what had happened that night, all she remembered was stepping out of the doors of the New Inn - after that, nothing.

Gayle Farrington had been exonerated from all charges and the police had drawn a blank as to who had committed the hit and run. There was a general consensus that Faye had just been in the wrong place at the wrong time. Faye was not so sure, something in her subconscious niggled at her and she could not eliminate the doubt.

A few days after she regained consciousness, Faye was moved to an ordinary ward. It would be weeks before she would get the plaster casts off and regain some mobility, so, Nathan arranged for her to be transferred to Cornwall. She was never so happy to leave Yorkshire as she was the day she was put into the ambulance for the transfer. Before she left, Ryan had requested permission to see her. He looked pale and wan as he apologised profusely about what had happened.

"Don't be daft Ryan, we did nothing wrong. It's these bloody reporters stirring up trouble. Why don't they leave me alone? I'm nobody. I just don't understand it."

"Well, the reporter I gave a bloody nose to is Joanne Tubbs nephew. He works for the Echo and is trying to make a name for himself. I'll tell you something Faye, if I ever meet him in a dark alley, he'll get more than a broken nose."

Faye touched him gently on the arm. "Don't get into anymore trouble. Nathan tells me you've already been charged with assault."

Ryan shrugged his shoulder and turned to the window. "I really don't care anymore."

"But what about the adoption you and Gayle are hoping for?"

He gave a short laugh and turned to look at her. "Well I've put paid to that, what with the GBH charge and all that." He sighed heavily. "Gayle wants a divorce."

Faye placed her hand on his. "I'm so sorry Ryan."

He shook his head. "Don't be, it's probably for the best. I'm going to travel a bit I think."

Faye nodded. "Well stay in touch won't you?"

"I will. I must say I'm glad you have Nathan in your life, he'll look after you." There was a slight hint of envy in his voice.

Faye smiled warmly. "He's been a good friend to me, I am lucky to have him in my life."

Ryan lowered his eyes and sighed gently. "Well goodbye then."

They embraced warmly. "Goodbye Ryan. You look after yourself," Faye said with tears in her eyes.

*

After six long weeks Faye's casts were finally removed and her real rehabilitation began. With the aid of physiotherapists, Faye began to walk again, albeit with crutches, and she longed for the day she would leave hospital for good.

"I've been thinking Faye," Nathan said one day, "How about we all have a little holiday in France? I have a good friend in Brittany, Gérard Duclos, who has a house near Dinan. We go most years and I know you will be welcome there too. This would be a perfect opportunity for you to recuperate. I should think you are heartily sick of these hospital walls."

Faye's heart swelled at the idea of leaving hospital. "That would be so lovely Nathan, thank you."

"Brilliant. Have you ever been to Brittany?"

Faye shook her head.

"Oh you'll love Brittany," Nathan said with great gusto. "It's about twenty years behind time - and I mean that in the nicest possible way. They call it the Cornwall of France. They have a long history with us you know, the Bretons, especially with the Cornish. For centuries locals identified far more with Britain than with mainland France. Wait until you see it. It's a misty land of lighthouses marooned off rocky coasts, with brisk sailing and cliff top walks, it's wonderful."

Faye laughed. "You sound like a travel guide."

"I will be a travel guide. I want to show you everything, the wild coastlines, and lovely beaches, and of course you shall sample the good food and ambience."

"Just remember I might be on these crutches for another few weeks."

"You'll manage, with my help," he said, kissing her softly on the forehead.

His touch sent a shiver of anticipation through her body, but she knew she must not let these feelings for Nathan grow. He didn't belong to her. She smiled softly at him. "I can hardly wait," she whispered.

Nathan stayed with Faye for the rest of the afternoon and they chatted happily about their impending holiday in Brittany. He left at four and Faye settled down to read her book, as she didn't expect any more visitors that day. But shortly after seven that evening, Faye was resting on her bed when she saw Nathan walking towards her.

She cocked her head and looked at him questioningly.

"You're back? I didn't expect to see you again today."

"I have a surprise for you," he said and her heart jumped a beat as she recognised the tall handsome man walking through the ward.

"Greg!" She looked from Nathan to Greg then back again.

"Hello sweetheart," he said kissing her warmly on the cheek. "Sorry I haven't been before Simon and I have been in Australia for eight weeks. I only found out today what had happened."

"So, is this the first time you two have been back together since…"

"Our silly estrangement you mean? Yes. We've had a lovely meal together in Truro and I'm staying over at Gwithian Cottage tonight, in your room, if you don't mind," he said cheekily. He sat down on her bed and reached for her hand. "Well in all honesty, I never thought I would see you again. You just vanished that night into thin air."

"I'm so sorry Greg, I felt awful after you had been so kind to me. I just didn't want to bring any trouble to your door."

"Mmm, it seems to me that trouble follows you everywhere. Did they catch who did this to you?"

Faye bit down on her bottom lip. "No, and I don't suppose they will. The police think it was just a random hit and run, probably some drunk."

Greg raised his eyebrow. "Really? What do you think?"

She pulled a thin smile. "I daren't think of the alternative. The police tell me they have put Crime Stoppers signs up in Burndale and Appletreewick in a hope that someone will have seen something, but I don't hold out much hope." She glanced from Greg to Nathan. "Anyway, I'm so glad you two are back together. You know, you're a real chip off the old block when I see you both together."

Greg laid a hand on his father's shoulder and Faye

knew the gulf that had separated them had well and truly closed.

51

Amos had been back in the boatyard only an hour when the police arrived.

"Amos Peel?" DC Cole shouted up to the boat.

Amos pushed the galley doors open, flicked his hood over his head and peered down to see who was shouting for him.

"Amos Peel?" Cole repeated.

Amos nodded.

"I'm Detective Constable Cole. I'd like you to accompany us down to the station."

"Eh?" He frowned. "What for?"

The officers had climbed the ladder and were now standing on the deck of the boat. "I'm arresting you on suspicion of the attempted murder of Faye Larson. You do not have to say..."

"What?" Amos wore a vacant look on his face and said again, "What? Who?"

The police exchanged glances. "Miss Faye Larson?"

"Faye?" A look of confusion paled his face. "No." He franticly began to look around for an escape route.

The other constable stepped forward, catching him by the sleeve to stop him, and then cuffed Amos's hands as DC Cole cautioned him. "Amos Peel, I'm arresting you on suspicion of the attempted murder of Miss Faye Larson. You do not have to say anything. But it may harm your defence if you do not mention when questioned something which you later rely on in Court. Anything you do say may be given in evidence. Do you understand?"

"No," he said, as he looked down at the handcuffs.

"Could you tell us where the keys are to your vehicle Mr Peel?"

Amos stood in open-mouthed bewilderment then whimpered, "They are on my table."

The officer went below deck then shouted down to his colleague, "I think you need to see this."

DC Cole urged Amos to go below and swiftly followed him. "Look at this lot."

DC Cole scanned the wall filled with images of Faye. Presently he said, "Photograph it."

A moment later Amos was being led off the boat and into the waiting patrol car.

*

It was such a relief to return to Gwithian Cottage after so many weeks cooped up in the hospital. Unable to do very much, Faye sat under a huge umbrella in the front garden to read. She felt happier outside when Nathan was not at home. The atmosphere indoors was decidedly chilly whenever she and Carrie's paths met. The air was still and hot, and thunder rumbled in the distance. A slow drone of a lawnmower in the distance; a bee buzzing in the flower bed; all indicated that summer was well and truly with them.

She came to the end of her chapter and reached for her crutches. It was so hot, and the little clothing she had on clung uncomfortably to her damp body. She decided a cool glass of Nathan's homemade elderflower cordial was needed. Slowly negotiating the front step she quickly had to steady herself as Carrie brushed past her brusquely and knocked her into the door jamb. Carrie sighed impatiently and continued out of the door without apology. Faye shook her head; she expected nothing less from her.

Turning the cold tap, she made herself a long cooling drink which refreshed her dry throat. She looked around the kitchen and thought it looked tired, drab and unloved. Carrie's standard of cleaning was not up to Faye's liking, but this was her domain and Faye had the good sense to hold her tongue, but oh, just a lick of paint and a good scrub would make it look so much better.

Feeling suitably refreshed, she limped her way back out to the hall. The thunder was a little louder now. A storm would soon engulf the west coast of Cornwall and hopefully fresher weather would give some relief.

She had just settled back down on her garden chair when the telephone rang. She struggled to the phone, hoping she could get there before they rang off. The journey hadn't been in vain. It was Pippa.

"Oh thank goodness it's you Faye; I hate it when the wicked witch of the south answers the phone. She is *so* rude. Hey you'll never guess what?"

As Faye listened, her face paled. "Are you kidding me?"

"Nope, Amos has been arrested on suspicion of trying to kill you," Pippa repeated.

"Amos! Are you sure?"

"I know we just can't believe it! They arrested him this morning and took him to Helston to be charged. The police have taken his Range Rover to do more tests on it, but apparently they have found blood on the front bumper and underside of the car."

Feeling faint and lightheaded, Faye leant heavily on the wall to steady herself. "That's absurd Pippa. Amos wouldn't have done it, I just don't believe it."

"Well, we just thought you should know."

*

In 'Interview Room One' Amos settled himself down on the metal seat and gazed around the stark grey room. He had a lawyer beside him, a pug faced man who blinked incessantly. "Think before you answer anything, my boy," he said. "I'll be right by your side."

"This interview is being recorded between Mr Amos Peel, myself DC Cole, and my colleague DC Tenna. The time is four-fifty p.m. on Wednesday the eighth of July 1998."

"Mr Peel, where were you on Friday the eighth of May this year?"

Amos's face paled. If it was a Friday, he knew exactly

where he was. He was dumb struck.

"Mr Peel, are you refusing to answer the question?"

Amos glanced at each of the officers and swallowed hard. He shook his head slowly and whispered, "I don't remember."

"I ask you again Mr Peel, where did you go on the night of the eighth of May?"

Amos remained silent as perspiration prickled his scalp.

DC Cole looked at his colleague then spoke into the machine. "Mr Peel refuses to answer the question.

"Well Mr Peel, we put it to you that you were in North Yorkshire that day."

A look of confusion flashed across Amos's face. "Yorkshire?" he said screwing his face up.

DC Cole exchanged glances with DC Tenna.

"We understand that on the night of the eighth of May you drove up to Yorkshire with the sole intention of harming Miss Larson."

Amos swallowed hard. "Why would I do a thing like that?"

"You tell us."

"But I really like Faye; I wouldn't harm her for the world."

"We understand you asked her out on several occasions, but she wasn't interested in you. Mr Peel is that why you stalked her?"

"I didn't stalk her," he answered affronted.

DC Cole cleared his throat and looked straight into Amos's eyes. "Have you ever been to Burndale, North Yorkshire?"

Amos bit down on his lip, he couldn't lie. "Yes."

"When exactly did you go?"

"Last year. It was the day after she was supposed to get married, to that other chap."

"Lyndon Maunders?"

"Yes."

"Why did you go?"

"I thought she might need me. It seemed everyone had turned against her. I wanted to help her."

"You thought she might need you? Even though she had slighted you, and thought you were odd?"

Amos shrugged his shoulders.

"Mr Peel has just shrugged his shoulders. Are you sure you weren't just stalking her?"

"No!" he said violently.

"Did you see Faye Larson?"

"No."

"Mr Peel, do you own the vehicle which you gave us the keys to yesterday, which is a Range Rover, registration N345 PRO?"

"Yes."

"Does anyone else drive your vehicle?"

Amos shook his head.

"Please speak yes or no into the machine."

Amos moved his face nearer the machine and answered, "No."

"Mr Peel, we have just received a forensic report on your vehicle, and traces of DNA were found on the front and back wheel arches and behind the front registration plate. The DNA matches Faye Larson's. I ask you again, were you involved in a hit and run incident on the eighth of May this year where Faye Larson received multiple injuries?"

"No!" he cried.

"Have you heard of Crime Stoppers."

"No."

"Two weeks ago we placed Crime Stopper boards in Burndale and Appletreewick in the hope that witnesses would come forward about the hit-and-run that Miss Larson was involved in."

Amos looked blankly at them.

"We had several people phoning in with information and twice your car and registration was mentioned."

Amos sat open- mouthed.

"I put it to you again Mr Peel, where were you on the night of the eighth of May 1998?"

"In Plymouth," he admitted.

DC Cole folded his arms. "With whom?"

Amos faltered. "No one."

"So no one can verify that you were in Plymouth that night."

"No."

"Why were you in Plymouth that night?"

"I was picking something up."

"From where?"

"Plymouth."

DC Cole sighed impatiently. "*Where* in Plymouth?"

Amos felt his lip begin to tremble. He knew he was a dead man if he told the police. "I'd rather not say." Amos broke down in tears. He laid his head in his arms on the table and cried for the next five minutes. When he raised his head, he left a trail of mucus from his nose on his sleeve. DC Tenna pushed a Kleenex box towards him.

"Were you driving your car that night?"

"Yes," he snapped. Then he stopped, looked into space as though in deep thought. "Oh, wait a minute, no, I wasn't. I'd borrowed Liam Knight's car. Mine had broken down." He felt the relief washing over him.

The two officers glanced at each other. "Did you call out a mechanic for your car?"

Amos shook his head.

"Please speak into the machine Mr Peel."

"No," he said softly. "Liam Knight said he would take a look at it for me. He said it was the alternator."

"And did he mend it?"

"Well I gave him a hundred pounds for an alternator, and the car started when I tried it a couple of days later, so, yes, he must have."

"This interview is terminated at five seven p.m."

"Can I go now?" Amos said getting up.

"No."

*

Liam had just returned from Helston when the police arrived. Pippa watched with interest from the office window as they exchanged words.

Owen opened the door and walked to the window to join her. "Now, what the devil is going on there do you think?"

"I hope they have come to arrest him. I am absolutely sure Amos has nothing to do with Faye's accident. It's more likely to be that bastard."

"Now Pippa, you can't go accusing people just because you don't like them."

*

DC Cole settled himself on the deck of Liam's yacht and refused the offer of a cup of tea. "We understand that you mended Amos Peel's car on the night of the eighth of May."

"Why, is that a crime?" he joked.

Keeping a deadpan face Cole said, "Did you?"

"No, I'm a businessman, not a mechanic."

"He said he borrowed your car that night, because his had broken down."

Liam snorted. "Like hell he did. I would never lend my car to him; I'd never get rid of the smell of aftershave."

"Mmm," Cole answered thoughtfully. "So Mr Peel did not give you a hundred pounds to replace the alternator?"

Liam laughed. "No."

"Did you speak to Mr Peel that night?"

"No, but he was having trouble starting it. But after a few attempts he was off, to wherever he went to."

"So you are saying he drove out of the boatyard in his own car?"

"Well, it looked like him."

"Thank you Mr Knight."

*

Amos spent a miserable night in the cells. He was cold and frightened and couldn't wait until morning when he would be allowed home. When the officer brought him breakfast he ran to the cell door.

"Can I go home now?" he asked hopefully.

The officer shook his head and laughed. "Probably in about twelve years, that's normally what you get for murder," he said sotto voce.

At ten forty-five a.m. that day, Amos was led back up the corridor to interview room one. Five minutes later DC Cole and DC Tenna walked in.

"This interview is being recorded between Mr Amos Peel, myself DC Cole and my colleague DC Tenna. The time is ten-fifty a.m. on Thursday the ninth of July 1998."

DC Cole sat opposite Amos and regarded him for a moment. "We have spoken to Mr Liam Knight."

"Oh good." Amos visibly relaxed.

"His version of that evening does not correspond with yours."

Amos looked puzzled.

"We have also had your car checked and it still has the original alternator. Mr Peel we are charging you with one account of the attempted murder of Faye Larson. Do you understand the charges brought against you?"

Amos was distraught. "I haven't done anything wrong. I love Faye, I wouldn't harm her for the world."

"Take him away," DC Cole said firmly.

*

Faye folded her arms as she listened to the police officer who sat uncomfortably at the kitchen table. She did not move or speak for a good half minute as she digested his news. Presently she said, "I think you have the wrong man."

"I can assure you Miss Larson, all the evidence says we haven't," the officer answered stiffly.

"I'm telling you, you have the wrong man. Amos would not have done that to me."

The officer screwed his nose and sniffed loudly. "Well, we just thought you should know, so you can put your mind at rest."

"What? How can I put my mind to rest, when a good friend of mine is behind bars, because you lot have made a mistake?"

"Faye," Nathan said gently as he reached for her hand. "They must have some evidence on him."

"No." She flashed her eyes at Nathan. "I am telling you, they have got the wrong man. Amos would not have done such a thing."

The officer cleared his throat. "Mr Peel isn't behind bars. Someone paid his bail this morning."

"Good, because if they hadn't, I would have paid his bail money myself, that is how sure I am that he didn't do it," she said adamantly.

The officer smiled thinly and reached for his hat to leave.

"Wait." She stood up. "Can we stop the investigation?"

"Stop it?" The officer eyed her cautiously.

Faye's mouth was set hard. "Yes, I don't want him charged."

The officer glanced between Faye and Nathan. "Well, that's highly irregular. We have put a lot of work into this investigation and it's in the public's interest to get people like this out of circulation. "

"Be that as it may, but you have charged the wrong man."

The officer sniffed again and nodded. "I'll pass your comments on to my seniors. I'll bid you good day."

Nathan got up and showed him to the door. When he came back into the kitchen he looked at Faye uncertainly.

"They have got the wrong man," she said adamantly.

He smiled and nodded, then gathered her up in his arms to comfort her.

52

Amos sat pale faced and thin lipped in the boatyard office, his hands cupping a mug of tea he had no desire to drink. Pippa, Owen and Gloria Barnes all looked on sympathetically.

"I didn't do it Owen, I swear I didn't do it."

"I know son, I know, we believe you."

"I love Faye. I know it's a hopeless dream, but I love her, I wouldn't hurt her for the world."

"We know Amos my luvver." Gloria put her arm around him. "Here, have a bit of my heavy cake, it'll make you feel better," she said pushing a plate under his nose.

"So," Owen said, "Tell me from the beginning, what the police said to you."

With a tremble in his voice, Amos relayed the whole sorry story to them. When he finished his eyes swept over the room to gauge their reaction.

"So, where were you that night then?" Owen asked.

He shifted uneasily in his seat. "I was in Plymouth." Owen raised his eyebrows for him to carry on. Amos sighed heavily. "I meet a man who does the booze cruise up there. You know, they get duty free cigarettes, booze and perfume on board. It's meant to be for your own consumption, but loads of people do it and sell it on," he added. "Well, every Friday night I pick a load up from a designated garage in Plymouth and then take it to another location, sometimes as far as Bristol. I don't sell it or anything, I just move it about, but I do get paid 'andsomely."

"So, if you have an alibi, why do they still think you were up in Yorkshire that night?"

"Well, I haven't got an alibi. I can't tell them where I really was. If the others find out I have dobbed them in, they'll kill me for sure."

"So, you're saying you are prepared to go down for attempted murder, just to save the arses of some petty criminals?"

"Language Owen," Gloria scolded.

Amos swallowed hard. "You don't know them; they can be a mean bunch if you get on the wrong side of them."

Owen raised his eyebrows again. "Well, prison will be no pushover you know." With this comment Amos promptly burst into tears.

Gloria hugged Amos tightly. "Well my luver, don't take on so, if it's any consolation, Faye doesn't believe you did it either."

He looked up and wiped the mucus on his sleeve. "Really?" he asked hopefully.

Gloria nodded. "She was on the phone just half an hour ago, wasn't she Owen? She is trying to get the charges dropped against you."

Amos's face crumpled again and this time they could not stop the tears.

*

Joe walked into the Chandlery the next morning whistling tunelessly. "Hello, hello, how have you all managed without me?" he said, happily sporting a suntan.

"Don't ask," Pippa answered, "….because you won't believe me if I tell you. How was Tenerife?"

"Hot, but, good fun!" He grinned. "So, come on, fill me in on all the gossip."

Joe stood in stunned silence as Pippa told him.

"What day did this happen?"

"Friday the eighth of May."

Joe pondered for a moment. "That was the night I went to the Hall for Cornwall to see Steeleye Span. I remember Amos driving out of Gweek in Liam Knight's car when I was putting my coat in my own car. I thought it was strange, but, I don't really have much to do with Amos, so, I never asked him why he was driving it. But, funnily enough, a few minutes later, I saw Liam driving Amos's car, in fact I followed him all the way to Truro."

Pippa's blood ran cold. "Knight said he never touched the car."

"Well, he was definitely driving it that night."

Pippa got up from her seat. "Watch the office for me Joe, I need to find Owen."

*

When Liam arrived back by bus from dropping his Range Rover in for a MOT in Helston, Owen Barnes served him with a notice to quit the boatyard. Liam tried arguing with him, but Owen was adamant. "I want you out of here, *now*." A small crowd had gathered to watch, Pippa and Gloria included.

He scowled coldly at Pippa for a moment, and then turned back to Owen. "Why?"

"Oh I think you know why," Owen said, crossing his arms.

Liam regarded him for a moment then said, "Where the hell am I supposed to go? I don't have any money to move this thing." He thumped the hull of his yacht.

"Sid will crane you in at high tide this evening, and then you can go to Hell for all I care, because that is where you belong."

"But….."

"But nothing, I never want to see your face around here again, you despicable bastard." And this time Gloria didn't scold him for his bad language.

*

As the Ina was lowered slowly into the water that evening, a keen wind had got up enough to ruffle the surface of the river.

Liam stood on the quay and watched the weather with trepidation. The forecast warned of unusually high winds for later that night, but although he had pleaded with Owen to let him stay one more night, his plea fell on deaf ears. Owen was adamant that Liam should leave the quay as soon as the Ina was fully afloat.

"You'll have to shelter on the other side of the river, until this storm blows over," Owen said to him. "But I don't want to see you or your yacht here after that, do you hear me?"

Liam ignored him as he watched the crane settle the yacht.

"He can bloody well drown for all I care," mumbled Joe.

In truth, Liam was not really a sailor. He'd only ever motored his yacht up and down the river, and he had never unfurled the main sail all the time he had owned the yacht. He didn't even know how. He knew he had about three hours of daylight left and with a bit of luck he could get down and pick up a mooring on the Helford before nightfall. He had been on the yacht before in high winds down on the Helford, so as long as he was anchored down and attached to a mooring he knew he would be fine.

*

As the yacht was uncoupled from the crane, Owen Barnes made a gesture with his hands as though to wipe them clean of him.

Liam could have done with slightly more water to accommodate the draft on his yacht, but leave he must. Barnes wanted him gone and there was no swaying him otherwise. He had no idea what had prompted this sudden outburst from Barnes, and when asked he had just stared at him with cold anger and said, "I don't like liars and I should never have let you stay here in the first place." And that was all he would say on the matter.

Liam seethed inwardly, as he manoeuvred the narrows with a degree of skill, and soon he was out into the open water. The sky darkened and heavy clouds lowered making it difficult to see where he was going. The engine coughed slightly and the yacht lurched and Liam wondered if there was enough fuel to get him to the Helford. He lifted the bilge lid and peered down into the depths. Down on his knees now he rummaged amongst the spinnaker and ropes, searching in vain for his five gallon can of fuel. "Damn." He slammed the bilge lid shut and hoped for the best. As he motored along, he felt the yacht begin to struggle. With wind against tide, the yacht felt heavy and the engine laboured even more. Within minutes the wind had strengthened and was halting all progress. The engine spluttered once again and Liam stared down at the cockpit willing the engine to keep going. He could see Tremayne quay to his right and turned towards it, but a running wave tossed the vessel sideways and half submerged the cockpit. The yacht lurched violently, but Liam managed to turn it back towards the quay, but it struggled to gain headway. Wave after wave rushed towards him, drenching the deck and unbalancing him as he fought against the elements. The engine coughed and began to smell hot then suddenly it gave up. Without power, the yacht was tossed about like a cork. The boom loosened and began to sway drunkenly. Liam reached out to tie it more securely, but in truth, he really had no idea of what to do for the best. The yacht lurched again and the stern became submerged sending Liam flying into the air. He landed heavily on his arm as the yacht climbed the next wave. Groaning in pain he grasped his arm just as a wave tossed the vessel sideways and the stern hit the quay wall with a sickening crunch. The cockpit was swamped by flood water, swirling and bubbling around him. As he struggled to his feet, a great wave slewed across the stern and knocked him clean off the yacht. As he flayed about in the swirling water he watched his beloved yacht smash once more against the quay, puncturing a hole in the hull. The mast splintered and the next swell turned her over, snapping the mast off. The sea was angry now; white water and foam swirled around him along with his belongings and the debris of his yacht. A piece of wood struck his head and a scarlet pool of blood surrounded him. He swam frantically towards the quay, but the tide and wind fought against him, pulling and sucking him underwater. So self-assured that he was invincible in all things, he never thought for one moment that he would not survive this horror, and then another wave engulfed him and quelled his arrogance.

53
Brittany, France

It was mid August and the overnight Bretagne ferry from Portsmouth to St Malo was packed with holidaymakers.

Faye lay in her cabin thinking about the news she had received about Liam. Pippa said he was missing presumed dead, but as yet, there was no body. When she was told, she felt nothing, not happiness at being free from him at last, or sadness for the loss of such a young man, she felt nothing for him. It was his children she felt sorry for. For all his faults, he was their daddy, and she knew only too well what it was like to lose a father at a young age.

She put her arms behind her head and smiled at the thought of Nathan and Greg's reconciliation. It was so wonderful to see her two favourite people getting on so well at last. Nathan's whole persona shone whenever Greg was around. It was as though Nathan had grasped a part of his past back from the brink. He found he was able to talk about his late wife Beth more openly, and he walked around with a new brilliance about him, as though a great weight had been lifted from his shoulders. The gulf had closed and healed and they once again became a family and they thanked Faye for that.

Faye's eyes felt tired now and her eyelids flickered shut, and as she drifted off to sleep, she hoped that Nathan was okay; she knew he would be missing Greg. Greg had been a regular visitor to Gwithian Cottage over the last few weeks. His partner Simon was away, teaching art in Italy, at an artists' retreat for the summer. Nathan had so wanted Greg to accompany them to Brittany, but Greg was adamant that he must get home to prepare for the new term.

Faye slept fitfully during the voyage; she had never been a good sailor and longed for the journey to be over.

She glanced out of her berth window at seven a.m. to see the wild rugged northern Brittany coastline before her. She quickly dressed and made her way up on deck and found Nathan leaning on the railings taking in the view.

Nathan grinned happily when he saw her approaching. He watched her face contort with concentration as she negotiated the slippery deck with the aid of her stick.

"Phew, that was hard work," she said, leaning on him for stability. "Where's Carrie?"

"No idea, I told her I was meeting you for coffee, but she didn't answer when I knocked on her cabin door. Maybe she's feeling a bit sea sick."

Faye smiled thinly. She knew exactly what was wrong with Carrie. Her coldness towards her told Faye in no uncertain terms that she was not welcome in the Prior household or on this trip. She sighed and pushed Carrie to the back of her mind, linked her arm in Nathan's and said, "I'm so excited Nathan, I've never been to Brittany before. I'm a bit concerned about the language though; I can hardly speak a word of French."

Nathan smiled warmly and patted her hand. "The Bretons have a fractured command of the English language, as we have of the French language, but don't worry; you will soon find they overcome the language barrier with warmth and passion. They are truly wonderful people."

They docked at eight a.m. and breakfasted on coffee and crêpes at the Brasserie des Voyages on Place Chateaubriand. At nine a.m. they called Gérard Duclos from a kiosk to tell him they had arrived and that they needed a couple of hours to explore. They then wandered slowly through beautiful walkways and narrow cobbled streets, taking in the shops and restaurants, which were in abundance.

Nathan was keen for Faye to walk around the granite ramparts of the medieval walled city of St Malo. Unfortunately she struggled a little, as her leg was still stiff from her injuries, and this held them back slightly, much to Carrie's annoyance. But Nathan had the patience of a saint. He was determined for Faye to see the outstanding views of the sea from the thirteenth century walls, and when she finally got there, she wasn't disappointed.

The views as promised were immense. The sea hadn't just gone out, it seemed to have evaporated, exposing acres of golden sandy beach and walkways across to tiny islands.

"Wow," exclaimed Faye. "If I didn't have a sore leg, I'd love to walk across to one of those islands."

Nathan laughed. "Yes you need to be quick on your feet just in case the tide comes back in though; otherwise you get marooned out there for six hours."

At eleven a.m. Gérard Duclos arrived to pick them up.

Gérard was not at all what Faye had expected. He was short and stocky, with broad shoulders and a slight bow to his legs. He had a flat moon shaped face, kind eyes, slightly lined by the years and a mouth which seemed to continually smile. From the evidence of his exposed arms and legs, he also had a liberal covering of dark glossy hair over his body. Not quite the suave, sophisticated persona Faye normally associated with the average Frenchman, but very pleasant all the same.

"Carrie ma chérie," he said, warmly kissing Carrie on the cheek. He took Nathan by the hand and shook it with great vigour. "Bonjour Nathan my friend, it is good to see you again."

Nathan patted the top of Gérard's hand in friendship. "Bonjour Gérard, it's good to see you too. Please, let me introduce my good friend Faye Larson. Faye, Gérard Duclos."

Faye stepped forward. "Bonjour, Monsieur Duclos," she said uneasily. "Ça me fait plaisir de vous rencontrer."

Gérard raised his eyebrows. "Bonjour Mademoiselle," he said, reaching for her hand to kiss. "Enchanté."

Faye beamed at Nathan, and then heard Carrie groan slightly behind her, but Faye ignored her.

"Come. The house is ready for you all," Gérard said, ushering them into his car.

Gérard's driving left a lot to be desired. He drove like a maniac, shouting abuse at anyone or any other vehicle which got in his way. Faye was quite sick when she arrived at the walled medieval town of Dinan, which was thankfully only twenty kilometres inland from the ferry port of St Malo.

Dinan was situated on the River Rance. IT was a pretty riverside port, filled with magnificent timbered buildings, which leant precariously towards each other across narrow cobbled streets. There were restaurants, creperies, bars, cafés and clothes shops galore, most of them housed in ancient buildings, which gave Faye the feeling that she had stepped back in time.

Gérard's house was a typical period Breton half timbered house, located adjacent to the River Rance in the Port de Dinan, so it was within easy walking distance of the town and quay. It was a large, airy, spacious building and Faye was shown to her bedroom which commanded a beautiful view of the river.

"You normally have that room Nathan!" Carrie protested under her breath.

"Well then, maybe it's time I gave someone else a chance to stay in it, isn't it?" Nathan said evenly.

"I've always wanted to stay in it!" she simpered like a child.

"I said Faye should have the room Carrie!" Nathan retorted.

"I honestly don't mind Nathan, if Carrie wants it. I don't want any fuss."

"The room is yours Faye," he said, giving Carrie a look to silence her.

Carrie flashed a look of contempt at Faye, turned on her heel and headed towards the rear bedroom. The door was closed with a louder bang than was necessary and she threw her bags onto the bed in anger.

Faye placed her bags down in her own bedroom and moved to the window to take in the much coveted view. The River Rance meandered lazily down the valley before her, accommodating several small sailing vessels, all moving gently in the late lazy morning sunshine; it really did look marvellous.   She turned to look at the bed, puzzled by Carrie's reaction. If Nathan normally occupied this bedroom, and they were, as she proclaimed, in a relationship, then surely they would have slept together here and she would have enjoyed this view. Things just didn't add up. Was Carrie telling the truth? With this happy thought running through her mind, Faye yawned noisily and crawled on top of the bed.

Nathan knocked on Faye's door five minutes later to tell her that lunch would be served on the terrace.   But when there was no answer, he carefully turned the knob and opened the door to find Faye fast asleep on top of the bed.

It was almost six p.m. before Faye woke from her slumber and she was famished.   She quickly showered and dressed and made her way down the elegant staircase and out onto the well kept terrace.

"Ah the beautiful Miss Larson is here!"   Gérard said, bowing slightly as she ascended the garden steps.

Faye blushed profusely.

"You are recovered from your journey yes?"

"Yes thank you."

"You like my house yes?"

Faye smiled warmly and nodded. "I like it very much Gérard."

"There are plenty of things to do here, I think you will like."   Gérard said, leading her across the terrace.   "You can stroll along the riverside walks.   If you ride, there is a nearby equestrian centre.   You can hire a boat, canoe, or bicycle, play tennis or simply relax on the terrace." He gestured to the sun recliner.   "If you prefer to go to a beach, there is one quite near.   St Cast Plage is the best; it has fine-grained sand, very beautiful and only perhaps twenty minutes or so drive from Dinan."

Faye looked down at her stick. "I think I will just be relaxing for the first few days thank you Gérard, until I can manage a little better."

"Of course, pardon. Nathan told me you had a very bad accident, you were knocked down with a car I understand?"

"Yes."

"And the person who did this, did not stop, is that correct?"

Faye nodded.

"Phaa drivers today, they do not care." Gérard wheezed as he took a long drag on his cigarette.

Faye smiled and raised an eyebrow at his audacity after experiencing Gérard's own driving skills.

"Ah, look here are the others!" Gérard exclaimed, as Nathan and Carrie came laughing up the garden path.

"Faye my love, how are you feeling?" Nathan said, as he sat down beside her.

"Great thanks. Have you two had a good day?"

"Yes we have. We've been out on Gérard's new boat. She's a fine vessel, Gérard. You'll have to come next time Faye."

Carrie folded her arms and said sharply, "I seem to remember her saying that she doesn't care for boats." She flashed a cold look in Faye's direction.

With a wave of the hand, Nathan dismissed Carrie's words as nonsense and said, "Oh I'm sure she'll be fine on this one. It's quite calm on the river." He looked at Faye and smiled warmly. "It'll be like the time we went mackerel fishing." He winked. "You were fine then weren't you?"

Carrie shot them both a steely look.

"Nathan?" Faye asked quietly. "Do you think we can have an early dinner? I'm starving."

"Of course we can," he replied getting up from his seat. "I'll go and have a shower now and get ready."

Carrie huffed loudly. "Well not all of us want an early dinner; I for one am not at all hungry. It's a pity you didn't bother to come down for the wonderful lunch Gérard had prepared for you Faye, you wouldn't be so hungry now if you had," she scolded.

Nathan threw a look of exasperation at Carrie, as she flounced off into the house. "Honestly, I don't know what has got into that girl," he declared.

They dined in a fine restaurant in the middle of the town. Carrie had reluctantly joined them, but refused to eat anything substantial on principle, though it was plain to see she was envious of the meals the others had ordered.

They drank fine wine all evening and talk was lively, and Faye found Gérard to be quite entertaining. They made their way home at ten-thirty after Carrie had complained of tiredness, but much to her annoyance she had to retire upstairs alone while the others joined Gérard in sampling his best cognac. At last Faye could unwind with Nathan. Over the last couple of weeks she had missed the intimacy they had shared while he'd cared for her in hospital. Faye was painfully aware of the resentment Carrie had of the close relationship which had developed between them during her recovery. Though there was nothing improper about their friendship, she knew in her heart that she must pull away from Nathan, for Carrie's sake, but for tonight, she was happy to snatch just a little bit of time with him.

During the next week, Carrie cajoled Nathan to join her in various pursuits, which would have been impossible for Faye to attempt because of her leg, and though he was reluctant to leave Faye, she encouraged him to go with her blessing. So with Gérard busy in his studio for most of the day painting, Faye found herself with lots of time on her hands to explore the old city of Dinan.

The first day she bought a map in the town and studied it over a coffee for an hour. Then she slowly walked eastwards towards the Place du General Leclerc to take a look at the old town, admiring the Convent of St Charles, a former convent of the Ursuline nuns, which boasted a beautiful formal garden. Then she turned south toward the Place Duclois, making her way carefully up the narrow and inappropriately named Grande Rue until she came across the church of St Malo, a magnificent gothic edifice, whose rear aspect is a riot of fifteenth century buttresses and carvings. She was too fatigued to explore any further that day, as her leg ached terribly. She slowly made her way back to the house, flopped herself on a sun recliner and vowed to stay by the house the next day and relax. She didn't of course - when Nathan and Carrie set off to go horse riding the next day, boredom urged her to drag Gérard away from his work and take her back into the town.

"But of course, I would love to spend the day with you; I was beginning to think you would never ask." Gérard smiled, disappeared into the house then just as quickly emerged with a haversack. He drove her to the Place du Guesclin, parked the car and walked with her along the Rue Ferronerie towards the Place du Guichet, until they came to the entrance to the castle, a fourteenth century fortification which formed part of the town walls. Faye was not normally too interested in architecture, but she had to agree with Gérard that the castle towers were amazing, one of which housed a quaint museum and some very spooky dungeons. They spent a couple of hours in the castle walking along the ramparts, and then they followed the Promenade around the town walls, to the magnificent church of St Sauveur.

"This is a wonderful place for a picnic, is it not?" Gérard suggested, looking out across the Rance valley.

"Yes it would be lovely," Faye exclaimed, immediately feeling her stomach rumble.

"It is good that I brought one then, yes?" He smiled, producing bread, cheese, beef tomatoes and red wine from his haversack. "From here, there is a winding stairway down to the port area of Dinan." Gérard pointed as he pulled the bread apart with his fingers. "There you can catch a boat downriver to St Malo; it is a journey of about two hours. Also, you get a wonderful view of the splendid viaduct, which now carries the road across the river. But, I fear you will not be able to climb down there today. So, we will stay here and enjoy the view, yes? Maybe do a little sketching? Nathan tells me you are an artist."

Faye had a wonderful day with Gérard. He talked a lot about his work and how he had met Nathan over fifteen years ago at an Art exhibition in Paris. He spoke warmly of Nathan's wife Beth, and how Nathan had struggled to get over her untimely death. He also commented that he felt Nathan seemed much happier in himself on this visit than he had been for a very long time. "Perhaps he has found happiness with Carrie at last?" he asked casually. "Though goodness knows why it has taken him so long, he has known her for over three years. Anyway, something has brightened up his life all of a sudden," he added scrutinising Faye, hoping she would divulge any knowledge of Nathan's obvious elation. But all she did was smile, although he thought he observed a flicker of sadness in her face. Presently he said, "And you Faye, why is someone as beautiful as you without a man?"

Faye looked at the ground. "I don't think I am any good at relationships," she said softly.

Gérard shook his head. "Nonsense, it must be because you have not met the right man yet." He winked.

Faye gave a short laugh. "I thought I had."

"Ah, you will know when you find the right man. He will dominate your thoughts day and night, your eyes will shine when he comes into a room, and the urge to touch him will overpower you."

Faye felt a tingle down her spine as he spoke. She knew only too well about the feelings he spoke of, but unfortunately for her, the man who triggered them belonged to someone else. She knew she must try harder to banish these feelings.

Gérard watched her for a moment trying to surmise what was going on in her head. "Are you all right Faye?" he said softly.

She inhaled deeply. "Yes I'm fine."

"Faye, would you be kind enough as to accompany me to dinner tomorrow night?" He tilted his head as he asked.

She looked up at him. "We always have dinner together."

"Yes, but I would like to take you to dinner alone, somewhere different for a change."

"Well..." There was a hesitation in her voice. This would give Nathan and Carrie an opportunity to have dinner alone for once, she thought. "Yes, I would like to go to dinner with you, thank you."

"Good," he said, with a satisfied grin, lit a cigarette and relaxed back on his haversack.

Nathan and Carrie were later than normal getting back that evening, so Gérard left them a note telling them where to meet for dinner, and he and Faye walked slowly down into the bustling heart of the town.

They had just ordered wine when Nathan and Carrie arrived, and Gérard took a great interest in Faye's body language as Nathan sat down. He noticed how her face blushed slightly as he greeted her, and how she touched her hair unconsciously in his presence. He watched when she smiled, and noted it was a smile for his eyes only. Throughout the evening her conversation was lively and animated, whereas Carrie's persona gradually became more subdued. Gérard was confused - Faye seemed to urge Nathan and Carrie to go off and enjoy themselves together, while she spent her days yearning for company. Then in the evenings when Nathan and Faye were together they were so obviously at ease with each other. Gérard decided that he must first speak to Nathan before he went any further with his plan to pursue Faye for himself.

When the girls had retired later that night, Gérard poured a couple of brandies. As he handed a glass to Nathan he said casually, "Nathan my friend, I have asked Faye out to dinner tomorrow night."

"Yes I know, she told me. You both seem to be getting on very well together."

Gérard paused for a moment and drew hard on his cigarette. "Yes we are getting on well. Tell me Nathan, how would *you* feel, if I pursued Faye a little further."

Nathan laughed slightly. "I can't think why you're asking me?"

"Well, I just wondered if you were perhaps interested in Faye."

Nathan smiled. "Nice thought Gérard, but I think I am a bit too old for her."

"Why, what is the age difference, sixteen, seventeen years?"

"Nineteen."

"Older men make better lovers." Gérard grinned.

"Well, that's what I like to think, though it's so long since I made love, I think I have probably forgotten how to do it."

"But, I thought you said Carrie came to your bed?"

"She did. Don't get me wrong, when she offered it on a plate to me I considered it, but I just couldn't. I just couldn't seem to get over Beth. I'm a sad individual aren't I?"

Gérard shook his head. "But you would like to make love with Faye I think."

"I told you, I am too old for her. We are just friends, really good friends at that. My life is certainly brighter since she came into it."

Gérard scratched his chin thoughtfully. "So you would not be offended if I pursued her."

Nathan shook his head slowly. "I love Faye very much and I'd like to see her happy and if you can make her happy, then you have my blessing, if that is what you're after." He turned and looked out into the night sky as his heart ached.

Nathan and Carrie decided to dine at home the following evening as Faye and Gérard were going out. But though Carrie retired to bed at eleven thirty, Nathan felt the need to stay up a little longer to wait for Faye to return. But he never heard her return.

It was four fifteen a.m.; a lone bird had begun to sing in the dawn when Nathan glanced at the clock on his bedside table. He sighed wearily and propped his head up with his arm; he hadn't slept all night. He had been listening for Faye returning home from her dinner date with Gérard, but as yet their car had not arrived back. Perhaps they had stopped in some small country hotel somewhere. He scolded himself for introducing Faye to Gérard. It had been so unsettling watching them drive off together that evening. He hated to admit it, but he was jealous, and now he felt lost and abandoned, lonely and wretched. He glanced at the empty side of his bed and sighed once more. Maybe if and when Faye found someone she felt comfortable with, he should try to forge a relationship with Carrie. After all, they had been together a long time and he really cared for her. But in his heart he knew that Carrie could not fill the Elizabeth shaped gap in his heart. Nathan was in love, but not with the woman who had desperately wanted to keep his bed warm for the last couple of years.

Faye had in fact returned home at one a.m., but she had asked Gérard to drop her off half a mile down the road, so she could walk back along the riverbank in the moonlight. Gérard was disappointed, but not surprised that she didn't want him to accompany her. Their evening, in a cosy restaurant in Forêt de Paimpont, had been very pleasant, though Faye had seemed a little out of sorts before the meal arrived. But the rest of the evening passed very pleasantly, although it had not been the success Gérard had hoped for. It seemed that romance was not in the air for him, and now he knew the reason why. So he had dropped her off as requested, then instead of returning home he drove into Dinan to spend the night with an old girlfriend.

After their dinner, Faye felt a desperate need for some air, and the walk along the cool riverbank was a welcome relief. She had a lot of thinking to do and needed some peace and tranquillity in which to do it. The evening she had just spent with Gérard had been one of shock and revelation.

The initial shock came as she sat down to dinner in Forêt de Paimpont and Gérard asked, "You like it here? It is a good place to drive to on a beautiful evening, don't you agree?"

"Yes it's very beautiful," she answered, watching the waiter as he poured the wine.

"We will have to come again in the day time to explore. The woods surrounding the village of Paimpont are all that remains of the once extensive Forest of Brocéliande, the heart of Breton Arthurian Country."

Faye felt the blood drain from her face. "Arthurian Country? King Arthur you mean?"

"Yes. Here can still be found L'Etang de Comper, the Lake of Comper, which adjoins the castle of the same name at the centre of the ancient Forest of Brocéliande. It is where the lady of the lake 'Vivienne' lived, mentioned so often in the Tales of King Arthur. According to legend, Vivienne was the foster-mother of Sir Lancelot and raised him beneath the murky waters of her Lake. Vivienne also presented King Arthur with the magical sword Excalibur." Gérard stopped for a moment. "Are you ill, you have gone very pale?"

"No, I'm fine," she said quickly. "I have a slight headache; it's nothing to worry about. I'm probably a little hungry."

Gérard nodded. "I'm sure we will eat soon. Now, where was I? Oh yes there is also Le Pont du Secret to see

353

where Guinevere declared her love for Lancelot."

Faye felt sick at the mention of Guinevere and suddenly stood up. "Excuse me a moment Gérard, I must visit the ladies room."

"But of course," Gérard said, rising from his chair.

Faye stood at the sink and swilled her face with cold water. All the old demons seemed to follow her around, even as far away as Brittany. Damn Guinevere! Would she never be free of Guinevere? She cupped her hands against her face and shook her head. She had thought that being the 'Face of Guinevere' would bring her fortune and happiness, but instead it had brought nothing but pain and misery. She took a few more minutes to compose herself then returned to the table to join Gérard.

"Are you all right? I was beginning to get worried."

"I'm fine now; I just needed to cool down a little to ease the headache. Please don't worry about me."

Faye sat at the edge of the riverbank letting the water gently lap and kiss her feet. Presently she glanced at her watch - it said three a.m. She sighed heavily. The last days of summer were fast approaching, and Faye felt desperately unhappy.

She knew she should not have hoped, but deep in her heart she wanted to hear that Nathan and Carrie were not, as Carrie made out, in a real relationship. They didn't sleep together as far as she knew, but it was obvious from the conversation that she had with Gérard over dinner, that the man she loved had no designs on Faye. Why else would he invite Gérard to court her? Her worst fears were coming true; Carrie had not lied. She couldn't help it, she was in turmoil. Faye loved Nathan with all her heart. She would like to have thought that it had happened gradually as she got to know him, but this was not true. Her feelings for Nathan had been instant and powerful, and it had been terribly hard for her to suppress them over the last eight months. She had probably loved him from the moment he rescued her from the car, that chilly night, but it was not to be. This holiday must have been a plan to introduce her to Gérard. It was plain to see that he wanted her settled with someone, so that the Gwithian household could return to normal. She sighed deeply again. Oh yes she loved Nathan, so much that it hurt, but she was not the home wrecking monster that Carrie and the gutter press had so venomously portrayed her as a few months ago. Yes, Faye thought, it's time to move on and make my own way in life again.

*

Gérard arrived home at nine a.m., breezed onto the terrace and scooped a piece of toast from Nathan's plate and grinned happily. "Any coffee?" he asked Nathan casually.

Nathan nodded and pushed a cup towards him. "Where's Faye?" he asked casually, looking behind him through to the lounge.

Gérard shrugged his shoulders. "She is not with me. She is probably upstairs in bed. It was after one when I brought her home last night."

Nathan frowned. "I didn't hear the car pull up."

"No, she … wanted to walk... to get some air, so she asked me to drop her off down the road."

"Oh," exclaimed Nathan. The relief wiped the pained expression from his face, and the reaction made Gérard smile inwardly. "So how did you get on? Did you have a good evening?" Nathan asked, feeling a little happier.

"Yes, we talked a lot. I think she is in love," Gérard said casually as he lit a cigarette.

Nathan's mouth tightened. "In love?" he raised his eyebrows. "So soon?"

Gérard laughed haughtily. "Oh yes, she's definitely in love." He moved to pat Nathan on the shoulder. "With you my friend, she is in love with you. I cannot believe you didn't know. She doesn't take her eyes off you. When you enter the room her face lights up - you must have noticed it for god's sake."

Nathan was speechless momentarily, and then shook

his head in disbelief. "But, she pulls away from me, if I try to touch her, even if it is just a comforting hug. It's as though she doesn't want me too close to her."

Gérard smiled as he lit a cigarette. "She thinks you are in love with Carrie, my friend. She doesn't want to split you two up."

"There is nothing to split up. Carrie and I are just friends." Nathan stood up, his heart swelling with emotion. "God, I can hardly believe it. I love her too, but was afraid to express myself for fear of being rejected again. What shall I do?"

Gérard smiled warmly and took a large drag of his cigarette. "Go to her you fool. My God, you English have no idea when it comes to love," he replied in a high-pitched wheeze that came from chain smoking.

*

Nathan tapped gently on Faye's bedroom door. He had never been so nervous in his whole life. He swallowed hard and gently called out, "Faye? It's Nathan. May I come in?"

There was no answer. He knocked again and the door was opened by the maid.

"Bonjour monsieur."

"Ah, bonjour Mademoiselle. Is Mademoiselle Larson awake?" he asked peering into the bedroom.

"Oui monsieur," she answered curtsying.

"May I see her?"

"Mademoiselle Larson left early this morning. She said….."

But in his panic, Nathan didn't wait to hear what the maid was about to say, and left her open-mouthed at the door.

54

Nathan rushed back to the terrace and pulled Gerard so violently by the sleeve he made him drop his cigarette.

"Mon Dieu," he said, "What on earth is the matter?"

"Gérard, she's gone, you must come and help. Can you drive me to St Malo now?"

The St Malo to Portsmouth ferry was due to leave at ten forty-five, but from experience, Nathan knew that tidal times could vary the ferry's departure. It could sail anytime from nine-thirty to eleven-thirty. He glanced at his watch - it was nine-fifty, the traffic was horrendous and they still had ten kilometres to go. Gérard was in his element driving like a maniac, and although Nathan was desperate to get to St Malo, he did rather hope he would arrive in one piece.

The port was heaving with holidaymakers when they arrived, which calmed Nathan's nerves slightly, as it was obvious the ferry hadn't sailed.

Before Gérard had even stopped the car, Nathan had leapt out of it. He ran frantically through the crowds of people. "Excusez-moi," he repeated constantly as he dodged and weaved around them. He made his way to the front of the queue, but Faye was nowhere to be seen. He paused for a moment to catch his breath, and then noticed a woman with auburn hair, fifty yards from where he stood.

"Faye? Faye?" he shouted louder as he fought his way towards her. She was in touching distance now, but still she didn't turn to acknowledge her name. "Faye," Nathan said, grasping at the woman's sleeve.

The woman turned and shrank back from his grasp; it was not Faye.

"Oh I'm really sorry, please excuse me. I thought you were someone else," Nathan said, holding his hands up in retreat.

The woman shot him a cold contemptuous look, and Nathan backed off until he was well out of sight of her. He stood breathless, in the middle of the crowd. This was impossible; it was like finding a needle in a haystack. For all he knew, Faye hadn't even come to St Malo, she could have decided to travel further into Brittany, but he thought that to be highly unlikely, so the chances were that she was still here. He started to look around again and before he knew it, he was shouting her name again and again. He made his way to one of the steel barriers and climbed upon it to get a better view.

He cupped his hands around his mouth and shouted, "Faye Larson, where are you?" Everyone looked up at him as though he was mad.

The ferry sounded its horn, the ropes were uncoupled from the harbour and the ferry moved off.

"Faye," he called out desperately, but the port police had moved in on Nathan and pulled him down from the barrier.

"You don't understand, I need to stop someone on that ferry," he protested loudly. "Please let me find her, I don't want her to leave."

"It is too late Monsieur; the ferry has left the port."

Nathan made his way back to Gérard's car and found him sitting on the bonnet of his car smoking. "Let's go back Gérard; it seems we're too late."

The journey back was as frenzied as the journey to the Port, but the time passed in a blur for Nathan. What a fool he had been to lose her, he berated himself. Suddenly the car came to a screeching halt and Nathan had to put his hand out to stop himself from hitting the windscreen. "Steady on old man," he said, shooting an anxious look towards Gérard.

Gérard was grinning. "I think you need to get out here."

They were about five minutes from the house. "Here?"

he looked puzzled. "Why?"

"Because I think you should." He grinned. "Look." He nodded towards the coast road. "I think you might just find what you are looking for over there."

Faye lifted her eyes as Nathan approached and he noticed she had been crying.

"I thought you had left on the ferry," he said gently, as he sat on the grass by her side.

She frowned and hugged her knees close to her chest. "Why did you think that? I told the maid to tell you I had gone for a walk." In truth, she had thought of leaving, but that would have been very rude of her after Nathan had arranged this holiday for her.

"I panicked I think. Thank God you're still here."

She smiled. "Yes, I'm still here," she answered sadly.

As he looked out into the ocean he said, "You know Faye, when I lost Elizabeth, I truly believed that nothing and no-one would ever fill the aching void she left within me. I never thought that I could love again, but, as time passed, the pain eased and my heart has opened up once again."

Filled with sadness, Faye smiled gloomily. "I'm happy that you feel you can move on again Nathan, Carrie is a good woman and you deserve to be happy again."

He laughed gently.

"What's funny?" Faye asked, frowning at his reaction.

"I was just thinking, how very charitable you are towards Carrie. I know you and her have not seen eye to eye in the past."

"No, well, I believe she thinks I'm queering her pitch."

A smile curled on his lips. "And are you?"

Faye lifted her eyes to meet Nathan to see if he mocked her. "Contrary to what the newspapers say, I don't wreck relationships."

His eyes sparkled as he smiled at her. "I never believed for a moment that that was the case."

Faye smiled gratefully. "Thank you."

They both returned to look out at the ocean. "I can assure you, there is not and never will be anything between myself and Carrie. She's been a good friend and companion, but I have no designs on her whatsoever."

Faye cast him a sidelong glance. "She believes differently."

"I know, and I should have nipped it in the bud right from the start, but…." He paused for a long time. "I don't know how to say this, but I know you like me Faye so I shall risk being very foolish by asking, if I can hope, that you and I ……." He cleared his throat and looked away momentarily. "I'm a lot older than you, and I don't expect for one minute someone as lovely as you would be interested, but…."

Faye felt her heart flip, she reached for his hand and his fingers curled around hers. The touch was electrifying and all consuming. "I love you Nathan, I love you so much it hurts. I don't care how old you are, all I know is that I love you."

His chest heaved with emotion. He squeezed his eyes shut as though his wish had come true. Presently he opened them and gazed at Faye with so much love. "I love you too Faye, more than you will ever know."

*

Anticipating Carrie's reaction to their news, Nathan advised Faye to go upstairs while he spoke to her. He found Carrie sitting on the terrace. She turned and smiled, running her fingers through her hair.

"Good morning," she said without turning around. "I was just about to send out a search party for you all." As he pulled out a chair to sit on, she realised he was alone, and her irritation that he and Faye had been somewhere without her subsided. She smiled. "I was just thinking we could spend the day on the boat, since it's our last day here."

"Perhaps later," he said, sitting beside her. He took a deep breath. "I have some news." Pre-empting her reaction, he tried to be as kind as possible as he began to gently tell her what she had dreaded since Faye had stepped into their lives. To say she was angry was an understatement.

"What about me?" She trembled with rage. "Do all these years we've been together mean nothing to you?"

"Of course they mean a lot to me," he said disarmingly. "You have been a special friend to me and I've enjoyed your company, I still do." He smiled softly at her. "I had hoped you would be happy for me."

She laughed and said chidingly, "Did you?" Her eyes flashed with fury. "Well if you think I am going to stick around while you play happy families with your whore, you are very much mistaken." She spat the words out like a nasty taste.

"That's enough," Nathan said stiffly. "I will not have you speak about Faye like that."

Much to Carrie's annoyance, tears began to tumble down her cheeks. "Do you seriously think that a woman like her could make you happy?" she sobbed uncontrollably.

"Yes I do," he said without hesitation.

Carrie's eyes narrowed as she scowled darkly at him. "How could you? Elizabeth would turn in her grave," she said, smacking him resoundingly across his cheek.

Nathan gasped as his face stung. He sat back, forcing himself to control his anger. "I think that's quite enough from you Carrie," he said his voice icily controlled. "Perhaps a little time on your own will help you to reconsider your feelings. I'll see you later when I expect you to have calmed down enough to be civil with both of us."

*

When Nathan knocked quietly on Faye's bedroom door, Faye thought he looked drawn and pinched around the mouth. She knew without asking that the deed had been an ordeal. She kissed him softly as he gently curled his arms around her waist. She had longed to be this close to him, to feel the softness of his lips, the smell of his hair and the firmness of his body next to hers.

"You're trembling," he whispered anxiously.

"Only in anticipation," she answered softly.

"It's been a long time since I made love to anyone," he confessed nervously as he picked her up in his arms and carried her to the bed.

Later, they lay together, spent, happy and content in each other's arms on that blissful afternoon. "You do realise I've loved you since the first moment I met you, when I rescued you from the car park, don't you?"

Her face was radiant as she turned her smiling eyes onto him. "Thank you for rescuing me."

"The pleasure is all mine my love."

55

The journey back to Cornwall was a dreadful affair. Carrie had been conspicuous by her absence during the crossing, and on the drive home had worn a face of stone throughout the journey. When they arrived back at Gwithian Cottage, Carrie immediately ran up the stairs and emerged ten minutes later with all her belongings in a holdall.

Nathan heard her footsteps and stepped out into the hall. Both parties paused for a moment and in the ensuing silence he stared at her bag. "Where are you going?" Nathan asked earnestly.

She laughed indignantly and tossed the hair from her face. "Well I'm not staying here if that is what you think."

Faye emerged from the kitchen. "I've put the kettle on, would anybody like a drink?" She paused and glanced first at Nathan, then at Carrie, then back to Nathan. "What's happening?" she asked quietly.

Carrie glared at Faye, her eyes cold and hostile. "You'll be pleased to know that I'm going!" she spat the words venomously at her.

"Carrie I beg you to reconsider," Nathan said exasperated. "This is your home, your job!"

Dropping her voice to a low hiss, Carrie said, "She can clean your house for you now. I resign."

Nathan moved closer to her. "Oh come on Carrie, surely we can sort this out?"

A terrific bitterness welled up inside Carrie. "No we can't. I'm leaving." She turned to Faye, her eyes blazing with anger. "But I'll tell you something lady; I'll make you pay for what you have done."

Nathan put his hand on Carrie's arm. "What Faye has done is made my life complete. Now I am truly sorry that our situation hurts you, but this hatred must stop now. I insist."

Carrie shrugged his hand from her arm. "She will break your heart one day, just you see if she doesn't." She swallowed as her words caught up in a desperate sob. "...and don't come running to me when it all goes pear shaped." The door slammed shut behind her as she left.

*

It was a slow day in Gweek, the weather was hot and movement on the river was minimal. Pippa greeted the postman cheerfully as he dropped an assortment of letters on the counter. As she sorted the mail into the various pigeon holes, she found one addressed to her with a Yorkshire postmark. Slitting it open with mild curiosity, it read:

Ryan Farrington
c/o Flat 95 Granville Villas
Skipton

Hi Pippa,

Just to let you know that the situation at home became intolerable and I have now moved out of the 'family' home. I don't have Faye's address and as you are a good friend to her I wondered if you could let Faye know that I have made the move as you both advised me to do. Having lost my job and now my home, I am living on a friend's sofa for the time being, while I reassess my life. The last year has been a terrible strain, and just making the move has eased a considerable weight off my shoulders. I do apologise for telling you all this, but I don't appear to have anyone else to speak to, and sometimes it feels better to write things down.

It was lovely to meet you again last May, though the ensuing circumstances were shocking. I trust Faye has made a full recovery. I understand that they have caught the bastard who did this, and if they ever let him out I am afraid I shall not be responsible for my actions.

I have it in mind to go travelling, and if you would permit me, I would like to write to you again and let you know where I am. I hope you are well and I hope that we meet again one day.

P.S I'm a marine mechanic by trade, if you hear of any work

going, let me know.
  Kind regards
  Ryan Farrington.
  01956 39392 (Temporary phone number)

As Owen Barnes entered the office, Pippa folded the letter, placed it in her handbag and said, "Do you know of any marine mechanic jobs going? I have a friend looking for work."

*

Although she would only admit it to herself, Faye was glad to see the back of Carrie that day. She glanced at Nathan as he busied himself at the kitchen sink. Her departure had affected him keenly, she knew that. He was such a gentle caring person that he couldn't hide his sadness at the end of a friendship. Faye stepped outside to put the rubbish in the bin and looked up into the night sky. "Gosh what a beautiful clear night it is," she said stepping back into the kitchen.

Nathan glanced outside. "Ah yes, a night for stargazing I believe. Come on, we could both do with something to lift our mood. We should be celebrating our love, not moping about here." In truth, he had been debating where the two of them should sleep that night. To share the bedroom he shared with Elizabeth, which still had all her personal things scattered about, seemed wrong somehow. He knew it was time to gather them up and put them somewhere until he felt he could part with them, but there never seemed any urgency before. His life had changed over the last twenty four hours, and now he knew it was time to move on.

Although it was August, warm clothing was essential if one was to go star-gazing, Nathan informed her, so, armed with coats, blankets and sleeping bags they made their way slowly up to the cliff top studio with the aid of a very powerful torch.

Once at the studio, Nathan lifted Faye with ease into

his arms and carried her up the stairs and through the hatch to the roof on the studio. It was eleven-thirty by the time they settled themselves. This was obviously something Nathan had done many times before, because he had a couple of soft foam mats and cushions to lay on in the studio for this very event.

When all was ready he beckoned Faye over to lie on the mat. She crawled carefully along the flat roof stopping whenever it creaked underneath her weight. Nathan laughed. "It's okay it won't give way, I promise. Now crawl onto the mats, then close your eyes and lay on your back. No peeping now." Faye felt Nathan lay beside her. A moment later he reached for her hand in the darkness. "Ready? Open your eyes."

Faye gasped at the wondrous sight above her. "Oh my Goodness, that is the most beautiful sight I have ever seen," she whispered, looking up at the huge vault of stars, all three hundred and sixty degrees of it.

As they lay, Nathan was pointing out Orion when suddenly a meteor shot across the sky. "Oh wonderful, did you see that? Make a wish Faye," he urged, but before she had a chance to make it, another one shot across the sky. "Oh, this is brilliant. I think we are in for a meteor shower. There will be lots of chances to make a wish."

"Nathan darling, I already have everything I could wish for," she said reaching tenderly for his hand.

For hours the night sky put on a show, better than any firework display. Eventually the meteors diminished and Faye yawned noisily.

"Time for bed I think," Nathan said squeezing her hand.

"I'm too tired to walk home," she said wearily.

"Then we shall sleep in the studio, it's really quite comfortable you know." Faye agreed happily. She too had been concerned that she was to share the bed he and Elizabeth had shared.

The studio radiated warmth as they stepped inside.

Laying their bedding on the floor they snuggled together.

"I'm sorry about Carrie, Nathan. I didn't want all this upset."

He kissed her tenderly. "I shall go and find her tomorrow and try to sort things out."

Faye sighed heavily. "She's going to go to the papers," she said quietly.

"I'm sure she won't."

"Yes she will and there will be reporters all over Zennor, you mark my words."

Nathan shrugged his shoulders. "Good, we can tell them we are to be married."

Faye sat up and looked down into the darkness at him. "Married? Have you just……"

"Proposed? Yes. Will you marry me Faye?"

"Oh Nathan, of course I will."

He pulled her back down and kissed her. "They can't hurt you anymore Faye, they have done their worst. We'll just ride it through; you won't be alone this time. I'm here and everything is going to be okay. Trust me."

Within twenty-four hours of Carrie walking out, a reporter was on the doorstep. But Nathan and Faye had been busy calling on friends and associates, and news of their forthcoming wedding was high on the village gossip agenda before the greasy haired journalist with the bent nose arrived.

The journalist had creamed as much information as he could from Carrie and she had laid it on thick about the break up Faye had caused between her and Nathan, but he found that everyone else in the village was frustratingly positive about Faye and Nathan's relationship. Hence the story only received minor coverage in the next day's paper, and was of little or no consequence to all but a smattering of people.

56

Faye glanced at the clock. Pippa was due at Gwithian Cottage anytime now. She could hardly contain her excitement at sharing a few days with her in preparation for the wedding. The cottage had undertaken a flurry of cleaning for her arrival, and Faye cast a satisfied smile over the place. A quick visit to the local shop to buy fresh bread was all that was needed now. Her heart sang with happiness as she walked through the village. The marquee was half erected and in three days time she would be Mrs Nathaniel Prior.

As she passed the pub car park something stopped her short in her tracks, and her heart plummeted. There, amongst all the other cars, was parked a black Audi car. The same car she had seen parked next to hers on more than one occasion. Feeling her mouth dry with fear, whoever had been following her before, had clearly found her once more.

Nathan was busy in the garden clipping the roses. He stood and stretched the stiffness from his back and looked towards Faye. She appeared to have dropped her shopping, but was making no attempt to retrieve it from the ground.

"Faye?" he called out, but she seemed rooted to the spot. Putting down his secateurs, he wiped his hands down his shirt and walked over to her. "Here let me help," he said, gathering up the bread. "Did you manage to get everything you needed because I'm going to Penzance shortly if you need anything else? Oh and Sarah and Jenny from the Tinners Arms rang, can you call in to see them about numbers for the buffet?" He stopped talking and scrutinised her face, frowning. He asked softly, "Faye? Whatever is the matter? You look like you've seen a ghost."

"Oh Nathan, it's that car there, the black one."

He followed to where she pointed. "What of it?"

"I've seen it before; it's the same car that used to follow me about."

"Are you sure?"

"Definitely."

Just as they spoke, PC Jack Saunders pulled up in his patrol car. "A very good morning to you both, I hope this weather stays good for your wedding."

"Thanks Jack. Actually you are just the person we need. Have you any idea who this vehicle belongs to? It's not local," Nathan asked.

"Why, is it causing an obstruction?"

"No, but Faye thinks the car has been following her."

Faye lowered her eyes and blushed in embarrassment.

"Really?" PC Saunders raised his eyebrows. Being a local bobby and not normally having anything decent to get his teeth into, he quickly got out of his car and walked over to the Audi, noted the registration and radioed through to the station. "This shouldn't take a moment." He nodded in satisfaction. "Hello Bert, check the owner of a car for me will you?" he said into his radio.

Faye and Nathan exchanged glances. "I hope I'm not making a fuss for nothing," she said nervously. "People will begin to think I'm a real drama queen."

Nathan smiled and kissed her tenderly on the forehead.

They watched as PC Saunders walked back to them. "Well success, the car belongs to Philip Morton! Do you know him?"

Faye spluttered, "Philip Morton? That was my father's name! But…" She shook her head utterly bemused. "He died years ago."

"I'm not entirely sure that is true Faye," Nathan said evenly.

Her head whipped round. "What do you mean?"

"I was confused when you told me he was dead. I was absolutely sure I had seen him at Elizabeth's funeral."

"But….why didn't you say anything?"

"In truth, I didn't know if I really had seen him. I used to think that I saw him on many occasions. He and Elizabeth were lovers before I met her, and he would never accept that she chose me over him. I believe he pestered her for ages after we were married. I didn't want to tell you this, but Philip Morton has been a thorn in my side for many years. When you told me he was dead, I rather hoped that it was true." He smiled apologetically. "Sorry Faye, I know he was your father."

"Do I hear my name being taken in vain?" A voice from behind them made them turn, and as the man approached, Faye felt her knees buckle underneath her.

He smiled softly. "Hello Faye. At last we meet after all these years."

Faye stood very, very still. "I thought you were dead," she whispered inaudibly.

He nodded. "I know. I'm sorry it's a long story, but your mother thought it was for the best. But, I've never been far from you Faye; I've always been close by. You just didn't know it." He smiled sadly. "I've watched my little girl grow into a beautiful young woman."

"You've been stalking her more like," Nathan snapped. "You've frightened the girl to death, don't you know that?"

Philip Morton shot Nathan a look of contempt. "Who rattled your cage Prior?" he said as he stepped forward towards Faye. But Nathan stood in his way to protect her.

"Get out of my way man. You've already stolen one girl from my life. I'm here now to stop you from doing it again."

PC Saunders stood agape at the exchange.

Nathan bristled with resentment. "What the hell are you talking about?"

Philip Morton's stance was defiant. "If you think I am going to stand by and let my daughter marry an old man like you, then you are very much mistaken. And while we are on the subject, how could you think of marrying again, so soon after Elizabeth's death? Have some regard for her memory man."

"How dare you…." Nathan lurched towards Morton, but seeing the threat in Nathan's eyes, PC Saunders stepped in to part the men. As he did, Faye took her cue and ran to the safety of Gwithian Cottage.

"Now come on gentlemen, let's have none of this," PC Saunders said as he held Nathan back.

"You just keep out of my way Morton, I'm warning you, I've had it up to here with you over the years," Nathan snarled at him before swiftly following Faye indoors.

Visibly shaken, Faye sat at the kitchen table with her head in her hands. She could not comprehend what had just happened.

Nathan was at her side a moment later. "Darling," he said pulling her hands from her head. "Don't take on so."

She looked miserably into his eyes. "Oh Nathan, I thought he was dead all these years. Mum told me he was dead, why would she do that?"

"I don't know darling. I don't like to speak ill of anyone, but my dealings with Philip Morton in the past have not been pleasant, maybe she had her reasons." He took a long measured breath then added, "He plagued Elizabeth, long after we were married, but she was very kind to him and always gently told him to leave her be. He never let me forget how angry he was with me for taking Elizabeth from him though."

She looked beyond the kitchen door to see if he had followed her. "Where is he now?" There was a frightened urgency in her voice.

"Jack Saunders is speaking to him. I don't think he'll bother us again….unless you want to speak to him of course," he added.

Faye shook her head. "No, I don't think I do." A moment later a car pulled up outside the cottage and Faye froze in fear. The car door slammed and footsteps could be heard running around to the back of the cottage. Faye stood up and backed towards the door. "Who's coming?" she said, her voice high.

"Hi, it's me." Pippa sang as she ran into the kitchen, dumped her bag on the floor and hugged Faye, making her burst into spontaneous tears.

Pippa stood back in astonishment. "Oh, what have I done? What's the matter? I didn't do anything." She held her hands in the air and glanced at Nathan for help.

"Faye's had a shock; her real father's turned up."

"No way," Pippa answered wide-eyed. "But I thought he was dead!"

"Apparently not," Faye said flatly.

"Why has he made an appearance now, after all these years?" Her eyes darted between them. "Is it because of the wedding? Is he here to give you away? Owen will be devastated you know. He was honoured to be asked."

Nathan cleared his voice, "I very much doubt it he wants to give Faye away. In fact he doesn't want the wedding to go ahead."

"Huh?" Pippa looked at him quizzically.

"He thinks I'm too old for her," he said raising his eyebrows.

"No way," she said elongating the words.

Faye relaxed and couldn't help but smile at her friend's reaction.

Pippa bristled. "I hope you told him to bugger off."

Composing herself now, Faye said, "No, but I will if he comes anywhere near me again."

*

Later that evening as they sat around the kitchen table, a knock came at the front door.

"I'll go, don't drink all that wine while I'm away." Nathan grinned as he pushed his chair back.

There was a chilly slightly autumnal feel to the air as he opened the door. "Evening Nathan, sorry to intrude, you look like you have company," PC Saunders said.

"No it's fine, come on in." Nathan stepped aside. "We are just polishing off a bottle of Shiraz in the kitchen."

PC Saunders took off his helmet and smiled. "I just popped by to see that Miss Larson is okay, after today's episode."

Nathan nodded and gestured him forward.

Faye and Pippa smiled as he entered and nodded a welcome.

The policeman cleared his throat. "I thought you might like to know that Mr Morton has left the village and he said he was very sorry for any upset he caused. I don't think it was quite the reunion he was hoping to have with you." He smiled sadly. "Anyway, he has gone now and I don't think he will bother you again."

Faye felt a rush of relief wash over her, tinged with a sense of uneasiness.

"However," he proceeded. "I had a long talk with him, and I must say he has one sorry tale to tell."

Nathan let out a huff of indignation. "He always could spin a good yarn," he grumbled. But Faye was unmoved as she looked at him with dark serious eyes, waiting for the next sentence.

"It's none of my business Miss Larson, but I think, if you can find it in your heart, then maybe you should speak to him. There are things you need to know."

Both Nathan and Pippa turned to look at Faye, who let out a long deflated sigh.

PC Saunders smiled and said, "Well, have a think about it. This is his phone number. But he said if he doesn't hear from you, he won't ever bother you again. He said to tell you he was sorry for what he said to you and Nathan. I believe there is some old gripe between you both which made him say those things. He told me to tell you that if you do marry, he would like to wish you love and happiness for the future. So, that was nice of him. Anyway, I'll leave you to decide, and bid you good evening."

57

As the knock came at the door, Faye's heart was thumping at the thought of seeing her father again. The decision to meet with him had not come easy and she'd crossed many emotions in the last twenty-four hours.

Pippa beckoned him through the door as the air prickled with nervous apprehension. The kitchen was large and warm, with a table at the centre that stood upon large stone flags. Philip cast a speculative eye over the room before sitting down in the seat Faye gestured to him. He glanced at Nathan, who glowered back.

"I'll leave you all to it then," Pippa said turning to leave.

"No," Faye said trying to keep the alarm from her voice. "Please stay, I'd like you to stay."

"Okay," Pippa said quirking an eyebrow.

Faye willed herself to keep calm. This was going to be an ordeal and she needed all the support she could get. She folded then unfolded her arms and stared intently at the father she had thought she had lost.

Philip cleared his throat nervously and smiled. "Thank you for allowing me to come and see you Faye."

Faye swallowed hard. "You need to thank Nathan, it's his house."

Philip nodded awkwardly in Nathan's direction. "I'm sorry about the other day. I over-reacted slightly." He glanced between Faye and Nathan.

"Slightly," Nathan said incredulously.

Philip bit his tongue. "I am sorry Faye."

Faye moistened her dry lips. "Be that as it may, but why are you here and why now? I thought you were dead."

"Nathan knew I wasn't dead, I'm surprised he didn't tell you," he said, raising his eyebrows.

Nathan stood and thumped the table. "I bloody wish

you were."

Now Faye stood. "Please, stop this at once, both of you." The two men turned away from each other and simultaneously folded their arms. Faye glanced at Pippa and rolled her eyes in exasperation.

"Why choose now to come back into my life after all these years?" she asked.

"I didn't choose not to be in your life. That choice was made for me."

"Go on," she answered, stony faced.

"I admit I never loved your Mum." He sighed heavily. "You were conceived one drunken night. I was drowning my sorrows, because the woman I loved had just married someone else." His eyes flashed angrily towards Nathan, but Nathan kept his eyes averted. "We were all at a party in Penzance, and one thing led to another and well, the next thing I knew, Marjory told me you were on the way." He lowered his eyes. "I felt trapped, but I knew I had to do the right thing and we were married soon afterwards. When you were born, I was so overwhelmed with love for you; I honestly tried to give up my wild ways. I was a father now, and you depended on me, I felt I had to make a go of it." He paused for a moment then continued, "Marjory was a difficult woman to please. She didn't like my bohemian lifestyle, or my friends." He laughed shortly. "In fact she didn't really like me! We had a nice home in Newlyn, small, but comfortable, I was a good photographer and brought good money home, but she was never satisfied. In truth, we didn't really like each other. But you, my darling daughter, you were the apple of my eye. You probably don't remember, but we spent an awful lot of time together out on the coast path. You would sit and draw with your crayons while I photographed the flowers and birds on the coastline. You had potential then; I hoped that you would develop that gift."

"Hum," Faye exclaimed thoughtfully. "Well my step-father put paid to all that. I was only allowed to read in the house. We didn't have a TV or any stimulus, and I was constantly discouraged from drawing on anything, though I did draw in secret, if I found a scrap of paper."

Philip gave her a pained look of sympathy. "Life with your Mum went from bad to worse. I had several affairs, nothing serious, but I think your Mum knew about them. I let you both down Faye. I had an accident on the fourteenth of June 1975."

Faye's eyes widened. "The fourteenth of June 1975?" she exclaimed.

Puzzled, Philip stopped and asked, "Yes why? Does that date have a relevance to you?"

Faye reached over for her bag and produced the photo she had kept all these years. "This, and a book of photographs of Elizabeth Trent's work, was all I had of yours. Mum destroyed everything else."

He took the photo and his eyes glistened. "Elizabeth sent this to me," he said quietly. "I was over the moon to receive it. It was cryptic, you see. There were only a handful of people who knew the studio was called 'The Blue Bay Café'. I knew Nathan was in America, there had been a piece in the local newspaper about him going. So, I thought my luck was in. I had hoped she had tired of him and wanted me back." He glanced at Nathan who flashed him a sardonic smile.

"But you were married to Mum."

"I know but I would have divorced her in a heartbeat if Elizabeth had wanted me back. But I was wrong. Although she was as kind as she had always been with me, she had brought me there to issue me with a final warning to stay away forever. I was devastated."

As Philip spoke, Nathan's brain was doing mental calculations. From what he could remember, Elizabeth had broken the news of her pregnancy when he returned from America. He was affronted that she had never mentioned that she had met with Morton. Why had she kept this meeting a secret? Morton had turned up many times early on in their marriage and she had always told him about the meetings before. Suddenly, his heart buckled, as the awful thought that Greg might not be his own flesh and blood jumped into his head. He heard a low sorrowful groaning noise; he wondered where on earth it was coming from and why it was so loud. Then he realised that everyone was looking towards him.

"Nathan?" Faye placed her hand on his. "Nathan, are you okay darling?"

He nodded regretfully. "I'm sorry; I don't know what happened there. I was just thinking of something."

Presently they all turned their attention back to Philip as he continued with his story. "The night of the accident, I was wallowing in self pity. Elizabeth had made it clear that she never wanted to see me again. So, I was drowning my sorrows with some random woman I had picked up. I didn't even know her name! I hadn't had a great deal to drink, but obviously too much to drive. My reactions were not fast enough, so, when another car came around the corner, there was nowhere for me to go, except into a granite wall. The woman with me was thrown straight through the windscreen and died almost instantly. I'll never forgive myself for that. I should have made sure she was wearing a seatbelt and I should not have been drink-driving. But there you go, I did it, I went to prison, I did the time, but I will never, ever, forgive myself for what I did."

Faye gave him a puzzled look. "Why did mum say you died in the crash? I don't understand."

Philip lowered his eyes. "She knew I would get eight years for manslaughter, though I only actually served four in the end," he added. "She wanted me out of her life forever. She told her solicitor that I had been a violent drunk for years, and that you were both afraid of me. I was told that if I relinquished all ties with you both, she would not bring charges against me for unreasonable behaviour. I didn't have a leg to stand on; I was already on a charge for manslaughter. She wanted a divorce, and I was told that there would be no more financial claims on me for your maintenance, and that I was to be dead to you from that day forward. If I came anywhere near you, charges would be brought, and I would go back to prison." He sighed heavily. "As I said, she didn't like me very much."

Faye did not move or speak for a long time as she digested his words. "I remember coming home from nursery school that day. Mum gave me a glass of milk and a chocolate biscuit and sat me down on the sofa. She said, 'I'm so sorry Faye, but your daddy isn't coming home anymore. He has had a terrible accident and has gone up to Heaven.' And that was that, she removed all traces of you from the house and you were never mentioned again. I was heartbroken, but I wasn't allowed to grieve for you, she didn't want to speak about you. If it hadn't been for the teachers at primary school, I would have floundered. I was only a little girl, but I remember their kindness."

Philip's eyes watered as he hung his head low. "I'm so sorry Faye. When I came out of prison, I came back to Newlyn, only to find you had moved up to Yorkshire. No one would speak to me, Marjory had done the business on me, and I was an outcast in my own village, so it took a while to find out where she had taken you. I knew I couldn't make any contact with you, but I so wanted to see that you were happy. When I finally located you, I learnt that your mum had remarried someone called Carl Larson. Oh Faye, I watched you from a distance, in your little grey school uniform. There was never a smile on your face and you looked so forlorn it broke my heart to see you. I know I shouldn't have done, but I sent you a Christmas present, I don't suppose you got it, but I marked it from Santa, in the hope that you would be able to keep it. It was a box of oil paints. Did you get it?" he asked hopefully.

Faye nodded slowly. "I remember opening it and the thrill of seeing all those brushes and paints and the smell of linseed oil. Oh I can smell it to this day." Philip smiled with joy at the scene, but then his face fell when she added, "It was taken away from me almost instantly. It was not on the list of acceptable presents we were allowed to have," she said bitterly.

Philip shook his head in dismay. "I did send you another box the next year."

Faye laughed dismissively. "I never got that one."

"No, I know. It was returned to the PO Box number I had sent it from with a solicitor's letter warning me to stay away. I think your Mum must had realised it was from me," he answered with dismay. "Over the next few years I would drive four hundred miles, five or six times a year just to watch you. I could not stop myself. From a distance, I watched you grow into a young woman. But it worried me how dowdy and downtrodden you always looked next to your school friends. I could see your beauty beginning to blossom, but you were keeping yourself under wraps."

Faye laughed ironically. "Believe me, if I had worn a hint of an accessory, I would have been grounded for weeks."

Philip pulled a thin smile. "I would lurk in the shadows, stealing glimpses of you. I thought you had seen me a couple of times when you turned unexpectedly, it's a wonder I wasn't arrested."

Faye's eyes widened. "You know, I always thought I was being watched, even then. I never saw you though. But, it did freak me out a bit."

"I'm so sorry Faye; the last thing I wanted to do was frighten you."

"Were you watching me when I went to work then?" she enquired.

He nodded. "I can't believe you went into banking."

Faye shook her head. "Again, I didn't have an option. Carl was the bank manager there and I walked straight into a job as a trainee cashier."

"Didn't you want to go to University?"

Faye just looked at him, and he knew the answer.

"I came in and opened an account with the bank, just so I could see you. I used to make a deposit several times a year, and always waited for you to serve me, but I couldn't make you look up at me. It tore at my heart to see you so shy and unfulfilled in that job. You were wasting away there; I knew I had to do something."

Faye knitted her brows together. "Do? What did you *do*?"

"I started to post you a copy of Cornwall Life magazine every month. You took some time to take the bait, but one year I walked into the bank and asked after you, only to be told you had moved to Cornwall." Philip smiled. "I promptly closed my account there and began my search for you again. I must say you remained elusive for a long time. I hoped that as soon as you came back home you would get the urge to paint. You did, didn't you? I'm not wrong am I?"

She gave him a wry smile.

"I knew it. I searched all the galleries in the hope that one day I would stumble across an exhibition of your work. But you were never there."

Faye smiled. "No, I was never successful as a painter. People always seemed to want abstract, but I prefer to make pictures of places you can recognise."

Philip nodded knowingly. "It was only when your name hit the headlines in the newspaper, when you were to be married to that Maunders chap that I realised that you had blossomed into a beautiful woman. I never recognised you in the 'Guinevere' adverts you know. They changed you beyond recognition, but you did look fabulous all the same. I was so proud of you when I found out. I'm so sorry everything went wrong for you at Lemmel."

Faye turned her head at the mention of Lemmel, and Nathan put his hand on her arm to comfort her.

"I drove up to Yorkshire the day after you were meant

to get married, but I felt so helpless, as I watched you being besieged by the gutter press."

"Oh don't remind me." Faye closed her mind to the memory of that awful time.

"I stood and witnessed your step-father denouncing you on his doorstep to a group of reporters. I was so close to punching his lights out, when he said he hoped this sordid affair would bankrupt you. So, I followed you to Skipton and then to the solicitors the next morning."

Faye shook her head in amazement and then a moment of realisation crossed her mind. "Did you pay my debts?"

Philip's silence said it all.

"Why?"

With a shrug of his shoulders he smiled. "I'm your father, and as your father it was my job to pay for my daughter's wedding."

"That debt was almost thirty thousand pounds!"

Philip raised his eyebrows. "I know."

Faye looked at him quizzically. "But how, where on earth did you get all that money from?"

"When I came out of jail, no one would employ me, so I started to work as a freelance war photographer. I've travelled the world, documenting war-torn countries with my camera." He sighed as if hating to admit the next part. "I'm a man of few needs. I have no wife, no family to care for. It's just been me these last years; in short, I've banked a lot of money."

Nathan regarded him suspiciously.

"Did you follow me all the way to Cornwall?"

"Well, I tried, but I lost you somewhere on the M5. It was only by chance I saw your car in Penzance a couple of months later and followed you to Lamorna."

Faye shuddered involuntarily at the thought of being followed. "I don't know what to make of all this. You seemed to have saved me from myself, whilst frightening the life out of me. You freaked me out when I realised I was being followed in Lamorna you know."

"I know, I'm so sorry for that. I just wanted to look out for you. Like a dad should look out for his daughter."

Nathan crossed his arms to his chest. "Well at least your flight brought you to me Faye, I have him to thank for that, if nothing else," he said smugly, catching Philip's eye.

Philip bristled indignantly. "I must admit, I never thought you would end up here. Talk about 'what goes around comes around'."

Faye gave him a reproachful look. "Nathan gave me a safe place to live. I have been happier here than anywhere else. It was good fortune that I ended up here."

Philip gave a mirthless nod of the head. "When I heard your Mum had died, I drove up to Yorkshire. I thought you would be at the funeral. I had decided it was time to come forward and tell you the truth. But you didn't show up. The next thing I knew you had been involved in that awful accident. I tried to visit you, but I wasn't allowed. Ironically they didn't believe I was your father."

Faye glanced at Nathan who said in his defence, "I thought it was your step-father, I didn't think you would want to see him."

"When they transferred you to The Royal Cornwall Hospital, I tried to see you again, but as you can imagine, I was dismayed to find your constant visitor was Nathan here."

Faye let out an exaggerated sigh. "What is it with you and Nathan?" she snapped.

"I've told you, I think he is too old for you!"

"Oh stop that nonsense at once. I love Nathan, and I will marry him."

"You are my daughter and you deserve better than him. Do you know he doesn't even put proper flowers on his dead wife's grave?"

It took a moment for the insult to sink in before Nathan stood up, scraping the chair on the stone flags, and roared at him, "So it was you?" He lurched forward to grab Philip, but Faye pulled him back down.

He turned to speak to Faye. "Mr Moneybags here kept stealing roses from someone else's grave to put on Elizabeth's. He didn't even buy them. He caused no end of upset and bad feeling."

"It was meant to," Philip retorted. "I thoroughly enjoyed the game."

Nathan started to rise again, but Faye put her hand on his arm and pleaded, "Please stop this at once." She regarded Philip reproachfully. "I will tell you this once and for all, there is nobody better than Nathan, and if you continue in this silly vein, we will never build a relationship with each other. Do I make myself clear? I will not put up with all this ill feeling."

Philip looked at her hopefully. "So, are you saying that you might consider building a relationship with me then?"

Faye pinched her thumb and finger to the bridge of her nose and said, "Only if you stop this ridiculous feud with Nathan."

Philip studied his hands for a moment as though sizing up his options, then nodded meekly. "Okay, I'm sorry Nathan, but you had better look after her." He held out a hand for Nathan to shake, which Nathan reluctantly took.

"Good, now, if you will excuse me, we have a wedding to prepare for," Faye said.

"Of course," Philip stood up to take his leave. "Would you?" he paused, not knowing how to broach the subject. "Would you mind if I came to the wedding? I would rather like to see my daughter on her wedding day."

"Not if you're going to cause any trouble," Nathan said crisply. "I want this day to be perfect for Faye, she has had enough trouble in her life," he added.

"I'll stay in the background, I promise." He sighed. "After all, that's where I've been for the last twenty two years."

58

September the sixteenth dawned cool and misty, but from the bedroom window in Gwithian Cottage there was a promise of sun filtering its rays through the haze, so Faye was not unduly worried that her wedding day would be anything but glorious.

They were to be married at the local church at three-thirty that afternoon, followed by a reception in the marquee erected in the field adjoining the pub. She turned to gaze upon her husband-to-be as he slept. A smile broke over her face and happiness filled her heart. She could hardly wait to become Mrs Nathaniel Prior.

As though Nathan knew he was being watched he smiled and said, "I know you are watching me," he whispered.

She clambered back into bed and kissed him, marvelling at the sensation of his touch. There was nothing nicer than sleepy morning kisses. She had never felt so much love for another human being before.

"Happy?"

"Ecstatic," she replied.

He kissed her again and smiled tenderly. "I'll be back in a moment," he said, pushing the bed covers from him.

She stretched sleepily. "Where are you going?"

He blew her a kiss as he moved around the bed to the door.

She watched his naked body as he walked, the muscles on his finely toned body rippled as he moved; he looked magnificent.

"Hey, don't you be looking at my naughty bits, we're not married yet," he joked, cupping his privates as he walked past her.

Faye smiled happily as she glanced around the newly decorated bedroom. Very subtly she and Nathan had restyled the room to make it their own. Only a marble sculpture of Elizabeth's remained on the dressing table. They both loved its form and decided to keep it in situ. There was never any intention of eliminating Elizabeth from the house, so most of her paintings and sculptures now adorned the other newly decorated rooms.

Nathan returned with a bottle of champagne and two glasses.

As they sipped their champagne in bed, Faye couldn't help but notice that Nathan kept glancing at the clock, and knew he was a little apprehensive about Greg and Simon's arrival later that morning. This was the first time Nathan had met Simon.

They had bought a new double bed for Carrie's old room and when Faye had made up the bed in readiness for Greg and Simon, she realised that Nathan found the thought of his son sleeping with another man in his house, a little uncomfortable.

"Nathan, they have been together for years, they do sleep together you know."

"I know, it's just that I always thought it would be a girlfriend he would bring home. I'm not homophobic; in fact some of my best friends are gay. It just seems strange that's all, just from a Dad's point of view. Do you know what I mean?"

Faye touched him gently on the arm. "Nathan, relax. It'll be fine. Simon is a lovely man; you'll really like him. He's just like Greg. They are just regular guys."

"Who sleep together?"

"*Nathan!*" she scolded slapping him playfully. "What am I going to do with you?"

He held his hands up in mock defeat. "I'm kidding, I'm kidding," he laughed.

*

As the morning progressed, Nathan took himself off to the marquee to set out the tables and chairs, whilst Faye and Pippa busied themselves in the kitchen doing the final preparations for the buffet. At eleven-fifteen, Faye wiped her floury hands down her apron and glanced around the kitchen. She had done some alterations to the décor in this room since Carrie had moved out. The once dingy room now had freshly varnished beams and whitewashed walls. A marmalade jar on the windowsill was filled with sweet smelling wild flowers, which a bee was gently humming around. At the window she had hung new curtains pulled back with matching ties, and there was a heady smell of garlic and herbs wafting from the savoury pastries she had freshly baked and placed on the kitchen table.

Nathan walked in and sniffed appreciatively at the aroma. "Oh yum, can I have one of these now?" he said, stealing a pastry then dropping it immediately when it burned his fingers.

"That serves you right." Faye tapped his hand to reprimand him. "Now leave them be, they're for later."

Nathan put his hands behind his back, suitably scolded.

She laughed and kissed him whilst untying her apron. "I'm just popping out to the shop to collect the French sticks to have with the camembert."

"Well before you do that I have a little surprise for you."

Faye smiled cheekily, and glanced in embarrassment towards Pippa, who raised her eyebrows. "Nathan, we haven't got time," she said coyly.

He smiled at her suggestion. "No this is for you, come on."

They made their way down towards the sea, picking their way along the rocky coast path, Faye taking things steady as she still had a slight limp and pain in her leg. "Where are we going Nathan, I have got a thousand and one things to do back at home."

As they passed the ruined building Faye coveted so much, he watched as Faye halted slightly. "Oh no, there's a sold sign on my building."

Nathan walked up behind her and rested his hands on

her shoulders. "Guess who bought it?"

She turned and looked deep into his eyes. "Have *you* bought it?"

He nodded. "It's my wedding present to you. This time next year, you will have your own 'Blue Bay Café'. I've had plans drawn up for a three bedroom dwelling, with a studio for you to work in, a café where you can serve your cream teas, and a gallery to show your work. When it's complete, we'll sell Gwithian Cottage. I think it's time for a new start. What do you think?"

Faye was dumbstruck and Nathan laughed heartily. "In all the time I have known you, I have never seen you lost for words," he said jovially.

Faye shook her head. "Words cannot describe how I feel Nathan, but, thank you from the bottom of my heart my darling wonderful man, thank you."

Turning to look out to sea they found each other's hand and stood in happy quiet contentment, quite forgetting the wedding plans for a moment, as they dreamed and planned their future life.

Presently Nathan broke the spell and they began to walk back up the coast path to the shop.

Dropping the French bread on the table, Faye put her apron back on and set about tidying the kitchen in preparation for their guests.

"I was just thinking," Nathan said. "I feel as though I should go and see Carrie. I know we haven't all seen eye to eye, but I'd really like to make amends with her, and I'd like her to come to the wedding."

Faye raised an eyebrow. "I think if she was coming to the wedding, she would have answered the invitation by now," she answered gently. "But I suppose there is no harm in going to see her. Good luck then, but I'm sure it will snow red ink before Carrie comes to our wedding."

"You're probably right." he said kissing her. As soon as her back was turned he stole a pastry. As he savoured his snack, he thought again of Carrie. In truth he was worried about her. It had been days since he had seen her. He really wanted her to be at his wedding, but as Faye had pointed out, she hadn't replied to the invitation.

Five minutes later he knocked briskly at the door of Oyster Cottage, the dwelling Carrie had rented since leaving Nathan, but there was no reply. He peered through the window but couldn't see through the net curtains. He looked back down the road into Zennor, towards the watermill. He knew she had found work at the Wayside Museum, and thought perhaps she was working today. As Nathan walked around the back of the cottage, he noticed Reuben Treen, tending his vegetable patch in the adjoining garden. Reuben was a small, balding man, who claimed to be the oldest inhabitant of the village.

"Morning Reuben," Nathan said. "You haven't seen anything of Carrie have you?"

Reuben stood up, pushed his fingers under his hat and scratched his head thoughtfully. "Not for a few days. Mind, she's got herself a boyfriend, I reckon they'll be busy doing whatever young couples do," he answered, flashing a toothless grin.

Nathan nodded. "Well if you see her, can you tell her I was looking for her?"

"Will do," he said, leaning on his spade. "It'll be 'appy day for you I reckon today. Am I right?"

"Yes Reuben, I reckon it will be."

"I'll be seeing you later for a drink then will I?" Reuben said winking.

"You're very welcome Reuben."

Carrie watched from behind the bedroom curtain, as Nathan walked back down the road.

"What does he want?" Liam asked as he stood behind her.

"Probably wants me to reconsider my refusal to attend the wedding."

Liam gave a short derisive snort and took another mouthful of whiskey.

Carrie turned and regarded him for a moment. "Isn't it a bit early to be on the hard stuff?"

He flashed a look of contempt towards Carrie. "Who the hell are you, my mother?"

"I'm just saying….that's all."

"You're just nagging." He took another swig from the bottle.

Carrie turned back to the window and watched with sadness as Nathan disappeared from view. She had no idea how she would get through today. Liam was no help. She'd had high hopes of a relationship when Liam walked unexpectedly into her life. But this handsome charming man soon turned out to be a hard drinking, deeply unpleasant bore.

Liam flopped back down on the bed and stared at Carrie. What a sad excuse for a woman Carrie was, he thought. Not so long ago he had his pick of beautiful women. In fact he had everything a reasonable man could ever want. But Faye Larson had put paid to all that. Christ, he had almost lost his life because of her.

His thoughts took him back to the evening he was banished from the boatyard. It was only good fortune that he survived that stormy night in the river. On the verge of drowning, a sudden swell had lifted and dumped him unceremoniously onto Tremayne quay. With his yacht wrecked and everything lost in the swollen river, except the clothes he stood up in, and fortunately his credit card in his pocket, he walked for almost two hours in sodden clothes until a local farmer picked him up and drove him to Helston. Collecting his Range Rover from the MOT garage, he drove to Penzance, sold it for cash, and with the money, he bought himself a dry set of clothes, a battered old VW estate to live in, and began to drink himself into a stupor.

His fortunes only changed when Carrie's interview with the newspaper had given him the first clue as to Faye's whereabouts, and because of his charm, and their common hatred of Faye, it had been easy to wheedle his way into her home and bed. He had to admit, her bed was a great deal comfier than the back of his car, but his residence here, in this grotty cottage, would be short lived, that was for sure. He was here for one reason and one reason only, because a few days after losing his yacht, the local paper had run the headline:

POLICE REVEAL THAT A LOCAL MAN WANTED IN CONNECTION WITH A HIT AND RUN, IS MISSING, PRESUMED DEAD, AFTER HIS YACHT SANK IN THE HELFORD RIVER DURING A STORM.

Well, if the newspaper thought him to be a dead man, he couldn't be blamed for the tragic accident which would befall Faye Larson, on this, her wedding day, could he? His lip curled maliciously.

It was lucky for him that it was common knowledge in the village that the newlyweds were honeymooning in the South of France, and that they were to drive there in Nathan's cherished Morgan car. He smiled inwardly and patted the knife in his pocket. It had been so easy to make the small adjustment to the Morgan, so as to ensure that there would be no happy ending to Miss Larson's fairytale.

59

Nathan checked his watch, it was twelve-fifteen. "Well, if you still want to marry me, I shall have to go and collect the wedding flowers from St Ives. I'll be back in an hour, in good time to make you my wife," he said, kissing her hand. "Look after my girl." He winked at Pippa and left.

Faye's old Sierra was hardly out of the garage before it broke down on Nathan. "Damn it, today of all days," he cursed, as he thumped the steering wheel. A moment later he was stood under the bonnet, spanner in one hand and an oily rag in the other.

"Having trouble?" a voice asked quizzically.

Nathan stood up and looked at the tall blond gentleman at his side. "Yep, the damn thing keeps seizing up. One day it's okay then the next it's as dead as a doornail. I've had it in the local garage but they can't seem to cure it."

"May I?" the stranger asked, pushing up his sleeves.

"Be my guest." Nathan sighed irritably.

The stranger peered under the bonnet for a moment. "Ah I see what the problem is," he exclaimed, reaching down to the depths of the workings. He fiddled for a few moments, grunted and groaned as he reached deeper. "Gotcha!" He straightened himself up, wiped his oily hands together and said, "See if she'll start."

It fired immediately and the engine purred like a kitten. Nathan laughed in astonishment. "Well I'll be damned. What did you do?"

"There was an electric wire loose; you couldn't see it, that's probably why it was missed at the garage. It was tucked right underneath, well out of the way. I had a car which used to do the same thing, sometimes it made the connection and sometimes it didn't. It drove me mad until I found the cause."

"Well I'm eternally grateful to you. Oh but look at the state of you, you're covered in oil," he said, handing him a cloth.

"No matter, it'll wash off."

"Are you here on holiday?" Nathan asked.

"No, I'm here for a friend's wedding."

Nathan's eyes widened. "Oh, are you one of Faye's friends?"

He nodded his head and held his hand out. "I'm also Greg's friend, Simon Jackson. I'm very pleased to meet you at last Mr Prior," he said as Nathan's jaw dropped open.

*

A steady stream of guests had arrived in Zennor by the time Nathan returned. Faye's kitchen was buzzing with people enjoying a pre wedding cuppa as she Pippa, and the staff from the Tinners Arms ferried the buffet across into the refrigerated cupboards situated at the back of the marquee. Thankfully the marquee was only fifty yards from the cottage.

At two p.m. they all took themselves off to the Tinners Arms so Faye could get ready. As Faye suspected, Nathan was perfectly relaxed in Simon's company. The two of them were getting on like a house on fire to which both Faye and Greg heaved a huge sigh of relief. As Nathan was getting a round in, David and Sarah Quintana entered the pub. When he saw David he was shocked by his appearance. He looked as though he had aged twenty years since he last saw him. When he voiced his concerns to Sarah Quintana, she told him that the shock of losing Jasmine had shattered both their lives, but the grief had weakened David's heart. "He's had three heart attacks. I'm afraid he is living on borrowed time Nathan."

Nathan felt his stomach drop. "Oh Sarah, I'm so sorry to hear that."

She smiled weakly. "At least you have found happiness again Nathan. Elizabeth would not want you to spend the rest of your life alone."

"That is so kind of you to say that. I know she was a good friend of yours and you must miss her as much as I do."

She nodded. "I miss her every day Nathan, every day."

He clasped her hand and smiled. "You and me both."

A sudden crash of glasses being broken made everyone look outside to find someone sprawled under one of the beer garden tables.

Duggie Martin moved swiftly from behind the bar and pushed past everyone. He grabbed the stranger by the collar and pulled him free of the broken glass. Once upright the gate crasher stared intently at Nathan who had come out to see what the commotion was all about.

"Do you know him?" Duggie asked Nathan, who shook his head. "Right bugger off and don't come back." He shoved the man unceremoniously away from the pub. As the other guests returned to their drinks, David Quintana gasped in disbelief as he watched Liam Knight brush himself down before staggering off towards the cliff path. A moment later, Philip Morton walked into the beer garden. "Oh my goodness!" Sarah Quintana pulled Nathan to one side. "When did Morton crawl out from under his stone?"

"A couple of days ago actually," he grimaced. "Would you believe he is Faye's father?"

Sarah gasped. "So he is here for the wedding?"

"I'm afraid so."

David Quintana interrupted, "Sarah, I'm just going out to get a breath of fresh air before the ceremony."

Sarah looked at her husband who seemed excitable. "Oh, are you okay David, do you want me to come with you?"

"No," he said emphatically. "I'm fine. I'm just going

for a little walk."

"Okay, but we will be going over to the church soon."

"I won't be long."

Nathan and Sarah watched him leave. "Oh I do worry about him."

Nathan cleared his voice, not sure whether to ask his question. But in the end he had to know. "Sarah, you were good friends with Elizabeth. Did she ever tell you that she had met Morton when I was over in America, you know, just before we found out that Greg was on the way?"

"Oh dear," she said unhappily. "Why do you ask now?"

"Morton mentioned it last night, when he came to see Faye."

"Oh!" Sarah unconsciously adjusted her hat.

"It's been on my mind ever since. I'm worried that Greg may not be my son."

Sarah bristled with indignation. "Elizabeth loved you unequivocally."

Nathan looked up sharply at her. "So why did she meet him in secret?"

She took a deep breath. "She told me she had asked him to come and see her - you were away in New York at the time. She was pregnant with Greg, and yes, I'm sorry but I knew she was pregnant before you did." She shrugged her shoulders. "She was bursting to tell someone and you know we never had any secrets from each other. Anyway, Philip had been married for about four years, but still he bombarded her with messages and phone calls. He was becoming a real nuisance and she wanted the nonsense to end once and for all. She told me she had arranged a meeting with him at the Blue Bay Café and asked if I would be close by, just in case. I hid in the toilet, while she read him the riot act. He took the news of her pregnancy really hard, and began sobbing like a baby, but Elizabeth stood her ground and refused to acknowledge his reaction. Then he got cross, and upturned the table, but still Elizabeth kept her calm. She had seen it all before with him and was thoroughly sick of his behaviour. She very quietly asked him to leave and warned him that if he ever contacted her again she would go to the police. Honest to God Nathan, I was having kittens in the toilet listening to all this, but it did the trick, she was never bothered by him again. From what I can remember, he got terribly drunk, picked up some woman from a pub and drove her home. They crashed and the woman was killed and Philip went to prison for manslaughter."

Nathan closed his eyes and sighed with relief. "Thank you Sarah."

"There is nothing to thank me for; all you need to do is look at your handsome son. He's the spitting image of you."

"Nathan?" Duggie called out. "Faye is on the phone for you. I hope she hasn't had second thoughts, eh?" He winked mischievously.

Nathan widened his eyes. "Don't joke of such things," he said taking the phone off him.

"Nathan."

"Yes darling?"

"Is my Dad there?" The word seemed so alien to her.

"Unfortunately yes," Nathan replied. "Why, have you changed your mind about wanting him at our wedding?" he asked hopefully.

"No, I actually need him to give me away. Owen and Gloria have just arrived and Owen has only gone and slipped a disc getting out of the car. They have had to go back home to Gweek. Can you ask him if he'll do it?"

Nathan ran his hands through his hair and gave a mirthless smile. "If I must."

*

In Gweek, under Faye's favourite tree, on the grassy banks of the Helford River, Amos sat in quiet, sad contemplation. Life should have felt good. The charges against him had been dropped and he was a free man, but he was desperately unhappy. The invitation to Faye's wedding was by his side, but his heart would not free him to attend. It was a bitter-sweet day for him. He knew from Pippa that Faye was happy, but, inside he was dying. Right up to today, when Gloria, Owen, Sid and Joe had set off to Zennor, he had hoped and prayed that Faye would have changed her mind and called off the wedding. After all, the man she was marrying was a lot older than she was. He scolded himself for not being happy for Faye, but he always hoped that maybe, one day she would see him and understand how much he loved her.

He looked up puzzled to see Owen's car turning into the boatyard, and then heard his name being called. He stood up when he realised it was Gloria calling. He frowned and checked his watch, why had they returned so soon? He shouted over to gain Gloria's attention. "I'm over here."

"Oh Amos, come quick, we need your help," she beckoned to him. She smiled gently down at Owen, who looked in considerable pain. "Don't you worry my luvver, Amos will help me get you out of the car and then we can get you somewhere more comfortable."

Amos's heart lifted. Faye must have had second thoughts after all. Why else would they be back so soon, if not to tell him the news? He ran as fast as he could towards the boatyard, hoping that his prayers had been answered and that there might, just might, be a chance again to win Faye's heart.

*

By three p.m. the house was eerily empty but for Faye and Pippa. All the others had gone on to the church. Faye sat nervously at her dressing table as Pippa carefully tied the sprigs of gypsophila and peach rosebuds into Faye's auburn curls.

"There, you look beautiful," said Pippa, resting her hands on Faye's shoulders. "He's a lovely man your Nathan. I just know you are going to be very happy with him."

Faye reached up and cupped her own hand over Pippa's and smiled. "Oh please let there be no hitches today," she sighed. "I keep thinking something will go wrong."

Pippa laughed. "It's just your imagination that's all, old demons coming to haunt you and all that. Everything will be fine trust me."

Faye rose, gave her a grateful smile and hugged her.

"Look your father is waiting outside."

Faye moved to the window to see Philip Morton standing proudly at the gate. "I still can't believe he's here, after all these years of thinking he was dead."

Pippa looked over Faye's shoulder at him and said mischievously, "I think you're going to have fun and games with him and Nathan though."

Faye shook her head. "Oh don't remind me."

"It must go right against the grain having to give you away to his arch enemy," Pippa said gleefully.

"Pippa stop it, you're doing nothing to calm my nerves," Faye said adjusting a flower in her hair.

Pippa's eyes twinkled playfully. "Sorry, can't help it. Oh, but poor Owen, he was so looking forward to giving you away. I hope he is all right. I bet he can't get out of the car when they get back to Gweek!"

"Talking of Gweek, has everyone else from the boatyard arrived?"

Pippa nodded. "Except for Amos, he didn't want to come in the end."

Faye sighed wistfully. "I feel so sorry for Amos."

"Don't fret so; I'm sure he'll be fine."

"I just wish he would find a nice girl of his own to settle down with."

"Well, it's funny you should say that…" Pippa declared proudly. "Owen has just taken on a new girl in the office, and she seems very interested in our Amos. I don't think it will take much to give them a helpful shove towards each other, if you know what I mean."

Faye grinned happily. "You're always the matchmaker Pippa aren't you?"

"Just you watch this space." She winked.

*

Faye stepped outside the door of Gwithian Cottage to greet a small crowd of people who had waited to see her off to church. They were not disappointed; she truly was a beautiful bride. She wore a simple gown of ivory silk, which fluttered softly as she walked. Her hair was left to hang in loose curls and she carried a bouquet of peach rose buds and gypsophila to compliment her hairdressings.

Philip Morton waited proudly at the gate to escort his daughter the short distance to the church.

They were watched from a distance by Carrie, who nursed her disgruntlement like a baby. She had thought Liam would have returned to watch. Maybe he had something else in mind to spoil Faye Larson's day - she sincerely hoped he did. He was certainly drunk enough to make a scene. She laughed acerbically; if he didn't spoil the wedding, then the honeymoon would be short lived. She knew Liam had something in mind to make Faye pay for ruining their lives, though she knew not what.

As Nathan waited patiently in his pew, he passed the time observing the new minister who was about to conduct the service. The Reverend Henry Trevan had moved into the village three months previously. He was a small thin man with a slight hunchback and a tortoise like appearance. He had a small round hairless face, and a wide thin-lipped mouth, which gave the appearance of him munching his words as he spoke. When the Reverend realised he was being watched, he turned his short-sighted bespectacled eyes toward Nathan. "Not long now," he chomped, then glanced and nodded slowly to some more guests who had walked down the aisle to take their seats.

There was a small commotion half way down the aisle as David Quintana rushed into his pew.

"Where the hell have you been David?" Sarah hissed. "And why are you so flushed? Are you unwell?"

"I've never felt better," he said, feeling the adrenalin pump furiously round his body.

"Where have you been? I was frantic looking for you."

"Let's just say, I bumped into someone I knew on the coast path," he said with a smile of contentment.

Nathan looked around the tiny church - it was almost full. His eyes met Greg's who was ushering the guests in and he smiled warmly at him. He thought of his beloved Elizabeth on their wedding day. They had planned to grow old together, but it seemed fate had other ideas for them. What would fate have in store for himself and Faye, he wondered?

Without him noticing, Greg came to sit by him, patted his pocket to make sure the ring was still there, then noted the expression on his father's face.

"You okay Dad?"

Nathan roused himself from his reverie. "I have never felt better," he beamed.

As the music sounded Faye's arrival, the Reverend Henry Trevan extended his long leathery neck, pulled at his dog collar as though to cool himself, then cleared his throat.

"Here we go Dad." Greg gently touched Nathan's sleeve and they stood up and moved forward.

As he heard her footsteps move closer, Nathan turned his head and the sight of Faye as she walked towards him took his breath away.

The service began and Faye could hardly contain the tears of happiness which welled up in her eyes as the Reverend spoke. She looked to her left where her father stood and then at her husband-to-be at her side. Nathan looked into her watery eyes and reached over to squeeze her hand.

".. Into this holy estate these two persons present come now to be joined. Therefore, if any man can show any just cause why they may not lawfully be joined together, let him now speak, or else hereafter forever hold his peace."

The church door suddenly flew open and Faye's heart sank. She closed her eyes as a cold chill ran through her body. This could not be happening to her again. The whole congregation turned, but Faye stood dead still, her eyes squeezed tightly shut to block whatever onslaught would come. In the background she could hear the congregation murmuring and footsteps walking towards her. The voice was familiar, but she tried to block her ears to the words he was saying. A squeeze from Nathan's hand urged Faye to open her eyes. She swallowed hard and looked slowly under her lashes toward Nathan. He was smiling. "It's okay darling, look," he said, gently aware of her apprehension. Slowly she turned to see Ryan making his way along the pew to sit with Pippa, apologising profusely as he picked his way past the guests. Their eyes met and his look requested her forgiveness for the intrusion. "Sorry," he mouthed.

The Reverend stretched his neck and once again he pulled at his dog collar. This was the first time anyone had ever halted a wedding during his time as a minister. "Who are you? Who speaks against this marriage? Do you have something to say?" he asked querulously.

"No he hasn't," Pippa said firmly. "He's just late that's all."

The Reverend moved to touch Faye on the shoulder. "Do you know this man?"

"Yes, I know him." She turned and raised her eyebrows towards Ryan. To which he mouthed, 'Sorry' again.

Nathan squeezed Faye's hand and smiled softly at her. "Are you okay?"

Faye felt her shoulders relax and she nodded happily.

He then turned to the minister. "I believe we are ready to continue."

There was a silence while Faye composed herself, but

in the far reaches of the church the sound of a pencil scribbling on paper told Faye she would once again be on the front page of tomorrow's tabloids, but, this time she did not care a hoot.

Outside, a smattering of people in their bright coloured finery chatted happily in the sunshine while the photographer flitted around everyone.

Ryan was the first to approach the happy couple, apologising profusely for the commotion he had caused. "I'm so sorry," he said, simultaneously kissing Faye and shaking hands with Nathan. "I thought I was going to miss the service; I was stuck on the M5 for five hours."

Faye looked at him holding hands with Pippa and smiled with happiness. "I don't deny you almost stopped my heart when you came in," she admitted. "But I'm so glad you are here. You do have a knack of having a big part at my weddings," she joked.

"Yes, for all the wrong reasons," he answered sheepishly.

"No matter, you're here now." She kissed him warmly on the lips to give the spotty reporter something to get his teeth into. "And I see you two have a little explaining to do as well." She grinned at Pippa. "You kept that quiet!"

Greg and Simon approached to offer their congratulations. "How's the car?" Simon asked.

"Works like a dream thanks to you."

"You will probably need to get the garage to check it out just to make sure I have secured the wire properly."

"I will." Nathan patted his arm in thanks.

"You're not taking that old heap to France on honeymoon are you?" Greg asked.

"Hey." Faye slapped him on the arm. "Don't talk about my car like that."

Nathan laughed heartily. "Fortunately not, we're going in the Morgan."

"Oh, is that your Morgan, parked over there? I was admiring it earlier," Simon said with some concern

"Yes, I've had it years, it's never let me down."

"Well, I think it's going to let you down now; there is brake fluid all over the road underneath it. If you set off in that, you'll be on the shortest honeymoon ever. I left a note on the windscreen to alert the owner, I didn't realise it was yours."

Nathan looked ashen faced. "Oh my God, thank goodness you saw it Simon. I have no idea how that could have happened. I only had it serviced a month ago!"

"Well, when I saw the pool of liquid underneath the car, I got on my knees to take a closer look, and it looks as though the brake pipe has been severed with something. Have you caught it on anything?"

"Not that I am aware of. I drove it out of the garage this morning to give it a wash that's all, but thank you Simon, that could have been fatal if you hadn't spotted it."

Once the photos were taken, Nathan glanced towards Elizabeth's headstone then at his new bride by his side. "A new beginning," he said softly.

Faye smiled brilliantly and kissed him, before they began to lead the guests from the churchyard to the reception.

Once in the marquee a fine spread of food was offered around and toasts were drunk to the health of the Bride and Groom. Faye looked deep into Nathan's eyes and saw a lifetime of happiness within them. Suddenly the peace of the warm afternoon was shattered as an Air Sea Rescue helicopter from the nearby Culdrose air base flew overhead.

"Gosh, that's close, I wonder what has happened," Pippa said.

"Apparently someone's fallen off the cliff." Philip said. "Duggie has just heard that it looks like that man who was drunk outside the Tinners Arms earlier."

David Quintana's lips gave a ghost of a smile as he took a glass of champagne and silently toasted the memory of his beloved daughter Jasmine. The icy bubbles fizzed in his parched throat, 'Revenge is always better served cold,' he thought happily.

ABOUT THE AUTHOR

Ann E Brockbank was born in Yorkshire, but has lived in Cornwall for the past fourteen years. Ann's first book, Mr de Sousa's Legacy, was published in July 2013. The Blue Bay Café is her second book. Her inspiration comes from holidays and retreats in stunning locations in Greece, Italy, France and Cornwall. When she is not travelling, Ann lives with her partner on the beautiful banks of the Helford River in Cornwall which has been an integral setting for both her novels. Ann is currently writing her third novel.

Ann E Brockbank

Made in the USA
Charleston, SC
07 August 2016